Zigmunds Skujiņš

Flesh-Coloured Dominoes

Translated from the Latvian by Kaija Straumanis

ARCADIA BOOKS

Arcadia Books Ltd
139 Highlever Road
London W10 6PH

www.arcadiabooks.co.uk

First published in the United Kingdom by Arcadia Books 2014
Originally published by Preses nams, Latvia, as *Miesas krāsas domino* 1999
Copyright © Zigmunds Skujiņš 1999
English language translation copyright © Kaija Straumanis 2014
Zigmunds Skujinš asserted his moral right to be identified as the author of this work
in accordance with the Copyright, Designs and Patents Act, 1988.

A catalogue record for this book is available from the British Library.

ISBN 9781909807525
Typeset in Garamond Premier Pro by Ned Hoste/2H Design
Printed and bound by CPI Group (UK) Ltd, Croydon CR0 4YY

The publication of this work was supported by a grant from the Latvian Literature
Centre, State Culture Capital Foundation and
Ministry of Culture of the Republic of Latvia

Arcadia Books supports English PEN *www.englishpen.org* and
The Book Trade Charity *www.btbs.org*

Arcadia Books distributors are as follows:

in the UK and elsewhere in Europe:
Macmillan Distribution Ltd
Brunel Road, Houndmills, Basingstoke
Hants RG21 6XS

in the USA and Canada:
Dufour Editions
PO Box 7, Chester Springs, PA 19425

in Australia/New Zealand:
NewSouth Books, University of New South Wales
Sydney NSW 2052

About the author

Zigmunds Skujiņš, one of the most renowned Latvian writers of the late twentieth century, was born in Riga, Latvia, in 1926. His work has been translated across Europe and several of his books have been made into films. He is the recipient of numerous Latvian and international literature awards, including a lifetime grant from the Latvian State Culture Capital Foundation.

About the translator

Kaija Straumanis is a graduate of the MA programme in Literary Translation at the University of Rochester, and is the editorial director of Open Letter Books. She translates from both German and Latvian. Her translation of Latvian author Inga Ābele's *High Tide* was published with Open Letter in autumn 2013.

Foreword

Jelgava, lying just a short distance south of the Latvian capital Riga, once the seat of the Dukes of Courland as well as being a western outpost of the Russian Tsarist empire, has historically been something of a cultural crossroads. Whereas Riga became prosperous and culturally heterogeneous as a Baltic trading port, Jelgava, or Mitau as the Baltic German nobility used to call it, absorbed its cultural influences through its German aristocracy and gained its political power through the intermarriage of the Dukes of Courland and the Russian Romanov dynasty.

Into this rich and many-layered historical background the reader is plunged by this fascinating novel, which appeared in Latvian in 1999 under the title *Miesas krāsas domino*. Remarkably, its author, Zigmunds Skujiņš, was by then 72 years old, with a long literary career behind him. In this respect, and also in his love of rummaging in the byways of Baltic history, he is reminiscent of his Estonian contemporary Jaan Kross. Like him, and perhaps also like the so-called 'magic realist' writers of South America from the same generation, Skujiņš is able to make his central characters also the central players in curious events which enhance the luminous strangeness of their time-worn and neglect-encrusted physical surroundings. And adding to the magic – the child's sense of wonder at all the treasures that can be discovered.

Skujiņš is a rare figure in Latvian literature in his willingness to delve deep into a wide range of times and places, in a variety of literary forms. Before considering his own career, it's worth remembering that at the time this novel is partly set – the late eighteenth century – Latvia did not have an indigenous literature. And it did not have statehood either; the area which is the setting of this novel was then the Duchy of Courland, and its educated class was German speaking. Latvian was the spoken language of the peasantry. There was a kind of vernacular literacy, but only insofar as a peasant might learn his catechism to please an 'enlightened' German pastor. This backwater of German culture and Russian empire, home to an unenfranchised Baltic peasantry, becomes in this novel scene of extraordinary sideshows involving some of the more notorious characters of eighteenth-century European history, such as the charlatan Count Cagliostro.

Zigmunds Skujiņš was born in Riga, capital of the then independent Latvia, on 25 December 1926. He was educated there, but at the age of seventeen, during the war, he was taken to Germany, returning to Latvia at the end of the war. After a year at the Rozentāls School of Arts, he became a journalist, and was involved in the broadcast as well as the printed media, rising to become first chairman of the national Radio and Television Council.

Skujiņš is a writer who is equally at home in longer and shorter fiction – he has been prolific in both. His collections of stories began to appear in 1956 with *Esmu dzimis bagāts* (*I was Born Rich*). The collections that followed established a characteristic trend in his writing: the blurred lines between everyday reality and dreams or illusions, and they range over many times and places, and include *Ciemiņš no viņpasaules* (*A Visitor from Beyond*, 1963), *Zebras āda* (*The Skin of the Zebra*, 1968), *Balzams* (*Balsam*, 1972), *Uzbrukums vējdzirnavām* (*Attack on the Windmill*, 1976), *Sermuliņš uz asfalta un citi stāsti* (*A Stoat on the Pavement and Other Stories*, 1980) and *Abpus durvīm* (*On Both Sides of the Door*, 1988). Some of his stories have been made into plays and even filmed, notably the novella *Kolumba mazdēli* (*The Grandsons of Columbus*).

In his longer fiction, such as the novel before you here, the author tends to develop broader themes: the contrast between youth and maturity: *Formarina*, 1953; *Kailums* (*Nakedness*, 1970), *Jauna cilvēka memuāri* (*Memoirs of a Young Man*, 1981, which has been translated into several languages); and later, as the author himself reached mature years, the reassessment of values that comes with age and experience: *Sudrabotie mākoņi* (*Silvery Clouds*, 1967) and *Vīrietis labākajos gados* (*A Man in his Prime*, 1974). But it was the novel *Gulta ar zelta kāju* (*The Bed with the Golden Leg*, 1984) that expanded the author's canvas truly into the historical dimension. This novel ambitiously dealt with a dynasty, tracing the destiny of a single family over the course of a century.

From there it seems a logical progression to this present novel: with the perspective of history, Skujiņš strives to throw into relief the uniqueness of Latvian identity. What makes a person a Latvian? By this time the author had accumulated a body of work in several genres and styles, but even in his more mature years he has been anxious to remain a quester after new forms, and fears stagnation: 'I'm most afraid that this novel has the smell of old age, which can easily happen at my age [...] The most terrible thing is to go into an old-fashioned nostalgic twaddle,' said Skujiņš in an interview published in the literary journal *Grāmatu Apskats* (1999, 6/7). His fear was unfounded; this novel has no trace of the smell of old age. Quite the contrary – the novel is very challenging. Some readers may be daunted by it, but as the critic Guntis Berelis said in a review of the book on its appearance, the voice of healthy common sense that is present in many places really is healthy, and not just the rumination of endless general platitudes. Berelis felt that this questing, restless and provocative work was perhaps Skujiņš' best novel.

The title of the novel well describes the process of its creation. First there is the game of dominoes, whose pieces fit together by matching patterns. Some of the pieces in the domino set are events at the end of the eighteenth century, intertwined in an extravagant Rococo manner; others are events of the twentieth century. And some are universal: those concluding sections in which the plot lines come together, and it becomes clear why the novel jumps between and across the centuries. These sections also contain broader speculations, reinforcing the novel's conceptual base. Some of these 'dominoes' may be read as separate short stories: for examples, the story of the funeral of Aspazija, the celebrated Latvian poetess (1865–1945), who was also the wife of Latvia's national poet Rainis and who became something of a Latvian national institution in herself. Skujiņš had already dealt with this theme in an earlier story, 'Satan's Angel', one of several semi-fictional reassessments of great Latvian literary figures of the past – but in this instance with a conscious sense of a game, as the domino pieces fall together revealing connections that were not immediately obvious. In this falling together of apparently unrelated connections, Skujiņš was applying a creative principle he had used in *The Bed with the Golden Leg*.

Another meaning of 'dominoes' refers to carnival costume. Yet, carnival costume in flesh colour isn't distinguishable from real flesh. A mask is transformed into a face, a face into a mask (recalling Skujiņš' earlier novel *Nakedness*). The author's underlying implication is that history is sometimes reminiscent of a comic carnival, or even a ghostly one, for whose participants the masks are indistinguishable from faces. The roles enforced by society on the individual become part of their natural existence. Doubts arise about the nature of what is 'real'. Sleight of hand with reality seems to be the extraordinary skill of one of the main characters in the novel, Cagliostro – was he a mage or just a charlatan? And who actually was the Pilot (the name by which Herberts Cukurs is unmasked in the novel), in whose character are united a servant of all the powers, a seeker of experiences, a shooter of Jews and a saviour of Jews? Seemingly disparate elements, the author suggests, go to make up the character of a Latvian – if such a nation really exists, he is suggesting, then it is an accidental blending of all kinds of bloodlines. In the twentieth century, the character of Jānis, of Japanese origin and with Oriental features, bears a passport that says 'Latvian'. The eighteenth-century figure of von Brīgen bears exactly the face that our narrator sees in the mirror.

What parts is a person made of? This is a question to which the novel pays special attention, starting from the nightmarish versions of the eighteenth-century soldier, sewn together from two parts by the surgeon, so which is the 'real' identity of the person, the upper or the lower part? The question is then posed: does the whole nation lack an 'upper part'? Skujiņš compels the reader to feel that it is history itself that poses these questions of identity. His gift lies in finding the illuminating anecdote from history, the little-known curious fact that throws light on history's grotesque domino-game with individual and national identity. It is a challenge for the author to provide a plausible background to the implausible mystificator Cagliostro, for example, and he rises to this challenge. The novel begins with his arrival in Jelgava in 1779 (an event also related by another modern Latvian author, Marģeris Zariņš, in a short story). The author/narrator places one of his ancestors in the story as a witness to events. Mystification is also the predilection of this ancestor, Count Bartolomejs Ulste; it is part of the mystification process that the narrator has come into the world after a long chain of generations. Mystification is a great leveller; it is not the exclusive right of the rulers or the ruled. It is a universal principle in world history, and it is comparable to cobbling a person together from several parts.

Skujiņš unmasks several myths and mystifications but immediately builds new ones, including his own self. The biography of the narrator in the novel seems suspiciously close to the author's biography. Are the differences and similarities between them to be taken seriously? Biographical veracity is interwoven with imaginative creation.

Flesh-Coloured Dominoes is easy and pleasant reading (especially thanks to this sensitive and finely-nuanced translation by Kaija Straumanis), but it is not facile reading. Skujiņš' assumption as a writer is that truth is stranger than fiction: the real events of history need little embellishment to seem to stretch the credulity of even an indulgent reader. The absurdities of history are here presented as the apparently random turns in a deadly serious game of dominoes: the apparent paradoxes are part of a logical structure at a higher level. The logical structure may be shaped solely by apparently impossible and at first glance incompatible paradoxes and absurdities. The arrival of Cagliostro in Riga in 2000 in the closing pages of the novel, again linking the centuries, seems to imply that the random operation of absurd events will continue into the future. Like dominoes being laid end to end to form a circuit, the pattern of history repeats itself.

As if to illustrate the capricious nature of the fall of history's dominoes, in a preface to the 2009 edition of this novel (as volume 8 in his Collected Writings), the author relates how, shortly after its initial publication, he was contacted by a reader who indicated that he had evidence that the ramifications of the extraordinary transfer of the court of Louis XVIII of France and his retinue to Jelgava in the late eighteenth century may lead down, through a complex set of family histories, to the author's own personal biography. Skujiņš digresses entertainingly on what is known of the families involved and their possible links between himself and the court of Louis. He has also been reliably informed, he says, that the greatest incidence of syphilis in Latvia for many generations after this 'second Versailles' period was concentrated precisely in Jelgava.

The intersection of a transferred French court, a charlatan from Sicily, and the local German aristocracy on the author's home territory of Latvia at a particular point in history is piquant and fascinating in itself. But perhaps, for a writer of Skujiņš' generation, there are further important signals from history. Up to the Second World War, when the author was in early youth, the ethnically German nobility formed the bedrock of the aristocracy in Latvia, though gradually waning in influence. Yet their life was swept away suddenly by the turmoil of the Second World War; Germans were no longer in the ascendancy, and new foreign masters swept in – the Russian occupiers who forcibly incorporated the still fledgling state into the Soviet Union.

In his later works, too, Skujiņš has continued to re-examine episodes from Latvian history. His novel *Siržu zagļa uznāciens* (*Entry of the Thief of Hearts*, 2001), embellishes the speculations about the life of the great Latvian dramatist and author Rūdolfs Blaumanis (1863–1908). The same author is the subject of one of Skujiņš' numerous plays, which have a habit of revisiting figures from Latvia's past and throwing a new, semi-fictional light on them.

A word about the transliteration of non-Latvian (essentially Baltic German) names. It is a peculiarity of Latvian that all foreign names are re-spelled according to the rules of Latvian spelling; this is so that that names can be adapted to the Latvian case-ending and gender system. The original of this novel was no exception, so the question arose for the translator whether to render the German names according to more orthodox German spelling. As not all of the characters are real, the question of fidelity to an 'original' doesn't always arise. So a compromise arrangement was reached between the author, the translator and the publisher. Other foreign names that are well-known from history, such as Cagliostro, are of course rendered in their familiar original form.

Christopher Moseley
Teaching Fellow in Latvian language and literature
School of Slavonic and East European Studies, University College London

I

I never knew my father or mother. I remember once when I was little, the topic came up over dinner with guests; grandfather said Ausma had gone off overseas with some circus act and disappeared without a trace, like a pebble down a well. After that I'd often peer terrified down the damp and darkened walls of our well, afraid I'd see a drowned woman.

The subject of my mother and father became an issue again when our teacher in junior school assigned us an essay titled 'My Family'. Grandfather just laughed: Write that your mother's a Siamese princess and that your father's Charlie Chaplin. And I wrote something along those lines. As she handed back our workbooks, our teacher joked that I'd be a writer some day, the next E. T. A. Hoffmann. But my nemesis, Consul Egle's son Fabian, spent the break talking loudly about how he doubted children of *those* kinds of women even have fathers. And that my *grand-père* was just a poor carter who made his living off transporting corpses.

That night, Grandfather and I had a long talk. The answer was split in two, like the tips of a fluttering pennant or banner. No child has ever come into the world without a father, and the matter of whose father was better, mine or Fabian's, could only be settled once it was clear what became of the seeds they'd sown.

'So kids come from seeds?'

'How else? Of course from seeds.'

'And where is the seed sown?'

'In the furrow of life, dummy. Where else?' Grandfather stared at me in surprise.

'Life furrows?'

'You've got to be joking,' Grandfather's temper flared. 'We've got seven mares and three stallions in the barn, and you have no clue where the seeds of life are sown!'

Grandfather's eccentric, old-fashioned ways were tied to exacting precision, his wild imagination to deep-seated knowledge. It's possible his old-fashioned ways weren't really him being old-fashioned, but a display of his disdain for conformity. The way Grandfather saw it, what the world needed was entertainment, rich theatrics. He didn't want to do anything the easy way. When performing in Paris, the singer Maurice Chevalier traipsed around in a flat-topped boater, which no one else did any more. When Grandfather worked with the carriages, he'd wear either a light grey English bowler hat or one of his many top hats. In cold weather he'd go out for firewood wrapped in his pelerine cloak. He'd paint benches in the yard while wearing white gloves. His tendency to wear a hat in any situation, it seemed, was driven by a modicum of human vanity: Grandfather was handsome, but his hair was thinning – a fact he either consciously or subconsciously tried to hide.

I've thought a lot about to what I could best compare Grandfather's personality. Maybe the old cash register that sits proudly on the Baroness's desk. Modern registers are definitely more practical, but this old machine was a monumental work of art, made of silvery metal, embossed with chains of flowers. When you cranked the handle and pushed the buttons, the beautiful redwood drawer would jump open with the ring of a bell.

The next morning Grandfather said he had to drive the small carriage to Riga and if I wanted a ride to school he'd drop me off.

The small carriage was incredibly enigmatic. In some ways it was similar to the black mares that pulled it. Now that I'm older and wiser, I'm able to elaborate a bit more on what, back then, were simply vague notions. The things we consider beautiful are, more often than not, a sign of conformity. The brilliance of perfection – be it the beautiful body of a woman, a boat in

3

full sail, a running deer or a luxury car – touches us like the warmth from a stove or the breeze from a draught. The feeling I got when I touched the door of the glistening carriage excited me no less than a lover's caress would ten years later. The cool, red goatskin seat sighed quietly under my weight. I sat between two crystal glass windows like a king on his throne.

The May sun shone brightly. The blossoming row of cherry trees along the Manor's stone wall created a white wave you could almost ski over. Grandfather came out not through the small side door but through the large main door, dressed in a new, light blue riding coat, indicating it was a special occasion. On his head, of course, was a silk top hat.

Five minutes before class started, the carriage swerved in a thin arc up to the school door. One of the classroom windows was open. Fabian's friend Alvis was sitting hunched up like a fat cat, using a pocket mirror to shine the sunlight into the eyes of girls walking by. As soon as he saw the carriage he fell back off the windowsill. And almost immediately several other heads popped into his place, like cuckoos from a clock.

That night, Grandfather and I talked again.

'Do you know what Fabian said? He takes back what he said about you being poor. But you still smell like a stable. Me too.'

'Ah-ah-ah! Tell him that stables aren't the worst smell there is. Foolishness, however, that has a nasty stench! Tell him it's easier to get into Buckingham Palace itself than it is to get into the palace stables. Ask him if he knows that Ernst Biron, the Duke of Courland and regent of Russia under Empress Anna Ivanova, was the Kalnciems Manor stable master's grandson. And ask him: What exactly is a duke, and what a stable master? Compared to the history of mankind, all of these distinctions are short-lived and trivial. One hundred, even two hundred years from now – which in the scheme of infinity is but a single breath – the scale of value will be different. What's a duke compared to Darwin, Kant or Harvey? Like Turandot, the history of mankind will give preference to those who can solve the riddle.'

I listened to Grandfather's words in silence, neither agreeing nor disagreeing. He studied my face and seemed to understand that I wasn't ready for this kind of discussion. He opened the table drawer and took out a deck of cards. 'You see,' he said, spreading the cards out on the table, 'each generation has to learn to play the game from scratch. But there's also genetic inheritance. A skilled player can give birth to children who then inherit an improved version of that player's skill. Do you think our beautiful mares fell from the sky? It's genetic! It doesn't matter where I am, in church or at the market – I can spot a fool from ten paces away. Stupidity, arrogance, violence, those you can see in people's expressions. And words can lie, but the hands never do.'

Grandfather owned what he referred to as a 'cart rental business'. Fabian's scathing comment about transporting dead bodies hadn't exactly come from nowhere. There were also catafalques in the carriage house, sitting in the half-light among the coaches, fiacres, landaus and phaetons that clients rented for weddings, baptisms and confirmations; there were both black and white catafalques, to which two, four or even six horses could be hitched. Put simply, they were hearses, and they looked no different from those used in the times of Mozart, Robespierre and Casanova. There was an airfield a kilometre from the Manor and commercial aircraft would fly over our yard daily as they'd take off and land; but, Grandfather would philosophise, eras always overlap in the end. It really was a fantastical sight when a two-horse catafalque rode out 'to work'. Above where the coffin lay rose a rounded, baroque roof supported by thick pillars and decorated with scalloped drapes and golden palm fronds. The horses were draped with black netting that reached to the ground. Large bouquets adorned the horses' foreheads. A coachman in a long black coat and a crescent-shaped, eighteenth-century hat sat on the coachbox. Four more coachmen, wearing the same black capes and the same crescent hats, were to walk on each side of the catafalque during the funeral procession. The men sat on the edges of the empty carriage as it drove out of our yard. But as they swung their feet back and forth you could catch glimpses of their legs from under their coats and the image was shattered: their trousers were completely of the twentieth century – probably bought from some Jew on Marijas Street or from the new flea market next to the Central Market. Either way, their clothes couldn't date back beyond the First World War.

These strange pretences that were so close to the frightening, intangible mystery of life and death held me tightly in their grip. The entertainment aspect of it didn't make it less real. It was theatre, but instead of plays people performed life. And those who were taken by catafalque to the cemetery didn't take their bows after the show.

The house we lived in also belonged to the era of Mozart, Robespierre and Casanova. It was no palace, even though it had initially been built as the Manor's central building. It was a simple two-storey structure with a great baroque tiled roof and a large fireplace in the middle. Clean lines and balanced proportions gave it a natural beauty, as did the ornately carved wooden doors, the ornamental metalwork and individually designed window shutters.

We – by which I mean Grandfather, the Baroness, Aunt Alma and I – lived in one wing of the Manor. The Pilot and his family lived in the other wing. Or rather, the Pilot's wife and two sons lived there, because the Pilot was usually off flying somewhere in the monoplane he had built himself, the 'White Fuzz'. To Africa, the Canary Islands, or Borneo. You could usually find out where he was by reading the first pages of the newspaper.

The kitchen and giant fireplace were used by both wings of the Manor. When the Baroness caught the Pilot cutting bits from the rack of her smoked ham the sharing stopped. The door to their wing of the Manor was walled shut. If there was anything to be discussed with the neighbours, it was done over the phone. We used oil and carbide lamps for light. There was no electricity in the Manor.

On the ground floor, along with the Baroness's room and the office, was a room that, for some reason, was called the armoury. What it really was, was a changing room for the staff. The walls were lined with large old cupboards which had most likely been built right there; there was no indication that they could be taken apart or that they had in some other way been brought in through the door. The massive, blacksmith-forged locks were no longer used, probably because the keys had long been lost. And the things you could find in those cupboards! Those same pelerine cloaks and grooms' liveries, thick cassocks, Friesian tailcoats and field jackets with bright buttons. The shelves were lined with top hats, bowlers and velvet huntsman's caps. Wigs rested on special wooden stands: a layer of dust and cobwebs indicated they'd lain untouched for some time. The corner of one cupboard was crammed with black mohair armbands and mourning rosettes to pin on hats.

Foggy mirrors in cracked Venetian frames stood between the windows, their mercury faces speckled here and there with bubbles. I'd sometimes sneak into the armoury and stand in front of one of the mirrors, where

I'd become Admiral Nelson, Napoleon Bonaparte, Gulliver, George Washington, Cardinal Richelieu. When combining the contents of those cupboards with things from the other rooms – a blanket, a broom handle, towels or kitchenware – the possibilities were endless. In my imagination I could turn into a musketeer, the Caribbean pirate Captain Morgan, an ancient Latvian soldier or Robinson Crusoe.

The Baroness knew about my pretend games; she'd even play along, sometimes, by letting the door open and close in a ghostly way or by beating eerie rhythms on a chair. We'd look at each other conspiratorially, the Baroness would press a finger to her lips and, carefully lifting her booted feet, would sneak out as quietly as she had come in.

Aunt Alma did the cooking, the cleaning, the laundry, and would introduce herself to strangers as the housekeeper. She couldn't stand the Baroness, not even the sight of her, and called her a crazy German behind her back, and, at least once a week, shouted threats of 'If this keeps up, I'll quit!' Back then I had no idea what she meant, and I didn't try to figure it out. There were no noticeable changes in our lives and Aunt Alma stayed on and continued her threats.

The Baroness was strange, that was undeniable. She wore riding breeches and knee-high boots whether it was winter or summer. She smoked cigarettes and wore men's ties. But at the same time, she went around with her hair curled, enveloped in the scent of perfumes that came from tiny bottles. Born and raised at the Manor, she had also lived there through the First World War and the disorder that came when power changed hands. She had no family. The Manor was technically still her property. Her relationship with Grandfather was complicated. On the one hand, he was her tenant; on the other, the Baroness worked for Grandfather, as the office manager of his 'business'.

The Baroness's family tomb was located at the top of a small hill in the Manor park; it was a concrete crypt with an iron door and marble lions. In Bermondt's time the iron door had been destroyed and the sarcophagi broken into; in turn, the lions had lost their heads to the Bolsheviks. When I was in primary school the tomb was vandalised by 'hooligans'. The lids of the coffins had been pushed down on to the ground, a fire had been made in front of the door. A row of skulls – four or five of them – was lined up on the stone threshold. The rest of the bones were scattered across the entire front of the tomb, along with threadbare rags and scraps of lace, as if there had been an explosion.

The Baroness picked up all the pieces, scraped them together, cleaned them off and put everything back in the coffins. Even the skulls were put back where they belonged. I asked her if she was sure she'd put them in the right places. What if she were wrong and the skulls were mixed up?

'Oh, no!' she answered. 'I know them. That's Bodo, that's Lieselotte, and look, there's Ulrich and there's Augustine ... I've lost count of how many times I've had to put them back! You could say that human bones are just as unique as people themselves.'

'But what if you weren't here?'

She smiled slyly and made our secret sign – she pressed her index finger to her lips. 'That's exactly why I *am* here.'

I was a bit afraid of the Baroness, but was also inexplicably drawn to her. Her room was unlike any other place in our wing of the Manor. A cave of secrets, filled with extraordinary and foreign treasures. The Baroness always had a new box to open, another secret drawer in her Louis XVI secretaire. I could inspect letters written with a quill and sealed with melted wax stamped with a signet ring. I could pin a real *Ordre de la Reconnaissance*, an Order of Recognition issued by the Duke of Courland, to my coat, or hang a real medallion of the mysterious Freemasons around my neck.

I didn't understand a lot of what she'd tell me, but it lent to the atmosphere of the Baroness's personality – the stifled laughter when inspecting strange objects, or the odd tendency to drift off during conversation and lightly, ever so lightly, brush my ear with the tip of her finger.

The Baroness used neither oil nor carbide lamps and instead burned candles. Sometimes one, sometimes three, sometimes more. There were candlesticks all around her room.

'I can't stand oil and carbide,' she said. 'When you let noxious smells into a room they overpower everything else. See how nice this sandalwood fan smells! Or this old leather journal. Candles burn nobly, each with its own character.'

I can see the candles in the Baroness's room, flickering in their silver candlesticks. I can even smell them, crying their tears of melting, yellow wax. And my thoughts weave in playful images like the tendrils of smoke that linger long after the flames are blown out.

II

Do you think the eighteenth century is a thing of the distant past? But this doorknob may have been touched by someone who personally knew Voltaire, the Marquis de Sade, Robespierre and Diderot, Cagliostro, Catherine the Great, Kant or Munchausen. It was only yesterday. Witches and wizards are no longer burned at the stake, but enlightenment and rational thought still mix with sorcery and magic. Educated people take part in table-turning séances, call on spirits of the dead and use occult rituals to try and reach a higher truth. Alchemy flourishes, the world is governed by a belief in secret powers, Kabbalistic symbols, the 'philosopher's stone'. In ballrooms sweltering with candlelight refined gentlemen dance graceful minuets with mannered ladies, as hot tallow drips from the chandeliers on to the plunging necklines of their gowns. Meanwhile, bloodthirsty vampires stir in their coffins in icy crypts; at night they steal out of cemeteries to prey on the living. Then, mechanisation takes the stage. Steam engines develop rapidly. There are disagreements on the classification of the guillotine – some associate the invention of the device with the development of mechanisation, others with the growing influence of humanism.

Then there were the Freemasons and Rosicrucians – champions of a borderless Europe for a like-minded, international partnership of brothers-in-ideas, 'in the name of spiritual enlightenment and well-being'.

Relationships take on a cultured, polished quality. The higher the social circle, the more refined the vices. In the homes of the socially prominent and in royal courts, marriage is as fanciful as the voluminous crinoline petticoats, like the turrets of battleships, worn by rococo women. The only thing touching their hips is the breeze; undergarments are for those who are old or sick. Concubines and mistresses enjoy respect. Marriage is a legal concept, not a moral one. Men and women 'sample' each other as one samples a newly discovered type of biscuit.

Am I mistaken? Is it maybe foolish to talk about virtuous and unchaste eras? There exists a belief that cosmic stability is maintained by the balance of positive and negative energies. Perhaps human society contains within itself a similarly balanced body of positive and negative drives. Maybe the only things that change are its manifestations.

The adventures of Giuseppe Balsamo, alias Count Cagliostro, also known as the Great Cophta, have been recorded to such an extent that to attempt to add one more page to the towers of documents would be like trying to increase the height of Mont Blanc by climbing to the top to dump a handful of sand on its peak. My intent isn't to talk about Cagliostro, but rather to draw attention to people who have yet to find a place in the records and to emphasise a few facts that could still be of interest and encourage people to rethink the present and the future. Even the writer Elisa von der Recke makes no comment on these facts in her book *Reports on the Famous Count Cagliostro's Time in Mitau in the Year 1779 and his Magical Activities*, published simultaneously in Berlin and Szczecin in 1787.

At one of Cagliostro's otherworldly séances, held in Jelgava (Mitau), at the corner of Ūdens Street across from the synagogue, on 21 March of the aforementioned year, Valtraute von Brīgen, who had lived for a long time without any information about her husband's mysterious disappearance in the war against the Turks, asks the Great Cophta to tell her the fate of Captain Eberhart von Brīgen.

Valtraute von Brīgen is visiting her cousin; Valtraute is from the Vidzeme region, born of the Baltic branch of the Līven family. Eberhart von Brīgen is also from Vidzeme, a nobleman from a family of Old Saxon warriors whose ancestors fought as far back as the Crusades in Palestine. Since 1721, Vidzeme has been included in Russia's double-headed eagle empire. Eberhart fights against the Turkish pagans under the Russian flag. His military career advances rapidly: cadet, junker, ensign, lieutenant. When he married Valtraute von Hān, a Līven on her mother's side, at twenty-five years of age, he was already a captain, adjutant general of the Grand Duke Constantine's regiment of cuirassiers. And suddenly – it was all over. The final battle before the Treaty of Constantinople was a fateful one for the fearless officer. In a letter of condolence, General Count Suvorin informs the baroness that von Brīgen has died nobly in battle; unfortunately, he was hit by cannon fire in such a way that 'there was nothing left to bury'. This doesn't sit well with the baroness. The news strikes her as unbelievable. Is it really possible to dissipate a person to the extent there's nothing left? No spurs, no buttons, not even a belt buckle. Is that possible? It's too horrifying. The Ancient Greeks and Romans were convinced that a corpse left unburied had to wander along the River Styx for a hundred years without crossing it. They believed at least three handfuls of sand had to be sprinkled over anyone who died. Only state debtors, temple robbers, traitors and suicides were denied the privilege of a burial. Why did Eberhart have to share their punishment?

Under the light of a lone candle in the spirit chamber, Cagliostro gazes into a crystal ball and spends several minutes murmuring incantations to himself. Then, as he wipes the sweat off his brow, he speaks in an almost agonised voice: 'The baron lives ... he just can't get to you.'

Having spoken these words, which momentarily daze Valtraute von Brīgen, Cagliostro abruptly announces that the séance is over and leaves to take care of the foundation of the Egyptian lodge 'd'Adoption'. The men in the spirit chamber take pity on the flustered baroness, but the majority of the women quickly follow after the Great Cophta. The idea he's come up with – to form a kind of Masonic lodge in Jelgava that would permit women to join – is essentially elegant flattery. But flattery, as is known, is the best pick for unlocking a woman's heart.

That night, after calming down and recovering, von Brīgen seeks out Cagliostro at Lord Marshal Medem's house and tries to learn more about her husband's whereabouts. Cagliostro turns her away. The baroness removes a diamond ring from her finger.

'You tempt me like Satan tempted our Saviour.'

The Great Cophta's smile is sinister, his dusky complexion not unlike the Lord of Hell himself. 'I am not all-powerful, I too must adhere to the wishes of the higher powers.'

'Count, it's a question of life or death!'

The count slips the ring into a hidden pocket under the lace jabot of his velvet coat.

'We shall continue the séance tomorrow.'

The next day, the spirit chamber is packed to the seams. The young Anna Dorthea Medem, fiancée of Duke Peter Biron, has come from Jelgava's Svētes Palace and sits in the seat of honour.

Shortly before the séance, Cagliostro asks Baroness von Brīgen to be patient. Tasks this difficult require the utmost sensitivity, which is not easily attainable. The audience can sense something, the tension builds and expands, women in tightly pulled corsets gasp for air in shallow breaths and nervously flick their fans. The men fiddle with their little phials of cologne, bringing their moistened fingers first to the tips of their noses, then to their earlobes.

Finally, Valtraute von Brīgen's eyes meet those of Cagliostro and she understands that the mage is ready. She is anxious, and the only candle in the chamber once again starts to waver before her eyes.

'If the spirits say that my husband lives, but is unable to come to me … would the spirits be so kind and let me know, through the Great Cophta … let me know … where the baron is right now … what happened to him? I beg of you … *S'il vous plaît! Bitte schön!*'

Cagliostro takes his place behind the candle. Thick beads of glistening sweat once more roll down his powdered forehead. It's understandable since the room is hot; everyone else is also sweating. But Cagliostro slides a silk handkerchief out from his sleeve, wipes the sweat from his brow, and then flicks the handkerchief into the air. Instead of falling to the ground, the white cloth spreads out like a kite and begins to rise. When it reaches the ceiling, it crinkles up and slowly floats back down to Cagliostro's palm.

Cagliostro's eyes roll around in their sockets and his head tosses fitfully from side to side for several moments. Then his movements settle and, as if reciting a passage from a book, he speaks with an icy indifference: 'Where there were two, now there is one. *Helion, Melion, Aldeberanion!* Sacred Osiris! Sacred Anubis! Sacred Bast! *Suton digotpu!* Where there were two, now there is one … That is all I have been given to say…'

The bridge of hope that had been stretched over the abyss slips away. Valtraute von Brīgen is surprised, frustrated, crushed. She tries to question Cagliostro after the séance, to get some explanation of the meaning of his strange words, but to no avail. The Great Cophta tells her dismissively: 'Keep searching!'

The baroness can't find peace of mind. She can't keep staying with her cousin in the sleepy manor, where croaking frogs serenade the windows and tomcats yowl at night. She has to do something.

The next morning she and Bon Esprit, her handmaid, board a stagecoach and head for Riga. An unsettling jaunt in a carriage from hell suits the mood. At the alarming sound of the post horn, the four horses pulling the stagecoach spook and dash ahead at a breakneck speed. Churning mud, splintering gravel.

It's said that the king of France plans to ban stagecoaches on the grounds that they're a menace to society. Newspapers run stories about cows, dogs and people that have been run over. Where a normal carriage rolls sleepily along, a stagecoach covers the distance with a monstrous voracity.

At the Vidzeme house of the knighthood in Riga, the baroness asks whether there is any news of the baron. They tell her he died in battle either near Makhachkala or Kalamakhacha. A treaty has been signed with Turkey. The fallen have been buried, prisoners freed, the regiment has returned to its quarters in Saint Petersburg. What more news could there be? The baroness can write to the headquarters or to the Grand Duke's office. If she hasn't already, of course.

'But they keep sending me his wages.'

'That's probably your widow's pension.'

'No,' the baroness energetically shakes her childlike, heart-shaped face. In fact, the childlike face isn't that of a child, but a regular young woman's face. The baroness is twenty-seven years old. It transforms into a woman's face under a big fashionable wig, with an even bigger hat on top of that. 'What are you talking about! I was told the baron is alive! And until someone sees his grave...'

The knighthood's assessor shrugs and humbly lowers his head and his own modest, official's wig. Almost as if he were showing the baroness the plait at his nape.

That same day, Valtraute von Brīgen writes a letter to the office of the Grand Duke. She decides to wait for an answer from Saint Petersburg right here in Riga, in a hotel. Two weeks later she receives a reply, which repeats Count Suvorin's letter, almost word for word. But there is a sentence at the end of the letter that catches her attention. 'When fording the river, a Turkish cannon hit the boat, the passengers on which were Captain Eberhart von Brīgen, one Captain Bartolomejs Ulste – a baron from Burtnieki (Freiherr von Burtneck) – and his horses.'

Now there is nothing left to do but return home, and at one point that's exactly what she wants to do. But the sentence about the boat sticks in her mind. She was mistaken to think that the mystery of the strange dissipation affected the baron alone. The family of Ulste from Burtnieki has the same problem. And what if they have more information?

Moved with a sudden inspiration, the baroness orders a carriage at the post office and heads with Bon Esprit for Burtnieki. It's a beautiful April day, though the road is full of potholes and bumpy after the spring thaw. They change horses six times and the carriage finally arrives at Burtnieki shortly before midnight. The baroness is exhausted. And it turns out that Freiherr Ulste's family doesn't even live at the Burtnieki manor. The Ulste property is just over a kilometre from the church. The baroness's spirits wilt. She's no longer so confident in her actions. To show up without warning in the middle of the night at a stranger's house, to reopen wounds that might already be healed...

The night is cool, bright and painted with angular shadows. The moonlight reveals a broad lawn with sturdy log buildings. It looks like a real farmer's yard. Strange. But who knows? Vidzeme is taking its time to recover after the long years of war and plague. Not everyone has the means to build new palaces like the barons von Ascheraden, Beļava and Stukmanis. Many families of nobility have moved into farmer's homes. Taverns, of course, are being rebuilt. And meeting places for religious fraternities.

Dogs tear around the carriage, barking madly. A bearded man comes out of the house, wearing a long coat thrown over a shirt and white linen trousers. He's carrying a sword in his hand, but casually, as if it were a cane. The dogs are shooed away.

'Allow me to introduce myself – Valtraute von Brīgen. Please forgive me for bothering you so late. May I please speak with Lady Freiherr Bartolomejs von Burtnieki?'

The bearded man studies the baroness with piercing eyes, but says nothing. She starts to think he hasn't understood her German. But that's not the case.

'Unfortunately that won't be possible. Lady von Burtnieki lives in Reval.'

'Really?' the baroness doesn't hide her dismay.

'But perhaps the Freiherr can help you?'

'Freiherr?'

'The captain.'

'Bartolomejs Ulste? But then ... Forgive me ... My ears are still ringing from the trip ... Is the Freiherr here?'

'You could say so – in a manner of speaking.'

Fear and disgust startle her, as if a spider had run over her naked breasts; what would it be like to meet someone who'd been hit by cannon fire? At the same time, she realises her trip hasn't been in vain. Things have taken such a surprising turn that it's clear she's about to learn something important.

The bearded man helps the women down from the coach. The baroness is unsteady on her feet, most likely from the long trip, but also possibly from what she's just heard. She has to hike up her dress and coat in order to get through the front door. The house is filled with darkness and all sorts of smells. This doesn't surprise the baroness. Since it's not a palace, it's natural for the livestock feed to be prepared in the kitchen. Valtraute von Brīgen is an eighteenth-century woman. She's used to there being a thick layer of smells wafting about wherever there is human activity – such intense smells that they can only be subdued in places where they are overpowered by Parisian perfumes or local fragrances, like crushed sweet flag or dried tansy.

The bearded man leaves them for a moment, then returns with a forked copper candlestick with burning tallow candles. Now they can see something. The room is wide, with low wooden crossbeams. In the centre of the room is a long table with benches on either side. There are a few decorative chairs, a stout little English carriage clock, and a framed oil painting on the wall, of a man in crusader armour.

'I'll go and announce you to the Freiherr. What was your ladyship's name?'

'Baroness von Brīgen.'

'Von Brīgen...' the bearded man murmurs. He takes a candle from the candlestick and, holding it above his head, disappears through the door at the end of the room.

The baroness is once again overcome by a sense of shame, or a sense of awkwardness. But there's no sound, nothing uncomfortable to overhear.

The lull of voices, a chair or stool scraping across the floor, the squeaking of floorboards, and the bearded Prometheus reappears with the candle over his head.

'The Freiherr will be right with you. Please, sit!'

This time the bearded man disappears through the door leading to the yard. The baroness waits. She can't catch her breath; the laces of her corset are digging into her back. She mentally crosses herself. But what is she protecting herself from? She doesn't know.

Finally, the chamber door opens. A hunched-over figure appears in the low doorway, blending with its own shadow. Once it passes through the door, the figure slowly straightens itself to its full height. It's much taller. Much. Good Lord, what a build! And he has a moustache. And long, grey hair, like a wig. The smile that reveals itself under the moustache is white, with one crooked front tooth. But the nose juts right out, sharp and straight like a whetstone. He has no visible scars.

The baroness stares at him, eyes wide. To say she is surprised would be inaccurate. It would be more accurate to say it was as if she had suddenly come across a bear on the road. She'd considered this possibility, meeting a bear, and in fact had hoped for it. But now that the bear is right here, she's not able calmly to assess the unfamiliar beast in front of her. She anxiously wonders what will happen next.

'Good evening, baroness. It's an honour.' The captain's voice is low and even. The warm fluency of his words falters only slightly, with barely discernible lilts of exaggeration, as if he were speaking to a horse, or a child sitting in his lap. The captain approaches the baroness, takes her hand, and bends to kiss it. The familiar, proper gesture puts the baroness more at ease.

'Please forgive us for bothering you so late. We came straight from Riga. You were with my husband in a boat ... Back then...'

'Madame, wouldn't it be best first to take off your coat? You're most certainly tired, and haven't eaten dinner. I assume you don't intend to continue your travels right away. Your home, if I'm not mistaken, is far from here.'

'But to stay on in the middle of the night without warning of our arrival. No, it won't do! When I received a letter from the office of the Grand Duke yesterday, in which you were mentioned as having suffered the same fate as Eberhart, I had the sudden desire to meet your wife. I thought that she would be as unhappy as I am ... The fact that I find you here instead is quite a surprise.'

'I understand! It would be strange if you, as a noble-minded wife, were to act differently. Yes, Brīgen and I forded the river together. Fording rivers isn't a pleasant task. But why are we still standing! *De l'audace!* Guests are guests, no matter the hour.'

Bon Esprit nods her head for the umpteenth time, as if confirming what the baroness has said. Though, most likely, in her sleep. Sleeping with her eyes open is her forte.

The captain claps his hands. 'Ede! Kaspars!'

The bearded man comes into the room, followed by an older woman in plain grey clothing but with a fancy silk bonnet on her head. The bearded man is fully dressed now, in a sweater and boots. The woman apparently dressed in a hurry; her unpinned hair sticks out of the bonnet.

'Set the table! Bring some wine! Ede, take the ladies to the guest chamber first, so they can freshen up from the road. They'll sleep there tonight.'

The baroness looks confused.

'We – '

'Madame, what is there to discuss? Only a monster would let you travel on after such a long journey, and in the dark of night. And what's more, you're justified.'

'Justified?'

'Yes. The justification of a loving wife. You wouldn't think of leaving without getting the last bit of the mystery out of me.'

'No, that I won't. Bon Esprit! Bon Esprit!'

'See, Voltaire was right – logic never fails!'

The captain peers at the baroness and smoothes down the tips of his pale moustache. It's as if the moustache itself is smiling. As are the captain's rough, soldier's lips. The baroness is back before long. She's dressed for dinner in a pointedly simple gown which is, of course, black.

One end of the long table has been set. The third place remains empty. Bon Esprit has excused herself, she doesn't feel well after the journey.

As the bearded man serves the table, there is a sound like a gunshot. The baroness lets out a scream.

'It's fine, it's fine,' the captain assures her. 'This new French wine, champagne, is so energetic that it explodes in the presence of ladies.'

The glasses bubble over with white foam.

'Kaspars, Ede, is everything set? You may go,' the captain calls to them over his shoulder, then turns back to the baroness. 'The first glass, to you! Crusaders enjoy a particular respect in this world. In your case, I commend pilgrims of the heart! Both are essentially driven by the same power. To you and to love, baroness! May your trip be not in vain!'

The captain reaches out and clinks his glass against hers.

'Oh ho, delicious! And what excitement in the glass!'

They eat, drink and converse. The baroness feels her anxiety, which until now has kept her in an uncomfortably tight shell, crack and crumble. Yes, she's still restless, but in a dreamy, bittersweet way, without tension, without feverishness. She wants to express herself, to talk about her feelings for Eberhart, to share her experiences and thoughts.

Captain Ulste appears to be a rather likeable individual and a skilled conversationalist.

'We were introduced by my aunt, Countess Stravinska, at a ball held by Baron Mengdens. My aunt was visiting from Saint Petersburg. Eberhart danced the *périgourdine* beautifully. Then he reserved my dance card for the *anglaise* and the *écossaise*. When we parted ways I said: "*Et voilà tout.*" He answered: '*Non, le coup de foudre.*' We had agreed that he would leave the army after the wedding. Eberhart said that his honour as an officer depended on his staying in the regiment until they won a victory over Turkey. How I waited for him! All hope and fear...'

Is the baroness telling all this to Captain Ulste? Of course, also to him. Though more to herself. Her story consumes her. Once spoken out loud, the words seem to carry some of the weight away with them. But maybe she's speaking out of cowardice, out of fear, in order to draw out the unknown, which could still end up being better than what she is about to be told.

The captain sits in a relaxed pose, his elbow on the table, his big, square jaw resting in one hand. He holds his glass in the other.

'Why am I wasting time with my own story, when what I truly want is to listen to what you have to say?'

'A truth doesn't become less true if you place another truth next to it.'

'Captain, sir, you know the reason for my visit.'

For a moment, Ulste's gaze wanders from the baroness. The hand under the chin pulls away. The glass is set down on the table.

What is the captain about to do? Nothing. He silently raises both hands, palms facing the baroness, as if to say – fine, if that's what you wish.

'I have to start with a brief introduction...' The baroness senses the captain's gaze close in on her once again, holding her tightly, as if he's just barely lifted her off the ground, allowing her only partial control over herself. Almost like when she was a child, when her father would lift her up by the armpits, and all she could do was wiggle her arms and legs in the air. A feeling that both frightens and excites you.

'We've all learned the Bible story about Jesus' trial before Pontius Pilate, when Pilate asks the Son of God: "What is truth?" A truly incredibly valuable question. Even in our all-knowing time of enlightenment, the answer was ambiguous and unclear. Truth could be an assumption that had yet to be overturned. When we use concepts like "possible" and "impossible" as arguments, we corner ourselves like a bunch of chickens jammed into a coop. Until the day the mystery of the circulation of blood was discovered, everyone thought man was a bag of skin filled with red liquid that kept the body from drying out and the bones from rattling around. In the past, if someone had said that the power that thunder and lightning create during a storm could be re-created artificially and put to use, that person would have been taken for an imbecile. Doctors tell people to vaccinate themselves against smallpox with cowpox. Does that sound believable? No! But vaccinated people don't get sick. Another example: everyone was accustomed to the fact that Louis XV's mistress Madame de Pompadour was practically toothless. But what do you know? One bright day Madame de Pompadour is once again smiling like a young lady in her prime. It turns out teeth can not only be pulled out, but also put in.'

'What are you saying? Really?'

The baroness's rapt attention is interrupted by her question, her voice full of disbelief and excitement. Teeth are no trivial matter to an eighteenth-century woman. The baroness's barber has already pulled two of hers, and who knows what will happen with a third. Luckily, if she doesn't open her mouth too wide, it's not noticeable.

'Yes, baroness, nothing ages as quickly as knowledge. We'll experience many miracles in our lifetime!'

'If only Comte de St Germain would share his elixir of life! It's not fair that he's already lived three thousand years, but won't reveal the secret of his elixir! Maybe he's a liar and the stories about those three thousand years are nothing more than stories.'

'In which case there are a few facts that are hard to explain. St Germain claims he fought with Count Charles of Anjou in 1268 against Conradin in southern Italy. Recently, in Versailles, St Germain described the armour Anjou wore. And a tenth-generation descendant of the count, who was privy to the conversation, confirmed that that's what the armour had looked like. Yes, it was stored in his ancestral palace.'

'Has he ever been married?'

'St Germain?'

'Yes. It would be interesting to know how old his wife is.'

'Count Orlov asked him that during a party with the empress.'

'And what did he say?'

'That three thousand years is a long youth. He'll marry some day. And he added that, in her time, he'd liked Cleopatra very much. Nefertiti had also been rather pleasant, even with the wart above her left eye.'

The captain refills their glasses yet again. The last of the bottle pours out. Another cork shoots into the rafters with a sharp crack.

'Oh, this champagne would be a wonderful wine, if only it weren't so military...' The baroness wants to say that the exploding corks frighten her. At night she wakes with a start when shots and blasts ring out in her dreams. She wants to talk about the uncertainty, the negative thoughts that turn life into a sombre game, as if she's searching blindfolded for the lost Eberhart. She can't tell the sad story without crying. She wants to cry right now, but to her surprise lets out a laugh, and her laughter sounds so lively that the candles flicker gaily.

The captain drains his glass and is silent for a moment, then speaks again. It's as if he's brought his strong shoulder forward to join the weaker one in the struggle upstream.

'Our regiment's surgeon was Almustaf Gibran, a Lebanon-born Christian. When he was ten years old, his father, a rich trader, sent him to school in England. After graduating from Cambridge, Gibran chose to work in India, even travelling as far as Persia, where he befriended the son of a Russian envoy and married the young man's sister.

'Gibran first gained fame in Saint Petersburg as a skilled post-duel physician. Then, when he delivered a live baby girl from the Countess Gagarin, who had died in childbirth, he was the main topic of conversation in the salons of high society. But when he saved the beautiful Princess

Volkonsky from a scandal at the court he unfortunately got mixed up in a surgical procedure prohibited by law and punishable by the church. It promised great trouble. His friends took care of it that Gibran became a regimental physician and left to fight against the Turks.

'Ask anyone in Saint Petersburg, Riga, Paris or London, what a war physician is, and they'll tell you: a glorified butcher, nothing else. On the battlefield, wounds are caused by lances and swords, lacerations from shrapnel, torn-off limbs. The distrust of doctors is so great that many refuse aid. How often have you seen one-armed or one-legged men in your so-called high society? In the case of more serious injuries, it's with honour and pride that officers forgo a doctor and find a priest instead.

'Gibran hated crude scalpel work; he was born an artist. Should that come as a surprise? The world is full of organ-grinders, and buskers. But this one wants to play differently because he's Haydn. Or Boccherini. Names are meaningless; we're talking about talent.

'When Ensign Lefevre lost his hand in battle at Gurjani, Gibran wanted to sew it back on for him. The only problem was that he didn't have the right colour thread to hand, so the seam was a darker colour and the young man was forced to wear gloves with longer cuffs.'

'How fascinating!' the baroness exclaims. 'Was it his right hand?'

'If I remember correctly, it was the left.'

'Well, then, that's fine! Men hold their left hands behind their backs in many dances...'

'But that was only the beginning. Lieutenant Narishkin was cleaved in half by some massive janissary. The top half, of course, fell to the ground right there. But the bottom half! It was something else! His boots in the stirrups. His arse in the saddle, as if it were glued there. His horse, a beautiful dappled mare, was spooked and galloped around the battlefield with his bottom half for some time. Thank God it didn't run into the Turkish camp. Gibran worked for forty-eight hours without sleep. We were stunned speechless. When Narishkin came to and asked for a glass of vodka, the commander removed the Order of St Andrei Pervozvanny from his uniform and pinned it on to Gibran's: "The world has never seen anything like this before." But Gibran answered: "Permit me to disagree, your grace. The possibilities of medicine are ruled by the unknown."'

'And that's what really happened?' the baroness says, her hands clasping her burning cheeks.

'What in my story, madame, strikes you as unbelievable?'

'It sounds so thrilling. This is the first time I've heard anything like it!'

'Luckily, like naivety in love, ignorance tends to be fleeting. The world is interesting precisely because it's possible to learn something new now and then. As a child, I often had to read the Bible, where there are miracles upon miracles. If I were to recite what's written in Holy Scripture, would you say it was possible or impossible? Like when God takes one of Adam's ribs and makes Eve. If God is all-powerful – and I don't doubt that he is – why couldn't he create woman the same way he made birds, animals, fish? Why did he have to open Adam's side like a surgeon, dig around in his insides, and disturb a finished product? But maybe that's typical of surgery as a method – to continue and improve on what was apparently finished. And what about the legends that are older than the Bible? The flying griffin – half-lion, half-eagle. Or the centaur – a combination of horse and man. Who created them? And why?'

The baroness fidgets in her chair. Is the captain really waiting for an answer from her? Oh, the room is so hot! They couldn't possibly still be feeding the stove; the swelter must be coming from the kitchen...

'Neither God nor the devil had wives, that's where the problem lay. The case of Mary is above suspicion!'

'You think Mary was the only one to become with child by the Holy Spirit? Look there, on the shelf is Abbé Checret's *De Resurrectione*, which includes an account of what happened in Avignon in 1317. The knight Fachon goes into battle against the Moors and, as was custom in those times, fitted his wife in an iron chastity belt. A year and a half later the knight returns home. The iron belt is where he left it, the key is around his neck, but his wife is pregnant! Very well, never mind Fachon. I was talking about Gibran...'

'Yes, yes, about Gibran!'

'At the battle at Chava, a junker named Hvastchikov lost an eye. His eyes were a peculiar colour – a silver that sparkled on sunny days like the blade of a sword reflecting the sun. Gibran took a look at the young man and said he could put in a new eye, but not one the same colour. There are both positives and negatives to being so different from the rest. What could he do? Gibran put in a new eye, but it was what he could get at such short notice – light brown, the colour of a walnut. And that's where the trouble started! Hvastchikov was, of course, released from duty. He returns to Saint Petersburg, where his fiancée is waiting for him. The first few days are spent intoxicated with joy. After a while the bride-to-be notices that her one of her fiancé's eyes is brown, and asks him: "Why is it like that?" The junker tells the story – it's the eye Gibran put in. The bride-to-be throws her hands in the air, and it takes her some time to calm down. "So it's not even your eye?" "No, it is. It's mine now." "But whose was it before? Some Turkish pagan's?" "I don't know, probably not."

'But she won't let it be. "It's like you're looking at me as a half-Turk. How awful! The eyes are a mirror that reflect the soul." "But it's just a reflection. A mirror can't change what it reflects." "Then you've never been in a carnival hall of mirrors! You can't trust what you see in the reflections!" The engagement is called off. Hvastchikov's parents file a complaint with the empress. They want to bring Gibran to court, but it turns out he hasn't broken any laws ... In the end, and just in case, they ask Gibran to relocate not far from the army camp.

'So! Now it's time finally to solve the mystery that you, your ladyship, so eagerly want to learn. The truth is self-conscious, with a feminine nature. It becomes flustered at the idea of its nakedness. And it can be just as flustering to someone who has to see that nakedness...'

'Good God! Dear captain, put an end to my uncertainty! What am I – a wife or a widow?'

'What are you? What does that mean – to be? As if a widow couldn't become a wife, or a wife a widow.'

'Please, let me be happy. Please, please!'

'Both happiness and sorrow are fleeting. It's just our imagination. To imagination!'

'Captain, sir ... Know that no matter what has happened, I will never give up Eberhart. I love him ... You must know that...'

'May you never lack the strength to love him!'

'May I never lack the strength!'

'Did you drink it all? Your glass is empty?'

'Empty. Please, tell me! Tell me, I'm listening!'

'When the snow melts in the mountains, the rivers overflow. The Çamur is fed by mountain streams, but it flows along a flat valley and is wide and deep. The Turkish troops led by Mustafa Şekeroğli weren't great in number, around one thousand men, but they were protected by the river. General Wrangel's plan of attack was quite bold. In the spring, fog settles in the valley every morning. The general ordered us to create smoke as well, by burning wet straw along the riverbank. And, of course, we had to build rafts for the infantry and cavalry. The boat mentioned in your letter isn't factual. Eberhart and I weren't in the same boat, but on the same raft. We had to nail flat boards to the rafts, because the horses weren't able to stand on the curved surface of the logs.

'We moved out at four in the morning. But even with the smoke and fog, the Turks caught sight of us once we reached the middle of the river. And that's when all hell broke loose! Their cannons were well positioned. The water boiled and the sky rained down.

'What happened after that – let me tell you, there is nothing simple about death on the battlefield. A sudden push, the raft under our feet was suddenly a confusion of lumber over our heads, and that was it...

'As I said, Gibran no longer lived with the regiment. He had relocated half a mile down the river. Woken by the sounds of the battle, he had come out on to the pebbled riverbank with his pipe for a morning smoke. After a few minutes, pieces of timber, men and horses, started to float past. Gibran called his servant, and they both watched for soldiers with lesser injuries. They didn't see any.

'Then the stream carried a strange jumble of body parts close to the shore. Two bodies had somehow hooked on to each other by the belts of their cuirasses. Here, your ladyship, I should explain that cuirasses are the heavy armour worn by mounted cavalrymen, which is where the name "cuirassier" comes from. One officer is missing his upper body, the other his lower body. It's not hard to imagine how things would have turned out under different conditions. But whether it was due to luck or to misfortune – it could go either way – this was Gibran, a talent leagues ahead of anyone else in his time. Once he was sure the ice-cold water hadn't deadened the tissue of the half-bodies, Gibran decided to salvage what he could. And in this case, in the only way possible – by combining the two halves to make a whole...'

The silence that follows Captain Ulste's words is long and meaningful, like at the opera when the spotlight falls on the soloist.

'Forgive me, captain, I don't quite understand...'

'There's nothing to understand. Both of us – Eberhart von Brīgen and I – are now one person. His lower body, my upper.'

The baroness grasps the table and stands up slowly. Her expression has changed to confusion. She can't grasp whether what she has seen and heard is happening in real life, or whether she's like an amateur actress who doesn't know that she's part of a ridiculous play.

'Later, of course, when they retrieved the fallen soldiers, Eberhart wasn't among them.'

'Captain ... please! Are you mocking me?'

'Madame, I understand. The situation truly is a bit unbelievable.'

'You understand?'

The baroness repeats the captain's words as if hypnotised. And immediately she wakes at the sound of her own voice. She looks at the captain as if she's seeing him for the first time, and her wide-eyed surprise and subdued expression turn to full awareness. There are two points in front of her – the thick, green champagne bottle and the captain's head with its ashen hair pulled back into a braid. The shortest path between two points is a straight line. With a distinctly feminine, yet simultaneously determined, motion, the baroness's hand connects the two points. The bottle doesn't break.

III

Even if the *I* of the daytime shines in its complete form and content, the *I* on the night side of things is never safe from danger. Dreams enhance desires, dramatise misgivings, reveal suspicions. The connection to society is illusory, we're forced to solve our deepest conflicts by ourselves. There's no good comparison. In the grand scheme of things, even so-called real life is just symbolic because we glide through time with causes and effects waiting in the inaccessible wings of the mind.

When I was still a boy, a large part of my world consisted of dreams. You could almost say that I lived more intensely at night than during the day. My life made the daytime seem colourless and insignificant. Not once during the day had I ever been frozen in fear, but in sleep I knew the feeling well. Not once during the day had I been tormented, but in my dreams I ran both from terrible beasts and from natural disasters: cliffs toppled down on to me, the ground gave way beneath my feet, I'd fall into dusky chasms for some unknown reason and from some unknown place.

I'd also run into my mother in the intensified night-time world. The attractive woman dressed in a long, shimmering dress and with a dog-training switch in her hand was faceless. But I knew she was my mother, and found her strange appearance fascinating. She'd walk along a tightrope strung between the stars. I didn't want her to go any farther; I wanted her to float down to me with her umbrella. Other times, a magician put my mother in a box and made her disappear, and once the act was over she was nowhere to be found. Everyone looked for her in a panic; uniformed arena staff lifted the tile floor. I still remember how, after the show, I'd be sitting all alone in the empty, dark circus tent, and how my heart would ache.

Later on, girls from school visited my dreams, as did the younger female teachers. One in particular. For example, the two of us would be in some kind of old warehouse, maybe an old mill. This teacher would climb up to the second floor and I'd stay downstairs. Suddenly, a few of the second-storey floorboards would collapse and the teacher would be hanging there above me. I couldn't see her face or torso, just her lower body dangling through the ceiling.

My dreams got to me. I'd feel uncomfortable when I was near the teacher and, either because I was embarrassed at myself, or because I wanted to hide my weakness, I started acting like an idiot: I'd speak in a defiant tone in class, I avoided eye-contact when she spoke to me, when we passed each other in the street I pretended not to see her. And at night I experienced even wilder scenes. I was fourteen years old, old enough for my sight to have been altered and, in the words of Ibsen's Troll King, for my world view to have changed.

One morning at breakfast, Aunt Alma handed Grandfather an envelope plastered with strange stamps. Upon reading the letter, Grandfather's response was one of laughter. Grandfather laughed often and about many things: when reading an article in the newspaper, when looking over my report card, when seeing a newborn colt in the stalls, when straightening his tie in front of the mirror. But over the course of time I'd learned to differentiate between the tones. This time his laughter indicated surprise.

'Well I'll be...' Grandfather chuckled, 'read it for yourself!'

There was a national coat of arms on the letter. It was a notification from the Latvian consulate in Rotterdam that Jānis, the son of Latvian national such and such (my mother) registered at the consulate and deceased as of a year ago, is at the orphanage located in such and such. The authorised individuals of said orphanage approached the consulate with the request to locate any family said orphan might have in Latvia. If the honourable sir such and such (Grandfather) would be willing to take on full legal responsibility for the health and well-being of the boy, he (the consul) requests to be informed of such via a notarised letter of response. Sincerely and with highest regards, such and such, Consul of Latvia to Rotterdam, Kingdom of Holland.

I handed the letter back silently and was surprised that I didn't feel like crying, which would seem natural considering I'd just been notified of my mother's death. I realised that I never had any real connection with my mother. That is to say, she had, in fact, been dead to me all these years. The idea of her existed only as a dream, but letters of notification don't apply to dreams. Nothing changed in my relationship with my mother.

'It looks like I've got a brother. Did you know?'

'I didn't know anything.'

'What happens now?'

'What do you mean "what happens"? You have a brother. We're obviously not going to let our own flesh and blood rot in some random country's orphanage.'

Our correspondence with the consulate brought us to one fine autumn day when Grandfather and I hitched up the little carriage and drove to the Riga shipping yard, where Jānis was supposed to arrive. Aunt Alma came with us, because there was not a word in the letters about how old Jānis was. What if he still needed to be dressed and have his nappy changed?

The trip, as you well know, had nothing to do with work. Grandfather was the coachman for personal reasons, but he still wore his light blue riding coat. And on his head, tipped forwards slightly in a casually refined way, was his favourite silk top hat. The thought of presenting himself in a banal and everyday manner at such a significant and celebratory moment would never have occurred to him.

The ship was already nearing the dock. A black cargo ship, loaded to capacity and sitting low in the water. One of those old-fashioned vessels with slender funnels, the kind that ran regularly between Riga and Rotterdam, set apart as a unique piece of shipping history with their strange names: *Everonika, Everanna, Everastrīda, Everelza*. Their usual cargo was lumber, coal or mineral fertilisers. They also often had a few inexpensive cabins available for less picky passengers.

A man in a sailor's jacket and a cap with an embroidered anchor on the front stood at the end of the gangway. Next to him was a boy of about ten years old. The boy looked exactly as I had imagined a Japanese boy would look – I had never seen one in real life. He had a round face, skin the colour of an onion, shiny black hair, narrow, black eyes framed by glasses and curved lips around bright white teeth.

Grandfather hurried in the direction of the steward, calling out: 'Any passengers on board?'

'Who are you looking for?' The steward responded to the elegant wave of Grandfather's top hat with a brisk, military salute.

'I'm looking for my grandson, Jānis.'

'Jānis's introduction to the Northern Sea was brutal. But he's back on his feet again. He's all yours!'

Then the boy spoke. In perfect Latvian.

'Greetings, dear Grandfather! I'm so happy! Mother told me so much about you.'

Grandfather's confusion lasted for only half a second. I was waiting for his typical laughter, a gesture showing doubt or confusion, at least a grimace of surprise. Instead, he slowly removed his ivory-handled magnifying glass from his breast pocket and lifted it towards the speaker. His other hand tightly grasped the little shoulder of the round-faced parcel.

'Forgive me, Grandson, for not recognising you. It happens. You see, it's been ages since I last saw you.'

IV

What stupid tales! Shameless, wicked mockery! Joking around when it's no time to joke. And that's not all! Claiming to be Eberhart von Brīgen's upper half! Without the least bit of respect for the decades-old generation of nobility. When he himself isn't even a registered Vidzeme landowner. He's most likely a descendant of local farmers. That's what Ulste is! An upstart. A cheeky military farmhand. Probably the relative of some Latvian dragoon officer who was transferred into Tsar Peter's troops along with General Löwenwolde of the defeated Swedes.

Inertia is taking over. It's so easy and tempting to give in. The inertia of these hateful thoughts rocks the baroness in smooth arcs as if she were swinging, a pastime that, through rococo fashion, has recently been greeted with enthusiastic approval in the eighteenth century. If only because, while gracefully flying through the air, ladies can show off their new and racy stockings.

But the smooth arc jams, gets caught, freezes. The baroness flies off the swing. Terrified, she remembers the words Cagliostro spoke in Jelgava: 'Where there were two, now there is one.'

Madness! Is she dreaming? Maybe that French champagne is to blame. It seemed like such a light, wonderful drink. Eberhart would never have let her have an entire bottle.

The captain lies on the ground, stiff as a board. His forehead is bleeding. His feet, clad in heavy army boots folded down just below the knee, are splayed out like the needles of a compass. The baroness is most disturbed by the way the supine captain's boots look in the candlelight, toes pointing straight up towards the ceiling. Like a corpse, the baroness thinks; maybe he really is dead.

She doesn't feel bad – not even a little guilty. It's just an unpleasant situation. As if she had suddenly tripped and upon getting up discovered her clothes had got dirty. But Cagliostro's prophecy bores its way through these instantaneous feelings – could the parallels be coincidence? What if she's killed not only Ulste but her beloved Eberhart as well! Rather, her beloved Eberhart's lower half. Something of him, in any event. Which is by no means insignificant, if he no longer exists in this world in any other way.

The baroness takes a few teetering steps towards the captain and wipes his bloodied forehead with a handkerchief. She has to hope for the best. A solid male forehead can't be that easy to break; it's not as if it's a raw egg. He's just a bit dazed. She should try to get him into a bed. Tomorrow he won't even remember what happened. And then she'll sneak into the guest room and slip in next to Bon Esprit. Then calmly think about what to do next. The day is smarter than the night.

She listens carefully for any sounds of activity. No, she doesn't hear anything. She grabs Ulste by the boots as if they're a pair of wagon shafts and drags him towards the door.

If the captain is telling the truth, the baroness is holding Eberhart's feet in her hands. Her heart jumps and the room spins before her eyes. She's made it to the threshold and pushes down on the door handle. The threshold is ridiculously high. The captain's limp arms catch on something in the half-dark. No matter, there's no stopping now, all she can do is keep pulling. *Lieber Gott*, is he heavy! The baroness tugs desperately with the last of her strength. She has to pry the captain's body off the ground one way or another. His head rolls with difficulty over the obstacle, landing with a loud crack against the clay floor like a stallion's kick to a stable wall.

Now she has to get the heavy lump into bed. She could just leave him on the floor; it would look more believable – he fell out and hurt himself. The weak glow of candlelight shines into the captain's room from the open door. The baroness wedges her hands under the captain's arms and tries to lift – but his sleeves and torso feel as if they're filled with cast-iron bullets. Looking for a better way to hold on to the limp figure, she finds his belt and tries to lift with that. Nothing. It gives her a better grip on his waist, but no leverage. The captain slides back to the floor. The baroness is tense from the effort, and at times recoils as if she's been stung by a nettle when her cheek touches a bristly chin, her breasts brush against the manly, barrel-like chest. Ulste isn't dead; life is literally steaming forth from him with his pungent male smells, the same ones she couldn't stand with Eberhart. They often reminded her of the rough life of the soldier: sweat, tobacco, wet leather, horse stables ... Suddenly the baroness feels the captain's arm, which until now had been hanging limply over her shoulder, slide down her side, and his hand takes hers.

'Close the door ... Kaspars is coming...'

The baroness jumps, snatching her arm away from him; she wants to scream, but the words 'is coming' cause her to freeze like a startled lizard.

'Close the door!' the captain repeats. 'You don't want to wake Bon Esprit.'

And risk scandal in the middle of the night in a strange man's bedchamber? Never! The baroness lunges to the door. The hinges aren't greased and creak horribly.

'My lord, did you call?'

'No, Kaspars. Blow out the candles and go to bed.'

Kaspars can be heard moving about for a few moments, then all is quiet. The surrounding darkness isn't so endless. The room has a six-pane window – a rather fancy house – and the moon shines brightly outside. Her back against the door, the baroness listens fearfully to the fading sounds, but her eyes are locked on the man sitting on the floor. As if, like Daniel, she were facing a pit of lions.

'Now, where were we?' the captain asks.

'You're a scoundrel!'

'Ah yes, the joining of bodies...' The captain's voice sounds a bit dream-like, but otherwise it's as if they were still sitting at the table, glasses in hand. 'Madame, come, come closer! Your soft hands have the opportunity to find tangible proof.'

His mysterious words shake the baroness like a strong breeze whipping a sail. But it's a force that doesn't come without an action. To keep herself composed, to keep from slapping the captain, Valtraute von Brīgen jerks back so violently that her head slams against the door just as loudly as Ulste's had against the floor.

'What proof?'

'Of Eberhart, of course. So you can see for yourself. I understand that's why you came here.'

'What are you talking about!'

'You don't believe me?'

'Of course I don't. I've still got my wits about me.'

But the edge in her voice is gone. Her fear subsides as well. Hasn't she sworn to brave fire and water for Eberhart?

'You're even more doubting than doubting Thomas.'

'Forget your Thomas! You've already explained one Bible story to me.'

'True. But come over and put your hand here. Here, here, right in this spot!'

It's not entirely clear where Ulste is pointing to. He unbuckles his belt and unbuttons his shirt.

'Don't you dare move! I'll scream until the whole house shakes.'

'You can scream once you've seen it. An examination requires composure. Obviously it would be better if your partner's lower half came to you. But considering the circumstances...'

'What circumstance? What examination?'

'Let's start by determining the border. With the seam.'

'Seam?'

'Yes, where the area that doesn't interest you stops, and where your rightful territory begins...'

'To say something like that!'

'I can also say nothing.'

What is happening under her massive wig and under her tightly laced corset? The whole thing reminds her of a hen house under attack by a fox. Everything that until now has remained complacently dormant is suddenly caught up in a whirlwind. Chaos and fluttering, a mess of feathers. Wings flapping in despair, fright and doubt, curiosity, excitement and anger. But maybe her femininity is playing hide and seek, to keep from ruffling its pride by giving in? In the end – if it is Cagliostro's prophecy ... After all, at the altar, she did promise to be with him in sickness and in health...

'Just don't try anything. I'll do it myself!' The baroness takes a few cautious steps towards the captain and slowly, slowly reaches out her hand. By her expression one would think she were about to sift through the remains of an unearthed casket.

'Closer, baroness, closer. What are you afraid of? You're the rightful owner, not a poacher.'

'Captain! Please!'

'With all due respect, madame. You remind me of the woodlands goddess Diana.'

'It's like a jungle! Oh-oh-oh...'

'And right there's the border.'

'Oh-oh-oh ... Where exactly?'

'Here, go on, go on.'

'*Lieber Gott!* And that's the seam? And it goes the whole way around?'

'Like a ring around a finger.'

'Unbelievable ... Inconceivable...'

'I'd sit down if I were you. You can't always rely on looking from afar.'

What she does next is beyond her own comprehension. Like being thrown from a horse and then dragged along behind it, your hands holding tightly on to the reins. You know you have to let go, but your fingers are cramped and won't move.

The baroness looks to the door, gathers her skirts with her left hand and carefully settles down next to the captain.

'This is only where your rightful territory starts,' Ulste urges her. 'Don't tell me this is your first time there.'

The baroness timidly moves her hand downwards. Her cheek is pressed against Ulste's shoulder. The strange weakness turns into shivers. As if she'd been pulled from the water and placed on an iceberg.

'And, do you recognise him?'

'What kind of absurd question is that!'

'Eberhart recognises you...'

'*Lieber Gott!*'

'Blessed are those who have lost, for they have hope to find again.'

'You ... You're lying! Oh-oh-oh!'

'See, Eberhart, your wife has already managed to forget you!'

'Captain, what are you doing? Captain ...'

'Try to understand Eberhart, your loving husband...'

'Please, no, it's not possible ... Oh-oh-oh!'

'Don't tell that to me. I'm not getting involved in your family affairs.'

There is the quiet murmur of Ulste's laughter; the dark sparks with Valtraute von Brīgen's gasps and sniffles. Then a sharp intake and exhalation of breath, as if a person drowning disappeared beneath the waves, as if a runner racing up a steep hill suddenly lost his footing.

'Eberhart ... My love ... How could I not recognise you...'

V

Jānis and I ended up sharing a room. Fourteen is a peculiar age. If my brother had shown up earlier, it's possible I would have experienced things differently. My ego would have been threatened, I would have begun a war of competitiveness, which could even have resulted in our hating one another. But at fourteen, it didn't even cross my mind enviously to hoard my belongings or, for example, to fight for a place next to Grandfather on the coachbox. Instead, my curiosity intensified regarding the veiled nature of his arrival. I wanted to know and understand everything because it had struck our family chord. My pride tingled pleasantly with the knowledge that I had reason to look upon myself as an adult. Nevertheless, my brother's sudden arrival was an even more exciting affair. Back then, adventures were at the top of my list of values.

When I use the word 'brother', it's not meant to be taken in a narrow context. I knew he was my brother and tried to accept him as such, though I could've just as well accepted storybook characters, like the Latvian hero Kurbads, or Michelangelo's David, as my brothers. Driving home from the harbour, it was as if we had a mysterious package with us, not a real person. Yes, the package could end up being my brother, but first we had to unwrap it, breathe new life into it, find logical connections. It was intriguing, even enchanting. I was almost sparking with excitement.

Years earlier I had stared into the well, trying to find my mother's face; now I looked at my new-found brother the same way. My mother in the well was just my imagination at play, whereas finding her face in my brother's had a certain amount of realness to it – in spite of how far-fetched the idea was. At least Jānis would know and be able to tell me things about my mother that no one else knew or would be able to reveal.

My mother had left Latvia as an assistant in my father's act, which in its time was considered a high-class one. My mother would sit on a chair that my father would balance on the end of a tall bamboo pole. My father, stage name Mario Rinaldini, was actually a young Latvian man from Valmiera. One day, as the circus tent was being taken down, one of the support poles toppled and crushed him. There was also a magician in the circus troop, Konishiki ('fine design' in Japanese). Every night of a performance he'd cut a pretty young woman in half with a circular saw and then put her back together again. When Konishiki's Japanese assistant fell ill, he asked if he could saw my mother in half. My mother was beautiful, with long, honey-blonde hair. She agreed.

The performance was an unbelievable success. Once the circular saw had sliced through her with a whine Konishiki would show the audience the two halves: my mother's upper body with its girlish face and flowing, angel-like hair, and, over there, the milky white legs with gold slippers on their feet. Children wailed, women screamed and men wanted to storm the stage to deal with this Frankenstein. But when the box was put back together and my mother climbed serenely and gracefully from it in one piece, the tent resounded with such sighs of relief, followed by such standing ovations, that contrary to circus tradition they would often perform an encore.

Jānis was born in one of the sleeper wagons; the circus was travelling to Spain at the time. His first memory is of an elephant rocking his cradle with its trunk. Its gigantic head and flapping ears loomed over him like a dark cloud. It's possible it wasn't a cradle but a rocking chair – Jānis was already two years old then.

Our mother's being sawn in half was kept from Jānis for a long time, but he ended up seeing the performance one day anyway. After the show, our mother hurried over to him, hugged him and asked: Were you very afraid? Were you very worried about me? No, Jānis answered. And then sensed our mother was upset. Her sweet boy sees his mummy cut in half, but he's not concerned. His father, on the other hand, is pleased. Of course he won't show fear; for a Japanese man to show his emotions is a sign of extreme weakness. But it's obvious Konishiki is delighted, and his words make it even clearer.

'*Akebono*' ('dawn' in Japanese), his father says to our mother, 'you forget there is also Japanese blood coursing in Jānis's veins. His ancestors were samurai in the Tokugawa shogunate era.'

After that conversation, our mother switched from speaking English to only Latvian, and Konishiki would listen calmly and participate in conversations by speaking Japanese.

Jānis never had trouble with languages. When asked what languages he could speak, he'd answer – all of them. And add, it only requires perseverance. Do you know what Konishiki used to say? With perseverance, a fly could eat a lion; in terms of perseverance, the Japanese are second to the fly.

Grandfather was worried that Jānis's knowledge wouldn't be sufficient for him in junior school, where some of the lessons were already being taught in French. Jānis hadn't attended school regularly while travelling the world with the circus. But after spending all summer being taught at home, Jānis was not only able to pass the tests but was moved up a year.

From the above you might get the impression that Jānis was a talker, someone who spoke freely and at length about all his adventures and experiences. But he was nothing of the sort. Getting Jānis to talk about something was like trying to untangle a net. On rare occasions he would speak suddenly, out of nowhere and without any prompting. Sometimes it would have nothing to do with the topic at hand. For example, when talking about football one day, he suddenly said: 'Just a game with a goal, that anyone could play. Now sumo, that's something. Sumo wrestling is for warriors!'

Jānis took a photograph of sumo wrestlers from his shirt pocket: bodies inhumanly large, two to three hundred kilogrammes-large, hard-cut expressions like the faces in Shinto art, and the quavering girth of Buddha in their massive bellies.

Behind his words were Jānis's sensitivity about his own small stature, as well as his desire to be tall and strong. And to a certain extent his way of thinking and how he perceived life. Sumo wrestlers were people like the gods, and that meant that he, Jānis, also had a chance. He just had to make the effort to change and to overcome his closest enemy: himself.

Jānis would often look at me with a smile on his face, his unusually shaped eyes rarely blinking behind his round glasses. The inner corners and upper eyelids of his eyes were covered by a crease not typical of European faces. It's possible he already imagined himself as having massive, powerful arms and legs, his hair pulled back in an ancient samurai knot and a thick, towel-like cloth around his groin.

'Have you ever seen a sumo fight?'

'Never. I've never even been to Japan.'

School life wasn't easy for Jānis. There were two reasons for that. First, his arrival at school caused a sensation, which means becoming a marked person. Second, because he was short and looked different, he was lumped in the category of those unlucky individuals who seem to be in the world solely so that those gifted with power and shamelessness won't die of boredom. And Jānis's introduction to school was even more difficult because of another factor. The indisputable leader and tone-setter of the school's gang of the powerful and shameless was Consul Egles's son, Fabian. And because Fabian and I were on bad terms, and because Jānis was my brother, our ledgers were combined.

Fabian took particular joy in working over the newcomers. He didn't attack them, and rarely used his fists; rather, he'd amuse himself with them, or – as he put it – just have some fun. He'd organise hygiene inspections and make them wash their faces in the toilet bowl, blackboard-licking contests, and school-bag inspections where he'd make the participants dump their belongings on to the floor or in the snow.

Everyone was used to assuming it was impossible to fight back. The way he looked and carried himself strongly affirmed this assumption, as did the convincing nickname of 'Buffalo'.

Fabian's main act was his so-called 'cock-fights'. The new boys were rounded up by the urinals and lined up with their trousers around their ankles and their penises out for inspection. Whoever was found to be the most endowed by Mother Nature was given a medal right there, as the *grand-seigneur* of the boys' lavatory. But the owner of the smallest penis was nicknamed the 'Dicklette'. Honourable mentions were given to the wrinkliest testicles and the most pronounced foreskin. Fabian was obviously hoping to gain some racy additions from Jānis's participation. He chose a moment when Jānis was at the urinals, but I was somewhere else.

Fabian operated with an unhindered conviction that he could do whatever he pleased. There was rarely someone among the school's quietly pattering lines of students who would stand up against his despotic behaviour. But Jānis was a lid from a different kettle.

When Fabian grabbed Jānis by the ear and placed him trousers-down in front of the bystanders, Jānis said, in his musical manner of speaking: 'Please don't make me do this! It's disrespectful towards one's fellow man.'

Fabian almost fell down laughing, but Jānis repeated: 'It's disrespectful towards one's fellow man.'

To add to the performance, Fabian threw his hands theatrically in the air and, doubled over with laughter, covered his face. And that's where he made his mistake, because in that second he got such a kick to the groin that he shot straight up like a goalkeeper and then crumpled on to the floor.

I had come into the lavatory at that moment and saw the rest myself. I've thought over what happened and have often wondered – what would I have done in Jānis's position? And I've often come up with the same answer – I would have used the moment of confusion to run away. Fabian was definitely stronger than both Jānis and me.

Jānis didn't run; he stood next to Fabian and waited. Jānis's face showed neither fear nor uncertainty. He wasn't calculating, he wasn't thinking of himself or what would come next. If your adversary doesn't back down, the fight has to continue. To the end. Until there's nothing left.

Jānis won. Fabian stayed on the ground until the bell rang, then dragged himself grunting and moaning to class. The bystanders had left quietly.

The event in the boy's lavatory altered my attitude to Jānis. If only the word 'attitude' could be replaced by something more appropriate. Nothing in our actual relationship changed. But the way the relationship was perceived did. Until that time, anything I didn't understand about Jānis's behaviour could be explained by our rather brief time as brothers. I figured the longer we lived together, the more time would wear him down, wear me down, and our family ties would grow tighter. His appearance no longer surprised me.

But then I understood – however strong our brotherly relationship might become, no matter how closely we looked at one another, we would always be two different people, and some impassable barrier would always be between us.

Each of us has an endless line of ancestors behind him. Even as far back as a trilobite in the depths of the sea (if the theory that all life started on our planet is true) – or in the expanses of the universe (if you believe the theory that man was brought to earth from some other cosmic object). Looking at history books about centuries and events far in the past, I ask myself – where were my ancestors back then, and what were they doing? Whether it was in the Middle Ages, the Stone Age, or the Genesis Flood, they definitely existed because otherwise I wouldn't be here.

Jānis and I were both carried and given birth to by the same woman, but Jānis was also made up of genes that I didn't have, and about the nature of which I hadn't the slightest clue.

And it's because of Jānis that I've spent my entire life trying to understand Japan and its people. The Second World War, with Japan's victories and defeat. The tiger-like leap in the economy, technology and art of the Land of the Rising Sun. Even its recent tumble into the war on money-laundering. I've been to Japan, have studied its philosophy and its customs. I could give lectures on the Tokugawa shogunate, the principles of ethics of the samurai Miyamoto Musashi – to overcome fear of death by 'being in a constant state of readiness to *hara-kiri*'. At the time of the incident in the boys' lavatory, all that knowledge was still beyond the curtain of time. And yet, Jānis's actions let me understand a little, both regarding what I respect and admire in the Japanese, and with regard to the things I don't understand about them and, it seems, never will. I have the overwhelming sense that, even back in that lavatory, Jānis would have been capable of cutting out Fabian's liver and eating it right then and there.

VI

A foggy April morning. It's misting rain, but the air is mild and warm. It's one of those days that greets you with green arms open wide as you venture out from the cramped indoors, your eyes full of wonder at the world.

Valtraute von Brīgen sees nothing. She walks quickly to the carriage, her arms wrapped tightly around her large, upside-down-pot-like taffeta hat. Then she stops for some reason, as if trying to recall something. Every movement, every facial expression indicates uncertainty and anxiousness.

Bon Esprit hurries after the baroness, tries to maintain her composure, but it's obvious that she is confused to the point of being terrified. Why are they in such a hurry? Why is the baroness acting so strangely? The confidante's submissiveness that has long been Bon Esprit's second nature is being overrun by the irritability of age. She pouts discontentedly, with open prudishness, but immediately replaces the expression with a tired smile meant for no one in particular.

The captain alone appears energised, fresh and calm. True, his face also reflects surprise, but one of mild astonishment, as if the rainy skies had just opened up with hail, or a strange bird had just landed on his shoulder.

'Can we leave?' the baroness asks.

'I don't see why not.' The on-going fight between submissiveness and irritability can be heard in Bon Esprit's voice.

'I wouldn't dare detain the ladies,' the captain says, 'though I still don't see what you would lose if you stayed for breakfast.'

'Thank you. Dinner was very filling.'

'But now it's morning. Heading out with only yesterday's dinner in your stomach is as reckless as threatening the Devil with a cross you signed over yourself yesterday.'

'One must choose the lesser of two evils.'

The captain doesn't seem to hear the edge in the baroness's tone and steps right up to her and extends his hand. She takes it, but then flinches and wants to pull away. She can't. The interlude is silent and the others present probably don't notice a thing.

'I'm trying to understand who you are. But the question isn't one that can be solved with several rounds of bottles. And absolutely not by lying down.' The baroness's voice grows quieter and quieter, the last words almost a whisper.

'What you are ... What we are ...' the captain says just as quietly. 'Once you have the answer, please, don't keep a discovery of this scale to yourself.'

'And now let me go. Or I really will cross myself. With a nice, fresh one.'

'Don't take the sweetness out of the honey.'

The captain's thick moustache brushes over the baroness's hand. She yanks it away and climbs into the carriage. Before the door closes behind her, she calls loudly: 'Thank you for your hospitality! It was a pleasure ... Coachman!'

'Thank you for the visit. On behalf of both Eberhart and me. Safe travels!' the captain's bow is ceremonial. 'To be on the safe side, Kaspars will ride with you through the forest.'

Why even bring up safety, when the baroness's head is spinning with ghostly images worthy of *Walpurgisnacht*. It's just as terrifying to ride through the forest as it is to ride along a flat plain, or down a busy city street, if the carriage is being followed by the whinnying of horses mounted by ghoulish riders – some with disembodied bottom halves in the saddles, and some with disembodied top halves hanging on to the horses' necks. Bon Esprit watches the baroness with beady, mouse-like eyes, speaks to her, tells her something, but the baroness doesn't hear her. Faces press against the carriage window and stare in at her, faces both familiar and foreign. Sweet Eberhart, is it you? It has to be. But the familiar gaunt cheeks and pronounced forehead break apart like oil on water and become a sneering mask. Oddly enough, Captain Ulste's face inserts itself now and then. It fades, disappears and then shows up again. Like the top halves of those ghostly riders, whipped up by the wind as they hang on tight to the horses' necks because the saddles and stirrups are empty.

The carriage pulls up to the von Brīgen manor around lunchtime. After the long bout of pent-up anxiety, the exhaustion, the brief moments of rest with fitful naps, only to awaken to the knowledge that nothing has changed and the journey is still under way, her ears pick up a familiar noise: the carriage wheels crunching over the coarse pebble drive. The baroness is overcome by an airy feeling of ease. Like when she had a nightmare as a child and her mother would take her in her lap and hold a wind-up music box to her ear to soothe her.

Valtraute looks out of the carriage windows – what she sees is like a cool compress on a feverish forehead. The old manor house with its four brick columns and red tile roof. A footman runs out, his white-stockinged legs flashing as he hurries down the steps. A chambermaid comes to the door. The pale face of Amālija Anna, the baroness's mother-in-law, flashes into view behind her bedroom curtains. The linden trees on either side of the manor are still waiting for their spring coats – for now they carry only a hint of change, coloured by the setting sun or by the silvery light of the moon.

The acrid scent of Bon Esprit's smelling salts wafts forth, stinging her eyes and throat.

'Welcome home, baroness! We're so happy! We've been waiting for you this entire week! Superintendent Aurelius will also be delighted. He stopped by this morning with greetings for baroness Amālija Anna from the princess and agreed to stay for lunch. At what time shall we set the table?'

'Later, later,' the baroness says, raising her hand as if to shield herself. 'Help me with my coat and bring me a bowl of warm water!'

Towards evening, Superintendent Aurelius decides to leave. If little Valtraute is awake and feeling somewhat refreshed after her trip, he would like to make his farewells. They're old friends. Uncle Joahim has known Valtraute ever since she was a baby. He's been a widower for several decades and never remarried. Now he's almost sixty. His stocky frame swells out, so there's no point in trying to button up his long black jacket. His face is rosy, round; his snub nose covered with red spots and tiny blue veins – a living topographic map. He walks about with a flouncy, old-fashioned Louis XIV wig placed haphazardly on his head. His face has been shaved carelessly, and his neckerchief is wrinkled. Letters from Aurelius are always stained with wax and decorated with ink-blots and holes from poorly sharpened quills. His handwriting is uneven, hard to read. But his benevolent character lovingly sands down the sharp edges of his shortcomings. Children and dogs are immediately drawn to him; even horses neigh softly and nuzzle him. Servants hurry to attend him with genuine smiles on their faces, and respectable gentlemen gladly spend time in his company.

Yes, Valtraute is awake and wishes to speak with her godfather. Would he be so kind as to come to her in her bedchamber? In the eighteenth century, receiving guests while one is still in bed is normal practice. And not just while one is in bed, but even while taking a bath. Even if anyone in Vidzeme is surprised by such behaviour, Valtraute doesn't want to lag behind Versailles fashion. It would be a spiteful display of egoism to conceal her exquisite, playful women's nightgowns and negligees from society at large. And why should graceful shoulders and lovely breasts be hidden from sight? By giving orders to his court while getting dressed, the king saves a few hours that could be spent doing something more worthwhile. What harm can there be if hospitality encourages hygiene?

Aurelius comes to her huffing and puffing, already calling: 'Little Valtraute, where a-are you-ou?' It's an old game, from when Valtraute was little and Uncle Joahim would visit; she would hide in an armoire or behind a door and he would pretend not to see her.

Her godfather enters the room and acts as if he can't see her. 'Little Valtraute, where a-are you-ou?'

They greet each other warmly as always, but Valtraute isn't in the mood for jokes.

'Sit here, next to the bed, godfather, and tell me truthfully – what is man?'

The superintendent lifts his long coat where the hem splits and carefully lowers his wide girth into the Venetian chair. He looks like a giant beetle fluttering its wings as it lands on a flower. The old gentleman gives the baroness a doubtful, surprised look. When her seriousness remains unshaken, he shrugs and thoughtfully tilts his head.

'What is man? A difficult question. It could have a three-part answer. That which is in man, that which is around him, and that which the Lord's dice will determine.'

'What do you mean, "that which is around him"?'

'It could mean the conditions. Take a seed, for example. If it's sown in the earth when it's warm, in spring, it's more or less guaranteed to sprout. But when it's cold, like in autumn, anything could happen to the seed. Why would it be different with man?'

'Man has a soul.'

'As a theologian, I believe in souls, and I take my belief from the Bible. But Immanuel Kant, a fellow student from my Kaliningrad days, believes that the existence of a soul can be neither scientifically proven, nor rejected.

'According to Spinoza, God exists in nature; but two manifestations of God can be seen everywhere in nature, including in man – namely, in the soul and in matter. *Ordo et connexio idearum idem est ac ordo et connexio rerum...*'

Aurelius comprehends that Valtraute's melancholy is a reflection of her widow's pain. Sensitivity has taken its toll on him in his old age. When faced with sadness, he just can't take it any more. Instead of standing by people in times of hardship, he'd much rather keep his distance and stay on the sunny side of life.

He pulls out his handkerchief with the intention of dabbing the sweat from his forehead, but he notices an inky fingerprint on the white cloth and, embarrassed, crumples it into his hand. 'Dear Valtraute, spring is coming, nature's time for celebration. Why mull over God's mysteries? The world is full of so many wonders that he lets us enjoy openly.'

The baroness doesn't seem to hear Aurelius's protest, her thoughts driven forward by her agitation. 'Can a person be put together by parts? One part taken from one place, and the other part from another?'

'Hm-mm-m. Everyone enters this world as a combination of both mother and father. Even Jesus Christ is more than just the Lord's son. He also has a mother. If this connection were trivial, would Christianity regard the Virgin Mary with such reverence?'

'That has to do with being born. I'm talking about a particular case. Is it possible for a surgeon to combine two half-bodies to create one that is whole?'

'That, my dear, is a question for a surgeon.'

'A surgeon? A surgeon's tasks are limited. What happens with the souls? Do they both continue to live, or only one of them? And if only one, then which one? What will happen come Judgement Day? Will both of them be called up, or just one? And what is the newly made person? Just imagine, one wife is left with the upper half of her husband, but a second wife is left with only the bottom half of hers. What do you see in their future?'

Aurelius sits frozen in his seat and stares at Valtraute; his peace and benevolent mood are dispersed. But Valtraute keeps talking. Questions that are – or aren't – directly in line with the critical conclusions of Kant's essays spill forth from her lips. Immanuel rejects the metaphysical investigation of the soul, the world, the universe and God. Valtraute is obviously no stranger to Kant's territory. It could be the basis for a new world view! If only … if only … dear, sweet Valtraute hasn't gone mad with sorrow. And if dear, sweet Immanuel hadn't lost his mind back in Kaliningrad … He always had problems with his health … And then that odd separation of his life into two periods, the first called his dogmatic slumber, and the second the awakening…

'My dear girl, I have no idea what you're talking about.'

'I want to know – if the human body be cut up and put back together however we want, can the same be done with the soul? What happens to the leftovers of the soul? Can a person be half alive and half dead? Is it possible for there to be a double person – like a pretzel with two loops, or an egg with two yolks?'

'I can only answer with the words of the Gospel: "He is not the God of the dead, but of the living." The soul is the part of man that connects him to God.'

'You misunderstand me. It's difficult to give in to the unknown, to accept the truth.'

'My dear girl! You can dream up many things, but is that reason to cause a ruckus in the world? The apple trees will blossom soon, there will be such beauty surrounding us! Kant says: "Two things fill the mind with ever new and increasing admiration and wonder – the starry heaven above me and the moral law within me."'

'"…with ever new and increasing admiration and wonder …" Good Lord! I'll tell you and you alone. Eberhart isn't dead! I was with him last night…'

Aurelius's hand flies to his head. It feels as if his short-cropped hair is forcing his wig up off his scalp. It's time for him to go. Back across the Daugava river. To the Vecsaule congregation to see Kant's youngest brother, Johann Heinrich. Maybe he has new word on the status of Immanuel's health.

VII

Word spread – Fabian Egle would be leaving the school and his family was moving to Germany. People had moved away before and no one really paid much attention. But it turned out that several students from the other classes were moving to Germany as well. It wasn't the Blumbachs, Tiefentahls, Delgavs, Egles and Millers as we knew them who were leaving, but *Germans*. That was a surprise.

As in any societal beehive, schools contain a complicated web of relationships, affinities and rivalries, attractions and repulsions. There had always been a wall that stretched between Fabian Egle and me, but I had never dreamed that our differing nationalities could play a role in it. In this respect the concept of 'our school' had always seemed like a well-built fort. But no! An entire side of our seemingly stable structure fell easily and quietly away, leaving a gaping hole, but also revealing a landscape we'd never seen before. We brought it up with our teachers.

'Is Egle really a German?' we interrogated our class teacher. Our question was the product of surprise, though the way the word 'German' was said now sounded different from before. As if we were talking about a suspicious lat coin that we'd found in our wallet.

'His mother is German.'

'And his father?'

'His father is Latvian.'

How interesting! My classmates' families aside, I knew many families with various national backgrounds, and I considered it normal. My friend Rihards's mother, for example, was a grand duchess of Tatar, and Edvards Zīlītis's mother was British. Proof of Sofija Gascēviča's Polish roots was in both her name and surname, while Harijs Kross spoke Estonian with his grandfather. Many of the boys in our class who came from military families had mothers who were the daughters of tsarist Russia's upper class. Men who had finished college in Russia but settled down in Latvia had married women from abroad. And the mixed families frequently mentioned in newspapers and books were accorded respect and recognition, and there was never any doubt about their being Latvian. Those families even personified Latvian identity: Goppers, Auškāps, Berks, Kalniņš, Kundziņš, Mediņš, Purvītis, Tentels, Tilbergs, Zaļkalns...

I contemplated the events of the past few days until, like a whetstone shooting out bright sparks as it sharpens a blade, my mind exploded with a thick cluster of questions. What does it mean to be Latvian? What has to happen for a Latvian to become a non-Latvian or for a non-Latvian to become a Latvian? Or maybe Latvian-ness could be divided into two states: the state of being a staunch Latvian and the state of being a weak Latvian, either of which could be undone under certain circumstances.

Based on conversations in class, in the halls and in the schoolyard, others were being hounded by similar questions. Where there used to be stories and jokes, now there were rumours. Hitler is planning on expanding his new Germany, which is already as big as a giant balloon blown up over half of Europe. The empire can't be filled with helium, so Germans from around the world are being called home. By hypnosis. The Krauts are ready to swallow nails and sit on hot irons under the spell of Hitler's magic. There was talk that the Germans weren't leaving because they wanted to but because they were being forced to. Germany's empty banks were the reason. The Germans can take only a few trunkloads of belongings with them. Factories, buildings, cars and land will be sold and the money will be converted into bombs. Other rumours sounded even more ridiculous – the Germans were leaving so the Russians wouldn't get them. Those who favoured the mystical attributed the Germans' moving away to Nostradamus's prediction of the 'time of boiling waters and raging fires'.

I felt strange. We were talking about tens of thousands of people. Could they all really be controlled by one person, waving his hand from afar, like a conductor? Thousands of years ago, Moses had lined up all the Jews to lead them out of Egypt to the promised land. Could an event like that repeat itself? Could talk of the Teutonic spirit be true? How had they arrived here in the first place? They boarded ships and came here. Now they were boarding ships and leaving. Back then, Rome's Innocent III gave the order; now it was the Reichskanzler and Führer rolled into one.

There was a kind of exaggerated light-heartedness, teasing and even a little arrogance going around. Newspapers wrote with a smirk, almost with a sigh of relief, about the Germans leaving. Magazines printed caricatures. At break time we'd hear hit songs from the humorists the Brothers Laivinieks, which had lyrics like: 'The Brits dance the Lambeth Walk, / the Krauts wave Riga farewell; / They bump their bums together – woo! / Good for us and good for you.' The last time I saw Fabian was in the staff room. It was possible he had come to get some papers, or to pay a fine. I was there to get the class folder. The teacher he was talking to had the folder on the table in front of her; whether I wanted to or not, I heard their conversation. She was asking Fabian about his documents. He said he just needed one page of information – a notice from the archive regarding his ancestors; that is to say, his bloodline.

'For how many generations?'

'Three.'

'Saying your ancestors were German?'

'No, what for? The clerks are interested in whether or not any of the immigrants' relatives are Jews,' Fabian's lip curved haughtily. He was obviously already living in the future; he was bored by the trivialities of the past.

That night I went in to see Grandfather. An oil lamp with a murky green shade brightly illuminated the surface of the large desk, which was stacked high with material proof of his hobbies. From ornate, leather-bound scientific volumes in four languages to clippings from the largest and smallest newspapers, unpaid bills and scrap paper resembling wood shavings, covered in notes and calculations. Also on his desk, as usual, were his telescope, his 60 × 20 Zeiss binoculars and a chessboard with a jumbled pile of pieces – a cake with curious decorations. Grandfather's love for chess, which had manifested in daily problem solving when there was a lack of opponents, had turned into a fast-spreading fire with the arrival of Jānis.

Grandfather didn't wear glasses, getting by instead with a magnifying glass. When I came into his office he was holding the thick lens by its ivory handle. He peered at me through the glass like a botanist studying the flowers in a herbarium. He was wearing a red damask coat with satin lapels which he casually referred to as his house robe, looking like the genie from *The One Thousand and One Nights* or a Santa Claus who'd forgotten to glue on his beard.

'Would you ask Jānis to join us?' Grandfather said. 'I haven't seen him today.'

'Jānis rode out with the Baroness.'

'Maybe you know why he brings flea powder home. Aunt Alma has complained and doesn't know what to make of it. Jānis gives her a packet every day.'

'Don't worry about it.' I wave my hand. 'It's just a thing. It's Nippon powder from the Japanese store on Kaļķu Street. I think Jānis just likes going there. Though he never comes with me when I go to the *Itālija* ice cream café.'

I was sure I had made a clever comment and that we'd both have a good laugh about it. But Grandfather remained serious.

'Well, then. My thinking was that no one buys flea powder without a reason.'

While we were talking, I accidentally brushed up against the rough, cool metallic surface of the binoculars. Maybe my fingertips craved the texture I had known since childhood. The toad-skin of the binoculars was tied to my earliest notions of the variable nature of distance, and how this object seemed to contain the powers of enlargement and reduction. It was forbidden to look through the papers and open books on Grandfather's desk. Objects, or things, as he called them, were open for inspection.

Grandfather watched me, but said nothing more.

'What's new in the sky?' I asked just to say something.

'You can see Mars rather clearly at night.'

'Are you surprised? You know Mars is going to be at its coordinates, no matter what happens.'

'That's exactly why it's worth looking at.'

'Is that something you discover over and over again?'

'It's something I verify over and over. To keep faith.'

'Sounds pretty religious. You don't exactly fit in with churchgoers.'

The cloud of seriousness that had hovered over Grandfather for a bit too long finally lifted. 'Churches have one flaw – roofs. Services should be held on clear nights under a starry sky.'

That's how we talked. If he started to discuss points of view, it meant I wasn't keeping him from anything important and the conversation would relax. At that time I wanted to talk about the continuing emigration of the Germans. Unfortunately, there was one factor that made that subject touchy – the Baroness was also German. Talking about the Baroness meant talking about his relationship with her. Since I was now technically an adult, skating on thin ice around Grandfather with certain topics was particularly exciting.

The relationship between Grandfather and the Baroness still felt like something special, half-obscured behind a waterfall.

I told him what Fabian had said about the three-generation bloodline.

'Is nationality determined by what's in your blood?'

The question must have been surprising, because Grandfather picked up his magnifying glass again and peered at me through it.

'Empress Catherine II, Princess of Anhalt-Zerbst, didn't see Russia once before she turned fifteen. Does that mean she's not the empress of Russia? Is Hitler not German because Austrian blood, or blood from who knows what other countries, flows through his veins? Around the year 900 the Viking Rollo founded Normandy in northern France. He had a son out of wedlock with some French tanner's daughter; the son became England's William the Conqueror...'

'Then is the concept of nationality non-existent?'

'No, of course not. It's just not one easily explained. The grouping of people into nationalities is a phenomenon in itself. Just like moisture in the air gathering into clouds, or the formation of waves. If you didn't know anything about the structure of a pipe organ, you might think that the holes in the pipes were useless, but it's thanks to those holes that the organ can make music. There are often centres of power that crop up in the world that collect and pump up the lesser powers. Until the moment when the totality starts to break up and separate. Connections create devastating tensions.'

'So maybe it's a good thing that the Germans are leaving?'

'I'm worried that there are some rotten goings-on behind it all.'

'No one's forcing them to go.'

'The reasons that do or don't force people have a surface and an underbelly. The Baltic Germans have always endured being far from Germany. For seven hundred years, being German in this area meant being the boss. It's not pleasant losing your privileges. Maybe that's why they're resting their hopes on Hitler.'

'The Baroness, too?'

I asked without thinking, but it was the one step needed to cross the line. Grandfather's eyes continued to smile under the contemplative knit of his eyebrows, but his jerky hand movements indicated my question had hit a nerve.

'The Baroness? I don't think so.'

It seemed as if he wasn't going to say anything else, but after a moment of silence he continued.

'See, not all Germans are alike. Johanna and Latvia have a special connection.'

He said Johanna, not the Baroness, which was a significant nuance.

'Among her ancestors are the little-known Baltic German Mecklin-Štaufs. When the barons were led by Patkul in protests against the Swedish king and tried to form alliances with Poland and Russia, the Mecklin-Štaufs refused to participate.'

'That happened ages ago! In the seventeenth century! How does that matter?'

'We're talking about particular individuals who refer to the past and believe memories to be their primary compass. They move forwards by moving backwards. The Mecklin-Štaufs fall into this category. They take pride in the fact that the battle that put Patkul's head on the chopping block happened on their property.'

'So the Battle of Spilve didn't happen over by where the Daugava flows into the sea?'

'No. Right here, at the Manor; it's where Charles XII lost his famous boot.'

I could tell that Grandfather was enjoying the historical turn of our talk. He went to a bookshelf and spent a while digging around, until he found an impressive leather-bound volume. He returned to his desk, brushing the dust off the book's cover.

'Here – the memoirs of the Mecklin-Štaufs, Johanna's grandfather and one of the merchants of Riga's Great Guild. *Die Grundlagen*.'

He opened the book to an already marked page.

'I suppose it's no use reading it in German; you're a French-speaker. In Latvian, it goes like this: "After the Swedes had cut down the Saxon-Russian army's 28 battalions and 30 squadrons like sheaves of wheat in front of the Manor under the hot July sun, thus claiming 26 cannons, 4 flags and the majority of their supplies, and having lost only 1,300 men themselves, Charles XII bathed in the guest room, changed his boots and drank two cups of water."'

Grandfather tapped his finger several times on the paragraph in question like a piano tuner, then snapped the volume shut.

'Maybe now you see what this house and this place mean to the Mecklin-Štaufs. The Manor has never been profitable. They made their living by serving in the army or by trading. They also owned a shipping company and a warehouse.'

'Why isn't Johanna's father buried in the Manor crypt?'

I took the liberty of referring to the Baroness as Johanna, as if underlining our conversation as one based on the equal standing of two adults.

'And that, good sir, is exactly what you need to know. Baldur Mecklin-Štaufs was a famous European archaeologist. No one had really studied the Baltics. The archaeological digs at the megalithic tomb sites in Vidzeme captivated this man, whom people called *Verrückte Baldur*, so much that he managed to get permission to be buried there, next to the burial site that he discovered near Lake Baužezers. And in the same way our ancestors were buried 2,500 years ago – in a dolmen. So it seems that, for the Mecklin-Štaufs, being *verrückt* is hereditary.'

'Johanna isn't a Mecklin-Štaufs. I've seen her passport. It says Holenders.'

My comment didn't rattle him, but the story which had been headed towards a specific point like a billiard ball to a corner pocket was suddenly nudged in a different direction.

'A woman can change her surname as easily as she can put on a new dress.'

'Was Holenders also an archaeologist?'

'When talking about archaeology, remember – layers aren't studied. Layers are simply dug up.'

Fascinating! The mystery of the relationship between the Baroness and Grandfather was part of the mystery of male and female relationships in general. There was much to discuss on this topic, but unfortunately at that moment Aunt Alma came in.

'Jēkab!' Her intermittent sniffling was a sure sign she was upset. 'I'm worried about that boy. They're not back yet. The Baroness had them saddle up that piece of rubbish Lēpis, and Jānis took Spēriens. They've never been in the forest this long...'

Aunt Alma was concerned for no reason. Grandfather probably knew that better than I did. What could possibly happen to them? True, it was a dark November evening, but as if Johanna could get lost! She'd ridden all over those woods, over every path, every firebreak in the surrounding fields and thickets. Even without the guidance of their reins, the horses would find their way back to the stables.

To my surprise, Aunt Alma's words caused an obvious shadow of unease to pass over Grandfather's face. There was no hope that our interrupted conversation would continue. And yet, it did – the change was a direct continuation of our conversation, and said more about Grandfather and the Baroness than could be put into words.

Of course, Jānis was with the Baroness, but Johanna was definitely at the core of the upset. Until now, my imagination had been missing some link and couldn't see sixty-something Grandfather and the fifty-something Baroness as lovers. What I saw now left no room for doubt – Grandfather and Johanna were emotionally engaged. It turned out that this match that he and I had supposedly been playing by ourselves all these years – with Jānis recently breaking in as brother and third player – had had another player in the game all along. The Baroness. At the core of it all. A person whom I knew and to whom I was attached. And yet, it was a hard pill to swallow.

In truth, what had happened between Grandfather and the Baroness, and what would continue to happen, was of less interest to me than what would happen between the Baroness and me. Would our relationship stay the same? The question was loaded with overwhelming uncertainty. The happy household in which I had felt secure up to now had already experienced a few cracks with Jānis's arrival. Now it was threatened with capital reconstruction. Unless the Baroness left along with the other Germans...

'I've told her not to ride at night. The old trenches in the woods are real wolf dens...'

In an effort to soften his words, Grandfather tried to make a joke.

'This is real Latvian night-time. In Egypt night is so thick you could rake your hands through it. Fine, good, good. Alma, thank you! I'll ride out to look for them.'

'Me too!' I sprang out of my chair. Things were getting interesting.

'Does anyone even know where to start looking...' Aunt Alma kept speaking.

'We'll find them!'

'The road to Kleisti,' I said with tempered calm. 'It's obvious. It would be foolish to ride into the forest at dark. A smart person wouldn't do that.'

'If it comes down to foolishness,' Grandfather nervously waved his hand, 'then the mistake of a smart person doesn't differ from that of a fool.'

VIII

A month has passed since the baroness arrived back home, but she's still being swept back and forth by that same swing – a swing she can't stop or get off. The world churns around her, the views are always changing. In one moment the upward sensation excites her, but then her heart is immediately gripped by fear of the impending fall. Valtraute is unable to think calmly and coolly. Who can, when high up on a swing?

If she recalls everything that happened between her and that man openly, with full disclosure and without taking anything else into account, she can't find anything to regret, or anything to make her suffer the reproach of her conscience. Quite the opposite. She's discovered new emotions, emotions she hadn't even been aware existed. And even if she had been a little aware, then it was because of the imaginary assumption that there must be something, since people talked about it so much. Now she's gone through herself, as if through a long-sought gate; she's been there and lived there (if that's the right word) overnight, has been turned into a different person. In retrospect, she's not certain if it was even her, Valtraute von Brīgen. Could something like that happen to her? Even though she's spent years pining as a love-starved soldier's wife, she's not without experience.

Yes, Eberhart wasn't his usual self. The smells were different, as was that silent dialogue in the dark when words are replaced by touch. But the part of Eberhart that she should have recognised with that particular sense that time gives to married couples, had she recognised it absolutely? Did Danaë recognise Zeus when he penetrated her as a shower of golden rain? She can't swear to it. Her memory is rather spotty in places. And how could it be explained that this compound body, which in the best case was half represented by her dear Eberhart, was able to accomplish what Eberhart as a whole never could? This conclusion could be broadened and applied to men in general. Because it wasn't as if she had known only her husband. In the end, there were long periods when Eberhart seemed not even to notice her. And the eighteenth century has its idiosyncrasies, after all! There are rumours that women at Versailles have peepholes made and little shelves for tiny flower vases built into the voluminous crinolines under their dresses in case their husbands come home unexpectedly and their suitors need a place to hide. Since that night Valtraute has had a recurring dream: she's naked and reclining on a chaise, like Boucher's *Resting Girl*. There is no one near her, but there is the distinct scent of a man's body in the air; it seems unfamiliar, but it means Eberhart is close.

Piecing people together has to be an insanely strange process. Even Valtraute, with her narrow education at home, knows that the body's lower half is closely tied to the parts in the upper half. Eberhart has pointed out to her more than once that one's manhood doesn't always listen to the brain's commands. More often than not, the brain defers to what one's manhood wants to do. That said, to say the upper half is more valuable or more important isn't justified. Would it be better if the top half were Eberhart, but the bottom half someone else? The foreign lower half could have an adverse reaction to her – to Valtraute – that might issue orders accordingly to the upper half. It could even end up with Eberhart's face, hands, thick neck and hairy chest being next to her in bed, but in combination with a eunuch.

She had once read a strange passage in the Bible which, at the time, hadn't really caught her attention. 'And Cain knew his wife; and she conceived, and bore Enoch.' So holy matrimony wasn't enough. A man had to *know* his wife. But how does that happen? Can the upper half know what the lower half doesn't? In turn, if the lower half knows, does it mean that the upper half knows as well? The thought stayed with her, and now whenever she's around one of the couples she knows, her imagination puts the two halves together and proceeds to evaluate them.

The family situation of her cousin from Kurzeme, Albertīne, is not ideal in any case. The relationship between Albertīne and her Maksimilians is poor. Valtraute can sense this whenever she visits. Albertīne is a flirt by nature and will take any opportunity to toy with her husband's emotions. It usually ends with hurt, with icy glares, hysterical sniffling and hiding in her room, while Maksimilians has his horses saddled and disappears for days on long hunting trips. Albertīne rages, yanks on the chambermaids' braids, has the manor staff and labourers flogged for no reason. In the summer she has Hans, her footman, row her out in a boat to the man-made island in the middle of the lake.

Valtraute's sister's family is entirely morose in this regard. Karina and Ferdinants live in separate wings of their manor and sometimes don't see each other for days. The chambermaids and footmen carry letters to and fro on silver platters. On Sunday mornings the married couple drive to church together, but when they return home they separate in the entrance hall. It's said their relationship took this turn immediately after their wedding at Christmas, when Ferdinants stood outside the bedroom door for almost an hour in his nightshirt, but Karina didn't let him in. After that he got sick with pneumonia, further confirming it was his lot to spend his nights in bed with heating stones instead of his wife.

Can she, Valtraute, say that her connection with Eberhart – the way it was before – was ideal? She shouldn't lie to herself! Of course, in their first years of marriage she didn't notice anything. With Eberhart in the army they didn't see each other often and each time he was home was like a holiday. But with time the harmony and the glow of happiness faded. Not to mention Eberhart's physical aggression – which, in the beginning, mixed with the ecstasy of his touch, had been arousing. It all seemed to belong to the new – the unknown – things that marriage disclosed, and which, overall, she thought beneficial. Yes, Eberhart was an egoist, with a narrow-minded view of the world. But those little faults, which came up only on occasion, weren't something she worried about.

The weight she had felt over the last years was the result of an overbearing feeling that she was able neither to explain nor to put into words. Now, recent events had somehow enlightened her. The constant flow of anxiety, the flutters of her heart when she was sleeping or awake, had all made her worry that her connection with Eberhart didn't fill up anything but left a large empty space. She had waited again and again for him to appear and take her so completely that the emptiness would disappear and she would become whole. But her hopes had been in vain.

But on that night, when she met Eberhart in a form that she still has trouble understanding, it happened. It really happened. Regardless of the place, the time, the conditions. In the hundreds of times she'd been with her husband, this was the first that she had been surprised with a new revelation – that she had been connected so encompassingly, so wholly, that she stopped breathing as a separate person. She had become a metaphysical figure that floated into a space and joined with another floating figure to form a new, far more complete creation, beyond desire and reason – one that neither needed, nor could have, anything else added to it.

No, that much she would swear to: she would have no problem with Eberhart in his new form if it weren't for this Ulste tagging along … No matter how fluent the captain's German and French, no matter how stately his shameless manners, his origins were pitiful. Common blood. Not a drop of nobility. It turns out that the title of Freiherr that he bears so defiantly is based on an error. When approving a war treasury loan from Ulste's father, instead of writing 'I received from a free man', the king of Sweden apparently confused the German phrases *freier Herr* and *Freiherr* and went with the latter: 'I received from a baron.' After that, Charles XII met his end so quickly that the entry remained as written.

A week ago, Uncle Joahim had brought some extensive information on Ulste's ancestry. Everything was as she had suspected: Ulste came from a local family of liegemen. Feudal rights from Grand Master Yorke. Served in dragoon regiments under the Swedes. Their second generation includes cuirassiers. Bartolomejs Ulste's wife, Barbara, is from a Riga family of lumber merchants. Lumber merchants are suspicious people in general.

Valtraute thinks and thinks, but can't decide what to do. She doesn't have documentation stating that Ulste is half von Brīgen, and she probably won't get any. What authority would issue a document like that? And it would be ridiculous to break into Ulste's bedroom waving those documents around, even if they were signed by the empress herself. But on the other hand, to refuse her husband – admittedly, a part of him – and ignore him … They had been joined in holy matrimony. If Eberhart isn't entirely dead, does she have legal right to be a widow? Of course, even in this case she finds herself in a silly situation. Ulste, a half-person just like Eberhart, can continue his life with his wife, but she's been robbed of the other half of Eberhart. Does Barbara have the same conflicting emotions? Who knows…?

With the start of the warmer weather, Valtraute has completely made up her mind – she must once more travel to Jelgava to see Cagliostro and ask for his advice. After all, he was the one who told her Eberhart wasn't dead. Yes, she'll ask the count to summon the half-living, half-dead spirit of Eberhart. It would probably be the first such event in Europe; and for that reason maybe he won't refuse her.

At the end of the week, Valtraute von Brīgen once again climbs into the stagecoach, accompanied by the prudishly reluctant Bon Esprit. It's a June evening, and a light fog settles beyond the carriage windows. As they near the Lielupe river, the fog thickens. The baroness is anxious, even a little frightened. The moon shines through the white veil with a blind eye.

IX

As we rode out of the stalls the darkness slammed into us with tangible density and embraced us as tightly as if we'd leapt into a black whirlpool. We couldn't see anything in front of us: not the horses' heads, not our own hands. But our eyes soon adjusted, and the darkness broke apart; we could make out the contours of the yard. The sky also proved to be more open than it had seemed initially; now and then the clouds parted to reveal a starry stream flowing with ink-blue fragments of ice.

The November dreariness whipped at our faces. Carpets of fallen leaves spread out under the naked black skeletons of the trees, looming before us like dull stains. It's hard to believe, but even through the powerful musk of the horses' sweat, through the leather scent of the bridles and saddles, the bitter aroma of autumn made its way to my nose – it's the most wonderful aroma in the world and belongs to the time between the first bird heading south and the first snowfall, when asters are still in bloom, the leaves fall and the prickly, green shells of chestnuts first burst open.

If you've never ridden a horse, any expectations you may have about it are probably untrue; it seems you could just climb into the saddle and let yourself be carried like a bird without wings. But riding is about as easy as ballet.

The horse is a large and powerful body that will only take pleasure in going out with a skilled rider. The combination of man and horse has a certain nobleness to it. This is demonstrated by the countless monuments that feature a horse and rider. Grandfather jokes that replacing this relationship with a new combination – man and automobile – wouldn't work out; no one has ever seen a great monument that portrays an important person sitting in a car.

Grandfather was the best rider. He seemed to change the second he mounted a horse. I'm not even talking about poise or stateliness, which Grandfather had even as a pedestrian. No, I'm talking about the transformation that comes over a person when you dress him in a priest's robes. It's hard to describe the relationship between Grandfather and horses. It definitely had something to do with a mental connection, which formed an almost cosmic understanding between them. Grandfather was able to work just as easily and gracefully with a fiery steed as he was with a stubborn, difficult mare. Though Grandfather never used words like 'steed' or 'mare'. To him, they were all 'ponies'. In other words, toddlers, children.

Grandfather was riding up ahead at an even gallop. The damp road thudded loudly under us in the surrounding silence, which was broken only by the rhythmic whizzing of the horses' hooves splattering through mud. Grandfather's worry gave our ride a dangerous feel. This time he wasn't worried about me, or even about Jānis, which would be understandable. He was worried for the Baroness!

He stopped at the intersection; one road led to the Manor park, the other split off to the nearby woods.

'Well – which way?'

'I'm thinking ... It'll be hard to look for tracks.'

'I wouldn't say that. Even a bird leaves tracks as it flies. So does a fish as it swims.'

Grandfather pressed the handle of his whip against the neck of the restless Cille. He held the reins very loosely, at chest height and with his arm straight out. Probably to let Cille decide for herself. Though he liked to remind us this style of riding was started in 5 BC by Xenophon.

The road led us along a clearing for a while. Beyond the local, little-used railway tracks, the road turned towards a large, sand dune-like hill, behind which the forest began. Here it really was as dark as a cellar. The forest road was lined with trees on both sides and ran along a black dale; in places the narrow crack turned into a tunnel. I had never ridden in a darkness this deep, but then again there wasn't much to see. I knew the area as well as my own bedroom. And I knew how far we had gone based on the heat radiating from my horse's back and the layer of sweat on it.

When we reached the edge of the forest, not too far from where we usually swam in the summer, Grandfather and I started in our saddles. In between the little fir trees and riverbank shrubs was a huge bonfire blazing happily away in its scarlet glow. The flickering light of the flames tore us from the darkness, illuminating the vibrant chaos of a gypsy camp and silhouetting the bustling figures. Covered wagons with ribbed frames, their shafts propped up. Low-lying gypsy tents made from a canvas sheet draped over slanted poles. Children and dogs running around the clearing. A bearded man in thick, black trousers and a red sweater playing the violin. It sounded as if there were other instruments as well, but I couldn't make out any other musicians in the eddy of people. Gypsy women were busying themselves around the bonfire with pots of all sizes. At times their flowing skirts flashed in colourful waves, leaving the impression that these swirling cooks with their rapid movements weren't preparing dinner but trying to put out small fires at their hems.

Grandfather and I immediately lost interest in the scene once we noticed Spēriens, who was trotting between the wagons and tents with a gypsy boy on his back. My heart stopped. Grandfather looked miraculously calm. Riding past the bonfire with his grey bowler hat raised in greeting, he steered Cille purposefully in the direction of the riverbank, from where Spēriens's happy whinnying was already hurrying towards us. And lo, there was Jānis, riding a strange, yellow horse with a long black mane and a long black tail – something like a cross between a pony and a workhorse.

It was as if a magnet were pulling the four of us together – the gypsy on Spēriens, Jānis on the mutt of a horse, Grandfather on Cille and me on Princis. Jānis's expression – at least this was how it looked to me – changed as if he'd been slapped. It's what I'd imagined waking from hypnosis would be like, when you start to comprehend where you are and what's going on.

'They travel just like circus people ... They used to have a bear, but it died of old age...'

'Where's Johanna?'

'Johanna ...? I was riding ahead, and when I looked back she was gone. I wanted to go back, but Spēriens just went further into the woods...'

'Eh, the devil should've got you!' The gypsy boy jumped from the saddle, but held on to the reins. 'Me and the heir already done a deal – I get one, he gets two. Quick as fleas, mean as tigers.'

'He's exaggerating,' Jānis protested, 'we never talked about a trade. He said it would be easy to turn Spēriens into a pony. It would be a new trick. He said he could fit Spēriens into a bottle.'

'A bottle?' the conversation started to interest Grandfather.

'I mean a magic trick. In the circus one magician dreamed of making the Eiffel Tower disappear.'

'Maybe this time we can try to fit this wise guy into a bottle?'

'Better yet, put him in a box and saw him in half,' I added.

'Hell and piss!' the gypsy spat, and tossed the reins to Grandfather. 'A gypsy camp's got no electricity; it'll take forever with a handsaw.'

Jānis switched over to Spēriens and the three of us rode into the woods.

'Now what?' Grandfather said once we reached the darkened road; it was part question, part thinking aloud. 'A man takes the Eiffel Tower and makes it disappear.'

'I shouldn't have done that ... I'm sorry.' Jānis's voice was dry; one could only guess how awful he felt.

Back at the intersection, Cille stamped in place, turning this way and that like a spinning compass needle, until she turned resolutely towards the edge of the forest through which we'd come in. The way back felt empty and uncomfortably long. Grandfather rode past us at the turn for the Manor park – either he'd seen something or changed his mind – and brought Cille to a halt so abruptly that she reared up on her hind legs and whinnied loudly.

'Let's circle once around the park!' Grandfather pointed with his whip, as if we didn't know which park he meant.

In truth, the park wasn't really a park any more. A few old trees rose high above a jungle-like thicket. The old pond and canal system were blocked up and overgrown, and were only filled in the spring when the snow melted, and later became overrun with tadpoles. There was one somewhat cleared path, which led to the crypt.

Which was right where we were headed. And I honestly couldn't explain it, but even I was now convinced that the Baroness and Lēpis would be there.

Lēpis was the first to come into view behind the whitish crypt wall. The Baroness was sitting on a box in front of the door – the box in which she gathered her ancestors' bones every time someone looking for valuables, or to cause trouble, came and upended it all.

Grandfather jumped down from his saddle.

'Johanna! What are you doing here?'

'It's a quiet and calm night.'

'Did something happen?'

'Only trivialities happen. No one says, "death happened to him". Or "birth happened to him".'

'Johanna, be serious! You just disappeared.'

'Lēpis twisted a shoe. So we came home.'

It was true. The horse's back left shoe – as far as we could see in the dark – was hanging on by a few nails. Grandfather pulled it off completely.

Lēpis didn't even limp with one shoe gone. We trotted back to the Manor. The interrupted conversation followed us like a torn ribbon – one end with Grandfather, the other with the Baroness. My suspicions were right. Having transferred the horses to the stable boy, Grandfather took the Baroness by the shoulders. The gesture, which I had never seen before, was like a seal on the document of a newly discovered relationship.

'Johanna, be so kind as to come to my study. The boys, too; they're not children any more. In the end, it has to do with them as well.'

I froze and pulled my head into my shoulders. It felt like a swinging Foucault's pendulum that, coming from the Baroness, could deliver a heavy blow.

'Very well, why not?' the Baroness's expression gave away nothing.

Grandfather's iron-clad love for tradition wasn't sacrificed; we had to wash our hands and change. Aunt Alma was asked to bring tea, while we went our separate ways and then reconvened in Grandfather's study. The oil lamp with the green shade was lit and blown out, in honour of the Baroness; then the candles were lit, their wicks crackling invisibly, momentarily warding off conversation, but also keeping it in sight. As he stirred his tea and then, intentionally or unintentionally, tapped his spoon against his cup, Grandfather began with a direct question.

'Well, Johanna, tell me once and for all, what's next? I see what's going on with you.'

The Baroness looked at Grandfather, and I saw in her dark eyes something I hadn't seen in anyone else's – the ability to change their brightness; something the light bulbs in the chandeliers at the cinema can do. The Baroness's eyes grew brighter and brighter.

'What *is* going on, then?'

'If you're going to leave, I'd want you to have that horseshoe to take with you. On the other hand, I understand what staying would mean for you...'

'It wasn't that long ago that Hitler called us degenerates. *Dekrepierte Nachkommen der alten Ordenstritter, die ja gar nicht heiraten durften.* Remember?'

But Grandfather went on.

'The Führer's words on the Reichstag stating that Germany has agreed on improved ethnographic boundaries still mean something.'

The Baroness listened half-heartedly. She was carefully trying to put a short roll of paper into a long, amber cigarette holder, but the paper kept falling. I'd noticed these short rolls at the store recently; they were called cigarettes. Once she had the cigarette in the filter, the Baroness lit it with one of the candles, inhaled deeply, and turned once more to Grandfather.

'It's absurd, dear Jēkab! Absurd! I'm reminded of my duty to Germany, but Germany has no intention of letting me get close to it. My German blood, it turns out, must take satisfaction from the Poles in newly cleansed Poland.'

'It's worth paying attention to the lies. Lies tend to have their share of truth. The Germans see eye to eye with the Russians! Just imagine,' Grandfather laughed and turned to Jānis and me: 'Hitler received a gift of friendship from Stalin – crude oil, iron ore and lead, which he needs for the war against France and England!'

'I'm not interested in transactions.' The Baroness blew out a bluish-white cloud, as if simultaneously creating a smokescreen, yet trying to dispel it.

'See what the *Rigasche Rundschau* says today.' Grandfather grabbed his magnifying glass and leaned closer to the candles with the paper: '"Those who break from the unified German people, are breaking from it for all time and will be responsible for the consequences themselves."'

'You're reading yesterday's paper, Jēkab. I can be neither broken off nor joined on. Turkeys come from America, but does that mean the turkeys in France and Belgium aren't turkeys?'

'I wouldn't use such a savory comparison if I were you. The Führer's vegetarian.'

'In his time, Schliemann gave my father the opportunity to work in Troy, and Carter to work down by the Nile. My father wrote in his journal: "Man must travel from his homeland under two circumstances – when he must do it, or when he wants to do it." I, thank God, neither have to do it, nor do I want to.'

After a moment the Baroness continued. 'You could give me the best advice on how to get rid of them. I'm woken by a call from the consular department almost every morning.'

'That'll be easy to take care of. You need to submit an application for repatriation as soon as possible.'

'Oh, great advice.'

'Of course, they'll deny you. And why? Leave that to me!'

I studied Jānis – what did he understand, or not understand, of what Grandfather and the Baroness were discussing? Did he understand that, in this moment, the future of the Manor was being decided, as was the future of Grandfather's business and – put simply – the future of the Baroness, Grandfather, Jānis, and myself?

'Any more questions, ladies and gentlemen?' Grandfather asked in a funny accent, though I couldn't tell who he was impersonating. Maybe Hans Moser or Theo Lingen.

Jānis raised his hand as if we were in school:

'Who, please, is Schliemann?'

X

Anyone travelling into Jelgava (Mitau) at the end of the eighteenth century would find a pleasant, medium-sized city with a population of twelve to thirteen thousand. After the devastation of war and the withering of Duke Jacob of Courland's once thriving commercial activities, the former port, Riga's competitor, still retained its importance. This was because of where the metaphorical clothes peg sat on the metaphorical clothes line connecting Paris and Saint Petersburg. Pretty wooden buildings with red tile roofs could be seen from the carriage windows. The main streets were cobbled. There were places of worship for Lutherans, Catholics and Jews.

Not too far from the cosy city on the bank of the Lielupe river was the New Palace. Maksimilians would joke that, much as Ernst Biron would often get confused as to whether his wife was lady-in-waiting Benigna Gottlieb or empress Anna Ivanova, so the empress's favourite had confused the Kurzeme piggy-bank with Russia's state treasury when commissioning the Jelgava Palace. The palace is big in size, its aspirations grand. After the empress's death, Biron ended up in Siberia and construction was halted. Now, Ernst Biron's son Peter is trying to finish his father's dream building. But it's merely a tying up of loose ends, not galloping into the unbridled power of the imagination. Even Duke Peter's *Academia Petrina* has been described to Valtraute as a temple of light that tries to ensure that the brightest minds and discoveries of the era don't pass over Kurzeme like the far-away formations of migrating birds, but instead settle down and nest.

Unfortunately, Valtraute's bright leads end in darkness. When a stator rubs against a rotor, electricity is created. It's fascinating. But what happens to a person when life rubs against death? The Frenchman Lavoisier recently discovered the law of conservation of mass. But then where does conserved mass go when it's wasted?

Religions are so lukewarm they're stagnant. Minds illuminated by knowledge are so shallow, so empty, though all the wonders of the world could be hidden in the deep, magical concept of 'mysterious forces'. Alchemy, theosophy, necromancy, communicating with the dead, leagues of werewolves and vampires, clairvoyants, bodily and spiritual transcendence, ghosts, wizards, witches and crones, chieftains, spirits, incubi and hags. The desire of Jelgavites to form connections with 'mystical powers' burns like a wind-fed fire. Disagreements between Kurzeme's aristocracy and Duke Peter drag on. If only there were someone who could provide more funds! And are the people of Kurzeme an exception in this case? Paris, Vienna, Berlin, Saint Petersburg are all experiencing the same problems. Promissory notes and masters of magic are racing back and forth like mad. Casanova, Magnocavalli, Swedenborg's apprentice Akselrod. Sent by those mysterious forces, the Saxon Moritz was elected by Kurzeme's landowners to be their duke, but Menshikov immediately came in and shamelessly and cruelly threatened Moritz's followers with the stick that was Russia.

Now Cagliostro, envoy to the European Freemasons, and his wife Lorenza, Queen of Sheba, have been living in Jelgava for several months. Cagliostro has opened the Egyptian lodge permitting both men and women to join. The rest of the things he promised the people of Jelgava haven't really been successful. Elisa von der Recke's pearls, which were buried in the ground, still haven't grown any bigger; the duke's silver still hasn't turned into gold. But the séances in the spirit chamber are inspirational, and the landowners of Kurzeme are seriously considering whether the intelligent yet magic-incapable Duke Peter Biron wouldn't be better replaced by the prophet's envoy Count Cagliostro.

This time, Valtraute von Brīgen doesn't waste any time. The market square – where they usually park the stagecoach – is filled with real market chaos. The coachmen drop off and pick up mail pouches, take trunks down from the stagecoach roof and hoist new ones up in their place. Exhausted from the journey, dishevelled, dusty, Valtraute is happy to see that Albertīne's carriage is already waiting for her. Compared to the stuffiness of the interior of the stagecoach, the clear evening almost seems brisk. Bon Esprit, as usual, counts their luggage out loud, reciting what each pack contains. Her voice is shrill and shaky. This is a result of worry, which has become the elderly woman's main activity in life and which amplifies the score of her pitiable feelings.

This time, Valtraute is in a hurry to get to Albertīne's manor, where boredom seems to seep from every nook and cranny with the smell of stale air (they live as if they had fallen behind a shelf). There are so many questions that need to be answered. She wasn't able to stay at home, waiting to see what tomorrow would bring. She has to do something, she has to start something. Of course, it's pointless to hope for any solid advice from Albertīne. And forget about that lout Maksimilians. But she'll be close to Jelgava, she'll try to meet Cagliostro once more and – if she's lucky – she'll learn what the astral part of Eberhart wants.

Maksimilians is off on a long hunting trip. Albertīne's eyes are dull; her joy at seeing her cousin is laced with nervousness. Albertīne's attempt to hide her foul mood is a role executed with a heavy limp. It doesn't worry Valtraute. She's on a mission. She's not going to give up halfway.

Albertīne prattles on about the dust from the road, dinner and the French onion soup only her chef knows how to prepare, but Valtraute cuts her cousin off in mid-sentence and announces that she is going out into the yard.

'Now? In the dark?'

'Yes. I want to smell the lilacs. They're not blooming yet in Vidzeme.'

When Valtraute returns, she leans against the door jamb and wipes her mouth with a handkerchief. 'I'm sorry, I got ill,' she says.

'Not a surprise, with such a long journey. I've told you before that you have to eat before you travel.'

'Please, don't talk about food! Please!'

Albertīne's eyes move at a snail's pace across Valtraute's face. Her gaze all but leaves damp trails in the powder.

'Oh-oh-oh! I'm familiar with those kinds of troubles!' Albertīne comes to life; even though her own married life is a source of bitterness, the ice over her feminine springs melts – in these matters her perception is sharp and her instincts alive. 'My dear cousin, you've got a man to blame…'

'A man!' Valtraute's exclamation sounds more like befuddlement than denial. Albertīne must be out of her mind! Valtraute's nerves are raw after the long trip, and her nausea pushes her straight into hysteria. 'What are you saying?' her voice breaks with such genuine offence that her crumpled handkerchief falls to the floor; her trembling hand covers her face and her shoulders start to heave.

Suddenly Valtraute freezes. The tears keep falling, but her hand slides slowly down her nose and lips. Her narrowed eyes study Albertīne. It's possible she's not seeing her cousin any more, but something else entirely.

'Valtraute! My sweet! What's wrong? Do you feel ill again?'

'It's nothing … I'm fine. Please, don't be offended. I suppose I'm not a modern person; I can't handle stagecoaches…'

But the Valtraute who says this is different. There's no anger, no spite. She's confused, upset, but deliberately calm. Even her voice is quiet. Her face has a pensive glow, like a woman in a Renaissance painting. She sighs, crosses herself, links her arm through Albertīne's and rests her head on her cousin's shoulder.

'If miracles weren't surprising, then they wouldn't be miracles.'

'What miracles are you talking about?'

'The miracles that happen to us.'

Valtraute spends a rough, restless night in a wide bed decorated with a peacock-feather canopy. A clock in the corner of the room keeps time, its rhythmic ticking sounding in her brain. Could she be pregnant with the child of Eberhart, who exists as only half a person? The thought crashes around like a bat trapped in a room. It's no use trying to fall asleep. When dawn breaks, it seems she hasn't slept a wink. But she remembers bits of strange dreams and understands that she wouldn't have seen those scenes while awake. Valtraute is absolutely certain of one thing: she must meet with the Great Cophta. It's mandatory. If Cagliostro knew Eberhart wasn't dead, then hopefully he can also tell her how to bring the legally deceased Eberhart's child into the world as the rightful heir to its father. Specifically as the rightful heir. Bastard children are born every other second. Even in royal circles. Stories about the Saxon Augustus say he fathered the children of at least three hundred and fifty-four women. Children are born, and no one cares who gave birth to whom. But she won't have that. She wants to keep her child, but it was conceived by an essentially non-existent person...

After her morning coffee and after help from Bon Esprit and Albertīne's chambermaid to make herself a bit more presentable, Valtraute von Brīgen announces that she wants to go into Jelgava. Albertīne has no objections. On the contrary, she plans to come along. The conversation will be silly and tiresome; Albertīne can barely contain her desire to shed some light on yesterday's topic. Although Albertīne, who has many friends and acquaintances in Jelgava's high society, could prove to be a more useful companion than the matronly Bon Esprit.

Valtraute's prediction is correct. Albertīne muses over the fate of menstrual cycles and the traps set for women by nature. Valtraute refuses to give in and steadfastly maintains her air of ignorance – I'm perfectly fine. Having dodged her cousin's noble efforts at an inquisition, Valtraute counters by asking what's new in Jelgava. Oh, a lot has happened in Jelgava! Count Cagliostro has announced that he's leaving for Saint Petersburg to sanctify the empress with the secrets of magic. Then she could take the Egyptian lodges in Russia under her wing. Everyone was convinced that little Elisa would go with Cophta to see the empress, but she declined. And the craziest of it all – Konstance, Elisa's relative who knows everything, says that Elisa got scared. At one of his lectures, Cophta said that magical objects could even be used to encourage otherwise unwilling women into committing sexual acts.

'Where do you think the best place would be to find the count?'

'He's still staying with the Medems. But we should find out if there's a meeting in the spirit chamber today.'

'Could we possibly stop over there?'

It's market day and Jelgava is teeming with people. From carriages to simple wooden carts, there is such a wall of them along the market square that the only way they can get closer is to walk. Pedestrians dart among the riders and horses in colourful groups. Women are wearing their summer dresses, lace gloves and parasols. Women from the countryside are dressed in whitish-greys. Stout cooks in the company of energetic basket carriers. Lowing cows, squealing piglets, the excited clucking of chickens.

Albertīne leans out of the carriage window and calls to the coachman: 'To the spirit chamber!'

The crowd in front of the synagogue is particularly large; the movement coagulates. Albertīne guesses it must be some Jewish holiday. But no, the crowd is surrounding the spirit chamber! Some people have even climbed up into the nearby chestnut tree.

Albertīne is already lifting her taffeta skirts in order to get out. Valtraute hangs back. The crowding is accompanied by vulgar whistles, howling laughter, shouts. Valtraute is repulsed by such behaviour; the crudeness frightens her.

'What's going on?' she asks, more to justify her hesitancy than with the aim of finding out.

'It looks like the count is doing something!'

Valtraute is instantly ready to rush out of the carriage, but she spots something that makes her stop in mid-step. Count Cagliostro, dressed in sparkling silver garb, as if he'd just stepped off a silver dollar, is waving his fists, hollering angrily and chasing a gaunt man dressed in green livery. If memory serves Valtraute, the man is the count's footman, the one who helps summon spirits and assists with the magical procedures. His skinny, stocking-clad legs and the flapping tails of his coat make him look like a giant grasshopper. As the grasshopper gestures defensively, the wig that has fallen off his head comes flying at him. A foot wedged into a fancy silver shoe tries to kick him in the backside.

The footman is finally able to escape into the crowd. The count freezes, breathing heavily, with one fist raised high, like an angry Zeus. His pose is frightening, his dark features commanding, and the crowd, which had been raucous up to that point, suddenly falls silent.

'...If anyone here dares to hire or talk to that scoundrel, there'll be hell to pay! Hell!' The count bellows in French; it's unclear if anyone present understands the meaning of his words, but the expressive tone of voice is enough. Then he disappears.

'We haven't come at a good time...'

'That has nothing to do with us,' Valtraute says, her resolve iron-clad.

'You don't know that. He's terrifying when he's angry!'

'I don't care!'

'I'm not going. I'll wait in the carriage.'

The coachman stands next to the open carriage door, his triangular hat tucked under his arm. Valtraute steps down the folding ladder with her head held high and, making her way through the crowd, heads for the entrance to the spirit chamber. The coachman runs ahead to open the heavy oak door for her.

No one greets her. Valtraute has only been here the one time, for the séance, and doesn't really know where to go. The stairwell is dusky; the only light filtering in through the window shutters is stuffy, tarnished. The magical room with the distorted mirrors and the acoustic aids must be on the mezzanine – that much she remembers.

Valtraute opens one door, then another. Not a soul! She opens every door in turn. And then unexpectedly, in a corner of a hallway, she comes face to face with Cagliostro, who is sitting on a small sofa with his legs stretched out before him and his arms stretched across the seat back. There is no sign of the sparkling silver garb in the sleepy half-dark of the hall; it's now more of a greyish, rusted tint. The spirit-summoner looks ahead with empty, indifferent eyes, as if he doesn't see her. Valtraute tries to put a finger on why she feels surprised. Then it hits her – the count is sitting alone! Well, of course, he no longer has his footman and helper.

'What do you want?' the question isn't exactly polite. The Great Cophta doesn't bother to hide the fact that she's disturbing him. His tired, worry-lined and stern face is without the slightest mask of civility.

'May I … May I help you with your footman problem?'

'You're too kind. I'm happy to be rid of the bastard.'

'I could offer you a well-mannered coachman, one good with languages.'

'That's not why you're here!'

Cagliostro makes no move to stand. Is that her punishment for her persistence, or a reminder that the conversation isn't taking place with his approval? Albertīne would faint from this kind of rudeness. But Valtraute doesn't care. There's no turning back.

'You are correct, Count. I hope you remember me?'

'I don't remember. I know. You're here because of your husband.'

'Yes. You're right. "Where there were two, now there is one." It turns out, be he a genius or an adventurist – call him what you will, but his name is Gibran – there is a man who is capable of such things.'

Her words seem to loosen something within the count. His sullen indifference changes to attentiveness. The Great Cophta moves over to one corner of the sofa and gestures for the baroness to join him. To put an end to the embarrassment of standing in front of this man, she carefully tries to sit, which is no easy task with the bulky crinoline.

'And this person doesn't want to be your husband?'

'Not quite ... I'm going to give birth to this new person's heir...'

These are things that Valtraute has never, ever discussed with anyone in her life. And definitely not with a man ... She stutters, blushes, speaks in circles. And yet she tells him. As much as she can. You can't keep anything from a Catholic father-confessor, either. And if a doctor asks questions, you have to tell him everything. Much like a clergyman or a physician, the count is a middleman, embodying the authority of a saviour who is beyond prejudice. It's possible he can even see right through to the secrets, so the questions are more of a ritual.

Valtraute admits that she would have nothing against Eberhart and Captain Ulste being combined, were the captain not married and – most importantly – if it wouldn't mean a mixing of class relations. She, Valtraute von Brīgen, as the count most certainly is aware, represents the most prominent branch of Baltic nobility. Her family tree starts with the Līven clan. Whereas the origins of the Ulste family are highly questionable. He comes from soldiers of the local liege lord...

As she speaks, the baroness nervously watches the thick wave of her skirts which, in spite of her efforts, slowly but surely are flowing in Cagliostro's direction, and are already moving across the knee closest to her. She raises her eyes to the count's in apology (*ah, cher pardon!*), but she stops short and turns to stone. The count's black eyes are eyes for only a moment. Then the bright, frozen irises melt into a dark stain that rises into the air like a spool of indeterminate size, pulling everything towards it as it spins on its own axis. Like a whirlpool, like the tornadoes she's read about in books. The baroness braces herself against its pull, digs her fingers into the back of the sofa, but her skirts and crinoline petticoat shoot up into the air. Her wig somersaults after them, as do the personal items that every eighteenth-century woman keeps tucked between her breasts: a handkerchief, light as a feather, a little bottle of smelling salts, a lice-pick.

Valtraute grows cold with the knowledge that everything is being stripped away from her like bark from a branch. Her fingers lose their grip on the sofa. As she floats upwards, her fear slowly fades and she hears the Great Cophta speak.

'Madame, you have received a great honour. You are the chosen one! Like the mother of Buddha, like the Virgin Mary, like Joan of Arc.'

Suddenly, she senses that she is once again standing on solid ground. A rosy fog swirls up around her; as the layers part for a moment, they reveal what looks like a corner of Arcadia with a colonnade and winding stairs. Now she is wearing a lightweight gown, with one breast covered and one uncovered, like Marie Antoinette in the Lebrun painting! Through the swirling haze, she can just barely make out a headless man. Or rather, he has a head, but he's holding it proudly in the crook of his left elbow, not unlike the way Albertīne's coachman had held his hat.

'That's Saint Denis,' Valtraute hears Cophta's voice. 'The patron saint of Paris. They offered to reattach his own head to his body, or the head of someone else – John the Baptist, Thomas Moore, the warrior Roland, Achilles – whichever one he wanted. But Denis stubbornly decided to stay as he was, the way he had been carved into the relief above the door of Notre-Dame in Paris.'

Little, naked, cupid-like beings leap along the stairs. Their bodies have been pieced together: one half of the buttocks is thin, the other plump and soft; one half of the body white, the other dark.

'The children of Judaea were chopped up by order of Herod. Almost every one of them was cut lengthwise. Not the best idea. Thank God it's not common practice.'

A gorgeous woman flanked by attractive young men floats by like a bright shadow.

'And look, Catherine of Alexandria in the flesh! A Christian martyr,' the voice says. 'Since she chose Mary Stuart's head for herself, Catherine has given up walking in her nun's habit. Even her personality has changed beyond recognition ... Yoo-hoo, Catherine, would you come here for a moment?'

The woman happily obliges, somewhat prudishly hiking up the front of her dress and skipping over with pointed toes. Her cheeks are flushed and her breasts heave from the short run, but it seems that every breath from her fiery-red lips carries with it a burst of excitement.

'... I had no idea there were so many different kinds of kisses! Deep kisses, my lord, what a dream! And if your mouths come together at an angle! Your lips stay where they are, but the kiss goes so deep that it moves through your entire body. Here, and finally, even here ...' Catherine looks to Valtraute, shrugs, gives a surprised laugh and gracefully slides her hand lower. 'And brief kisses, just with the corners of the lips. How they trail down your neck, along the inside of your forearm...'

Valtraute finally notices the Great Cophta. Until now he has been hiding in the background, but now he steps up next to her, wearing a white coat tied at the waist with a rope, like a monk's habit. In his hand is a long, elegant staff with a violet bow tied at the tip. Like a Versailles dandy, or a dance instructor. 'Catherine, are you happy with your new state?' Cagliostro interrupts the excited chatter with authority, regardless of good manners.

Catherine looks at him, eyes wide. Confusion snakes so clearly into her surprised expression that it seems certain she won't answer. But that isn't the case. Catherine finds her voice.

'I'm very happy. Ve-ry! Yes, I died by the sword, proving my faith in the Lord, but that hasn't kept me from gaining a broader perspective on the world today. As a little girl I prayed to God to be beautiful and to be loved. But with the looks I inherited from my mother and father, that dream never came true. Life as a nun renders love unrequited.'

'There are a few things I don't understand,' Valtraute fidgets. 'Now you have Mary Stuart's head, but you answer to Catherine of Alexandria. Does Mary Stuart continue to live without her head?'

'My lady, the head Mary's mother gave her hadn't yet fallen into the sawdust on the platform when she had set her sights on the head of Catherine Howard, the fifth wife of Henry VIII. Do you know why? Mary thought she sang like a crow, but Howard's voice was sweet as honey.'

'People are rarely content with what they have,' the Great Cophta says. 'The poor want to be rich, the rich want to be happy. The rich desire power; those who have power lack the money to enforce it. One person thinks his nose is too long, another thinks his is too short. One person works all day every day, but has nothing to eat. Another eats all day every day, and dies from sloth. Envy grows, distrust spreads, hatred is rampant. The world has everything, but it hasn't been put together the right way. The ancient Egyptians knew this and it's up to us to discover it once again...'

The Great Cophta is no longer standing next to Valtraute. Catherine of Alexandria with the face of Mary Stuart has also disappeared. The rosy fog thickens rapidly and she hears echoing words.

'Holy Horus as the golden eagle! Holy Bast of Bubastis as the cat! Almighty Shu as the lion! Seth trapped Holy Osiris into a box and threw him into the Nile. Isis searches for her husband's body and the fish tell her where the box has washed up. Isis finds Osiris and hides him, but Seth finds him again, cuts Osiris into four pieces and scatters him to the south and the north, to the sunrise and the sunset. Holy gods, help us find the body of Osiris and put him back together again!'

The voice stops. The gentle whisper of the forest can be heard in the silence. A slow breeze quietly rustles the leaves as it steals through the trees. Valtraute comes to and looks around. The Arcadian garden reveals itself through the mist, with its colonnade and winding marble staircase. A man dressed in silver walks gracefully down the steps; he leans on a long staff with a violet bow tied at the tip. Is it the Great Cophta? It is, but it isn't ... The head of the French King Louis XVI sits on his shoulders. Strange indeed – can you change the heads you wear, first one, then another?

'Help righteousness and reason prevail! Deliver the world from destruction! ... *Fraternité, égalité...*'

XI

I've never been able to learn more about how Grandfather and Indriķis Skangals met. When the Germans started leaving Latvia, Skangals could have been around, or a little over, thirty years old. His pleasant, distinguished face was made even nobler by the golden rims of his glasses and the bristly moustache above his mouth, which was considered a sign of intelligence. Skangals was a theology student and both his respectable manner and his conservative dress corresponded with his chosen occupation. He often wore pinstriped trousers with his longish black jackets. In cooler weather he wore light grey spats over his shoes. His shirts were always snow-white and starched stiff as a board. The narrow, high collar with the folded-down corners was always adorned by a dark tie.

Indriķis couldn't have come from an upper-class family because he was paying for school himself. And in a fairly odd way at that. He made clever use of his German language skills and his God-given talent for reading indecipherable handwriting in order to dig up information about family histories in archives, old church records and the civil registry for his clients. Some were piecing together their family trees and wanted to know the whos, whats, and whens of marriages, births and deaths. Others needed to determine their legal rights to inheritances or property for court cases, and wanted information about their ancestors' immigration and their ownership of this or that homestead. Skangals researched and found all of it. For generations, clergymen had been recording significant events, not only about their congregation's spiritual lives, but also about their worldly lives, including ancient customs, the work of magicians, moral deviations and political events.

Grandfather referred to the hard-working student as the Sherlock Holmes of the archives and believed Skangals possessed exceedingly extraordinary skills in that field. Anything uncommon appealed to Grandfather's heightened perception of the world. But I thought the explanation was simple. This was another case in which the heart put a wandering mind back on the right path. Skangals's calling wasn't theology, but rather symbology, and around symbols he was happy as a worm in flour. The first level of knowledge helps one orient oneself – which can also be referred to as the ability to follow a lead. Working at the highest level of knowledge triggers the subconscious, allowing the senses – or, put simply, the intuition – to have an input.

Grandfather himself told me later that he contacted Skangals right after the conversation with Johanna and asked him to look through three generations of the Mecklin-Štaufs family tree. The main goal – to find a Jew amongst her relatives. A Goldfinger, a Zeligman, a Nathanson or, even better, a Rothschild.

When Grandfather let out a laugh indicating the last one had been a joke, the Sherlock Holmes of the archives answered very seriously that the task wasn't a hapless one. Intermarriage with rich Jewish families, most often to the daughters of rich Jews, particularly amongst merchant circles of the Riga aristocracy, wasn't as uncommon as people thought. Intermarriage between the Rothschilds and a Baltic landowner was a possibility because there was no difference in social class. After the French Revolution the Rothschilds had become incredibly wealthy and all five sons of Mayer Rothschild, a former resident of the Frankfurt ghetto, were given the title of baron for their services. The question was how probable and how close was the marriage to the Rothschild family tree, and through which son – Germany's Amschel, Vienna's Salomon, England's Nathan, Naples's Calmann or France's Jacob. In her time, Nathan's daughter had married the Baron of Southampton, and one of his granddaughters married Count Rosebery, who later became the British prime minister. One of Calmann

Rothschild's daughters married the Duke of Gramont, another married the Duke of Wagram. Unions that great, of course, wouldn't be found in Riga, but the Baltic barons were by no means worse off than the barons of Schleswig-Holstein or Hessen, and we could feasibly find the granddaughter of some third cousin from the Rothschild family.

After a few days Indriķis Skangals called Grandfather with a whoop of victory: 'Fo-ou-nd it!'

'A Rothschild?' Grandfather's laugh conveyed joy and disbelief.

'Johanna Mecklin-Štaufa's mother is Ada Hedberga, and her mother's name is Zāra! Ada is also a Jewish name. In Hebrew it means "to adorn". The name Ada was first registered in Latvia in 1882, in the city of Krustpils.'

'And what's her ... ah, Zāra's surname?'

'It doesn't say. The only thing we know about her maternal grandmother is that she died in childbirth. It's safe to assume she was an immigrant. When a mother dies in childbirth, it's tradition for the child's middle name to be his mother's name. The church register says: Ada Zāra Hedberga.'

'Mmm, yes.' Grandfather was doubtful. 'Ada Zāra Hedberga ... It's a little weak. Can we possibly certify the notice? For example, Ada Zāra Hedberga, daughter of Zāra Hedberga, née Rothschild?'

'We can't,' said Skangals.

'What you *can't* do is put your trousers on by pulling them over your head,' Grandfather answered angrily. 'Don't tell me you haven't dug up proof of pure German bloodlines for dozens of Bērzingi and Kļavingi.'

'That's different. Especially if you can show they were christened in a German congregation or went to a German school. In this case, we lack proof.'

'In this case, the proof is in her maternal grandmother's name, Zāra! From what I understand, there's no real word on her father.'

In the end, Grandfather broke down Sherlock Holmes.

'Fine, I'll keep looking,' Skangals said. 'Ada Zāra Hedberga, daughter of Zāra Hedberga, née Rothschild...'

Johanna was surprised when she received notice from the archive. Everyone in the family had been convinced that Ada Zāra was Swedish. It was something they often discussed, joked and laughed about. She even had relatives in Sweden; they wrote letters back and forth. There had always been some Swedish book by the playing cards on the little round table next to the cosy armchair *maman* liked to sit in. They'd often celebrate Saint Lucy's day at the Manor.

The newly discovered Rothschild ties didn't elicit any stronger emotion. The Baroness only asked: 'Did you already know?'

Grandfather answered firmly. 'Of course!'

'Then that changes everything. Problem solved.'

'Nothing is solved yet. You need to submit an application.'

Grandfather was right. While the Baroness idled, clerks came to the Manor to inventory both personal and estate property. For the time being the appraisal was being conducted from outside. The Baroness pointed out to the clerks that her papers weren't yet in order. The specialist, who had come in from Germany, answered with German logic that, once the honourable countrywoman (*gnädige Volksgenosse*) finally got to that point, there wouldn't be enough time to do everything properly. On paper she was German, and that's why she was subject to repatriation. The Führer's orders were not debatable.

'All right, I'll submit those papers,' the Baroness told Grandfather. 'I'm tired of these idiots hanging around.'

Two weeks later the Baroness received in the mail a large envelope made of yellow, waxed-looking paper. The Reich eagle spread its wings out on the upper left corner, a wreath and swastika gripped in its talons. The same eagle was on the white, typewritten page of the letter inside. The letter itself was short: 'The consular department of Greater Germany's Foreign Ministry has deemed your request to move to the State as undesirable. Heil Hitler! Department Director Wurst.' The signature, short and abrupt with an upward loop, had been made with schoolboy precision.

Having read the letter, Johanna tilted her head and, as if the paper were dusted with poison, slipped it carefully into her jacket pocket.

'So far, everything has worked out. God help me in the future as well. Because now I have two – the Christian and the Hebrew one.'

XII

It is with some effort that Valtraute von Brīgen shakes the leech-black stare. She feels the desire to shield her eyes, as if she were stepping out from a dark cellar into broad daylight. Cagliostro's face shows intense calm. Could she really have fallen asleep? Valtraute looks with horror at the thick wave of her dress, which has now covered both of the Great Cophta's knees. The baroness gathers up the piles of silk and retreats to the corner of the sofa.

'What you tell me, I already know,' says the face turned towards Valtraute. Strange: if she had to enumerate the count's defining features, the only thing she would be able to describe is this feeling that sometimes burns cold, and sometimes hot, but in any event completely overshadows all else. It's doubtful that the profile of his nose or the contours of his lips would make one come out in goosebumps or break into a sweat. Cagliostro's gaze hits her like a wolf's eyes reflecting in the night.

'What did I tell you?'

'Facts are not difficult to find. The truth is.'

Full circle and the conversation is over. Getting answers from Cagliostro is harder than threading a needle. But the baroness is relentless. Her curiosity is driven by more than just uncertainty; the baroness's honour is her weakness, and now that it's being threatened it's set off warning bells.

'Did I say anything about an inheritance?'

She guessed correctly. The mention of money immediately grounds Cophta.

'No. You're with child. The child of an unusual father.'

Valtraute shrinks further away from the count, leaning over the golden-rimmed back of the sofa. But she relaxes immediately. She has to be strong. She won't get any closer to the truth without further discussion.

'Forgive me, I'm upset...'

'How nice. You're sincere, you're sensitive. But that's no reason to do nothing.'

'What should I do? Inform the district administrator? Appeal to the council? Write to the governor general?'

'The ancient basilisk, a crowned vulture with a serpent's tail, was hatched from a rooster's egg by a toad. It will shoot out its reeking tongue and swallow you like a fly.'

The Great Cophta speaks these blood-curdling words in a measured voice and thoughtfully rubs his furrowed brow. His white-powdered wig is pushed above one ear, revealing short-cropped, curly black hair. Suddenly he grabs the baroness's hand in his hard, gnarled fingers and meets her frightened eyes, then speaks sharply: 'You will come with me to Saint Petersburg to see Monsieur Gibran!'

'Monsieur Gibran?'

'And then to Brussels, to London!'

The baroness hears Albertīne's words – Elisa von der Recke refused to go with the count to Saint Petersburg. And now *she* was on the line!

'Why? Why should I?'

'You are the chosen one!'

'Chosen for whom?'

'What is written in the constitution of the Egyptian lodge? All people are connected, even disconnected and reconnected. Preference is given to combinations that lead to a more complete and improved community. Monsieur Gibran's connection must be repeated a hundred, a thousand, ten thousand times over! Your arrival in the European courts will make quite an impression. A charming young woman carries within her the fruit of a harmonious creation, designed by the highest of intellects!'

Upon hearing the word 'fruit', Valtraute von Brīgen's vision swirls again. As if she had opened a door to find something she should never have seen. She should close the door, look away, leave. Her heart trembles, her embarrassment leaves her breathless, but the temptation is so very strong. She looks on. And what does she see? Herself. Naked, with a large, pregnant belly. Cagliostro stands next to her (dressed, of course!), as if they were about to dance a minuet, he holds her hand in his as he spins her round and round on display.

That will never, ever happen! Only she has no argument with which to object. No, there is one! There is!

'Is the connection harmonious if it muddles class distinctions? Captain Ulste isn't one of us.' The baroness slightly exaggerates the disappointment she feels when thinking about Ulste.

The smoulder in the count's black eyes flares up. The baroness's feminine instinct senses that her words have struck a personal chord with Cophta. It's possible he's wondering whether what she said wasn't partially aimed at him.

'What's wrong with the Freiherr?'

'The title has no meaning.'

'What does, then?' The question drips with mocking curiosity.

'Blood. Ulste doesn't hide his common background.'

The corners of Cagliostro's lips curve into a devilish smile. The baroness had noticed it before. Devilish is precisely what it is; no other word describes it better.

'Is the baroness so sure that she would be able to walk into a steamy sauna and tell an emperor from a servant? As far as I know, all people are descendants of Adam and Eve.'

No matter how great the baroness's reverence for the Great Cophta, his tone offends her and tears spring to her eyes.

'The King of Shinar and the King of Ellasar are mentioned in the same place in the Bible as Adam and Eve. And right with them are the slaves Abraham took with him into battle...'

Cophta doesn't seem to hear. It's apparent that Valtraute von Brīgen's attempt to argue with the count has angered him. If her protests can't be completely quashed, they at least have to have their noses and ears chopped off, like idols in a coveted temple.

'A crimson, ermine mantle today, a prisoner's flaxen trousers tomorrow. A swineherd today, a member of the court tomorrow. Or perhaps the nobility are born into the world with a special mark on their foreheads? Perhaps they're born the most chaste, the most honest, already trained to wipe their own noses and use the lavatory?'

'What is all this! You, count, are purposely trying to twist my words. Nobility is the selection of generations, a class formed by specific assignments. With its own view of the world, its lifestyle.'

The count laughs, but not kindly. The baroness's arguments are obviously greatly annoying him.

'Class distinction is an illusion!'

'Count! *Mein Gott* ... and this coming from you! Your ancestors...'

The baroness is unable to finish. Cophta interrupts her.

'The nobility I boast of doesn't hang by the thread of our leaders' mercy.'

The verbal slap the baroness has received for the feminine naivety of her comment is followed by a postscript.

'Russia's great Alexander Menshikov started out as a baker's apprentice, became a duke, then a grand duke, then a field marshal, then a generalissimo and finally an admiral. But he died a common, lice-ridden convict in Siberia.'

Whatever tolerance the baroness has left is now gone with the wind. She wants to scream and stamp her heel against the floor. But she controls herself.

'I don't know how things are in Russia. But everything with us, the Germans, is in order. The chronicle of my mother's ancestors – the von Līvens – for example, goes as far back as the thirteenth century. There are no bakers' apprentices in our lineage.'

Cagliostro's black eyes widen, as if he's only now seeing the baroness for the first time and is surprised.

'If I were you, I wouldn't emphasise "us, the Germans". There is no basis for saying Kaupo of Turaida, the first of the von Līven family line, was a German. Yes, he converted to Christianity and went to Rome to see the Pope, but he was "*Undutsche*". "*Von Liven*" – of the Livs.'

The baroness notices a cloud of fog once again starting to swirl around Cagliostro, and a burning cold flows towards her. It sends a chill through her body. Maybe she misheard him? But no, he said what he wanted to say, and meant what he said.

'Count, what an awful joke!'

'I didn't realise this was news to you.'

'Your insults will be checked!'

Her pride breaks down in the wake of Cagliostro's laughter like a wilted rose. She feels the urge to escape – which a rose, most likely, does not. She feels shamed and exposed.

'Even if you could prove that the von Līvens are descended from locals or, as you said, from the Livs, which is pure fantasy, even then you would be wrong. The ancestors on my father's side of the family tree include the von Hāns.'

'Yes, indeed. The von Hāns are also descendants of locals. Having migrated to Prussia, this family also shows up with the surname "von Gayl". But it doesn't matter, baroness! We must find Gibran!'

XIII

On 14 June 1940, the Germans marched into Paris; three days later, Hitler's then allies the Russians thundered into Riga with their tanks. Latvia, until then an independent state, had also been a member of the League of Nations. The weather was hot and sunny. Jānis was away at a scout camp in Sigulda. I don't know what happened in the city centre. Not far from the Manor, a Russian tank racing along the narrow, sandy road missed the turn and drove through a two-storey wooden house.

The Baroness had brought her radio into the office. I thought it was strange, the way she did nothing but sit in front of the radio with her hands folded on the table. The only thing being broadcast was music.

I ran to the airfield. The football field was locked down and dusty armoured vehicles were parked in front of the hangar. A few planes I'd never seen before flew over the silent field – short, fat monoplanes with stub noses. They passed over and disappeared.

That evening, Grandfather came home in one of the four-horse catafalques from working a particularly fancy funeral. He brought news that an enraged mob of Orthodox Pentecost celebrators had fought with police by the central station in downtown Riga. He hadn't driven right through the chaos, but had heard the gunshots with his own ears. He'd also seen one policeman on a horse leading a second horse that was covered in blood.

The Baroness sat daydreaming in front of the radio.

'What's happening to the world? How will it all end? It can't be that this many people can actually all lose their minds at once.'

Grandfather sat down, pensive, and took off his crêpe top hat to press his handkerchief to his sweaty forehead. Up until now I had only noticed his wrinkles when he laughed, and was surprised to see his facial expression reflected exhaustion and the weight of his years.

'Reason works like an icebreaker – it pushes and pushes forwards, and then retreats.'

This pessimistic assessment wasn't about to undermine Grandfather's love for life. Leaning his tired back against the chair, he added: 'Time had already been derailed in *Hamlet*, but the gravediggers kept hard at work. We have to keep living on as well. People will still get married, babies will still be born. Man wants to live!'

Daily life at the Manor really did continue as usual. Carriages drove newly-weds, and catafalques the deceased. The fall of President Ulmanis wasn't met with any particular reaction at our house – dictatorships are like ships in tropical waters: they quickly come to a standstill and are taken over by algae and snails. Grandfather laughed loudly about the new president, Kirhenšteins, and called Lācis's cabinet a defective deck of cards that had only a couple of aces and too many jokers.

Maybe it was the uncertainty of the future and all these questions hanging in the air that was at fault, or maybe something else, but we all wanted to be in the same place, to enjoy the new-found togetherness. At least, that's how I saw it. In the evenings Jānis and I would go to see Grandfather for no specific reason and our conversations lasted for hours. At first it was unintentional, but later on even the Baroness joined in.

Summer was turning into autumn. Evenings were still relatively light and pleasant, but there were an increasing number of stars. In the same way as the sweet *Reseda* and *Matthiola* gave the dusk-swaddled yard a strange and alluring scent, our meandering, contemplative night talks lent a tantalising vibrancy to our imaginations which the daylight was unable to illuminate.

Jānis had the enviable ability to anchor any topic three, four generations deep. I, for example, knew nothing about Grandfather's parents. His father, Daniels Ulste, had served in the cavalry and worked with a man from the Kurzeme region named Kristaps Helmanis, who had been the main veterinarian to the mounts of the tsar's bodyguards. When Helmanis was the first to create a serum to treat glanders in horses, he himself contracted the disease and died in 1892. Daniels Ulste then moved to Riga and took a position managing Kristaps Morbergs's stalls. Morbergs owned the most luxurious buildings in Riga, but he also wanted the finest horses. Finer than the ones pulling the six-horse carriage owned by a man named Strickis, the city's second-greatest horse-lover and owner of the Wolfschmidt brewery.

The Baroness's experience with the Bolshevik regime in 1919 turned out to have been quite bad. Starvation, yes, she remembered that. Being frozen in the small, heatless gable-end attic, from which she could only venture out at night because she had supposedly 'fled abroad'. Three other people in addition to Johanna lived in the Manor – her old nanny and former wet-nurse, the coachman, who by then was almost completely blind, and an unbelievably emaciated man who for some reason was called the Piano Tuner. The cows had been slaughtered, the horses commandeered.

Grandfather turned out to have had even less contact with the Reds. At that time he had been putting his partial knowledge of the veterinary field to use in Kurzeme, where he looked after the horses in Kalpaks's battalion. Later, with papers issued by Defence Minister Zālītis, he had gone on a sea-bound odyssey from Liepāja to Ainaži to organise a medical service for the horses of the Northern Latvia army.

Grandfather had heard much about 1919 from his father, who had spent the Bolshevik years housed with Morbergs in the building across from Bastejkalns Park. One night there was an authoritative knock at the door. Morbergs was convinced he'd be taken away to be shot; he put on and took back off his winter coat with the fox-fur lining, and gave it to Ulste. But the intentions of the new regime turned out to be different – the expropriation of Morbergs's apartment and possessions. The rescued coat served Morbergs well in later years when he lived in the former street-sweeper's apartment – the winter was cold and his firewood had been taken along with everything else. A truck pulled up in front of the building the next day. Riflemen tossed Morbergs's personal library down a wooden gutter from the third-storey window and into the back of the truck. The ornate volumes rained down in a flutter of covers. Morbergs hadn't been able to stand the sight and approached the commander: 'Those aren't bricks, they're books and demand respect!'

Grandfather didn't beat about the bush when he talked about the new regime, using terms such as communist, the Soviet rule, Bolsheviks. To him, everything fell under the heading 'the Reds'.

I remember the day the lat was taken out of circulation and replaced with the Russian paper rouble – it was almost midnight when we left Grandfather's office. Jānis and I were heading up to our room when there was a loud knock at the front door. We had heard and talked about these late-night callers recently so we should have been prepared, but we still felt surprised and shocked. Grandfather looked completely confused. On his way to open the door, he stopped for some reason and put on a top hat – which was considered a class enemy and was mocked in newspaper caricatures. What's more, it was the crêpe top hat he wore for funerals.

Three men came in. Two in uniforms, one in civilian clothes. Unarmed. Russian military could be seen in Riga on every other corner, but it was still hard to get used to their odd appearance. Their greyish-green cotton shirts fell down to their knees. Their rounded hats had square peaks. Their boots were bunched in countless folds around their ankles. And it was as if they'd been ordered to use large amounts of sickly-sweet cologne.

'We're looking for citizen Johanna Holendere.' The private spoke, gargling the 'r' in the back of his throat.

The Baroness was the only one who hadn't come out of her room. Even the knocks on her door seemed to go unheard. When she finally came out, she gave the impression that she had been expecting the late-night visitors. She was fully dressed, down to the necktie, down to the earrings. Every curl on her head in place.

'Can I offer our guests something? Tea or coffee?'

'Another-r-r time,' the private said, his right hand raised in a half-salute. He seemed ready to greet her with the standard military gesture, but stopped himself because he wasn't in uniform. 'We r-r-require the answers to a few questions. About your r-r-relationship to one of our allied countries.'

'By all means, come in.'

'Not here. At the commissariat.'

Stopping in her tracks, the Baroness looked back sharply.

'Does that mean I'm being arrested?'

This apparently wasn't the first time the private had heard this question. His answer came automatically, like a train ticket from an automated kiosk.

'Not at all. But it wouldn't be proper to require you to r-r-rely on yourself for transportation.' His tone almost sounded pleasant.

We didn't sleep that night, waiting for the Baroness. She came home towards morning.

When she'd got out of the car she had found herself in front of a familiar building, where the respectable Ministry of Internal Affairs had once been housed, and where tourist posters reading 'Explore Beautiful Latvia!' and 'Meet Your Homeland!' had once been displayed facing Brīvības Street. She had been there once before to take care of some formalities with the fire brigade.

They brought her into a room where a military man sat behind a desk, looking as if he had stepped right out of a Chekhov play: a tousled mop of hair, a clip-on pince-nez on his nose. He didn't speak Latvian; the private who had brought the Baroness did the interpreting. The private's knowledge of Latvian proved minimal. So, like it or not, they ended up switching to Russian. The aggressive tone of the conversation didn't bode well.

'Why are you hiding the fact you are Baroness Mecklin-Štaufa?'

'I was Baroness Mecklin-Štaufa. When I married Jozefs Holenders in 1928 as a citizen of the Republic of Latvia, I became Johanna Holendere.'

'Who is this Jozefs Holenders? Where is he? What's his social background? Occupation?'

'Jozefs Holenders is dead. He's buried in Mārtiņa Cemetery.'

'You're German. What was your purpose in staying here? Why?'

The questions were ceaseless. The men spoke both at once. Even the pince-nez one gargled his 'r's. It sounded as if they were mimicking one another, chattering like an excited flock of birds. The verbal outpouring was reminiscent of the aggressive vendors at the Marijas Street kiosks and was shockingly out of place in a respectable government institution.

The Baroness understood that making excuses would be as useless as explaining topography to the roadside mileposts.

'I have a document of rejection.'

The men spent some time poring over the German foreign minister's letter, muttering 'deemed undesir-r-r-able', 'deemed undesir-r-r-able'...

'There's no explanation here. What's the decision based on?'

'I believe it was based on my relatives. My maternal grandmother Zāra Hedberga...'

As if silenced by an invisible conductor's baton, the men froze for a moment, exchanging meaningful glances.

'Wha-a-at! You're not German?'

'Blood can tell you how much alcohol you've consumed, but scientists haven't yet discovered how to determine percentages of nationality.'

The conversation continued in its initial harsh tone, but the Baroness sensed that the men's hostility had waned. In the end they announced that the investigation would continue and she would be summoned again if necessary. Everything she had seen and heard was classified.

'And that took all night?' Jānis was surprised. It was after seven in the morning. He and I were already dressed in our school uniforms.

'Oh – oh, it was a boring process. They recorded every question and answer. There was something wrong with the pen, there were ink splotches on the page. The first "r-r-r" stepped out a few times, probably looking for something, but he didn't find it. At times they'd both step out and leave me while they discussed the situation. I think they were trying to decide whether or not to ask their director what to do.

'Do you know what surprised me the most?' she added as an afterthought. But as she asked the question, the Baroness's expression changed so quickly that the real meaning of the last hours instantly became clear. Just as water keeps pouring down the wet face of a swimmer surfacing from the waves, so terror, disgust, confusion and exhaustion rolled down the Baroness's forehead and cheeks. 'Towards morning when the military "r-r-r" filled out the pass and the first "r-r-r" led me to the exit, the entire building was lit up like a textile factory at night. I could hear voices behind every door. Dark games in the daylight...'

'Working at night is economically advantageous. Electricity is cheaper at night,' Jānis thought aloud.

The Baroness smiled as she went by to go to her room, stopping to reach out her hand and lightly touch Jānis's earlobe. She had touched me like that many times before, but this seemed to be the first time for Jānis.

'Ah, yes,' the Baroness looked back, 'what's also curious is that I saw the Pilot there. On my way out he and one of those uniformed longshirts passed me in the hall. It was definitely him. He pretended not to see me. I'm positive it was him. In a black Latvian army pilot's uniform. Without the captain's ensign, but with a red star on his hat.'

XIV

There is no room for words – the trip to Saint Petersburg is a mad adventure. She would have never come up with the idea herself. And certainly not in her current state, but turning down the Great Cophta is not within her power.

To Valtraute von Brīgen's surprise, the journey turns out to be quite pleasant. The road is tolerable not only in both parts of the Vidzeme region, but also past Pliskava and Luga. And they're not travelling in a stagecoach. One carriage was lent to Cagliostro by Duke Peter of Courland; the other is from the Medems. The plush red velvet of the cabin gently envelops the passengers like pearls and gemstones in a jewellery box. The fear she had contracted from Elisa von der Recke that the count would turn dangerous in the close quarters of the journey proves to be unfounded. Cagliostro is travelling with his life partner, Lorenza the Queen of Sheba. Their party is a small and curious one. Lorenza's only attendants are the negress Jo, her chambermaid, who could be a man or – most likely – a hermaphrodite, and the three-foot-two-inch dwarf Fulla, the animal-keeper; Lorenza always goes out with a white dove perched on her shoulder and a bronze-coloured adder named Homer wrapped like a fat bracelet around her arm. Then there's Cagliostro's chef, a fat, smiling German with five chins, the new footman hired in Jelgava shortly before their departure, and a dishevelled, raven-like astrologer named Midas, with whom Cagliostro converses in King Solomon's language.

The men of the entourage sit outside on the coachbox with the coachman or at the back of the carriage on special seats. The baroness and Bon Esprit ride alone. Except for the times the Great Cophta steps in to announce something, or Jo comes with refreshments from the travelling provisions provided by the duke.

In accordance with Russian law, five dragoons are stationed at each post office. As they draw nearer to Saint Petersburg, the count requests that they accompany him. Dragoons in bluish-black tunics, their spears facing outwards, ride in front of the golden carriage; the cavalcade is impressive.

The surroundings grow increasingly sullen. As if there is a large spider's web covering everything. The forests are pitiful, flattened to the ground, sucked dry of all life. Colours tarnish and darken to grey. Marshy meadows, dead and bare tree stumps. Lonely gulls in the wind-ravaged, cloudy skies.

And then, suddenly, a *Fata Morgana*, a dream-like vision reveals itself from a flat hillock: an enormous city with a golden tip rises up in the distant blue haze like a spade sinking into the sky. It's at least ten Rigas and Jelgavas put together! Palace upon palace, bridge upon bridge, tower upon tower.

Valtraute thinks of her nanny's story about the boastful fisherman who, arms spread wide, told how big a pike he had pulled from the lake. The braggart's friends tied him up so he could move only his hands, but that didn't stop him – he spread his palms open to the size of a cabbage and said: 'The pike's eye was this big, look!'

A city that had grown on top of numerous islands, reflected in the waters, was also something like an eye. A giant eye that gives you a sense of the size of the body to which it belongs.

Cagliostro is met at the city gates by Senator Yelagin, grand master of the Saint Petersburg Freemasons, and several high masters. Either afraid of the winds coming off the Gulf of Finland or, more likely, fulfilling some ritual, the welcoming party stands at the side of the road wearing black hooded cloaks over their ornate silk costumes.

Senator Yelagin climbs into the carriage with the Great Cophta. Lorenza the Queen of Sheba and one of the welcoming party – a tall, lean, pale, middle-aged man – ride with the Baroness von Brīgen for the remainder of the journey.

'Allow me to introduce myself – Quartermaster of the Kunstkamera, von Schnitzler.' The pale man's voice sounds hollow, as if he were speaking from the bottom of a barrel. To say that the conversation is engaging and flows freely would be an exaggeration. The quartermaster mostly names the visible buildings.

'Peter the Great's palace ... Elizabeth's palace ... Catherine's palace...'

'How many palaces are there in the city?' Valtraute asks.

Von Schnitzler, as if rocked by an invisible wave, turns his curly-wigged head from one side to the other. 'A lot. And more are being built.'

'Why does each new ruler build a new palace?'

'Maybe because of ghosts. Bad memories are undesirable neighbours...'

The Queen of Sheba wants to know about the biggest scandals at the court, what everyone is talking about.

Schnitzler hesitates, fidgets, his Adam's apple bobs up and down nervously. But Lorenza's smiles and sweet tittering do the trick. The quartermaster slowly relaxes, comes alive.

'An inexplicable tragedy – Princess Saltykova has given birth to a blue baby boy. Entirely blue, as if he's been dipped in ink. She's had only girls up to now, and she could finally have an heir, someone to carry on the family name – but no.'

Valtraute bites her lip; how terrible! Unbelievable! What if she gives birth to a horrible monster? Hairy, or with two heads...

But the Queen of Sheba is quick to calm her. She does the same for the fool Schnitzler, even touching his hand in assurance.

'Now, now, it's nothing! The Great Cophta can take care of these things. The governor general of Corsica's son was born green, and even cried green tears. Now he's all better. Tell Princess Saltykova she can rest easy. Is the empress's relationship with Potemkin still passionate?'

'Lately, the empress has been seen more with the young Savadovsky. But in state matters Grigory Aleksandrovich still has the lead role. He's tempting her with his "Greek Project"; he wants to defeat Turkey and turn the Byzantine throne over to Catherine's grandson. Matushka' – Schnitzler says this word in Russian – 'says aptly: "Grishenka, when it comes to women you're like a broken net, letting everything fall through." But the prince answers cleverly: "Except for the greatest fish, which is in my net for life." But Potemkin is insatiable, now he has a son from one of his cousins.

But what news is there from Europe?'

'I don't even know if I'm allowed to say. The Great Cophta prophesied Saint Germain's death. No one really knows how old he is. Saint Germain claims he's four thousand years old, though his footman says he's exaggerating by at least a thousand – but that he had been to Nebuchadnezzar's banquets in Babylon.'

Captivated by what he is hearing, the quartermaster wheezes and nods his large, gaunt face in time with the Queen of Sheba's words.

'He'll have to die some day...'

'Everyone must die once. The Great Cophta also foresees the death of Maria Theresa in the near future. Then Emperor Joseph will be free of her. He's one of ours. Austria is headed towards great changes.'

'If only our beloved Russia were also headed towards change!'

'There is much talk of Russia in Europe!'

Schnitzler pulls his disproportionately thick lips into a wry smile.

'Russia's reform is like a rainbow; it's not a bridge you can drive over.'

The week flies by quickly. Something new always comes up, something yet unheard, yet unseen, unexpected. A moment of rest, and then the next round. Visits and excursions, theatre performances and balls. Life in Yelagin's palace is like a dream. When the senator decides to show them his horses, fifty footmen lay out Bokhara and Kandahar rugs on the marble steps and tile floors of the palace, and the horses are paraded into the ballroom. At the card table Cagliostro announces that he understands the language of the Moors; Yelagin immediately claps his hands and several dark-skinned dancers dressed in colourful bird feathers rush into the room.

The white night skies of Saint Petersburg dim only a little before the sun starts to rise anew. Valtraute wakes suddenly from a brief nap. The room is bright and a nightingale sings loudly, longingly, outside the window, almost like the nightingales in Vidzeme. If this is a place where everything is possible, where all your wishes come true, then she wants – really wants, not just would like – for Eberhart to be next to her, here in this bed as wide and long as a garrison parade ground! And she doesn't care how, with his own face or Captain Ulste's broad chin and light-coloured moustache, which she can still see, smell and feel against her cheeks, neck and breasts. She needs a live man, whole or, if not, two-pieced, three-pieced, four-pieced, but one who is here with her and will let her live like a young woman should. A refined woman. Why does she, Valtraute, have to sacrifice her youth for the greater good? She doesn't want to be the mother of Buddha, the Virgin Mary. After giving birth to Jesus, the Virgin Mary gave birth to four or five more children as was normal. So God had mercy on her. Doesn't she, Valtraute, deserve His mercy? It's strange, humanity will get new opportunities, but she won't get anything. Her child won't even be of the Holy Spirit, but from the bottom half of some body. Dear Eberhart, where are you? How wonderful it would be if we were both here to listen to the nightingale! I'd lie in your arms, and you'd …

She shouldn't torture herself! The baroness tosses and turns. She rubs her throat as if she's parched, touches her hard, swollen breasts. Oh, how sad, how unbearably sad!

Each day, Valtraute von Brīgen tries to learn when they'll finally meet with Gibran, but the answers are evasive – 'we need to determine a few circumstances', 'it's not the best time'. She can see Cagliostro's mind is elsewhere. Things don't seem to be going quite the way he'd like. He summons spirits in the Freemasons' lodge, gives astrological readings, says he can change one substance into another, but the idea of an Egyptian lodge receives weak support from the ladies of Saint Petersburg. And the empress is taking her time acknowledging the arrival of the guests.

The count truly is busy, that is undeniable. The great city is presented as paradise itself, but the gentry have no shortage of troubles and worries, and everyone wants Cophta's help. Men who are years older than their young wives need astral energy. Men who have outstanding debts from card games want to turn bronze into gold. Ageing women want an elixir for youth. It's true that the Great Cophta turns some of them away rather brusquely, if not rudely, but he tells everyone who comes to him something that makes their eyes become wide and their hearts jump. There is no doubt: Cophta can just look at a person and read them like a book.

Saltykova's blue baby is a special case. News that Cagliostro can rid it of the affliction spreads quickly. Everyone waits to see what will happen. But serious tasks require serious preparation.

Count Cagliostro travels around the expanse of Saint Petersburg in the Duke of Courland's golden carriage, feeling out the wellsprings of energy and simultaneously establishing contacts with like-minded people. The Queen of Sheba has become the quartermaster Schnitzler's bosom-friend.

Amazing things happen with this man. The oafish German, stoked by Lorenza's temperament, has become a fervent admirer, and his persistence doesn't go unrewarded. It's no secret. Dear Eberhart always said that sperm and a dying person's sweat were two odours you didn't need a nose to smell.

Finally the day arrives: the Empress Catherine requests Count Cagliostro's presence at her new palace at Peterhof. The Great Cophta arrives in five carriages with a full entourage. The leader of the local Freemasons, Count Yelagin, is also invited.

With their small dimensions, the long row of halls through which they walk to be received appears to express modesty. At the same time, the luxury, wealth and extravagance are piled on so densely that it feels as if the only way they can manoeuvre through it all is to press against the walls and move sideways. A thicket of paintings, porcelain, crystal, gold, tapestries, amber. On the walls, on the ceiling, on the floors. Flowing, wavy, curvy lines, as if based on the female body. The glimmering clusters of chandeliers, the inviting lounges, chaises longues, and card tables with suggestively curved legs. Historians will later call the rococo style a frenzy of provocative excess, of unbridled lavishness, but at this moment the nervous baroness is the only one who senses that she has stepped out of the familiar baroque into an entirely different and wonderful world.

The empress is standing in the middle of the room: an older woman, with thick-set cheeks, soft neck and sunken, manly chin, a thin upper lip and cool, blue, calculating eyes, dressed in a simple, striped, bordeaux-coloured moire costume. The rumour that they don't wear wigs here any more turns out to be true. Catherine's natural hair is gathered in thick curls. Prince Potemkin does have a wig, but it's strangely smooth, with just a few curls by the ears. Potemkin's chubby face is comical: wide eyebrows that look as if they've been painted on, close-set eyes and a long, cork-like nose with a stubby tip. A black ribbon is tied over one of his eyes. Though stocky in build, the prince still looks small when standing next to the empress. But his thick shoulders look tense with energy; like a cat stalking a mouse, he looks ready to pounce any second.

Baroness von Brīgen doesn't notice the others in the room. Maybe some day she'll find herself standing in front of the almighty Lord God – Him willing – or maybe she won't. But right here, right now, not three steps from her, are Catherine the Great and the famous Prince Potemkin!

After the introductions, the empress invites everyone to the adjacent room – a salon with a crackling fireplace. The welcoming rituals differ from those Valtraute is accustomed to in less grand society. Potemkin flops into a chair and immediately lights a long Dutch pipe; Count Cagliostro removes a tin of snuff from his vest pocket with a flourish.

'Spitefulness is a bad advisor. Intending to spite the Swedes, Peter built his capital in a place where everything freezes in winter, but rots in the summer. A good place for the Russian capital would be Riga,' the empress says and, as easily as if she were chatting with close friends at a garden party, turns to Count Cagliostro. 'What do you think? Will England declare war on Holland?'

'Absolutely,' Cophta answers nonchalantly. And only after a moment adds: 'Your Majesty...'

'Are you sure?'

'More than sure.'

'The British blockade won't cut off the Americans?'

'It won't.'

'You can predict that?'

'I can. And Russia will get the warm south.'

'See that, Matushka! And you doubted it!' Potemkin shouts, sitting up taller in his chair.

'No, Grigory Aleksandrovich, I didn't doubt it. I just don't want you and your army to get too hot in the warmer countries...' The empress doesn't change her tone.

Valtraute tries to understand what they're talking about. It definitely doesn't have anything to do with her mission. Whenever she'd pass card tables, she would always listen in confusion to what was being said: 'I fold!', 'Hit me!', 'Deal!' Here, the phrases 'call a truce with Sweden', 'Lord Southampton's opposition' and 'Beaumarchais' ideas' are just as nonsensical to her. The empress and Prince Potemkin clearly enjoy the game, and are skilled at it.

Strange that Yelagin doesn't take part. Valtraute forms the impression that the empress doesn't even see him.

And Yelagin does nothing to remind them of his presence. He sits frozen, his portly body jammed crookedly into the chair like a misshapen candle in the socket of a slender candlestick.

The Queen of Sheba has also been silent. But she isn't excluded from the game. Lorenza's white dove sits on her shoulder and Homer the adder sleeps wrapped around her forearm. Every now and then one of the animals stirs, drawing the attention of the others. One could think the animals only move by command of Lorenza or Cagliostro.

All of a sudden Valtraute feels something like a draught. She senses Cagliostro's eyes on her and knows that it is the precursor to something bigger, and that something is happening now. The baroness feels her cheeks grow warm, as if she were a blushing girl again. And just as when she was a girl, the warmth spreads from her cheeks down along her neck, to her corset, and takes her breath away.

'If I may ask, what is Monsieur Diderot doing?' Cagliostro's voice sounds distant.

'Monsieur Diderot is our librarian and is still in Saint Petersburg. He's been having health problems lately.' They can sense the subject isn't one the empress enjoys discussing.

'When Monsieur Diderot had trouble publishing the Great French *Encyclopédie* in Paris, you took the publication into your protection. You were even looking for opportunities to publish it in Riga...'

'The necessity to do so didn't arise.'

'The brightest minds in Europe valued your responsiveness. It was an inspirational gesture – to buy the impoverished Diderot's library and bring him to Saint Petersburg. Why did you do it? ... Your Majesty?'

'A curious question,' the empress says, with emphasised disinterest, and shrugs her somewhat hunched shoulders.

'It's not a question ... Your Majesty. I know the answer. With the help of the encyclopaedia, you wanted to change their heads.'

For a moment the empress's expression freezes in surprise, but it is immediately worn down by the whetstone of irony into a cool stare.

'Cleverly said.'

'Truthfully said.'

'I don't disagree. Progress means change.'

'I'm offering you a new opportunity...'

'To publish the encyclopaedia?'

'To change heads.'

'Ha, ha. Your *emploi*, it seems, is broad. More literary matters?'

'No, surgical. Permit me an example. A few years ago in Moscow, Pugachev bade his head farewell. His punishment was just, but barbaric, and not everyone was pleased with it. Wouldn't it have been more convenient to put another head on his shoulders? Replace the rebellious one with one more trustworthy. Just imagine: he becomes an obedient citizen and goes to fight against the Turks. Under his command soldiers would go through fire and water!'

The empress's pinched smile shines like a pair of pliers. Catherine struggles to weigh and evaluate what she has heard. The comparison with Pugachev, that disgusting man, is unpleasant.

'Do you know of any cases where a head was switched?'

'A head and other parts of the body. As necessary.'

'A strange joke.'

'Not at all!' the count makes a sweeping gesture towards Valtraute. 'Behold, I give you Baroness von Brīgen, a relative of the noble Līvens. Her husband, Eberhart von Brīgen, adjutant in the Grand Duke Constantine's regiment, lost his head in a heroic battle against the Turks. Together with his shoulders and chest. The lower part of his body was attached to Captain Freiherr von Ulste's upper body, and the combination functions normally. The baroness is three months pregnant with her husband's heir...'

Valtraute doesn't know what to do. The ice-blue eyes of the empress observe her with close intensity. As a precaution, Valtraute stands, curtsies deeply, then sits back down.

'From a national perspective, the options are numerous,' Cophta's voice grows increasingly enthusiastic as he continues. 'An increase in spiritual ability among the society at court, bringing back decorated generals of legend, grafting youths and men of the lower classes with pre-worn but titled heads! It would be a step towards the equalisation of humanity, a goal that has been lauded by the most prescient minds of our century of enlightenment.'

Count Cagliostro wants to embellish his speech with more examples, but the empress cuts him off impatiently. In listening to the count's words, it's possible that she's thinking the same thing as Valtraute: *Lieber Gott*, what would have happened if Catherine's idiot husband Peter III had changed his pathetic brain-barrel for a more powerful one? Most likely, Catherine would have been the one executed, and Peter III would have remained alive and villainous, sitting on the throne with Liza Vorontsova by his side as his wife. Now that would be rich!

'There are miraculous things happening in our country, but we don't know any of them! Grigory Aleksandrovich, perhaps you know something?'

'News to me! It's all news to me!'

Finally, the empress has reason to notice Yelagin.

'And you, Count Yelagin, do you know anything? The improvement of society smells like your rose garden. I wouldn't be surprised if you were to decide whose head should go to whom...'

Count Yelagin's breathing wheezes loudly like a tired logger pulling a saw back and forth. He jumps to his feet with his fat hand on his heart.

'Great Intelligent Mother of the Motherland! The Freemasons are your most loyal subjects. Philosophically, we support the brotherhood of man, the enlightenment of the mind and the well-being of society. But if we're talking about surgery...'

At this moment Count Cagliostro shouts 'a propos', interrupting Yelagin like an impetuous jailbird, a shameless refuter of etiquette, then loudly clears his throat and continues evenly.

'...Your Majesty, I am here to take care of the problem. Yes, we kept the situation a secret. Your Majesty knows how quickly rumours spread and how devastating the consequences can be. Now, yes, that some experience has been acquired...'

The empress's hand flies up like a strike of lightning. Even the Great Cophta stops short at such a resolute gesture.

'We wish to know who has this experience!'

'The person is no stranger to Saint Petersburg.' Cophta's matter-of-fact answer sounds a bit offended. But he doesn't want to be angry with the empress. No, he's more open-minded than that; trivialities are beneath him. 'I'm talking about the surgeon of Grand Duke Constantine's regiment, Almastaf Gibran.'

'We've never seen him here!'

'Yes ... Your Majesty! The regiment was headed in the direction of the Black Sea.'

'More new information!' The empress claps her hands and knits her brows with slightly exaggerated wonder. 'Grigory Aleksandrovich, we didn't give the order for the troops to assemble.'

'True, true, Matushka. There was no order. But when you go to sleep in a barn loft and there are sometimes girls around, undoing a few buttons now and then isn't a sin.'

'Prince Potemkin! You are not in a barn loft!'

'Apologies, Matushka. My mind wandered...'

'We also haven't seen that ...' the empress hesitates. 'That ... kind of fate. With a new head.'

'Not just the head. One person's head, and another person's lower body.'

'It doesn't matter! We haven't seen this person.'

'Exactly ... Your Majesty.' Count Cagliostro is unshakable. He speaks with confidence and almost in a tone of voice as if he, not the empress, were controlling the conversation. 'The newly formed body you speak of returned to serve in the cuirassier regiment. He is probably stationed where the surgeon Gibran is – near Taurida. By your Majesty's order, their arrival in Saint Petersburg would be a matter of weeks. Pythagoras and Newton's discoveries would pale in comparison to Gibran's.'

There isn't a single trace of a smile left on the empress's face. Her full lips are as tightly puckered as a trumpeter blowing his horn.

'We understand your enthusiasm. We advise you to understand our responsibility. Before overshadowing Pythagoras and Newton, the sceptre and the crown require that everything be considered carefully.'

Once that is said, a trace of thaw flits over the empress's icy face.

'...and now, see, the prince has spitefully got it into his head to become Potemkin of Taurida. If he starts a war in the Crimea, he's going to need soldiers and surgeons.'

'Your power and your will ... Majesty, you gain Europe's favour by inviting Monsieur Diderot to Russia. Perhaps you'd like to gain similar favour by permitting Monsieur Gibran to travel from Russia to France?'

Here, the empress and the Great Cophta wage a little battle. They are both so tense that they're shaking. A long silence fills the salon. The empress hears a short cry and, turning her head, sees an unnaturally pale Baroness von Brīgen slide from her golden chair on to the rug. Cagliostro rushes to her and takes her into his arms. He does this with incredible ease, as if von Brīgen weighed nothing. But the baroness seems to grow smaller and smaller in the count's arms, until she looks like a small girl who has fallen asleep in her father's lap.

The Great Cophta leaves the salon. His entourage bows and leaves as well. The Freemasons' grand master, Yelagin, is the only one who hesitates – he turns his head, stands, sits and then finally, wheezing and wiping his forehead, follows the others. But in accordance with court etiquette, he exits the room step by step, with his back to the door.

The empress shivers as if dizzy.

'Grigory Aleksandrovich, what happened here?'

'What happened!? Nothing happened, Matushka. Everything is fine. You said ... You said the visit had come to an end.'

'Strange indeed ... We saw something else ... We don't like it ... Call for Gozubov!'

The director of the Secret Chancellery enters the room. Catherine II has a weakness for swarthy men. Gozubov is just that, a real Hercules in an eighteenth-century dandy's clothes. With the brains of a mole.

'Yes, Majesty?'

'Keep an eye on every move Cagliostro makes! Watch his entire entourage! We'll talk about Yelagin later.'

'Understood!'

Gozubov has a strange gait. He walks with his chin in the air. It looks as if his small nose is sniffing out something that only he can smell.

XV

Johanna was never called back for questioning. In broad retrospect, it seems that the explanation was to be found in the rapid development of the larger situation. The number of enemies grew continuously. Life teaches us that not everything happens logically. A plane crashes, killing ninety-nine passengers but leaving one survivor. A forest fire advances towards a house, just a few more inches before the swirling embers reach the roof, but suddenly the wind changes and the flames are carried in the opposite direction. Why does it happen? Those hard to explain things are always rolled into a single, expansive concept – luck.

The Manor, too, was saved by luck.

In documents from way way back, it had been registered as a rural estate; expropriation of buildings did not apply to rural homes. Grandfather's carting business was nationalised, but essentially nothing changed. A local committee was formed among the coachmen and pall-bearers. The Baroness continued to work as bookkeeper and cashier. Grandfather was no longer the owner, but the executive director. The commissariat issued an order for the horses to be transferred to the Automobile and Horse Rental Station – a new-fangled institution that was unique within a ten-kilometre radius. But people went on being born, getting married, christening their children and dying. People still needed funeral catafalques. And there were still newly-weds who wanted to go for carriage rides.

Jānis and I were primarily occupied with changes at school. Our teachers changed, our curriculum changed. New words bubbled and washed over us: the great victory of the working class, the weight of the bourgeoisie has been shaken off, the sun of Stalin's constitution. The vocal orgies burst forth in a turbulent stream. And only now and then between the churning waves did the pale, frightened face of someone drowning become visible. Some of the students' fathers or grandfathers had been arrested the night before, while others received summons for questioning. And the parents of yet more had simply disappeared, and there was no way to figure out what had happened to them.

Jānis's classes ended on 14 June. Those of us who were ready to don the gold-striped cavalier caps in the autumn, which would mark us out as secondary-schoolers, still had classes.

It was a warm, sunny morning. There was an open platform at each end of the old Belgian tram-cars, as if they were made for riding in good weather. After the tram had crossed the sandy plot of Uzvara Square and turned at the Torņakalns Depot towards the Pontoon Bridge, it ran for a stretch alongside a car which carried a strange cargo. Sitting among numerous packages were a man in a winter coat and a woman in a grey rabbit-fur coat, with a small girl in her lap dressed more for summer. In the far corner was a Red Army soldier, holding his bayonetted gun between his knees. The sight drew our attention, but more out of surprise than anxiety. Because – as I mentioned – the weather was beautiful and school had finished. Like the majority of my countrymen, I was incapable of grasping the tragedy that was taking place in Latvia that day. With my upbringing and my notions of the laws under which the world functions, I never would have thought that something so unfair, inhuman and horrifying could happen in broad daylight and in plain sight.

At school the teachers were acting strangely. About one third of our classmates hadn't shown up for lessons. No one knew if that day's classes would take place.

Several days later, my notions, which were apparently outdated, received a new and even more crushing blow. Jānis and I had gone to visit a friend on Lībiešu Island. On either side of Zaķusala Island, an archipelago of romantically named islands bordered both banks of the Daugava river: Grāpju Island, Putnu Island, Jumpravsala Island, Zvirgzdu Island, Kazu Island, Muižas Island, Mūksala Island, Beņķu Island. Lībiešu Island was connected to Maskava Street by the man-made Krīdenera Dam. We bared our spring-white bodies to the sun and lay on the beach, from where we had a broad view of the Daugava and the Riga skyline. The arcs of bridges sat low on the horizon in the distance. Fishermen in their motorboats, sailboats and rowboats zigzagged along the river. Little steamboats pulled rafts and heavily laden barges. The sun illuminated carefully stacked piles of lumber on the islands along the riverbanks. The whine of sawmills and the thick scent of sawdust reached us over the peaceful water.

Around noon, aeroplanes appeared over the left side of the Daugava, coming from the direction of Kurzeme. They flew in the direction of the sea, in perfect triangle formation as if they were part of an aerial display. When the anti-aircraft guns started firing and white shrapnel clouds rose up around the squadron, we realised something wasn't right. The sounds of the explosions didn't reach us, but we saw a wide pillar of smoke rise up from beyond the bridges, cutting diagonally into the sunny June sky. Fuel tanks were the only things that could burn that thick and black.

The war had begun.

The air along the road that led to the airfield was acrid with the fumes. We saw gaping, smouldering pits, glass fragments, torn wires, shattered branches of trees. Plaster and boards were decorated by shrapnel holes. The dead and the injured had already been taken away. At the small restaurant across from the stop at the end of the tram line, a woman had been turned into a bloody smear against the building's wall. Any one of us could have been in her place – me, Jānis, Grandfather or the Baroness. In my eyes, any transgression against human life was a punishable crime, but now I saw that human life depended on a lucky roll of the dice. Whether the dice landed on life or death was determined by the invisible shifting of the numbers just before they were rolled. Our minds refused to let us comprehend it, our survival instincts refused to let us accept it, but the individual drive of each of us no longer held meaning.

The Manor had only been partially hit as the blanket of bombs fell. The two-centuries-old linden tree sprawled in the yard as if it had been felled by an axe; shrapnel had reduced the greenhouse behind the stables to rubble.

Quoting Montaigne, Grandfather reacted to the beginning of the war with unshakeable calm: 'So you may neither flee from life, nor run to death, I have tempered both the one and the other with sweetness and sourness.' He was convinced that the air raids would continue and searched the park for a passable bunker. In the end, we decided that the Manor's cold cellar would make for a good enough shelter; the floor was a thick layer of dirt, the vaulted ceiling sturdily built and supported by stone beams. The Baroness thought her ancestors' tomb would be safer, and asked for a few chairs, a small table and a hammock to be brought there.

The air raids continued one after the other, for the most part at night. The choir of wailing sirens sang a funeral hymn, and then the bombs dropped. My body shook with shivers as I jumped out of bed and dressed in a hurry to run to the basement. I told myself it was because of the cold night air, but it was the eerie chill seeping from the sky itself as the skeleton-white fingers of searchlights combed through the blackness.

Sunny days were replaced by dark rainy ones. The textile factory building, which had towered over the area like a grand castle, stood smoking, the burnt-out walls and pitifully mangled metal beams now a depressing monument. There were no signs of life at the airfield. The trams ran for a few more days, then disappeared all together. We heard talk that the Pontoon Bridge was closed to local traffic and that only small groups of pedestrians, escorted by armoured cars, were allowed to cross.

The Baroness sat in her usual spot by the telephone with a Scottish plaid shawl around her shoulders, smoking cigarette after cigarette. Tormented by the lack of employment, the coachmen and catafalque escorts played cards in the coach-house. Grandfather announced that he was going on a reconnaissance trip and had them prepare a two-horse funeral carriage. When he got back, he told us trenches had been dug along the Daugava. Exhausted, dirty, pitiful men with blackened, fallen faces sat in their posts. It was as if they didn't understand where they were or why they were there. They voided their bladders and bowels right there in the trenches, either due to orders to stay where they were, or out of complete and utter despair.

The sirens were silent on the last evening of June; the anti-aircraft guns held their fire, the German planes flew so low you could see the white crosses on their black wings. Now and then the air shook with a long and low rumble: something somewhere was being blown up.

In the morning, the coachman who lived on Jūrmala Avenue rode over on his bike to tell us that the Pārdaugava area was now under German control. Grandfather went to the pile of firewood and dug out the radio he had hidden there. We were able to catch the final words of the national anthem: '... to live there happily, in our Latvia!'

'The Reitera Choir,' Grandfather said. 'Six singers ... Just listen how clean the sound is!'

The dark grey clouds had dissipated like the nightmarish burdens of the night. A warm wind was blowing and the sun shone in the airy, summer-blue sky. Around noon the next day, Jānis and I got into a boat at the Zunda gangway and sailed across the Daugava to Riga. Every bridge had bombed-out sections in it. The city itself, particularly downtown, had been hit pretty hard. On both sides of the Freedom Monument red-white-and-red flags waved at the tops of newly erected flagpoles. Flowers were heaped up at the base of the monument. The Honour Guard was back in its place. People came together, laughed, cried, hugged one another. Even I was overcome by a strange sense of elation; maybe it came from those around me, maybe it came from the feeling that everything I was seeing and experiencing was a big revelation. As if this were the first time I was seeing the Freedom Monument, the red-white-and-red flags, the people and the flowers. But even the familiar things now appeared in a different light, because nothing was the same any more. Even the Riga I was seeing, feeling and taking in, was a Riga unfamiliar to me, entirely different. I even sensed myself as new and different.

Jānis was intrigued by the German technology – the hitched-up anti-aircraft guns, the cannons propped on motorcycles. He asked if the war was over. I said it wasn't, but what we saw wasn't necessarily indicative of war.

Stately German generals – decorated, fingers covered with rings, deer-skin mittens in hand – walked freely and without care along the boulevards and parks. Now and then we'd catch a glimpse of a Latvian army general or one of our instructors as they passed by. Local bigwigs had once more come out of the woodwork, not to mention the elegant women. Among the rubble and ruins, which reeked of fire and smoke, sat artists in German military clothes – painting with watercolours and oils, sharpening their pastels. The self-aware, open Europeans were a stark contrast to the shabby, dishevelled throngs of people who had left Riga. Upon entering a café, a German general would toss his hat and heavy, gun-laden holster to the cloakroom attendant with careless elegance. There was the scent of expensive cigarettes; soldiers marched in formation and whistled cheerfully. In the brilliant light of day, the eye could still spot tiny shadows, remainders of yesterday's darkness – though it might not have been worth paying attention to them. Armed men herded some people along the street to who knows where. Prisoners of war cowered behind hastily erected barbed-wire fences. They were filthy, exhausted; they could have been the same men Grandfather had seen in the trenches.

On the third evening after the Germans assumed power, they took the Baroness away. Jānis and I had spent all day wandering the city and were sleeping so deeply that we heard nothing. Come morning, we didn't understand why Grandfather was sitting at the kitchen table in his underwear with his pelerine cloak around his shoulders, and why there was a lamp burning in front of him when it was daytime.

'This whole mess is my fault,' Grandfather spoke in a dull, choked voice as he took his head in his hands. 'Why didn't I see it coming? Why didn't I think of it?'

His explanation was stilted, disjointed.

'Gestapo, in the most banal guise ... Leather jackets, black caps ... hands in their pockets ... Baltic German and Schwabian accents ... "Sir, we'd like to do this without causing a commotion – where's the Jew?" At first I didn't know who they were talking about. "What Jew?" I asked ... "The one who's pretending to be German and wants to smuggle herself back into Greater Germany ..." One of them is holding a paper, I can see it's a copy of the letter Johanna sent to Berlin. "Don't tell us Frau Holendere has left for the weekend..."'

'What does that mean? What'll happen?' the questions came out as stuttered fragments. Grandfather had probably been wrestling with similar questions all night. When something didn't work out, when he had to admit weakness, he was bitter. Even then, he looked at me with near-disdain.

'What's going to happen? We have to get her out! Or else we're just a bunch of sheep!'

'But is a sheep necessarily a bad thing?' Jānis didn't understand. 'A sheep can have horns – a ram; rams are confrontational, vengeful, stubborn...'

Grandfather cleared his throat, thought for another moment, then stood and blew out the lamp.

'You're right! This time we have to be rams. Real rams!'

He looked glum, but the darkness under his knitted brow did a somersault. As if moonlight were reflecting off a frozen lake. As if light had broken through grey winter clouds.

Grandfather drove around, made calls, met with Indriķis Skangals, packed packages, wrote letters, but he was unable to track down Johanna. I couldn't shake the certainty that, just as unexpectedly as she had disappeared, the Baroness would turn up again. And would sit in her room or at the desk in the office. In my mind, such concepts as prison, crime, punishment, could not relate to the Baroness. If she were in a prison, it meant that sooner or later the misunderstanding would be cleared up.

We heard a lot about prisons. Newspapers and journals wrote about nothing else, bringing to light the horrors committed by the now-defeated Soviet powers. Mass graves were dug up in prison yards, unearthing those who had been shot dead over the last year. The images of mounds of uncoffined bodies struck a nerve. Almost every photograph contained the face of someone who had previously been in the newspapers or journals. Well-known ministers, generals, directors, cavaliers and philistines now stared up, with empty eyes, lipless mouths, black bullet holes in their foreheads. The already decomposing hands were bound with barbed wire, nails had been ripped off their fingers.

We'd heard of similar torture in the inquisitions of the Middle Ages, which still gave us a chill centuries later – but they were guesses at best, rumours, questionable whispers. The class-cleansing institutions had been operating unbeknown to the majority of society, almost like the gurgling underground sewers, which it is hard to believe exist beneath the smooth surfaces of the boulevards and streets. Now the manholes were off, the sewers were open. What we saw took our breath away.

Grandfather, sombre and ragged, stopped bringing newspapers home. Jānis and I would run to the kiosk ourselves. Every page revealed something new and entirely unbelievable. Lists of those deported, farewell letters thrown out of trains, eyewitness accounts. One night, almost fifteen thousand men, women and children – babies included – had been herded into six hundred and sixty cattle cars to be deported from Latvia to Siberia. Six thousand had been held in captivity, shot dead or sent to prisons abroad. Anyone could go into the basements of those torture centres and see with his own eyes the electric-shock equipment, the hooks hanging from the ceilings, the execution rooms with gutters in the cement floors to drain the blood.

'Grandfather, what do you make of all of it?'

'There's nothing to make of it. Out of one pair of claws and right into another. We got to know one psychopath, God help us survive the next.'

His predictions were spot-on. Hopes for Latvia's renewed independence dissolved within a few weeks. The Germans talked only of unifying Latvia, Lithuania, Estonia and Belarus into a region of the west. Lieutenant Colonel Deglavs, who was the most adamant about reinstating the Latvian army, was found in his apartment with a bullet hole in his neck.

Former militiamen, employees of communist institutions, school principals, people who sang songs of revolution and anyone who carried a red flag were all persecuted. Their fates were unknown, but it just so happened that the prisons were once more overcrowded.

Absolutely everyone blamed the Jews. In some way, the threatening shadow had fallen on Johanna, and subsequently affected us. The newspapers said nothing about how, after the Germans took Riga, synagogues were burned to the ground, with the people still inside. But you can't cover up those kinds of things. Jānis walked around with a stony face; Grandfather huffed and threw his hands up.

'Just imagine it, in Riga! Where the only people fighting in the name of the Latvian nation were the drunks outside the pubs! What would Blaumanis, rest his soul, make of it, he who married the Jewish Zāra and Joskis on stage right alongside the Latvian Elīna and Aleksis in his *Skroderdienas Silmačos*?'

The radio and newspapers spilled forth accusations as if in argument with Grandfather. Who let communism loose on the world? Who were Karl Marx, Rosa Luxemburg, Leiba Trotsky, Lenin's mother Miriam Blanc? Who greeted the occupiers with red roses? Who helped the Russians on those nights of mass deportations, leading them to the right doors in the foreign labyrinth of streets? Was it perhaps Simons Šustins, who signed off on hundreds of death sentences in the Riga Cheka? All of the communists had fled or had been locked up, but the Jews walked around unpunished, bought up the best products and plotted new conspiracies. In order for the world to be ruled by order, the root of evil had to be weeded out...

Initially, the commandant's office had ordered Jews to register themselves. Then they were forbidden to use public transport or go into shops. After a while, the order was given that they weren't allowed on the pavements and could only walk in the streets, and they had to wear a yellow Star of David the size of a hand on their clothes. By mid-October the Jews of Riga had to relocate to life in the ghetto – an area of the city's Moscow Fortstaat neighbourhood that was surrounded by a high barbed-wire fence.

Discussions about these orders and others turned into a kind of daily ritual for mentioning Johanna. We didn't say grace at meals; instead, one of us would always say: 'I wonder how Johanna is doing.'

One late night an older woman on a bicycle rode into the Manor courtyard, probably a teacher, and gave Jānis a torn strip of newspaper. A sentence in the Baroness's handwriting informed us that she had been transferred from prison to the 'people pasture'. By the time the shocked Jānis managed to find Grandfather, the old woman had disappeared, and we didn't learn anything else.

Grandfather reprimanded Jānis in a gruff voice for this mistake, but he couldn't hide his joy. He read the note over and over again, gave it to us to see, then took it back and read it once more.

'It's good to have some clarity! An end in sight!'

At the breakfast table the next morning, Grandfather announced that he was going to try to do something to help the Baroness.

'How can we help?' Jānis threw me an excited look, ready for anything.

'You're staying at home this time. Though the Führer has said that the Japanese are the Aryans of Asia, Germans still have a mental block about darker skin.'

'And me?' An uncomfortable heat rose to my cheeks. Anything that touched on the physical difference between Jānis and me made me feel a kind of internal resistance, even something like shame.

'You'll come with me as material proof. You're the epitome of the authentic Aryan.'

I understood my blond hair was the stamp of authenticity. During the first years at school I'd been nicknamed 'Butter'.

Grandfather sent for the open two-horse carriage, which for some reason was called the steward-mobile. Even though the weather was cool, Grandfather carried his pelerine cloak over his arm. He wore his tailcoat with the rounded corners, striped trousers and a dark neckerchief under the collar of his starched shirt. And resting at a chic angle back on his head was his silk top hat.

Unfortunately, I no longer remember the name of the institution we went to. The titles of German institutions were long and complicated. It was located in downtown Riga, in a ministry building constructed in the last years of the free state. Grandfather was certain there wasn't a higher civil office in Latvia than this one. The gentleman Grandfather asked to see 'in regard to a matter that would personally interest Reichsmarschall Göring', was called Dresler, or Drehsler. Or something along those lines.

The outer doors were guarded by armed men holding machine guns. The two gentlemen who pulled up in a two-horse carriage and referred to the Reichsmarschall got by them fairly easily but it was harder one storey up. The staff were different. Our footsteps were silenced by plush rugs; the aroma of waxed parquet and leather furniture filled the space. The quiet murmur of voices could be heard from behind tall oak doors, along with the steady clacking of typewriters.

It took some time for several clerks in olive-green 'Golden Pheasant' uniforms and swastika armbands to understand Grandfather's authoritative demand. They studied both of us carefully, spoke among themselves, shrugged their shoulders and scratched their heads. Grandfather stood tall, his chest puffed out and stomach sucked in. His top hat balanced elegantly on the crook of his bent left arm.

Eventually one of the clerks went out, and upon returning asked us to follow her up one storey. The peace and quiet, as if there weren't a single living soul around, was palpable. No sooner had we entered a larger room decorated with an oriental rug, paintings on the walls and a marble sculpture on an Empire-style podium, than a small, grey being, who could best be described as a nun in uniform, scurried quietly as a mouse from the adjacent room. Of course, she was wearing glasses and shoes with a modest heel. She exchanged a few almost soundless words with our escort, then disappeared through a door masked by a heavy curtain. After a while she came back through it and motioned for us to follow.

The first thing the eye was drawn to in the expanse of the enormous room was Adolf Hitler. The gesture of his extended arm could be taken as a greeting, a motion for silence or as a warning – stay back! Back – that could mean away from the desk below the portrait and the man now standing in front of it. Wearing the same kind of coat as the Führer, the same Iron Cross on his chest, the same dark blue trousers. Strange, but the most impressive part of his head was his neck: a scarlet stack of muscle, on to which his face was plastered like an animated mask. The mass ended with a tapered skull. His hair was parted on one side, like Hitler's behind him, smoothed down diagonally across his forehead towards the left eyebrow. But this man's hair didn't glisten; he had a kind of turkey-like crest at his crown.

Without wasting time on introductions, perhaps worried he'd lose the unlikely opportunity to get a word in edgeways, Grandfather blurted what he had to say, like a trigger-happy dueller. My basic German-language skills let me follow most of the conversation. His litany went approximately like this:

'...When the Reichsmarschall hears of this, certain somebodies will probably wish they were in someone else's skin. I assume you are aware of the Deputy Führer's weakness for preserving the memory of his first wife, the late Norwegian – Carinhall Palace – close relations with Birger Dahlerus – I'm shocked that the advisors haven't informed you of this. Back in the twenties, in Riga, the Norwegian embassy employed her close relative, Arne Hedbergs. At that time, one Zāra Leandere, née Hedberga – which you should know, but which you possibly don't know – stayed in Riga for a longer period of time. And why was Leandere-Hedberga in Riga? She loved her old godmother Hedberga, which is where she got her name, Zāra ... What's your name, honourable sir?'

'My name?' The fat neck reddened deeper, the crest of hair turned this way and that. 'Johann ... And so?'

'Well, see, from the Bible! Johann, Johanān, Jānis's appearance in the Bible, John the Baptist...'

'It's a German name! Johann Sebastian Bach. Johannes Gutenberg...'

'I'm talking about origins. Doctor Goebbels's name, Joseph, is also from the Bible. But because of that does anyone say that the chief of propaganda is a Jew? The calendar is full of biblical names: Pēteris, Jēkabs, Ādams, Sīmanis ... Marta, Zuzanna, Marija ... Various nations have various approaches to them. The Swedes favoured Izaks, Ābrams, Absolons, Zāra. It doesn't mean anything.'

'Did anyone say it means something?'

'Precisely, honourable Lieutenant Commissioner! Precisely. Ada Zāra Hedberga's daughter, in a hearbreaking insult to this Aryan youngster's bloodline' – here Grandfather indicated me with a broad sweep of his hand – 'is locked up in the ghetto. How do you like that? First she, Baroness Mecklin-Štaufa, was denied her request for repatriation to Greater Germany because of her grandmother. And now...'

The vicegerent's block neck reminded me of a raw hunk of beef. As material Aryan proof, I had apparently convinced him. He glanced at my butter-blond hair, then shook his narrow head.

'Interesting...'

'Interesting until the moment Miss Leandere learns of it. The Reichsmarschall just organised a triumphant debut in Badelsberg for her newest film *Grand Love*, which you've probably heard. The Reichsmarschall just organised a triumphant debut in Badelsberg. If word of this reaches Doctor Goebbels, whose feelings about anything that affects said diva's fate is a public secret, then...'

'Yes, yes,' the fat neck hurried to agree, 'Miss Leandere's films are brilliant.'

'The question is short and simple – what's going to be done about Miss Leandere's god-daughter's daughter?'

The fat neck stiffened, then resolutely straightened.

'Zāra Leandere's relative will be released. We'll issue a written order. Honourable sir, the ghetto is under Jekeln's jurisdiction. Let him find her. I don't stick my nose in the group leader's territory.'

'Thank you!' Grandfather said, waving his hand in farewell. 'You've got yourself an alibi. You're an intelligent person. The right man in the right place. With a written order, we can locate the Baroness ourselves.'

At the time, I didn't understand Grandfather's parting words. '*Was ich besitze, seh ich wie im Weiten, / Und was verschwand, wird mir zu Wirklichkeiten*.' Now I know they're from Goethe. 'That which I possess, from afar I see, / And what has disappeared, has become reality for me.'

XVI

Valtraute von Brīgen can sense that the once warm waters of Saint Petersburg's court surrounding Count Cagliostro have now iced over. Séances with the higher powers are still held at the Happy Union lodge, but events in honour of the Great Cophta dwindle. And the few that do still take place are characterised by careful restraint.

Valtraute asks if, while awaiting Gibran's return from the military camp in the south, she absolutely must remain in residence at Yelagin's palace. Maybe she can go and stay with her relatives. Her mother's sister is deceased, but her two cousins are still living at the Moika Palace. The Great Cophta won't hear of it; their work is only just beginning. A week from now, when, with the help of astral energy, he'll transform Princess Saltykova's blue infant – a prisoner sentenced to death – into a healthy heir, it'll be a big occasion, like when the prophet Elijah rode into the heavens in his chariot of fire. The church will organise services of thanks, Italian masters will shoot fireworks over the town squares.

The count is in high spirits. He's picked up the trail of another genius as great as the surgeon Gibran. The resident of some Russian province, a blacksmith and bath-house attendant rolled into one, has invented a steam-operated machine and made it work for forty-three consecutive days. The man's name is Ivan Polzunov. With his invention, mankind is on the path to betterment through mechanisation. In France, other geniuses are also working for the good of mankind: Doctor Guillotine and the Arras lawyer Robespierre. Doctor Marat is also very active, much as Saint-Just is the voice of humanity at large. Pretty soon there will be only one thing remaining to change the world – to get the blessing of the Pope in Rome. The golden age of enlightenment will soon begin in the history of mankind.

'It seems to me that you were unable to get the empress's blessing,' the baroness says curtly. Things haven't gone the way she had expected. She doesn't doubt the count's abilities, not at all, but the baroness still has no clarity regarding her fate from here onwards. And the worst part, it turns out, is that the count doesn't seem to care. This is why her displeasure breaks through her outer countenance.

'The time hasn't yet come.' The Great Cophta closes his heavy, walnut shell-like eyelids. 'The monarchy intends to secure its power, drowning its citizens in poverty and lack of rights, and yet they break free, give in to the sceptre of a more powerful rule...'

'Do you mean Empress Catherine?'

The count must not have heard her because he continues calmly.

'...It's not fate, everything is achieved with the mind and by individual choice. But the outcome is always the same. Always the same...'

'The same how, count, how?'

The eyelids open slowly, but his gaze remains dreamily disconnected.

'When we do one thing, another remains undone. What we do and don't do is important.'

'Then what should I do? Or should I do nothing? Has the long road travelled been for nothing?'

'What must happen, will.'

'But perhaps it can happen a bit faster?'

'The empress believes it's important to conquer the southern lands. In reality, it's important for Russia not to turn its army against Prussia and France. Nothing is separate, everything is unified. Empress Catherine, you, the changing world, Egyptian lodges, the betterment of mankind...'

Valtraute doesn't understand much of what the Great Cophta is saying, but her wonderment and loyalty flow and flow. She becomes concerned that her rather direct questions may have affected the count, and she hurries to add to the discussion the innocent tone of salon chatter, which the French describe by the endearing term *causerie*. 'Those who understand science are usually referred to as scientists,' the baroness smiles cheerfully, and searches Cophta's face. 'Do you consider yourself a scientist?'

'A scientist? What foolishness!'

'A prophet? An ambassador of God? A representative from another world?'

The thick, black eyebrows on the count's powdered forehead shoot up. No one has ever asked him such a question. But the count is in a good mood, and the question playful. Hah, interesting!

'And if I said I was an artist?' The count adopts the baroness's tone.

'I'd say that was wonderful. And I'd ask, what does it mean to be an artist?'

'To be able to do that which not everyone can do. To be able to do what only a few others can do. Maybe only one person on the entire planet.'

'Like Leonardo da Vinci? Like Michelangelo?'

'Precisely.'

'They both lived at the same time, so you can't say they "did what no one else could do".'

Count Cagliostro laughs in delight. It's obvious he is fond of von Brīgen.

'Two such great souls never compete among themselves.'

'Do you, count, have a counterpart?'

'Two, even,' the count lowers his voice theatrically. 'One is named Mozart, the other Beethoven. Little Ludwig is still just taking lessons from Salieri. He's ten years old...'

The healing of Princess Saltykova's blue infant takes place at the Happy Union lodge of the Freemasons, the Rosenkreuz and the Illuminati, in the company of the unfortunate parents and their guests. Priority has been given to women of an older age, for whom anything related to birth, death and healing is close to their hearts, and who are able to empathise with and appreciate everything. Of course, preference has also been given to their escorts, experienced gentlemen; for whom the rejuvenating power of life has heightened their interest in the mysteries behind the births of their grandchildren and great-grandchildren.

The lodge members greet Count Cagliostro with a celebratory rite. Men in black silk cloaks and tapered hats line both sides of the staircase, swords raised and crossed ceremoniously over the steps. Count Cagliostro arrives with the Queen of Sheba, the dwarf Fulla and the astrologist Midas in tow. Baroness von Brīgen follows at a distance; she doesn't feel she truly belongs in the count's entourage.

Darkness reigns inside. Not a single candle is burning in the chandelier overhead. The path is marked by servants dressed in livery and holding silver candlesticks. Flickering shadows move with the ghoulishly illuminated figures heading up the creaking wooden steps.

In the spirit chamber, only a single candle is lit next to a small altar. On it there looms a yellowish skull, a masonry trowel and protractor, a stuffed owl, a parchment scroll and an angular crystal prism.

Gemstones glint in the twilight of the shifting shadows, wigs shine dimly and there is the swishing and shifting of brocade skirts and military sashes. Then the servants, the guides to the pathway, disappear and the grand master Yelagin locks the door from the inside.

A lithe flute melody starts to play. The Great Cophta approaches the altar. The astrologist Midas presents the crystal prism to him. Lorenza the Queen of Sheba releases a white dove into the air, which, its wings flapping, flies once around the room and then returns to settle on her shoulder. The dwarf Fulla totters quickly towards a door that leads to a sort of sacristy. The flute stops abruptly and with it, it seems, the collective breath of the audience. Silence drops like a stone in a well; it thirsts for an echo.

Suddenly, a child cries out. Shrill, frightened, loud. They hear long gurgling breaths drawn between cries. And as suddenly as it started, the crying stops. The Great Cophta takes the crystal prism in his hands and begins to recite unintelligible, magical verses in a strange voice. The language could be Ancient Egyptian, or the language of the wise Chaldeans. It clearly requires great effort. The count drips with sweat, his entire body shakes and his words are interspersed with low moans.

From the darkness of the sacristy, a servant floats forth holding a white bundle, and places it solemnly on the altar in front of the Grand Cophta. Slowly, gingerly, the count unfolds the white cloth corner by corner, until a feeble infant is revealed in the middle, like the stamen of a water lily. The infant is wrinkled, limp, blue. Compared with its body, its head looks frightfully large and hangs at the end of a thin, wrinkly neck like that of a baby bird that has fallen from the nest. The black hole of its mouth gapes open and closes, but without any sound.

Still chanting in the mysterious language, the Great Cophta picks up the blue infant, lifts it high, then lowers it back on to the cloth and carefully, corner by corner, refolds the white bundle. A black velvet canopy descends on to him from the darkened ceiling; the altar, the white bundle and the only burning candle are cloaked in the thick, dark material.

The moment of blinding darkness is brief. The drawn-out and tense silence is broken by the rich, deep sound of a gong; the air rings for some time afterwards. A light flares in the back left-hand corner of the chamber, in a spot to which no one had until then paid any attention. From it, a glowing and ghostly skeleton, bony arms spread wide, glides over the heads of the audience.

Then the reverberations of the gong stop, and the skeleton disappears. Darkness. Those present turn back to look at the canopy and are rewarded. The black velvet is being raised. Everything is as it was. The candle burns, the white bundle is on the altar. The Great Cophta stands in front of it, arm raised. He makes a sweeping gesture. The flute trills once more. With eager, impatient movements, Cophta unfolds the layers of white cloth: the first corner, the second, the third, the fourth ... And lo, in the centre of the swaddled cloth is a squirming, rosy, angelically plump infant.

The flute trills on, but no one hears it over the unified cry of surprise that springs forth from the audience. People sniffle, touched; they applaud, shout their bravos. Princess Saltykova, who had been following the healing procedure in a kind of half-daze, now presses an airy, orange blossom-like handkerchief to her mouth, cries out and throws herself on the child. She takes it, presses it to her bosom and sobs tears of joy. Canes fall from the hands of speechless gentlemen. Princess Volkonsky has fainted.

'Unlock the door!' the duke shouts. 'Water, quickly!'

Even Valtraute von Brīgen is looking around as if stunned. What has happened strikes a personal chord. If the Great Cophta can help Princess Saltykova, he can also help her. This is a man whose abilities cannot be comprehended. Then she's shaken to the core by a new-found realisation – or, more precisely, her understanding has been dissected; the pedestrian term *realisation* wouldn't be enough to cause this kind of feeling – she doesn't yet know what she will give birth to! What if she brings into the world something as horrifying as that blue wretch with its wrinkled skin and long, limp neck? Or a being with two heads like the eagle on the Russian crest? Can the everyday concept *it's a child – I'm with child* – contain what has happened to her? If a blue, deformed creature could be begotten within matrimony blessed by sacrament, what could be expected from a world-improving experiment, from lying with a combination of two men instead of one regular man?

Valtraute presses her palms to her stomach and for the first time physically feels a maternal hope. The rapid pulse beating warmly through the silk of her gown is not hers alone. It's also the pulse of another, the new life inside her, which is taking up more and more room and which will tear and stretch her with the force of its growth.

Why did this occur to her only now? Why does she truly grasp her new situation in the exact moment when Princess Saltykova presses her healed heir to her bosom with joyous ecstasy? Or perhaps she simply finally understands the broad expanse between the signposts *happiness* and *unhappiness* in which the concept of *child* is hidden.

Valtraute is torn from her shivering reverie by an embrace. The door is unlocked. A line of servants enter the chamber one after the other, carrying silver candlesticks. There are so many candles that a wave of heat pushes forwards; the melting wax fills the room with the scent of honey. Valtraute is momentarily dazed and at first she doesn't understand who is kissing her so fervently. Then she comes to. Aleksandra, her dear Leksīte! They've found each other in the end! But she shouldn't be surprised – it would be a greater surprise not to see Leksīte in Saint Petersburg. Leksīte and Natālija.

After she kisses her, Aleksandra steps back and looks at Valtraute with a somewhat confused expression. They haven't seen each other in ages and they've both changed over the years. The initial outburst of joy is quenched by a sense of foreignness that they must get over.

Aleksandra explains that they've just arrived from Gatchina this morning, where they're spending the early summer. And they'd heard about Cagliostro, and yes, even Valtraute, while there. Her words tumble out in bunches. Her elegant, youthful face is still glowing and rosy from her excitement; not even the layer of powder can hide it. Above her large, bright eyes, the high arch of her eyebrows gives her the same pleasantly surprised and somewhat pretentious expression she's always had.

'Oh, forgive me, dear Valtraute, I haven't introduced you to Fjodor Pavlovičs. When we introduced him to mother, she immediately wanted to know which Nikulins he was from – from the grand dukes, or the counts. But Fjodor Pavlovičs answered – from the chemists. Fjodor Pavlovičs' father was assistant to Lomonsov, and Fjodor Pavlovičs was head of the chemistry faculty at the academy.'

The spirit chamber is filled with people; everyone is milling around so closely that Valtraute only notices now that the young man in the long, dark coat with the thick plait of natural hair is with Aleksandra. They exchange greetings.

'We also have Aleksejs Fjodorovičs. Our fifteen-pound golden nugget. Three and a half months old. When you come to Moika, you'll see him. We'd be happy to take you there now.'

Valtraute doesn't think long. A bell rings and reverberates until the next ring flows into the one before it. The healing of the blue infant and thoughts about her own future offspring intensify her emotions, and she hears the continuation of the subject matter *child* in Aleksandra's invitation. Actually, she doesn't think at all; she's led by the irresistible desire to look at a small, healthy child. To hold a round, tangible bundle, to feel the smooth skin against her cheek, to breathe in the sweet smell of a baby. To regain her courage, so that everything in this crazy world spinning in chaos will fall back into place.

'Very well, my dear,' she says. 'Let's go!' Then she remembers Count Cagliostro. She should probably let him know, but the Great Cophta is like a moated castle.

Slowly heading towards the door, Valtraute feels almost weightless. She's being carried along by invisible currents of air like a dandelion seed.

'Fjodor Pavlovičs, I know you don't believe in Cagliostro,' Aleksandra says. 'But the event was marvellous, and we found Valtraute.'

'Yes, I'm delighted,' Valtraute says.

'That's not what I meant,' Fjodors Pavlovičs shies from the issue, caught in the incongruity between his desire to defend his opinion, but not to argue with Aleksandra, who is still madly in love with him. 'I'm surprised by the strange connection – foolishness isn't possible without intelligence, and intelligence exists thanks to foolishness.'

They are helped into the carriage by attentive men dressed in something that looks like civilian clothes combined with a uniform. They inspect the passengers, even look under the seats. Valtraute doesn't pay it any attention; she's heard much about the strange behaviour of Russians.

The following day Aleksandra and Fjodors Pavlovičs bring Valtraute back to Count Yelagin's palace. The grand master looks upset; he's short of breath and can barely speak.

'Good God, haven't you heard?' The count presses his fat, ring-bejewelled hand into his left side and shakes his head like a horse plagued by flies. 'The Great Cophta has left! He's gone! I'm afraid to even think how it will end!'

'Left? Gone? End?' Valtraute answers, frightened. The surprises that fuel her fear fall over her like a freezing shadow. 'What does that mean?'

'If only someone knew. Matushka is clever. Not even Gozubov would risk his neck doing something like this!'

'Please, count, if you could elaborate.'

'They're saying the child wasn't healed, but switched. They arrested a woman with a sick infant.'

'How can a child be switched?'

'Gozubov knows how to play his trump cards beautifully. And the empress will tighten the reins...'

Aleksandra and Fjodors Pavlovičs don't leave Valtraute at Count Yelagin's palace. Bon Esprit has already packed their things. The return to Moika is solemn, like coming home from a wonderful party that ended with an unexpected death. They all look at each other, but no one speaks. The women are in shock, Fjodors Pavlovičs is uncomfortable.

At tea time, Aleksandra's friend Countess Volkonsky arrives with new rumours. The Great Cophta has been thrown into a private cell in the Peter and Paul Fortress. When the church tower struck for the twelfth time at midnight, the guards heard the sound of a heavy, barred door opening. They'd run to look and were suddenly blinded by a bright light, as if they'd looked right into the sun. When their sight returned, there was no sign of Cophta. Count Volkonsky had been present when the incident was reported to the empress. The empress had given a sour smile, shrugged and said:

'Doesn't this strike you as a scene from a comedy?'

The Duke of Courland's golden carriage had disappeared along with the Great Cophta. Luckily, Lord Marshal Medem's carriage was still in Yelagin's carriage house. Baroness Valtraute von Brīgen can be on her way as early as tomorrow. Why would she stay another day in Saint Petersburg? How horrible! Hor-ri-ble!

XVII

Grandfather hurried down the stairs, whistling and so energetic that it was hard to keep up. I'm saying that less in regard to myself and more for the Golden Pheasant who escorted us from the high director's office to the door. At the main doors, Grandfather shouted something happily and waved his top hat. The guards holding machine guns to their chests exchanged quick glances with one another, and returned the farewell. Their wide-set boots snapped briskly together then they returned to attention.

'Now to that Italian invention!' Grandfather shouted once we were back in the carriage.

'Where?'

'The ghetto! It was Pope Paul IV's idea. He created the first ghetto in 1550 in Rome. And do you know why? To protect the Jews.'

'The popes have their hands in everything!'

'It is what it is. Even financially speaking, the Vatican's merits are indisputable. In 1179 the pope prohibited Christians from handling currency exchange or loans.'

It was a cool, sunny day. The wind plucked the final leaves from the lindens along the boulevard, scattering them across the asphalt and cobblestone pavement. Where groups of pigeons used to gather in front of the Opera was now empty. Rumour was, the German soldiers had eaten them. The trams looked strange – the windows had been painted over in thick layers with only a hand-wide stripe left clean across the middle. The honour guard no longer stood in front of the Freedom Monument. Even the red-white-and-red flags were gone.

We passed under the railway viaduct in front of the central station. Anti-aircraft guns sat on the grassy embankment, their slender muzzles angled towards the sky. A little way beyond the Church of Jesus Christ a tall barbed-wire fence blocked the road. I'm not entirely certain, but it seemed to me that the word Grandfather spat out at that moment was not one to be used in public. It was the first time I had heard him speak that way.

'Nothing in the world is more stupid than a blocked-off road,' he sputtered angrily.

Even today, at the age he was back then, I have to agree with him. Truly, when a road is blocked by a wall or barbed wire, it's indicative of a loss of sensibility.

An absurd scene unfolded before us. Cement gateposts rose up in the centre of the rapidly erected, transparent hedge. Their massive size and texture reminded me of pictures of the tank traps of the Siegfried Line that I'd seen in magazines. Next to the gate was a small guardhouse and checkpoint, built from freshly cut boards. A long chimney, like the chimney of Stephenson's locomotive, sat atop the roof. Maybe not exactly like it, but that's the impression I gained from the spotlight affixed to it.

No death marches had been led out of the ghetto gate as of yet, and there were still various pretexts given for the rounding up of all the Jews in one place.

As far as I could tell, the neighbourhood on their side of the barbed wire in no way differed from the side we were on. The checkpoint functioned like an open sluice – people kept coming and going. In groups and individually. Only their faces had an unhealthy pallor to them, and their movements were tired and unsteady, like the movements of patients walking around the halls or gardens of a hospital.

I was convinced that Grandfather would park the carriage on the side of the street and we'd continue on foot. Instead, he waved his white-gloved hand, whistled, and halted the horses' fast trot right in front of the gate; this meant he wanted to drive inside.

'Hello! Hello!' Grandfather called. '*Schneller!*'

A man, probably a policeman, came out of the little guardhouse, took one wide-eyed glance at the carriage and scrambled back into his post.

'Hello! *Schneller!*' Grandfather bellowed persistently.

Some minutes later, a second man emerged from the ghetto building closest to us and, leaning on a cane, headed towards us with stiff, reluctant steps. What military division and rank he represented was, and remains, a mystery to me. Green military trousers were tucked into his short boots, and a silver band decorated the collar of his field jacket. That supposedly meant he wasn't an officer. The German asked what business Grandfather had here. Grandfather answered that he was delivering a letter from Lieutenant Commissioner Dresler-Drehsler, and that he must speak with the ghetto's Chief Director Commander. His voice, which clearly indicated that this was no discussion, was sharpened by another shout.

'*Schneller! Schneller!*'

The German listened to Grandfather, scratching the wrinkled back of his neck with one hand. He listened and nodded, which could be interpreted both as agreement, and as a gesture of comprehension. Then he motioned to some guards.

'*Losfahren!*'

They opened the gate. We drove into the ghetto.

The German clambered into the guardhouse, most likely to make a phone call. We waited for a longer time, and then a small man dressed in a rubber raincoat pulled up in a grey military vehicle. Add a tin crescent pin to his lapel and a helmet on his head and you'd have a regular gendarme. But his plaited shoulder straps and parade cap meant he was of a higher rank than the formations that wore caps with a skull for a badge. The man didn't get out of the vehicle. If there was anything to be read in his motionless face, its features cut as if out of dried-up glue, it would have been mouldy, fly-flecked arrogance and a complete lack of interest in the scene in front of him.

Leaning with his back against the carriage, and with equal disinterest, Grandfather held out the letter from the civilian authority between two white-gloved fingers. Their conversation went something like this:

'Yes, and?'

'It's all in the letter! Ms Holendere is to be released immediately!'

'By all means, I have no objection.'

The officer spoke apathetically, as apathetically as is humanly possible. But not for long. After a few seconds, the bored expression imploded. The frozen face screwed up, puckered and warped through a series of grimaces that expressed hatred, contempt, dismay and jeering. Not towards Grandfather. Not even towards the aforementioned Ms Holendere. But towards the absent Dresler-Drehsler!

'He can come down here himself and find the lady! Smart-arse! Hot-shot! Does he have any idea what a ghetto is? Does he understand how many thousands of people are in here?'

Once he had finished shouting, there was silence, which Grandfather interrupted with a polite, almost gentle objection. All that was missing was for him to put his arm around the shoulders of the rubber-raincoated bundle of nerves, pat its head and smooth its hair as if it were a frightened little boy.

'We're talking about someone very close to the Reichsmarschall, almost a relative. Don't make this worse for yourself! What each of us feels is our own business. Duty is duty...'

The officer was visibly growing tired of the conversation.

'Henke!' He barked in a voice made for giving orders. 'Find this woman! Do what you need to! No stalling!'

A few words were jotted down on the notice and the letter was tossed to Henke, who remained standing with the wind-blown paper in his hand, like a railwayman holding a flag alongside the tracks. The little grey car turned around and disappeared as quickly as it had arrived.

'Ah well,' Grandfather rubbed his gloved hands together. 'Go on! We don't have much time.'

'It won't be that easy,' Henke stamped his cane against the gravel lot. 'Reading through four hundred house registers isn't the same as reading a wartime menu at a restaurant. And they don't even stick to the registers. They purposely cover their tracks. Things get heated, especially at night. They clean out the rich, chase pretty women.'

'Who cleans who out? Who's chasing who? Aren't there police around?'

'That's the thing, there are.'

'Despicable!'

'Of course it's despicable. The guards get the leftovers.'

'Excuse me?'

'I can't make any promises.'

'In which case we'll find her ourselves!'

We had taken up the entire road – the carriage with both horses, me, Grandfather and Henke. A group of older people entered the ghetto on foot, yellow Stars of David pinned on their fronts and backs, and shepherd's sacks slung around their necks for food or whatever else. When they reached us, they stopped and drew together into a tight bunch. It was as if they were surrounded by a cloud of exhaustion and melancholy.

'What're you waiting for? Why aren't you moving on?' Henke shook his cane.

'We've been ordered to walk in the street.'

'Don't play dumb! You're in the ghetto!'

A two-seater sports convertible drove through the main gate – a fat yellow gherkin with an angled windscreen at the front. There was only one custom-built car like that in Riga. We didn't need to ask whose it was. I was willing to bet that neither the Pilot, nor Grandfather, were pleased to see one another. They seemed perplexed, as if the Montagues and Capulets had crossed paths in a place where interaction was unavoidable.

I had nothing to do with the conflict between the Baroness and the Pilot, and God only knows what role Grandfather played in it all. But the two of us were a team, on the Baroness's side. What was the Pilot doing here, if the Baroness had seen him with a star above his brow at the Cheka? Judging by the way the gate was opened for him, he was his own man in the ghetto.

Grandfather pulled over to the side of the street, letting the yellow gherkin steer past. As if to taunt us, the Pilot only drew his car closer to our wheels.

'What's this? I thought only the fire brigade answered false alarms. And now you too...'

When he spoke, the Pilot had the habit of squinting. The outer corners of his eyes crinkled, drawing fine lines in his sunburnt face. He could have been around forty years old. Dark hair, thick eyebrows and a prominent nose made him look Italian or Spanish. Or Jewish. But maybe the thought occurred to me only because of where we were.

'There's a real fire, all right,' Grandfather spoke warily, not yet having decided whether the question dignified a response.

'Well?'

The Pilot leaned towards Grandfather like a volleyball player waiting for a serve. 'So ... you're here...'

Grandfather hadn't wanted to speak, but the Pilot's gaze pressed home.

'So? I'm in charge of transport here ... Petrol is harder to find right now than water in the Sahara,' the Pilot kept on, as if this were information we needed to know.

'An odd little desert ... with transport.'

They stared at one another like two rams on a narrow path.

'If it's of any interest to you,' Grandfather relented and beat the brim of his silk top hat with a broad gesture, 'we're here for the Baroness. I have a notice stating she's to be released. Only one small catch – it'll be like finding a needle in a haystack.'

What surprised me wasn't the Pilot's shock, but that his shock quickly turned to anger. He cringed and sat back, his bushy eyebrows deeply furrowed.

'The Baroness is here? Don't be ridiculous! Why?'

'Why? ... Jesus Christ would be here, too. I'm not speaking for his Father in Heaven...'

The muscles clenched under the Pilot's tanned face. It looked as if his jaw had clamped shut and was struggling to unclamp itself.

'You, gentlemen, don't understand where you are. This isn't a haystack. This is a shit-stack.'

He told us to wait where we were and drove off. An hour and forty-seven minutes later – I kept my eye on the clock – the Pilot returned with an old woman dressed in filthy rags. Upon closer inspection, I grew terrified. It was the Baroness.

XVIII

Valtraute von Brīgen has returned from Saint Petersburg, but the recent experience still weighs heavily on her. Like a shipwreck on a survivor – or a kidnap victim who sees his life flash before him in the knife at his throat – she can't shake off the sensation. Days go by, the distance between the present and those events grows greater, but every now and then she slips back into the past.

Such shame! Such scandal! Valtraute can't believe that Cophta is a fake; it's a mistake, a fateful turn of bad luck. His talk about malevolent forces hadn't been unfounded. A moment of inattention, the blink of an eye – and *voilà*! She cannot, absolutely cannot, stop thinking about poor Princess Saltykova. Can a woman's heart withstand such cruelly shattered hopes? How happy she looked holding that healthy, angelic boy in her arms! Even Valtraute had been lifted up and carried on the wings of this miracle. And what a merciless fall! She's embarrassed for the princess. Embarrassed for everyone.

Valtraute wasn't directly involved in what happened, but her name will come up in the shadows of memory. 'Back then, when Cagliostro and Baroness von Brīgen...'

Aleksandra and Fjodors Pavlovičs try to act as if nothing had happened. But their behaviour expresses their discomfort and embarrassment. How the palace winds blow determines the climate in the courts of Versailles, Potsdam, Vienna and Jelgava. Saint Petersburg is no exception.

It's strange, but in addition to the bitterness of being back home, alone, she's starting to doubt the origins of the Līven and Hān families, which Cophta had dismissed in their conversation. But now isn't the time for her to dwell on that. If, like normal people, Cophta makes mistakes, why couldn't he be mistaken when he talked about the origins of the Līvens and Hāns? Her ancestors definitely belong to the famous tribe of warriors entrusted with a noble task, like the one written about in the famous legend of the Holy Grail about Lucifer's crown jewel, which King Arthur's knights guarded in the castle on Purification Hill. As a young girl, she'd more than once heard how the German knights had come to battle with the Baltic pagans after the Crusades in Palestine. Even that was proof of a distinguished beginning – knights were the idealists of generations past.

Valtraute tries to extract some information from Baroness Amālija Anna. The result is sad. Eberhart's mother is completely disgusted, her bony fingers feverishly wave a lace handkerchief as if an invisible ghost, or something even worse, enveloped in the nauseating stench of compost, were advancing upon her. It seemed as if the old woman was about to have a heart attack, but thankfully it only ended in tearful sobbing.

'*Trautchen, schämen Sie sich!*'

Uncle Joahim arrives at the end of the week. It's been a while since they've seen him; his body has grown rounder. Now his bluish-green, rosy face truly resembles a globe in a curly wig propped up on his shoulders. The superintendent gasps for air, winded by the excitement of his visit and the rapid movement so ill suited to his body type. The tiny eyes sunken into plump cheeks flash playfully; his spirits are high.

This – this is a person who comes when he's needed, Valtraute thinks. No matter what, Uncle Joahim must know the answer.

She opens her mouth to ask about the origins of the Līvens and Hans, then remembers her mother-in-law's cry, 'Traute, for shame!' and catches herself.

It really could come out as a strange question – and so be it, but should she be ashamed of her desire to know the truth? She's certain that Uncle Joahim will confirm what Cagliostro said. Is that what she wants? Maybe Amālija Anna is right and she has no call to be asking silly questions. But it's not just about her, Eberhart or the Great Cophta. There's another person for whose sake she has to learn the truth. For that person alone!

'Uncle Joahim!' She locks eyes with her godfather. He's lounging in the guest room's large armchair, his hands folded on his large stomach as if in prayer. 'Uncle Joahim, tell me the truth, is it true that the Līven and Hān families are descendants of this country's people?'

The superintendent laughs to himself with a clucking cough. As is often the case with older people, who have seen children move into adulthood, Valtraute is still a little girl in Aurelius's eyes. Well matured, with some experience, but still a girl. The question itself doesn't surprise him; her desire to know the answer does. And as is often the case when children first ask about the relationship between a man and a woman, the problem isn't finding an answer, but in choosing the right words with which to do so.

His official's resolve takes the upper hand, and the ambiguous sounds become freely flowing sentences.

'Dear girl, what we think we know about history is in fact incomplete. German ships didn't drop anchor off the coast of a country of savages, and our ancestors needed more than swords to accomplish what they did. Livonia was created in a game of intrigue between the locals and the newcomers, who were a force to be reckoned with. The fate of Riga was determined in 1210 when Kaupo, king of Livonia, sided with the Germans. Rome and the Order were also fighting against the Livs. They had their leaders, their nobility. If we hadn't been able to make peace with them, the knights who arrived from Germany would've been eliminated, easy as that. On the other side were the kind Kurlanders and the organised Zemgalians, as well as the Latgalians, who had trained like Roman gladiators in battle with the Estonians. The Germans made it their priority to find allies among these groups.'

It seemed as if Aurelius was settling into his lecturing tone and preparing to talk for some time, but Valtraute's feminine impatience wasn't tempered for long lectures. 'You mean that the Līvens and Hāns really are the descendants of Kaupo?'

'I don't know about the Hāns, but the Līvens were vassals to the Order at the time Livonia was captured. In the fourteenth and fifteenth centuries, recruiting local fighters was still a common practice. They started using guns. The significance of knights decreased and they were replaced by dragoons, musketeers, cuirassiers. Haven't you ever heard anything about the liegemen, the Freiherrs, the Curonian kings?'

Valtraute should be shocked, she knows that, but her emotions are divided. It's not like the disappointment of discovering her doll has a stomach full of sawdust; she feels incredibly offended. She wants to pull herself together. She doesn't understand much of what Uncle Joahim has said.

'So you're saying we're not German?'

'No, why would you think that? You're German. More German than people from Germany. They're Germans because they're German. Your ancestors became Germans because they wanted to be German. In this country, the identifier *German* has always referred to class more than to nationality. Rulers. People with opportunities. But the sturdily built building is starting to show some cracks. What is at fault is the disease of western fashion and the desire to improve society ... Jānis Šteinhauers, one of the richest landowners in the Vidzeme region and the area surrounding Riga, died last year. If he had called himself a German, they would've made him mayor. But he hired a history expert to prove that he had the right to succeed as a Latvian as well. The Kurzeme region had an even crazier situation. My colleague from Sunākste, Gotthard Friedrich Stender, by ancestry undeniably German, requested in his will that his gravestone say he was Latvian! And what that did for him, I don't know, but cases like that aren't without consequences.'

'My mother was definitely a German! And my father was a German! You know that as well as I do!'

'My dear girl, I've already told you – it isn't that simple.' Joahim looks truly unhappy. 'After this country was conquered, life didn't change for some time. The locals had to pay taxes, that's all. The first landlords came from knights who didn't want to return to Germany. And did all of their wives come over from Germany? Even hostages, the sons of local leaders, were raised in Germany and brought back with Christianity in their hearts. They joined the upper class. There are places in Vidzeme and Kurzeme where district names are the same as the surnames of barons. And who knows any more if the district was named after a baron, or the baron after the district ...? For centuries, the Germans' mask has been like a domino cape in a Venetian carnival...'

Uncle Joahim trails off and waits for Valtraute's objections, but is met with a confused and startled look.

'I don't believe those are ancestors to be ashamed of. Most likely, you really are born of nobility, while the ancestors of a good many knight are straight from the lines of highwaymen. The men of this land are strong, live long lives. Vidzeme and Kurzeme are filled with beautiful women. The classic example of the Baltic hybrid are the von Biron ladies or, for example, Marta of Alūksne, who charmed Russia's most powerful men and became Catherine I ... That's how it goes ... That's...'

The conversation is over. Valtraute's head is spinning; she doesn't understand, doesn't know what else to ask. Aurelius can see what's happening to her. He's embittered and saddened the dear girl. God help them! He feels broken, and all that remains is a piece of advice from his childhood days – if you've done something bad, run for it.

Their parting is strange. They sit, each occupied with their own thoughts, make eye contact, and remain silent. In the end, Aurelius pulls himself out of the chair. He waits to see if she'll say anything, try to convince him to stay or make a joke in farewell as a sign that she's not angry. But Valtraute wrings her hands nervously. Aurelius bows and heads for the door. He sensibly and carefully lifts his fat, black stocking-clad legs and thick, silver-buckled shoes high as he walks. As if Valtraute were sleeping and he is afraid of waking her.

The shock Aurelius has caused is nothing compared with what happens a few days later.

It's an oppressively hot summer. Valtraute snoozes for hours on end, reclining under the arbour on a soft blanket and cushions. A book lies open next to her. Etchings and paintings of eighteenth-century women in elaborate dress – squeezed into corsets, hips swathed with piles of crinoline and silk. Valtraute also likes getting dressed up. But not in the summer, while idling about outside where prying eyes can't see her. Lately, she's heard wild rumours about special garments for sunbathing and for swimming outdoors. Hopefully under a parasol, so the face, shoulders and arms would be protected from the sun. The best thing to wear when relaxing is a chemise, which is sometimes also called a nightgown, dressing gown or bathrobe. Valtraute is wearing one right now under the arbour; it ties together at the neck, drapes loosely and fully around her like a bell around its clapper. Lately she feels best in chemises. Not just because of the heat. Stuffing herself into a corset, being tightly laced up, constricted – she doesn't want that any more. Her body is changing. She's reminded of the overwhelming feeling of growth; like a bud being pushed by an unstoppable force, she's ripening and expanding. It's so wonderful to give in to complete freedom, to listen to both sets of heartbeats as the breeze slides across her sensitive skin.

She feels as if the loose garment is a temporary cover, because she still hasn't told Eberhart's mother. For the simple reason that she can't think of the best way to explain to Amālija Anna that she's going to be a grandmother. She can't ask that other – well ... that other one, who besides her is the only person who could speak of the matter.

Then there's Gibran, true. But she has no hopes of getting Gibran to come here. And would Amālija Anna even believe their testimonies? She doesn't believe that the earth rotates, that, in relation to people in the northern hemisphere, people in the southern hemisphere are walking around upside down. Oh it's better not to think about it! Valtraute again visualises Eberhart's mother's bony finger shaking at her and her reprimanding cry: '*Trautchen, schämen Sie sich!*' She has no idea what will happen once she has to register the child in the church records and the registry of land ownership. No, she shouldn't think about it, shouldn't, shouldn't!

Valtraute gets to her feet and, leaning against one of the arbour's posts, looks around. What the von Brīgen manor proudly calls its park is in truth a small copse of centuries-old trees with a thicket of wild lilac and lush grass, which isn't mowed but instead used to graze sheep. Right now the sheep are grazing in the far corner, where there are fewer bushes and the view opens up over the hillside and down to the river snaking below. From a distance the woolly beasts look like white stones scattered across the clearing. The bare-legged shepherdess with her grey skirt and staff runs about, dancing in her own way and singing happily. Valtraute doesn't know why the girl has caught her attention, why her heart is warmed by such tender feelings. Then it hits her – the little girl's song! When Valtraute was little, her nanny Made would sing it to her when they were alone and could play as they pleased.

Valtraute doesn't realise she's started singing along. Memories of her nanny become paintings that blend strangely with reality. Free from daily concerns, from the uncertainty of doubt, the memories float in their own anti-gravity.

Baroness Kornēlija, who replaced Valtraute's late mother, was capricious, ruthless and had an unpleasant smell. But the scent that wafted from Made was pepperminty, like meadowsweet or tansy. Made was strong, ruddy, smooth, and Valtraute never felt as safe as she did with one of Made's bare arms around her. At night she could wake from the worst nightmare and fall right back to sleep if Made was by her. Gentle fingers stroked her head: 'Sleep, sleep, here come the good dreams.' Made would sew colourful dolls, *kunnas*, from rags. When she was in a very good mood she'd undo her braids and let Valtraute brush her hair with a boar-bristle brush or comb. Along with Made, Valtraute remembered the blue porcelain chamber pot. When Valtraute sat on it and had a hard time going, Made would kneel next to her and gently put her arm around Valtraute's shoulders.

Valtraute's thoughts are understandable. In the eighteenth century, life without chamber pots is unimaginable. Bathrooms are only just being introduced. Versailles doesn't even have those amenities yet. There's talk that Rastrelli is piecing together something similar for the palace in Jelgava. People of lower social classes are content to do their business in a barn or outdoors, right alongside their beloved livestock. The nobility use a *pot de chambre* which, covered by a monogrammed handkerchief or a silver lid, is carried ceremoniously by chambermaids and servants through manor and palace halls, like some mysterious sacred vessel. In even more urgent situations, baronesses and barons, dukes and duchesses, would make use of castle corners or hedges. It was easy for the ladies in particular. Hoop skirts are wide. Undergarments weren't in style; all they had to do was stand with their feet slightly further apart. They could do this without even pausing in a conversation with a female companion; it was a matter of character and habit.

Baroness von Brīgen doesn't like slinking around corners. She keeps to pots that the chambermaids bring in and take away. Even now, reclining under the arbour, there's a pot within arm's reach. A fancy Meissen porcelain production with a vibrant butterfly on the lid in place of a handle. But she's not thinking about that now. Right now she's mesmerised by the little singing dancer. Sun, sheep, a blossoming field! A glorious pastoral! The tantalising proximity of nature! Marie Antoinette herself couldn't go a day without shepherds' songs accompanied by flute.

Valtraute watches the little waif in the linen skirt and her restless heart grows still. Oh, how she'd love to be a girl again, carefree, without memories. She doesn't even notice that she's started to wade into the pasture that has grown thick around the arbour. Valtraute sees the dancer stopping glancing around, hiking up her skirt and squatting. Valtraute watches, watches, and gathers up her voluminous chemise and squats as well. Buttery meadowsweet, goosegrass and clover sway in front of her eyes. A bumblebee climbs heavily up one of the stalks. Grasshoppers chirp...

Suddenly, a horse whinnies. Valtraute von Brīgen stands abruptly, startled. A horseman rides into the park from the direction of the courtyard. He rides closer, and now it's impossible not to recognise him: Eberhart von Brīgen, her husband! *Lieber Gott!*

XIX

After the ghetto, Johanna physically bounced back quickly. Only her scalp had some scabs that wouldn't heal. Then she cut her hair short, applied mercury salve and sat under a sun lamp, and it got better.

And yet she was no longer the old Baroness. Jānis grew confused and didn't know how to act around her any more. As if the Baroness had forgotten to put on a dress and were instead standing in front of him in her underwear.

'Y'know, I've got the feeling they swapped our Baroness in there.'

'You think?'

'Haven't you noticed?'

Of course I'd also noticed the changes. Grandfather's business continued to operate, and the Baroness sat at the desk in the office every morning as usual. But sometimes the phone would ring, and ring, and she would sit frozen, her stare drilling into some point only she could see. When one of us would pick up the receiver, the Baroness would look surprised. She'd take order after order with a business-like amicability and then thank us.

'I didn't even hear it!'

What was strange was her new tendency to confuse events. She talked about what had happened with the Russians as if it had been under the Germans. And about what the Germans had done – as if it had happened under the Russians. Immigrants from the east and the west were referred to as 'elements', a kind of two-legged, chimeric effervescence. The Cheka, the Gestapo, the *istrebiteli* and the *Schutzmannschaft* were ghost-like kobolds. According to ancient belief, kobolds were omens of bad luck – on board ships they meant destruction, in houses they meant death; a spectre on a black horse riding through a town meant the plague, cholera or leprosy were nigh.

At first Grandfather assumed the Baroness was confused, suffering from a typical kind of feminine inattention. He tried to pinpoint the time, or the differences in her kobolds, depending on the situation. The Baroness listened calmly, but went on talking.

'Giant rats danced all around us there. Īzaks started to feed them. The only food was a dead cat, and Īzaks tossed it into an open tin barrel. The rats jumped in to get to the cat and couldn't get out any more. While there was still something to eat, the rats were friendly enough with each other. But once they'd eaten the cat, they turned on each other ...'

'Exactly! A real kobold's trick,' Grandfather confirmed. 'Poland was swallowed by rats coming in from both sides. Now Stalin has been accepted into the gentlemen's club.'

'And that makes him not a rat?'

'Johanna, dear, you're right, but where is this coming from? You didn't talk like this before.'

'Live and learn. Īzaks often said that clarity is the waste product of a life lived. There wasn't paper to write on, so he graced us with oral renditions. Memoirs could be the vaccine against falling ill with old delusions. The ex-kobold, it turns out, had a lot of experience.'

'What do you mean – ex?'

'Yes, yes, he never hid the fact that he helped cleanse society in '38 in Lublanka. Now and then the persecuted and the persecutor trade places.'

It was as if the world had split into separate parts. Newspapers, magazines, the radio and even books used statistics, journalism and irrefutable documentation to drive everything to one side. When no other country would admit Jewish refugees fleeing from Germany, Latvia let many of them in. But they repaid this by destroying their freedom. Of the illegal Communist Party's thousand members in Latvia, almost half of them were Jews. After the Russians came in, they even worked in the Cheka. Unable to fault Latvians for anything else, in 1940 they persecuted them for using the word 'Jew'.

The Baroness's stories, and countless things she'd experienced on a daily basis, pushed her in the opposite direction. It was as if a thick, poisonous haze were filling the air, slowly fogging over my vision and making my ears ring with strange sounds.

'Why didn't I know that "Jew" was a bad word?' Jānis asked, displeased.

'It's a manufactured offence.' Grandfather wasn't fazed in the least by the question. 'The way I see it, you can also call them Israelites. All of these terms are antiquated and none of them can be eradicated. Language is a living thing, and it changes. Supposedly, the first to use the word "Jew" were the Canaanites. The Greek *hebraios* means "on the other side", meaning "those who live beyond the river". Here they don't live across the river, they live among us. Boys, haven't you figured it out? Latvia had a Jewish theatre, Jewish organisations, Jewish schools. If the word was offensive, would they have used it themselves?'

Even though she was at home with us, the Baroness was still living in the ghetto. She kept informed about what was going on there, asked questions of people who stopped by the office or who phoned.

One day, tenderly pinching my ear, she said: 'You should know, too. It's starting. A woman who reserved a half-carriage this morning for a wedding was complaining that she caught cold last night – they couldn't get across the road. Armed guards were driving a long, long line of people in the direction of Biķernieki Forest...'

Another time Grandfather came home and told us he'd heard about women and children herded by armed guards in the direction of Rumbula. It was a starry autumn night, the air crisp and still; later there were sounds like those of a battle. Aunt Alma was quick to tell us that silver fox and seal furs and fancy clothes had shown up on the black market. As if by magic, women of ill repute had suddenly accessorised themselves with strings of pearls and real gemstones.

The Latvian language took on a new concept: *Jew-killer*, a synonym of the times for *murderer*.

To which people this concept applied and what it was based on, not even the Baroness could explain. There were rumours and guesses, so gruesome and fantastical that they seemed unbelievable.

And it was in this way, it seems, that the belief that the Pilot was on this team of *Jew-killers* was solidified into an almost irrefutable truth. I considered whether our having run into him at the ghetto didn't confirm it. In our evening discussions, neither the Baroness nor Grandfather ever brought it up.

Recently, we hadn't seen much of the Pilot at the Manor. He probably had an apartment in downtown Riga; Latvian pilots had been pushed aside, and there was no good reason to live near the airfield any more. The adventurous aura that had often surrounded the Pilot like a black cloak, and Grandfather's opinion that he was someone from whom you never knew what to expect, didn't change with the course of events. That's how he'd always come across: half-pirate, half-Pizarro, some kind of temple-treasure thief.

I ran into the Pilot once at the Opera. He was wearing his old leather flight commander's jacket with the breast pocket for maps, and his black forage cap with the velvet rim. I remembered the red star and looked to see if he didn't have yet another badge sewn on to it. But no, nothing had changed since we'd met him at the ghetto. It was safe to assume that with wartime thriftiness he had probably worn out his old Latvian military uniform.

Sundays were the busiest days for Grandfather's business. It wasn't yet fashionable to hold weddings or funerals during the working week. I think it was mid-December. A light dusting of snow covered the ground. Because it made no difference to me where I did my algebra homework or studied French grammar, I sat down at the office desk in front of the telephone. Jānis and I would do that from time to time. The Baroness would thank us, throw her fox-fur coat over her shoulders and go out. Silvery snowflakes drifted through the rays of sun – tiny, tiny flakes like mothball shavings. It was the powdered sky that caught and held my attention, otherwise I probably wouldn't have looked out of the window at all.

A little later the Baroness came back into the office. She looked upset.

'Did something happen?' I asked.

'I went to see my family,' she replied to no one in particular, her gaze focused on the cigarette paper in her fingers, which she couldn't get to roll straight.

'Right,' I said. 'Why wouldn't you go see them? Bodo, Lieselotte, Ulrich.'

'Of course.'

'And so?'

The Baroness ground the ruined cigarette paper on the table, and our eyes met. 'Now there's also a girl.'

'What girl?'

'She was brought over tonight, from the ghetto.'

'The ghetto? Who brought her?'

'She wouldn't say. And won't say, even if you drove needles under her fingernails.'

My limbs felt heavy. In the crypt ... In winter! Luckily the snow wasn't thick and there weren't cross-country skiers sliding around. Someone could accidentally find her.

'We have to wait for Grandfather,' I said firmly.

Grandfather came home exhausted, but the news about the girl immediately revived him. Anything that tickled his fancy and was out of the ordinary, as he put it, lit a fire under him. After proclaiming something was 'very dangerous', only someone who didn't know Grandfather would expect him to then back down, stay out of it, hold back. But what those words really meant was that he was already committed, heart and soul.

Grandfather said he'd go and inspect things on his own, but the Baroness, who knew where the girl was, refused to stay behind and stood up to go with him. In the end we took Jānis's advice that all four of us should go. If the girl were still in the crypt, we'd give her Jānis's coat and hat and bring her back to the Manor with the rest of us. Jānis would sneak back home a little later.

As it does in December, the night came on quickly. Imagination is a powerful thing. This time, the road that we'd walked so often without the slightest concern echoed every one of our heartbeats. We went quietly, in single file. The Baroness, Grandfather, Jānis and I. The ground was frozen. The thin layer of snow mixed with the sand and stuck to our boots. Our footsteps felt heavy. And not because of the sand.

In the dense blackness, the crypt looked hopelessly abandoned. It seemed absurd to think we'd find anything living there. I was hard pressed to imagine the dank grotto as a temporary place to stay. Yes, it was possible to wander into it, like an attic into which a butterfly might flit, or into which a canary might escape its cage.

As if he'd picked up my thoughts, Grandfather stopped in front of the crypt and turned to us to whisper: 'I don't think anyone's here.'

'Wait here. I'll say something, so she doesn't get scared.'

The iron door creaked loudly as it opened. Never before had that sound seemed so clear, so sharp.

'Don't be afraid...'

A weak, childish voice called out from the dark. The person whose voice it was was shaking so intensely that her words tumbled out in stutters like the clattering of an old sewing machine. Grandfather couldn't keep his voice to a whisper in his excitement; he spoke, but with a hint of charm which lent his words a sense of security. The Baroness wanted a smoke and she rolled a cigarette. In the match-light I saw the girl's face. Or rather, two giant, bright eyes.

The girl turned out to be as tall as an adult. She wore a second, hooded coat over her coat, the kind rural folk wore on long horse rides. Probably subconsciously sensing that she didn't have to be afraid of us, she calmed down. She was going to be transported further on. Yes, she had biscuits to eat, but she was thirsty.

Suddenly, we were illuminated by a beam of white light.

'Hands up! What's going on here!'

All activity and sound stopped short, as if the film in a projector had caught fire.

'What's going on? That's what we'd like to know.' Grandfather was the first to regain his composure.

The bright light swayed, shedding some light on whoever was carrying it. The Pilot stood in the doorway.

It felt as if I had been thrown into one of the adventure stories I'd read as a child. Everything that I'd heard about the Pilot's mysterious doings suddenly made sense. He'd been secretly and patiently following the Baroness's every move, waiting for the perfect moment to take his revenge on her for the embarrassment of stealing that ham. Like a cue ball, his carefully aimed shot hit three balls at once: the Baroness, ourselves, and the unfortunate girl who was exposed because of us. We'd brought the hunter straight to her.

'Oh, it's you! Just you!' The Pilot seemed no less surprised than we were.

What strange, unbelievable things can happen in a lifetime! Steel structures collapse, the voices of angels are heard between the panting of

147

hate, the adder slinks away with the king's crown on its head, and a newly realised truth slides across your face like a breeze that barely stirs even your eyelashes.

The Pilot hadn't followed us, hadn't recognised us, wasn't here because of us.

Grandfather wanted to say something, but stopped himself, keeping quiet with his usual dignity. The Baroness smoked steadily. The Pilot went to the girl.

'This is Lea,' he said. In a voice that, to be honest, sounded a little too brazen and friendly to me. 'She has to stay here for a few days.'

The Pilot waited a moment for a response; when he didn't get one, he added in the same tone: 'We're talking a couple weeks, until the opportunity comes to get her out.'

'I think it would be better to discuss this at home,' the Baroness said.

When the Baroness and I played Black Peter or dominoes, I'd experienced complete surrender to the heat of the moment. The nightmare slowly receded into my subconscious, but it didn't disappear entirely.

We went back quietly through the dark. Like black ghosts, I thought.

XX

No, truly, she's not mistaken! And it's certainly not a matter of a midday witching hour, either. Eberhart jumps down from his horse and walks towards her, smiling brightly and rhythmically tapping his riding crop against the leg of his boot. Exactly the way Valtraute has hoped to see him, and once more to have him, in her dreams and desires.

...She wakes up, and Eberhart is next to her in bed; she opens the door and Eberhart falls into her arms; she runs towards a carriage out of which Eberhart has just stepped...

And now here he is! And what's more, with all his upper body! As if nothing had happened. Or maybe this is another combined version of Eberhart? O Lord, why doesn't she feel like fainting? Ladies are supposed to faint at moments like this. That would be the polite way out. Instead, she continues to gawk stupidly, on legs that stand strong. Joy doesn't describe the feeling that paralyses her; surprise, yes, undoubtedly surprise. Valtraute could die from curiosity about what will happen next. As if she were standing on a lake shore, watching a strange creature swimming towards her, something familiar but also foreign.

Eberhart seems to feel the same thing. His behaviour is equally hesitant. After such a long time apart he doesn't show the slightest sign of tenderness, not even the desire to feel her against him which is normally characteristic of him. He doesn't even move properly to embrace her. Upon closer inspection, the cocky smile is more of a pained, melancholy grimace.

'Look, I've returned.' Eberhart – apparently Eberhart, who else? – stops a little way in front of her, now almost violently thwacking the leg of his boot.

Oh, he's being considerate of my negligee, Valtraute thinks suddenly. She quickly pulls a lacy silk robe over her chemise, but Eberhart doesn't seem to notice and continues: 'I'm back.'

'So it seems…'

Somehow everything feels wrong. She doesn't say what she should, or what she wants to say. Secondary thoughts dart aggressively through her mind and even the words come out wrong.

'I hope you won't be too strict a judge. I don't harbour any illusions that our relationship could be the same as it was before. Much has changed. But placing blame on anyone in a situation like this…'

'Who's to blame? Do you mean that surgeon? And the cutting in half?'

'What surgeon? What does a surgeon have to do with it?'

Eberhart forces a laugh. His gaze travels restlessly back and forth, flicks away from Valtraute, and then back to her.

'Some situations really do make you want to get cut in half… I'll tell you everything sometime, but not now, please, no. Let's draw a line through the past and start again.'

'Are you saying that one half of you was here all along? Then tell me right now – where was the other half?'

'Dear Valtraute, why are you adding more stones to my pile? Extra weight won't help. But, if you insist, I'll tell you. At first I was in Denmark, then later in America.'

'America!'

'Why are you surprised? Lafayette recruited volunteers. Without support from the French, the Americans would've never broken free from the British.'

'Without support from the French? The British? What does that have to do with … with…'

Valtraute stops short because she doesn't know how to put into a few words the feeling that comes crashing across the train of her thoughts like a giant landslide, blocking the path ahead and the road behind.

'Traute, I'm begging you! Let's save it for later. I don't deny my guilt, but the story is rather long.'

And Valtraute understands immediately – a woman is involved. As unbelievable as it may seem, this thought thoroughly rattles her. Not because she's surprised by Eberhart's infidelity, but because she realises: if Eberhart was being unfaithful in America, he couldn't have been here with her! It would be a strange infidelity, without the lower half of one's body. Given that, the child she's carrying has nothing to do with Eberhart!

Now Valtraute doesn't want to think any more. Eberhart is right, let it be. Her understanding is like a broken necklace; the pieces fall, roll, scatter in all directions.

'Let's go inside,' Valtraute says, and hears her voice fall flat. So she doesn't betray herself, she looks encouragingly into Eberhart's face and curves her lips into a smile. Eberhart sighs deeply, takes her hand and kisses it. As he straightens, he turns away, but Valtraute manages to see it – the sun shines off tear tracks on either side of his nose. A long-lost tenderness momentarily darkens her vision like a gown sliding over her head as she dresses. She doesn't see anything, but her body dives into that familiar garment, the familiar scents, the worn-in contours.

It would be natural for Eberhart to embrace her. In any case, it would be preferable to speaking again. The desire for closeness overcomes Valtraute so strongly that she feels her cheeks flush. But Eberhart is apparently satisfied; he cools and gathers himself. He's not thinking of her.

'Thank you,' Eberhart is saying. 'It would be good if you could go in first and prepare Amālija Anna. My arrival could be a huge shock to mother.'

The monotonous, boring life at the manor is spun into a whirlpool that separates them from one another for a while, placing distance between them. Other people with their thoughts and conversations appear in the interim. Valtraute is thankful for the time alone. While Eberhart talks with his mother, while the servants draw the baron a bath, while the family eats a feast in celebration of the miraculous return, Valtraute waits for the excitement die down. Of course, she's not able to look at Eberhart and pretend that what happened is meaningless or that their relationship will be what it once was. But the questions no longer constrict her chest like a fever. She doesn't take part in the conversations, but does that mean people won't go on talking? Life will keep moving forwards, even while she's somersaulting in the air like a storm-whipped leaf, without the faintest idea of how to get back to earth or what will happen once she's found her way home. Eberhart visits his mother, bathes, feasts on roast rabbit, elegantly smokes his long Dutch pipe. She, Valtraute, fans herself, dabs her lips with her handkerchief, gestures to the servants to clear the table as usual. Even the baby, the living treasure in her womb, acts normally, kicking now and then as if to protest at the dark, uncomfortable and narrow space it inhabits. Interesting – has Eberhart really not noticed anything? He used to pay close attention to her waistline.

The whirlwind settles in the late night hours. Amālija Anna has gone up to her room. The rest of the guests have filtered out. Valtraute and Eberhart head for bed. Just in case, Valtraute has declined the services of Bon Esprit and Emma. Who knows what Eberhart has in mind.

And she's right. Eberhart doesn't move to say goodnight to her at her bedroom door, but follows in behind her. It would be silly to turn him down, saying she's too tired or in the middle of her monthly cycle. And would she want to, anyway? What would be gained? There has to be some clarity, one way or another.

Emma has turned down the covers on the wide bed. The candles are lit. Valtraute takes a few steps towards the bed and stops. Eberhart follows. He stops, too, but a few paces back. They stand in silence.

'Traute, what are you thinking about?' Valtraute hears Eberhart's voice behind her. It's a voice she hasn't heard since the first months of their marriage – gentle, sweetly hesitant. She knows from experience that, when it's that voice, there's nothing to think about; all there is to do is to turn around and fall into his outstretched arms.

That's exactly what she's thinking about. That. But it's a terrible thought. So terrible that it scares her. She looks back and is happy – even worse – is thrilled to see the person standing behind her is Bartolomejs Ulste!

What am I thinking? Valtraute turns around and, of course, finds Eberhart standing there. I'm thinking that, in a way, days are like lottery tickets – most of them are worthless, and only a few are winners.

'We can establish a new way of keeping time, and start from this exact moment. But with whole days.'

Slowly, as if he were fighting a powerful headwind, Eberhart crosses the space between them and hugs Valtraute tightly to him. But she realises that even in that moment Eberhart's face turns into Ulste's face and, ashamed, she gives in to Eberhart's kisses with such burning surrender that what follows is no longer in her control...

The first clear thought in her sensation-jumbled mind is the baby – *Lieber Gott*, did it survive that? If anything bad happened to it, it would be her fault alone, Valtraute's. It seems Eberhart still isn't aware of her true state. Strange indeed, if he didn't notice anything with her clothes on, that he wouldn't notice now, when there wasn't even a nightgown between them ... Eberhart's fingers had always been so sensitive...

Valtraute is lying somewhat diagonally and reaches one hand towards the edge of the bed to search for the blanket, and the other under her back for whatever is digging into her buttocks. She finds her corset wedged between the pillows with the tangled sheet.

Eberhart is lying face down on the edge of the bed, arms splayed, trying to catch his heaving breath. Leaving her right after being intimate – that unpleasant habit is typical of Eberhart. Quickly getting off her, and almost running away. It used to bring Valtraute to tears. Until she saw everything that happened in these situations in a chilling, backward light. Did Eberhart's manic passion, his strength and at times brute force indicate his desire to be closer to her, to feel her more completely? Maybe it was a desperate fight to tear away from the abyss of their hips, from the tenderness of her hands, aching to touch him? A fight between life and death, diving deeper and escaping again, relinquishing the nectar of life and yet not surrendering. When the battle was over, Eberhart left her with a long sigh like a strangled opponent and rolled away to the edge of the bed.

They're separated like this for some time, until everything falls back into place and the calm interrupted by the battle of intimacy resumes. The way they're lying in bed makes her think of people lying in coffins. The blanket is the only thing they share; their bodies don't touch. Arms crossed over their chests. Their heads on pillows, faces turned straight up.

'Who was she?' Valtraute knows there's no point in asking, that it's her feminine jealousy that moves her to pester him and that it's silly to show it. But her curiosity, or maybe her desire to satisfy her ego, are stronger.

'She?' Eberhart repeats, but it's as if the sound comes of its own accord, because his lips don't move. 'The wife of a fellow soldier.'

'And she stayed there, in America, alone?'

Eberhart's clipped laughter breaks into the darkness.

'Caucasian women don't stay alone in America. Don't worry about her. She's probably already the wife of some plantation owner or general.'

'What an awful country!'

'The land of opportunity.'

'But you didn't stay.'

'No, I didn't. I'm an aristocrat. I didn't understand before what it meant to be an aristocrat. Now I know. It's not about the title. Kings can be transplanted, aristocrats can't. In America I could've been a millionaire, the owner of large plots of land. But as an aristocrat I'd fail there. There was nothing left to do but come back to what makes me an aristocrat – this land, the traditions of our class, the world view that is my own. Yes, to you, too, Traute, because you're part of the soil where my aristocracy has its roots.'

Valtraute is unable to keep listening in silence. She sits up in bed so abruptly that her silk nightcap slumps comically on to one ear, revealing her natural hair, which stays hidden under her white powdered wig during the day.

'And you've never been by the Çamur River? You've never been hit by a Turkish cannonball?'

'Why the bizarre questions? Since when were you familiar with the geography of the Caucasus campaign?'

'Please answer me! It's incredibly important!'

'Of course I was there. That's where I was injured. And how I ended up at Reval.'

Valtraute ties the ribbons of her nightcap under her chin with clipped movements. She ties a bow, unties it, and reties it again.

'Was Bartolomejs Ulste there, too?'

Now Eberhart sits up abruptly. He tries to hide his surprise behind an ironic smile, but it comes out rather thin, and his honest shock glares through it.

'You know Bartolomejs Ulste?'

Valtraute doesn't know what to answer. She feels her body stiffen, but her fingers keep fiddling with her nightcap ribbons.

'Yes, Ulste was there,' Eberhart continues, understanding that Valtraute isn't going to provide any explanation. 'He was injured more seriously. In the stomach. Stomach wounds are terrible. I think he died.'

'Died?'

'Why are you so surprised? People rarely survive stomach injuries. All right, let's assume he didn't die. What does it matter? We didn't have the kind of relationship where we'd each take an interest in the other's life. That said, I don't know anything more about that man.'

Baroness Valtraute stops tying and untying the ribbons. Her hands drop on to the blanket in front of her. It's as if even her eyes are frozen.

'Eberhart...' Valtraute says after a long silence, a silence that seeps in like the venom from a snake bite, when it's too late to change the course of events and all you can do is wait for the end. 'There is something you have to know about...'

'About Bartolomejs Ulste?'

'About him, too.'

Valtraute folds back the blanket, lifts her nightgown, takes Eberhart's hand and puts it on the swell of her belly. 'You're an experienced man, you should understand – if a woman is this round, she's with child. I'm no exception. Even this morning, I was still convinced that the child was yours. Or at least a part of yours. But after what I've just heard, there's nothing to do but accept that the father is Bartolomejs Ulste.'

There's nothing further to tell here. The reader already knows the story of what Valtraute told Eberhart next.

But 'tell' isn't the right word. She doesn't tell him, she lets go like a woman in labour who has reached the final moments of birth and can no longer be contained. No fear, no mental calculation, not even the threat of death. She doesn't think about what will come next. All she knows is that she feels a release, the weight lifts. It's strange, this bubbling stream that spills forth from her, a real waterfall of sin.

With her feminine instinct, with a sixth sense that Albertīne calls 'fever vision', Valtraute knows that Eberhart would be able to accept a pregnancy from outside their marriage (it's the eighteenth century, after all!). But the snare that has ripped into his soul with iron teeth goes by the name Bartolomejs Ulste.

For three days Eberhart von Brīgen grinds away at his aristocratic soul, like a wolf caught in a trap trying to gnaw off its own leg. He doesn't succeed. On the morning of the fourth day, shortly before sunrise, the baron loads the 18-calibre French cavalry pistol he brought home from America and shoots himself in the manor garden.

On a cold, blizzardy January night, Baroness Valtraute von Brīgen gives birth to a son, whom she names Johans Amadejs. They're still in the period of mourning. The entry in the local church register notes that Valtraute was wearing a black lace chemise from Bruges at the time of the birth. The entry also notes that Johans Amadejs was born prematurely. How prematurely, it doesn't say. And what does it matter? What matters is that the new von Brīgen is in good health and a hearty eater.

The wet nurse, Šķērsta, holds Johans Amadejs to one breast, and her little Jānis to the other.

XXI

Grandfather liked to joke that German-occupied Latvia's self-government was a new world wonder – a government that functioned like a glove that the true leaders slipped on when there was dirty work to be done. And in turn, maybe the self-government's own wonder of wonders was there to keep the balance: a gigantic Rolls-Royce, like an opera house on wheels. The car the Chinese embassy in Berlin was showing off with a few years ago. Then, when Germany teamed up with Japan, China closed its Berlin embassy. In Berlin they were unable to sell that ghoulish car, which guzzled petrol like the Niagara Falls did water. So it became even ghostlier – with an additional firewood gas generator – and eventually it ended up in Riga.

Imagine our surprise as we watched this amazing limousine pull into the Manor courtyard one dreary, grey November morning in 1943.

Jānis and I watched, intrigued to see what would happen next. It didn't occur to us that the visit might have something to do with Grandfather's business.

A few minutes later two men in black were standing in front of the Baroness's desk, asking to speak with the director of the business.

'We have the honour of representing the Department of Culture and Social Affairs,' one of the men said, turning his black, mothball-scented Borsalino fedora in his fingers.

'Yes. To represent the self-government, in the matter of the Latvian nation losing the poet Aspazija,' the other man added.

'What? Has she gone missing? Or do you mean to say she died?' Grandfather's surprise proved more powerful than his tact. He didn't usually throw his hands in the air when he was shocked.

'Unfortunately, it is our task to organise a funeral service befitting the poet. Your business has a four-horse catafalque in working condition. Would we be able to take a look at it?'

'Of course,' Grandfather said. But, knowing him, it's safe to say his mind was most definitely anywhere but on the catafalque.

'We can't afford a very extravagant funeral. The Chief Officer of Propaganda has set aside two thousand marks, but that limitation shouldn't be made obvious.'

The men looked at the black, four-horse catafalque, leafed through the album with the options for equipment, took notes about the costs and then left. The Funeral Commission would make a decision, and the final order would be sent later.

Having seen off the visitors, Grandfather came back, thoroughly worked up. He'd already put on his matte top hat; his face had an animated look, as if he were ready to jump up on to the coach's box right then and there.

'Cheapskates! Penny-pinchers! And that's how they plan to bury Aspazija, our greatest poet! How d'you like that?'

The Baroness argued that the fault was probably not in the two thousand marks, but rather that the Germans just didn't want to draw widespread attention to the event, to keep the patriotic emotions of Latvians from swelling up, so people wouldn't come together en masse, and so on.

'What do you mean "don't want to"? They don't want to, but we do! A dog doesn't want to eat mustard, but smear some under its tail and suddenly it's ready to!'

Grandfather went to his room and didn't come out for the rest of the night. We could only guess at what he was doing in there.

The next morning – I remember it was a Saturday – Grandfather said: 'You're going to be late to school today, and with good reason. Let's go and take care of things.'

'Where are we going?'

'Where we went to take care of things before.'

Grandfather was once again wearing his tailcoat and striped trousers. And of his head, almost as if he'd slept in it, was his matted top hat. We drove to the important German institution in downtown Riga, where a couple of soldiers stood guard at the doors and where, above three storeys of secretaries, a man with a thick neck made decisions about the fate of the district at large.

Grandfather had them announce him as the man 'already known to his excellency as the relative of Zāra Leandere, who is here on no less significant business regarding the case of the Rozenberg family'.

The same thing happened as last time, only a bit more dully, maybe because the element of surprise wasn't there. Maybe because it wasn't 1941, but 1943. Even the conversations in the front offices no longer seemed mysterious, because I had a greatly improved grasp of the German language.

The Lieutenant Commissioner stood in the same spot where we'd left him last time. The difference was that, instead of raising one eyebrow at us as we entered the room, this time he took a few steps towards us and extended his hand to Grandfather in greeting.

'You remember us?' Grandfather asked.

'I believe we resolved a delicate matter,' the Lieutenant Commissioner said, watching Grandfather with his head tilted to one side.

'Precisely. And were there any negative consequences?'

Silence.

'There, see! But it could've caused some trouble.'

More silence.

'Now, this time ...' Grandfather continued after a thoughtful pause, not lingering for small talk. 'Do you know what's happening with Aspazija's funeral?'

'Aspazija's funeral ... Yes, I've heard something.'

'I'll tell you what you should know. Aspazija, real name Elza Rozenberga, mother of Reichsminister Alfred Rozenberg...'

Another pause. The Lieutenant Commissioner watched Grandfather with eyes that looked foggy. It was impossible to know what was going on inside his pointed head. After a few moments something gurgled in the depths of his throat and a sound not unlike a belch rolled out through his lips.

'E-e-e-eh...'

'Yes, sir!'

'Don't you think you're reaching a little high?'

'Not at all.'

The viceroy walked back to his desk with a still unreadable expression on his face and pressed a button. I can't say the moment was pleasant. I was sure the men with the automatic rifles held to their chests would come in and ask us to follow them out. But instead, the uniformed nun entered the room, that same boring secretary.

'Bring me the information on Rozenberg's parents.'

'Right now?'

'Now.'

'It won't be that quick.'

'Call Windecker.'

The secretary disappeared. Tension filled the large office like a piston in a motor cylinder. The Lieutenant Commissioner, his hand hooked in the buttons of his coat, paced back and forth behind his desk. I only noticed now that there was a clock in the office; a shiny disk swung lazily to and fro in a massive cabinet, like a moving target. Grandfather, surprisingly, didn't say a word, and sat with a bored expression on his face. Later, I understood that, tactically speaking, this was a move of genius.

The secretary returned and placed a sheet of paper in front of the Lieutenant Commissioner. We could see there were only a few words written on it. Its contents were reluctantly revealed by the book the secretary had brought with her: she had been unable to find any specific information. The standard official biography, nothing more.

The secretary opened the book at a marked page. This is where Grandfather interrupted the quiet murmur like the powerful trombone fanfare in Tchaikovsky's 5th Symphony.

'I can tell you exactly what it says ... Rozenberg was born in 1893 in Tallinn ... his father came from a family of Northern Vidzeme Latvians, his mother was a German ... He studied architecture at the Riga Polytechnic Institute ... He was a senior member of the "Rubonija" student fraternity ... In 1918 he emigrated to Germany ... As of 1934 he was the Führer's deputy in issues of ideology ... That's the official story! I'm talking about the truth.'

Sweat broke out on the thick red neck. 'The truth is written here ... right here...' the Lieutenant Commissioner stabbed his index finger into the book. 'And I'm not interested in anything else. Especially if it involves the Reichsminister.'

'What is unfortunate is that the Reichsminister himself knows the truth. And God alone knows whether he will be indifferent as to how his mother is buried. You can write what you want and how you want it. But at heart, your mother is always your mother.'

'Mother, mother. Why suddenly his mother?'

'Those are the facts. In her youth, Miss Rozenberga was married off to a man she didn't love, but then he was sent to America. Then she meets an officer of the tsar's army named Kucevalovs. In 1892 – I repeat, 1892 – their relationship is quite serious. Elza submits an application for divorce to the court. The new couple consider themselves engaged and prepare for the wedding. The only obstacle: Elza can't get her documents in time. And then she accidentally learns that the officer is still involved with some former ladyfriend. The wedding is off. Elza leaves, head held high. But in those days an unmarried and pregnant woman was no trivial matter. Elza quits her post as governess in Jelgava and moves to Northern Vidzeme. Yes, yes, the aforementioned Northern Vidzeme. And there, on 12 January 1893, she gives birth to a son. The young mother finds someone she can pay who will be willing to care for the boy for a while. Just for a while, then she'll take him back by adopting him or some such. But the saying "man proposes, God disposes" proves true. In 1894, Elza – by this time the poet Aspazija – meets the love of her life, Rainis, Latvia's Goethe. Rainis's relatives look down on the divorcée. The child would be the last straw. Aspazija was already versed in the deceptions of love. So she won't seem too old for Rainis, she claims she's three years younger than her real age. This time there was only one choice, to raise the child secretly ... There you have it, the truth about Herr Rozenberg's mysterious parentage.'

'You're saying that Party Member Rozenberg isn't a German?'

'I'm saying what's reflected in his own official biography. I doubt Napoleon would have wielded power so passionately had he been a pure-bred Frenchman. As you know, he was from Corsica – and short, to boot.'

The Lieutenant Commissioner's eyes were growing rounder and rounder until it looked as if they were pushing past his eyelashes like fast-growing puffballs. It was obvious that the conversation both horrified and bewildered him.

'Then later, why...?'

'Surely you've read Shakespeare. Who led the Venetian fleet to victory in battle? The Moor Othello!'

'That doesn't prove that Aspazija's funeral would be of interest to the Reichsminister.'

'Pardon, but who ordered a ceremony for her seventy-fifth birthday to be held in the National Theatre? Not you?'

'That ridiculous thing? That Aspazija didn't even attend?'

'She took the liberty of not attending.'

The Lieutenant Commissioner paced behind his desk, back and forth, back and forth. Then he'd move to sit down again, but immediately returned to walking first in one direction, then the other. His thoughts were probably doing the same inside his head. Finally, banging both fists on to the glossy surface of the desk, the director and representative of power announced his decision.

'Forget about the questions that aren't within our area of authority. But there's one thing no one can deny – Aspazija is an important poet, and her funeral has to be worthy of her.'

'I agree! She deserves exactly what she deserves, nothing more.'

Grandfather's voice had a tone of 'There, you see, we agree on yet another issue' about it.

With the green light from upstairs, the poet's funeral committee flared up like a bonfire fed with kindling. The head decision-maker, some gentleman from the self-government, listened to Grandfather's suggestions and put them into action.

Grandfather's fantasy shot freewheeling into the air like a majestic eagle. Despite the dreary weather and the gloomy mood of the people, everything had to be white. Six white horses with white, mesh covers and white bridles. The carriage, of course, was to be white. The pall-bearers in white coats and white crescent caps, which the French called *incroyables*...

Our carriage house held a white carriage, and it got a fresh coat of paint. The additional horses needed were hired from the Salomonsk Circus, which was currently hosting Viennese horse-trainers. Milzis, from the theatre, would supply the white coats and white *incroyables*; he'd been included in the funeral committee as a friend of the poet and – naturally – was elected artistic director. In him, Grandfather had found a like-minded person, someone with a deeper understanding.

The casket with the poet's remains had already been sent to the Māra Church. The cathedral was in partial dusk. The large chandeliers hadn't been lit; only a few side lights flickered here and there. Workers placed stands around the casket, with forked silver candelabras and laurel saplings in round pots. Laurels were in fashion now – no big event took place without them. Afterwards they were taken back to their greenhouses.

When he first saw the coffin, Grandfather slapped his left palm against his face. (The right hand, of course, was holding his top hat.)

'Aspazija with a cement-grey pauper's coffin! Never!'

The committee deemed Grandfather's disappointment justified and took the decision to transfer the poet to an oak casket with a tri-vaulted lid and bronze detailing.

This was my first close-up experience of a funeral. In truth, I'd never been that near to a dead body. I gazed at the poet's thoughtful, frozen expression in shock, with a strange curiosity, as if I'd stepped out of the realm of the world I knew.

'Look closely and remember – this is the first and last time you'll see Aspazija as a person. Ten years ago I met her at the seaside. On an autumn day as miserable as this one. She was walking along the beach and I was watching her footprints in the sand. Look how small her feet are, like a child's. A size thirty-five shoe, no larger.'

'That explains a lot,' said Jānis. As usual, his assessment was odd. 'According to Shinto belief, women with small feet are able to walk on moonbeams.'

The oak casket was ready the next morning. The undertakers were able to transfer her body quickly.

There was no indication yet of the storm to come. It started around noon. Either just because he wanted to boast, or for some other reason, the Lieutenant Commissioner had contacted Berlin. Unfortunately, the text of the conversation will forever remain a secret, with no hope of it being revealed. Grandfather had just happened to stop in to see the director of the funeral committee when the Lieutenant Commissioner called. The phone conversation lasted five minutes and consisted mainly of words that have no equivalent in the Latvian language. Of course, the Lieutenant Commissioner was the only one doing any talking, but the director had shuddered, flinched, frozen and trembled.

With that, the grand farewell for the poet became nothing more than a dream. Grandfather was banned from participating in the funeral. The poet was brought to the cemetery by a plain black hearse. But in that beautiful oak casket!

I had always placed Grandfather on a pedestal, and the fall he took at that time in no way accorded with my beliefs. As painful as the arrows that pierced Saint Sebastian, the suspicion bored into me that Grandfather was only human, like the rest of us, subject to successes and failures. That, like everyone else, he had weaknesses, made mistakes, had his inconsistencies and eccentricities. Old age also came with rust. But Jēkabs Ulste never dragged his feet, never crawled into a corner and never felt excluded. Things were never boring with him, and even in the face of defeat he never gave up hope of a reprieve.

Years later we'd rehash the incident more than once. With time, Aspazija's funeral, which in my mind had been a sombre event in an overcast city, gradually took on different colours. What I understood later gave me a broader perspective on those distant November days. Aspazija only gave the appearance of lying in her coffin with her turbulent life behind her. In truth, she had set in motion an opposition movement to this oppressive occupation; she became the flag waving on the front line, calling and summoning, more alive than ever. The thick layer of asphalt was cracked open by a pale little mushroom of freedom. This, much to the surprise of many who didn't know her.

Grandfather's contribution to this incident was just an episode. But he took satisfaction from it and laughed heartily.

'Never forget who Aspazija is! But, more importantly, never say she's just tucked away under a simple mound of sand!'

XXII

Just as an umbrella changes the paths of raindrops, legends often push reality to one side. Who doesn't know the legend of Peter I conquering the Baltics? But Grandfather proved that it wasn't true. The Northern War was over, but the Duchy of Courland continued to exist as an autonomous state. Russia only took Kurzeme in 1795, buying the throne from Duke Peter von Biron for 2.9 million roubles, or approximately 8.4 tonnes of silver. Those kinds of transactions were frequent back then. In 1867, America bought Alaska from Russia for 7 million dollars (the cost of a modern-day small commercial plane). In turn, Duke Jacob Kettler of Courland acquired Tobago and Gambia in the seventeenth century.

Grandfather said the idea of the Duchy of Courland had by and large been trivialised – the German was a lord, the Latvian a servant without rights. It hadn't been and couldn't have been like that. Books I read later in life confirmed what Grandfather said.

There was a local class of vassals in Kurzeme. The region's manufacturer was recruiting skilled workers, who ended up being drawn from the rural population. And it was the city folk who supported the duchy in its arguments with the nobility. The division into Germans and Latvians in Kurzeme wasn't justified. Kurzeme was inhabited by Courlanders, with the class distinctions typical of the times, but without any boundaries to cross. Biron's own origins are proof-positive of that – as are the histories of the kings, the Latvian scientists of Kurzeme, the clergymen, literati and the notable employees in all stations of life.

The Courlanders Mancelius and Fürecker wrote their works in Latvian. It was known that Fürecker was married to a 'well-to-do and independent' Latvian widow. The highly educated Fürecker was just Fürecker – but his Latvian wife was 'well-to-do and independent'. The barons and farmers in the Duchy of Courland usually spoke Latvian with one another. In the same way, Grandfather found that the dukes of Kurzeme knew Latvian, including the last duke Peter's widow, Anna Dorothea – with whom the eighteenth century's most skilled politician, Talleyrand, later fell madly in love. The poet Elisa von der Recke of European renown spoke Latvian, as did Beethoven's friend Karl Amenda, born in Talsi, and Kant's youngest brother, Johann Heinrich, who lived in Vecsaule.

The ability to speak Latvian in the Duchy of Courland was considered a matter of course. Even one hundred and twenty years after it was first published in Jelgava in 1789, old Stenders's German–Latvian Latvian–German dictionary helped enrich the knowledge of the Latvian author Rainis. The names Antiņš, Gatiņš, Bierns, Lipsts, Tots and others came straight from the Duchy of Courland, from the dictionary of old Stenders...

...It's June of 1799, just before midsummer. After a very long break, Baroness Valtraute von Brīgen once again travels to spend the summer with her cousin Albertīne. Everything looks like the Kurzeme of years past, and yet it's completely different. *Mein Gott*, how the world changes!

Kurzeme is in its fourth year of being under the Russian empire. The revolution in France continues. Europe is ruled by chaos. King Louis XVI and Queen Marie Antoinette lose their heads to the slanted blade of the newly invented guillotine. One Paris newspaper writes that 'the unlucky souls feel only a breeze at their napes'. At least thirty thousand French 'have their heads and bodies separated'. The surrounding countries are deeply troubled by the lake of blood that has pooled in central Europe. And a horrifying creature has risen up from the red depths: Napoleon Bonaparte, the swift-handed go-getter of the French Republic, who desires to rule over everyone and everything.

The brother of the guillotined Louis XVI holds stubbornly to his conviction that the rightful rule of France still belongs to the House of

Bourbon. After the death of the Dauphin Louis XVII, he crowned himself Louis XVIII, king of France. He hopes to hold off the usurper 'with the help of God and trustworthy friends'. His powerful group of allies includes the somnambulistic emperor of Russia, Paul I.

And so, having fled France, Louis XVIII has spent a year in the Jelgava Palace, allotted to him out of pity by the Russian tsar. Jelgava, of course, isn't Versailles, but even while living off the charity of others, Louis XVIII's group of attendants numbers around 250 people. Ministers, chamberlains, secretaries, equerries, dukes, viscounts, marquises and counts. Albertīne wrote: 'I've never seen anything like it in Jelgava. People walking along the streets call out to each other *"bonjour, comte!"*, *"bonjour, comtesse!"* In the pastry shops, women part company saying they hope to see one another soon at the Tuileries or the Palazzo Farnese. When the weather is good, the courtiers go on trips around Zemgale or to the garden parties of the region's richest landowners. But Louis XVIII is always too busy to join in. He writes letters, on paper on which he himself has drawn the lines, to all the leaders of Europe, urging them to wage war against the evil that has been unleashed. The letters are stamped with the Great Seal of France, which he had managed to grab when fleeing from the Tuileries.'

Yes, time does not stand still. Valtraute is already over forty. Idle women wither in mid-life, wilt, lose their lustre. Valtraute doesn't want to have to say the same about herself. She isn't content with the life she has led until now; she's still waiting for something. Her life is a jumble of fiery discontent and hope. It could be that that's why her eyes are still bright, her movements graceful and spritely, her acumen sharp and perceptive.

Despite the prejudices against everything currently coming from Paris, Valtraute finds the new fashions appealing. The freedom her body enjoys without corsets reveals favourably its soft but defined contours. That's undeniable. Of course, she doesn't plan on ordering nightgown-like dresses like Madame Récamier. Let the excitable ladies of Paris have all that. She has heard that lately they walk around almost naked. Last winter, many style-conscious women in Paris caught cold, contracted pneumonia and died in the name of fashion. Lord keep her from that kind of foolishness!

The first thing Albertīne tells her after she arrives is that there will be a royal wedding in Jelgava, and Maksimilians has procured an invitation for Valtraute as well.

'That's mad! What are you saying? I don't have a dress for that!'

'Don't worry, we'll get one. We have a week.'

'Isn't the Eighteenth already married?'

'He is, yes. But he's childless. To retain the French throne for the House of Bourbon, Louis XVIII has wheedled permission out of the Pope to marry Louis XVI's daughter Marie-Thérèse to his other brother's son, Louis Antoine Bourbon.'

'Well, thank you, my dear! It will be truly wonderful! I can't think of a better time of year for a wedding.'

The birds are singing, the sun strolls across the land; Jelgava reminds her of a bridal bouquet. The chapel, located on the ground floor of the palace, smells of roses and lilies. The surrounding streets are packed with ornate carriages. Throngs of people, as if at a fair. And the people! In velvet, lace, brocade, silk. Ostrich feathers, decorative medals, galloons and epaulettes. Many of Kurzeme's aristocracy and Jelgava's most notable residents have been invited to the wedding. Paul I of Russia has sent governors Driesen and Fersen as representatives. It's no secret that they will present the bride with a gift from the tsar – a diamond necklace.

Valtraute has found a good seat in the chapel. She would be able to see everything if it weren't for Maksimilians, hanging around Albertīne with his old-fashioned powdered wig placed haphazardly on his head. Now and again you'll still see someone wearing a bird's nest like that; the people of Kurzeme are trying to display an unshakeable connection to the noble Europe of old.

'The one in the red suit is Cardinal Montmorency, the head bishop of France,' Albertīne whispers to Valtraute from behind her fan. 'And the most fascinating part is that he's deaf...'

There's a mob of clergymen in front of the altar. There's one Orthodox parish priest dressed in gold, like an icon, with a golden mitre on his head. And one Lutheran pastor like a black rooster in a muster of peacocks.

The king himself leads the bride to the altar, followed by his adjutants and courtiers. Attractive he is not, that much can be said. Even Louis XVI – as far as can be gleaned from stories and etchings – was as corpulent as a chef with a fat rump. But this man here – *mein Gott!* – like a plump Rubenesque woman, and with the face of an ox. And His Majesty is wearing long trousers under a plain blue tunic! An invention of the *sans-culottes*!

Perhaps, as he's strolling along the bank of the Lielupe river, he also wears a red Montagnard hat!

The bride is wrapped in white like an arethusa rose. She must be a copy of her unlucky mother, the charming Marie Antoinette. The groom isn't anything special. The Bourbon beak, of course, is there, but at least the rest of him is what a man should be. Valtraute wonders if his red hair is naturally curly or curled by hand. They've invented heatable rollers precisely for that purpose; sadly, they haven't yet made it as far as Jelgava.

Old Cardinal Montmorency slowly stumbles through the wedding ceremony. Thankfully he doesn't give a sermon. A tall clergyman comes to the front, looking like a monk in his simple smock, with a cross hanging from the belt around his waist. Tension builds in the packed chapel from his first words; they wait in the drawn-out silence for what he'll say next, as if waiting for the booming thunderclap after every flash of lighting.

'Abbé Edgemont de Firmont,' Albertīne whispers.

The force of the abbé's words silences her. It's not as if evil alone has symbols. There are also symbols of trust and decency. Abbé de Firmont never forsook his ruler, not even on the scaffold, when moments before Louis XVI met the guillotine's blade, the abbé cried the words that travelled across the world: '*Fils de Saint Louis. Montez au ciel!*'

Valtraute draws her phial of smelling salts from her bosom and takes a refreshing sniff in each nostril to prevent her becoming dizzy with emotion.

The abbé's words have also affected the beautiful bride, Marie-Thérèse, daughter of martyrs, now the Duchess of Angoulême. She's sobbing gratuitously. It's a bit much; one mustn't treat a wedding as a funeral. True, the memory is still fresh and the abbé is a living reminder of the horrific event. But nevertheless, it's not as if the guillotine will be going along into the newly-weds' bedchamber.

After the ceremony the guests are invited to the Festive Hall in the southern wing of the palace. Ever since she first started travelling to Kurzeme to visit relatives, first with her father, then later as a young lady, and later still as a married woman, the Jelgava Palace has always been a mysterious entity to Valtraute, simultaneously intriguing her and frightening her. Like the glens and thickets of the road through the Kangari Hills, or the dark Pope Forest between Riga and Olaine. This building stretches on continuously, yet also continuously comes apart. Like a snake swallowing its own tail, symbolising eternity, the palace wraps around the square courtyard and seems both to grow from and to consume itself. It's been repainted several times, but isn't finished yet. Many of its windows are without panes, many balconies without railings.

It occurs to Valtraute that this palace reminds her of her own life. It started out beautifully – it has burned down, broken down, been mended. Even the steps are just temporary.

But she has nothing immediately to complain about. The court ruled in her favour in the von Brīgen land inheritance case. Her relationship with her son, Johans Amadejs, could be better, of course. Their disagreements are metaphysical, difficult to put into words. The young von Brīgen is so different, is like a persistent reminder of that one moment of weakness in her life. She and her son don't see each other often, and they've never had reason to live together. May God give everyone such an understanding father figure as Johans Amadejs found in Uncle Aurelius. She wonders how the old wiseacre is doing. He seemed a bit ill when they last saw one another. He's a man of years, Methuselah's age!

But Valtraute isn't exactly at ease. She's always had admirers. But this time is different. The district administrator, Baron von Klapmeijer, has proposed to her twice, but she still doesn't know what to say. Is there any point in trying again, after all this time? Cohabitating in mid-life with an undomesticated person encased in a hard outer shell of his own habits would not be easy. If they were younger, yes. Then two people can be put together, as a gardener plants two saplings side by side and, if the bonds of love hold them together for a while, they grow into one another. You can't combine two grown trees like that.

However, if the idea of marriage isn't completely dismissed, Klapmeijer is an acceptable candidate. Firstly, he's not too old and there is nothing military about him (God forbid!). Secondly, the Brīgen and Klapmeijer properties are adjacent to one another and would be easy to manage jointly. Thirdly, Klapmeijer is a widower with no children; he has no close relatives who would meddle and stir up trouble. A woman needs a man. Any statement that refutes that is all prattle and hypocrisy. Valtraute thinks once more about gardeners: while new flowers grow and sprout leaves, they don't need a stake for balance. When fully grown hydrangeas or rose bushes sway in the wind with clusters of blooms, a stable support doesn't detract from them but actually lets them be more themselves. Yes, to be themselves. She can even see that in Albertīne; to say her foppish Maksimilians is the model husband would be an exaggeration. What is she waiting for? For a man, Klapmeijer in his prime.

On the second floor, a procession starts immediately beyond the large grand staircase, then the throne room that she's heard so much about. Maksimilians has been to the palace both before and after the fire and knows many things. Unfortunately, his diluted way of thinking and his indiscretion quell any pleasure in listening to them.

And lo, past the rooms with the Dutch-tiled walls, finally they reach the Festive Hall. Butlers in orange livery stand on either side of the double doors, next to large vases of white lilies. Either as a symbol of purity or as a Bourbon heraldic symbol. Either carries the scent associated with the Bourbons, which both delights and causes a headache.

The walls of the hall glow golden, and the freshly waxed parquet reflects the light from the large window so brightly that their feet stop in their tracks of their own accord.

Valtraute's attention is drawn to the paintings. Zeus sits in a rosy-yellow throne of clouds on the ceiling; he doesn't seem so severe, or mighty. Isn't the sombre wrinkle between his eyebrows more a sign of exhaustion and boredom? Muscular Mars, who is drowsily lounging next to flirtatious Venus, isn't about to lead an army into war any time soon. That much is certain. Just like the carnivalesque marshal of Louis XVIII's guard, who kissed Valtraute's hand, and who has an army – if Maksimilians isn't mistaken – of fifty men. Has the painted Neptune in his triton-drawn seashell chariot arrived from a world less realistic than this one here, made up of these doll-like marquises, dukes and counts? Earlier, she thought the mural on the ceiling was purely decorative. But no! It's a valuable reminder that every world view is symbolic and based on assumptions. Until Galileo proved the earth spun on its axis, everyone assumed it didn't spin at all. And they were happy. Ptolemy's world was as flat as a pancake. But did that mean that the sun didn't shine, that the moon didn't wax and wane?

Valtraute looks around – where's the line between the fiction of the nymphs and dryads flying overhead and the reality of the king standing right over there, who inhabits his kingdom only in his imagination? Valtraute is unable to describe this strange sensation. A few years later, in

London, she'll be overcome by the same feeling. It'll happen in Madame Tussaud's museum, which doesn't yet exist. But at this moment she has yet to experience the future, and all she knows is that she feels strange.

Though she will hear Madame Tussaud's name here and now, in the Jelgava Palace.

The celebration slowly casts off its ceremonial stiffness and the gloomy shadow of memory. It's overcome with a carefree feeling typical of the French, and apparently also of the Courlanders. The hall bubbles with dances – a sea billowing with silk, lace and the eccentric movements of the gentlemen. The refreshment parlour next to the great hall is like a peaceful gulf, a calm port where the enthusiastic dancers can stop and catch their breath, and a place for the more tranquil revellers to drop anchor, meditate and take in the view.

Valtraute is sitting across from a seventh-generation chamberlain to the king. The Marquis Covuer de Montpensier is a man of indeterminate age, with such a thick layer of powder on his face that it reminds her of stucco. Even his powdered wig looks as if it has been borrowed from a plaster sculpture. But his eyes twinkle. The impishness and gaiety fizzles when he tells her he received the saddest gift on his last birthday, when he was in Paris: news of his wife's death. She had shared a prison cell with the widow of General Beauharnais, Joséphine, who was now Napoleon's wife. Joséphine had been spared because the guard took a liking to her, but the marquise hadn't been so lucky, and had died a month later alongside those who were fated to meet the blade of the guillotine.

'Wait, but her head wasn't chopped off?' Maksimilians asks from the table. His French is shaky, and he hasn't understood much of what has been said.

'No, *mon cher*. Her heart couldn't bear the proximity of death.'

'That's horrible.' Valtraute shivers, as if an icy draft had just blown through the oppressive room.

Albertīne wants to know: did Marie Antoinette's executioner really lift the decapitated head by the hair and publicly slap her face, only for her death-pale cheek to turn crimson?

Everyone gasps at Albertīne's question. Silence falls over the table, the jolly dance music still playing in the background. The marquis sits with eyes wide open, his powdered face frozen. His slack features are like a corpse's.

The thought occurs to Valtraute that maybe his is yet another decapitated head, lifted from the bloodied sawdust of the scaffolding and carelessly tossed into the lace neckerchief of a raised collar. Had Marie Antoinette been buried without her head? They must have placed it in the casket with her...

It can't be that the marquis hasn't heard Albertīne's question. Albertīne is fidgeting nervously in her chair. Finally, the marquis opens his eyes. They are as joyful and alert as those of a child who has just woken from an afternoon nap.

'Don't believe everything you hear. Marie Antoinette's head couldn't have been lifted by the hair. Before women ascended the scaffold, their hair was cut off. The documentary proof is in the death mask Madame Tussaud made from Marie Antoinette's decapitated head. I have the pleasure of knowing Madame Tussaud. Madame was Louis XVI's sister Élisabeth's drawing and sculpture teacher for nine years at Versailles.'

Nit-picking Maksimilians speaks up haughtily, trying to trap the marquis: 'I'm interested to know how you, your grace, have seen this mask? It would be logical to assume that it's located in Paris, where, if I'm correct, you haven't been since Marie Antoinette's death.'

The marquis doesn't seem to notice the tone of disbelief in the question. He summons a servant with a noble wave of his hand and has their glasses refilled.

After a long discussion about wine in general, and the Amontillado and Beaune du Château Paul I has sent from his cellars for the wedding, the conversation veers purposefully back to Marie Antoinette.

'Madame Tussaud learned how to make death masks under the artist Philippe Curtius, who was preoccupied with sculpting anatomical objects out of wax. At the time, she had a colleague from Russia who had the same passion for that type of work. When Curtius died in 1794, the Russian – or whatever he was, he didn't look Russian – left France soon afterwards and took a copy of Marie Antoinette's death mask with him. Our king had the idea to use the mask as the basis for an artwork. Many are familiar with the Spanish artist Alonzo Cano's bronze sculpture – a bowl with John the Baptist's head in it. Our ruler had the idea to install, upon his return to Paris, a tray with Marie Antoinette's head upon it on a marble pedestal in the cathedral of Notre-Dame. It would be a memorial to the martyred

queen and serve as a reminder of the blindness of obsessed minds. The king has one request – the head must look real.'

'Real?' Albertīne repeats in disbelief. She's like a little girl asking for a ghost story, only to tremble in terror.

'Not literally. We're talking about a new approach. Yes, that was his request – Marie Antoinette's decapitated head had to look realistic!'

'And made of what?' Maksimilians's question is a challenge.

'That's a secret. The work isn't finished yet. But the result is expected to be something entirely non-traditional. Just like the artist himself. The sculptor is also an anatomist, physiologist and eschatologist.'

'An eschatologist?' Albertīne has never heard the word before.

'Yes. Eschatology, which, of course, I won't have to explain to anyone here, scientifically studies life and death, the immortality of the soul, the resurrection of the body and so on and so forth...'

The interest in what the courtier is saying works like wind on a windmill.

'The hope was that the head would be at the altar during the wedding ceremony, where it would remain until the restoration of legal order in France. Yesterday it was revealed that some obstacles have arisen. I had the honour of being in attendance at the king's conversation with the artist.'

'So the head is being made right here in Jelgava?' This question is blurted out by baroness Valtraute von Brīgen. She can't shake the feeling that the marquis, turned towards Albertīne, is actually speaking only to her – that what he is saying is somehow a secret, but that it has a significant connection to her, Valtraute's, past and future.

'Not just here, in Jelgava, but in this palace.'

'What's the artist's name?'

'I doubt his name will mean anything to you. Monsieur Gibran is little known in broader social circles.'

Did she hear correctly? The sounds coming from the Frenchman's mouth creak and churn like the unoiled wheels of a stagecoach.

'Monsieur Gibran ... Monsieur Gibran,' Valtraute repeats to herself and feels her body stiffen, as if she's been turned to ice.

XXIII

It's difficult to order events by their significance. The assessment is largely determined by one's point of view, and how the events affected the assessor.

In October 1944, Riga saw another change of landlord.

The Germans had built an explosives warehouse at the edge of the airfield, in the oak forests between the Manor and the railway tracks. It seems as if they'd managed to take some things with them, but then blew up the rest. We spent a week living as if we were at the foot of Mount Vesuvius. The series of explosions was particularly heavy at night. The air trembled, the ground shook, the sky lit up in short, cutting bursts. A third of the Manor's window panes shattered, but the weather stayed warm. We still had the double-paned winter windows up in the attic where they had been stored in the spring.

The windows were the only thing immediately affected by the change of power, but the first actions of the new rulers shook our life at the Manor to the core. The Baroness was arrested once again. This time it didn't even seem personal; they just gathered up and deported anyone whose documents in one way or another connected them to Germany. Johanna – at the time she was fifty-six – had been listed in the registry of the Martin Church's German congregation. Unlike Hitler's bureaucrats, Stalin's bureaucrats weren't interested in bloodlines. The church registry was good enough for them.

In my archive of personal experiences, there is no entry for Johanna's arrest. At the time, I was in hospital with typhus, in a kind of anaesthetic stupor. When I returned to the Manor, the Baroness's arrest was like a scabbed-over wound. We never saw her again.

Many years later, something of her fate was revealed by the poet H. H., who had been deported with his family in a similar manner – in consequence of an entry in a church registry – right after the Russians arrived. In the third or fourth year of deportations, he was at the market in a small communist town when he met an old woman who didn't have any hands. It was common in the north to lose limbs to frostbite. She was trying to sell photographs of a young girl in return for a loaf of bread. One of the pictures showed the teenage girl in a swimsuit on the beach near Riga. Drunken miners were staring at the pictures in wonder: 'Look at that lovely, naked bird!' The woman told the poet she used to live in Riga, near the airfield. He couldn't remember her surname, but said it could have been Holendere.

Grandfather's business suffered a fatal blow. The remaining horses were nationalised – this time for real. The young mares were taken to the racetrack. Logic didn't go hand in hand with Soviet rule. What they'd allowed once, they didn't the second time around. The racetrack was later forbidden, though it had operated before. The totalisator turned over large amounts of money.

Having lost the Baroness without trace, Grandfather, like a gymnast standing in front of a broken beam, was unable to pull himself together. He was no longer the capable, self-confident man he'd once been. Even when making decisions his reactions were confused and muddled. 'The carriage is fine with three wheels. Two wheels make it a gig. But if there's only one wheel left, it's just a wheelbarrow,' he said.

But of course, he wasn't talking about carriages. With no employees, no horses, no opportunity to work in the way he wanted and to which he was accustomed, Grandfather would spend his time in the carriage house alone. Then once, when he'd gone to the racetrack stables to see his mares, Grandfather got himself a position as a night watchman. The stable commander, a retired lieutenant colonel of the tank corps, was shocked to see the night watchman show up dressed as a jockey and wearing a black bowler hat. Then, apparently remembering that people in England went to the Derby wearing grey top hats, he shrugged his shoulders and said: 'Riga ... the devil only knows – these westerners!'

Jānis and I continued our studies. Our school had lost its elite status and was now just a regular secondary school. The road there and back was an adventure. The hastily built wooden bridge over the Daugava river couldn't accommodate the tram lines. We had to travel the distance between the relaid tracks on either side of the river on foot.

The city was empty of locals, but filled with newcomers. A line of air force officers showed up at the Manor with orders for 'living quarters'. In the beginning, they took over one wing of the building, where the Pilot used to live. Later, men showed up with orders for the office and the armoury. Grandfather, Jānis and I were left with two rooms. Aunt Alma, who had never been able to stand the Baroness, unexpectedly announced that she would never let those Russian skunks take Johanna's quarters, and issued her own order to take the room for herself.

In the mornings, the unpredictable Poļina would be in the kitchen in just a nightshirt, yawning and mussing her uncombed hair with both hands. Card games with Lieutenant Colonel Rumjancevs sometimes ended with a fight and a broken mirror. The same mirror I once stood in front of, imagining myself as Nelson, Gulliver or Richelieu.

The last room on the left resounded with the roars of lions. The moustachioed Major Gogo had obtained a gramophone in Germany, with a single record – the sounds of various animals. The babbling of camels and lowing of zebras went almost unnoticed, but the lions rattled the entire floor. Gogo always had masses of relatives coming to visit, bringing smoked mutton, wine and southern fruits. Godmothers, sisters-in-law and female cousins sat behind the closed, but often not entirely shut, door, praying in loud, sobbing voices for God to stand by their relative in his test flights. But their prayers went unheard. They found a piece of the plane and one of Gogo's hands about a kilometre from the crash site.

When Poļina was in a good mood, she'd make pancakes for Lieutenant Colonel Rumjancevs, and bring us *blini* slathered with American condensed milk. When she was in a bad mood, she'd yell at us – call us fascists, bound for Siberia – and yell at the Russians with unintelligible Tartar or Kazakh words, which not even Grandfather could translate. These bad moods tormented Poļina often.

Jānis picked up Russian almost without realising it. He also had an easier time getting to know people – crossing a threshold that, so far as our neighbours were concerned, always seemed to trip me up. So, of course, Jānis was the first one to learn about Poļina's troubles. She was Rumjancev's war wife. Now the lieutenant colonel was demobilised and was getting ready go back to his real wife. But Poļina was pregnant.

'She told me everything,' Jānis said with surprise. He was almost seventeen, but was slow to grow taller. His voice was still changing, and it would break, jumping ridiculously between falsetto and bass. His smooth, round chin was sprouting a few facial hairs.

'Yes, you seem closer to them,' I spat foolishly, thinking of Jānis's Russian. But Jānis shrank.

'Possibly. Grandfather is right; the Russians and all those like them are trapped in the same immigrant complex. But they don't see me as a Latvian, they see me as their equal, an immigrant.'

'Don't be silly.' I reined in my bravado, embarrassed. 'Try telling a Russian that Pushkin was an immigrant to Russia.'

'Grandfather tried to reassure me, too: "How are you not a Latvian, when you have a Latvian heart?" But no one sees your heart. They see your face.'

'So?'

'Then it's all bug eyes and slack jaws. Every time I speak Latvian. Not in school any more, but in the shops, in the trams, on the street. Do you know what our class teacher told me yesterday? That I have very little chance of getting into university.'

'Why?'

'"Why" isn't a polite question in the Soviet Union.'

It was a strange time. The war was behind us and we ran from it without looking back. With the changeover of power, our perceptions of wrong and those who were in the wrong, of rights, responsibilities and fairness, were so muddled up that not much made sense any more. The easiest thing to do was to explain the unacceptable and the incomprehensible by the fatal concept *war* – which, quite possibly, had before now brought an undetected but contagious clouding of reason. But it seemed as if, now that the worst was over, the healing could begin. The shadows of our memories still snaked around our ankles, dragged like heavy hems – but we had to move beyond them. Latvia wasn't alone: a large part of the world, altered beyond recognition, was resuming a life of peace.

Grandfather kept repeating: 'Boys, what can I say, this is your time, you won't have another! From a historical point of view the French Revolution was a miserable interim, but millions of French people passed their entire lives in a chaos that lasted "only" seventy years.'

Talk about university was in truth talk about dreams of the past, considering the reality of the awakening. The knotted birchwood box where we kept our joint funds was usually empty. Grandfather's salary was enough to buy our rations – a few loaves of bread, a handful of sugar and cooking oil. And so our empty stomachs wouldn't stick to our spines, Aunt Alma stuffed us full of her rutabaga mash.

I talked to Vladimirs the most about the future. No one knew where he'd come from; it was as if he'd fallen from the clouds. When I went into my classroom under the 'new conditions', he was just there. Wearing an old, patched-up suit and worn lace-up boots. At times it felt as if he wasn't really our age, but an experienced man. Once when we were talking, I told him that I'd go to university no matter what, and Vladimirs gave a strange laugh, saying: 'You, buddy, have guts!' This phrase emanating from the naive, simple-minded Latgalian boy became as indispensable to me as food. The confirmation that I was brave was something I wanted to hear again and again, because I wasn't that convinced of it myself. So it became my custom to bring up the subject of university almost daily. And every day Vladimirs would repeat 'you have guts ...', 'you have guts...', like Skaņaiskalns Hill echoing my own calls.

Was I driven by bravery? I doubt it. More likely it was stubbornness. Stubbornness combined with the world's worst mathematician – optimism. Grandfather would refer to Jānis and I as riders of the night – I suppose, meaning we were riders who galloped on without paying attention to the road.

'That's not true,' I argued. 'Did Veidenbaums have it any easier during his studies? "I had a thin time of it..."'

'You, boys, won't have it that bad. Steamed rutabaga is good for you.'

That autumn I was accepted into university. When Jānis left school, he didn't follow my example; he looked for work and would study as an external student.

The factory where Jānis took a job – without much choice, if his pockets weren't to be forever empty – ended up being a trailblazer in the semiconductor industry. Jānis heard the unexpected fanfare of trumpets announcing a meeting with fate. He threw himself into the secrets of diodes, thyristors and transistors like a newborn turtle that has never seen water throws itself into the churning ocean. New industries have a rare quality – both beginners and experts start on the same level and work simultaneously to open new doors to the unknown.

Pretty soon, Jānis had made a name for himself. When people talked about him, they rarely used the words 'he is'; they usually said 'he'll be'.

When he was twenty years old, Jānis fell in love.

Little is known even now of the nature of love. As little, in fact, as is known about the universe, which people have inhabited for at least 270,000 years. The newest theories about falling in love explain it prosaically – through the effects of dopamine and noradrenaline on the brain's limbic system. Nevertheless, chemistry has never had the answers. The switch that sets the chemistry in motion when we see not just any old person but *the one*, is still swathed in secrecy.

I don't know where Jānis met Guna, but that's not important. He changed beyond recognition and displayed signs of the limbic system in motion – a person grows wistful, their awareness of the surrounding world decreases, they become particularly stubborn.

Guna wasn't especially beautiful. She was taller than Jānis, with freckles and thin lips that gave her a look of determination; she didn't use powders or make-up (back then, women seldom did so in any case). She wore her mousy hair pinned up in a wave over her forehead. When it was cold out, she'd wrap a woollen scarf around her head, which many woman did in the post-war period.

I think Jānis started talking to girls sooner than I did – and, true to his character, ambitiously, thoroughly, and in a way scientifically. With that certain persistence that drives researchers into the Amazonian rainforests and the African deserts.

Ever since we had lived together, I believed Jānis had never taken a great interest in clothes. One night, he took a button-down shirt from his briefcase and showed it to me like some wondrous object.

'Look, it's my old shirt, but look at the colour now! And the collar!'

Jānis ran his fingers carefully over the perfectly sewn seam, as if he were holding a golden Aztec diadem.

Though it wasn't perhaps by means of those tiny, well-threaded, needlepoint stitches – which revealed a femininity, in the tenderness of the everyday task, with which our family was little acquainted – that Guna tied Jānis to herself; the magical glow was already there. For Jānis, a wandering circus performer's son and the representative of our male-dominated family, Guna embodied a world that surprised and enticed him. This showed in the phrases that sometimes slipped from him: 'It takes Guna half of the summer to visit all her Vidzeme relatives', 'Guna likes home-grown flowers', 'If only you'd had Guna's home-made *pīrāgi*!', 'Guna says freshly washed bed sheets should smell like the wind'.

My idea of how relationships form these days is hazy. Based on cinema and literature, the process has shortened, become pathetically businesslike. When we were growing up, people in love literally strolled though those initial sparks of emotion. They'd wander the streets, search out quiet, romantic corners, frequent out of the way cinemas. Maybe that's why I first ran into Jānis and Guna together when I was out visiting a gravestone at the cemetery.

'I didn't realise you also knew Akers!' I said in surprise.

'Akers? No. Guna came to clean up her godmother's gravestone, and then we just ... You can only experience spring in Riga at its fullest in the cemetery. Sometimes you can hear nightingales at Arkādija Park, but you can hear the cuckoo only here.'

She looked around with alert, observant eyes; when she spoke she had a slight provincial accent. For some reason, she reminded me of a little girl caught misbehaving.

Later, Jānis told me more about her. Guna's family still led a rural life. For years her father had maintained the Čiekurkalns neighbourhood water tower; they lived right in the area. Her mother took care of the family and their cow which spent the summer grazing in the nearby fields along the railway tracks. Children of city employees received their secondary education free of charge, and Guna had wound up at one of the city's most prestigious schools, with the children of factory owners, bankers and high-ranking officials. Naturally, Guna's parents' hopes for the future were tied to the prospects of their only daughter. The war and the political carousel didn't change anything in that respect. Everything twisted and turned, but their hopes were based on a well-marked path: Guna was studying medicine.

It's not hard to imagine how Jānis's first encounter with her parents went.

'Have you lived in Latvia long?'

'Almost ten years now.'

'And where were you born?'

'Hard to say exactly where. But in a circus wagon.'

'What's your father do? And your mother?'

'I live with my grandfather.'

'And your grandfather?'

'My grandfather works at the racetrack, taking care of the horses.'

'I see, I see ... Yes ... And what do you do?'

'I work in a factory...'

Most probably, her parents' confusion would have stopped at the shrugging of their shoulders, had the strange guest's appearance in their home represented nothing more than their daughter playing around. When it became clear that the knot of their relationship was growing tighter, however, panic ensued.

Guna and Jānis's relationship lasted two years. The game that had started out so playfully, of its own accord, became over the course of time a difficult trial for all involved. They had a choice – to give in to fate or try to break it.

A twenty- or twenty-one-year-old woman's ideal man is nothing more than a dream. He's a part-imagined, part-tangible dream man, and he'd probably already made his appearance in Guna's world, allowing her to experience life's first desires and hopes.

In my opinion, Jānis was a far cry from this ideal. But on the other hand, he was real, you could spend time with him, care for him, and she had room in her world for desire. Young boys aren't the only ones driven by a longing to appease their hormones – young girls are driven just as hard by theirs.

Jānis didn't seem to notice the icy manner in which Guna's parents regarded him. Upended by love, the fanaticism coded in his genes played its part. The hunger that carried him to Guna was insatiable; that could have been what set it apart from the hunger he knew from previous experiences. As Mephistopheles said, 'Blood is a juice of rarest quality.' Love turns the red nectar of life into the strongest glue that can seal two into one. An almost complete stranger had become a part of him, letting him experience a new-found sense of togetherness.

As they got to know each other better, Jānis's character revealed itself to Guna – one would imagine – no less vibrantly than his appearance. Love is deceitful. Like groundwater, it doesn't flow on the surface, but through deeper layers consisting of different slopes, different dams.

But Guna was unable completely to ignore the undeniable truth of her parents' severe and constant opposition. Both in regard to Jānis's uncertain future, and the chance of her bringing yellow children into the world – God created races that are separately defined for a reason. After a while, these warnings start to sink in – and even if your conclusions aren't altered, your thinking is.

One night I walked in on Jānis as he stood in front of the mirror, comb in hand.

'Thinking of a new hairstyle?' I asked in passing.

I expected him to indicate to me with a wave of his hand that it wasn't worth flapping your tongue over every little thing. But he answered with a rather serious question: 'Does my hair look like varnished telephone wires?'

It was probably something Guna had said teasingly during their drawn-out farewells at the front gate. Jokes often indirectly reveal what would otherwise go unsaid; they express what we don't mean to say. The subject of Jānis's hair had been brought up. It had been thought about. It already weighed down in the scale of fate.

Not long before the midsummer holidays, Jānis announced that he was taking a holiday and would be staying at the Rietumbuļļu beach, where Guna and a girlfriend of hers had rented a veranda.

'How are the three of you going to stay there?' I was confused.

'The friend is just there so her mother won't worry.'

He came back home on midsummer eve. He sat down at the table, put Guna's photograph in front of him and buried himself in his lecture notes and books. When I got home several hours later, the notebooks and textbooks were right where they'd been, and Jānis was sitting frozen, still looking at the picture of Guna.

'Why didn't you stay at Buļļi?'

Silence.

'What?'

'Why didn't you stay at Vakarbuļļi?'

'Guna had to go to the countryside. That's what her family does at midsummer. She'll be back soon.'

Jānis was acting strangely. It's how I imagined people acted when they go crazy at a full moon, climbing out of windows and on to roofs. The limbic floods reached their climax when the postman brought a registered letter. A curious letter. Later, the white page stood next to Guna's photograph, and I looked at it many times over. There was a single phrase written in the middle of the page – Love You. No date, no greeting, no signature. That kind of letter is written in a particular state of nerves, before a suicide or as a ship is sinking.

I didn't follow the shock waves of their relationship over the coming months, as I was preoccupied with my own matters. Jānis and Guna kept on seeing each other, and I already viewed them as an unwed wedded couple.

It was a grey, rainy autumn day. The streets were flooded, puddles splashed underfoot. I ran into them downtown at the colonnade. I found it strange that in weather like this they would just be standing there, next to each other. There was a kind of oddly sombre and stiff atmosphere about them, the inertia of broken clocks and boats bobbing in place along a dock.

('Does your girl kiss with her eyes closed?'

'You taking a poll?'

'Guna always closes her eyes.'

'Does that bother you?'

'No ... But...'

'What d'you mean, but?'

'I'd like to know why she does it.'

'Each of us lives in a real and an imaginary world. The imaginary one is probably more comfortable.'

'That's the thing ... That's the thing...')

'Greetings, young lovebirds! The windows are streaming with tears, and there's a fog rolling in. Classic Aleksandrs Čaks weather...'

As if moved by my words, Jānis removed his glasses and carefully wiped them with a handkerchief. His face, with its shallow-set features and narrow, half-lidded eyes, was bared as if in naked embarrassment.

'Fine for him,' Guna said, 'he's staying in Riga. But I have to go and dig up potatoes.'

'Don't worry, Jānis, the students will be done digging by Christmas.'

Jānis again took refuge behind his glasses. The frames became too small for him long ago; they were the same ones he'd worn when he first arrived on that ship.

'Guna's father was taken to hospital yesterday.'

'Oh, don't start again. He's already better this morning.'

It was hard to tell from her voice if what she said was a reassurance or a reproach.

She was gone three weeks. Then Jānis said she'd caught cold out in the country. No, he wasn't going to visit her, Guna didn't want him to, it wasn't the right time.

After a week, however, he did go. This time he was welcomed with unexpected warmth. The room smelled of *pīrāgi*. Guna's father sat at the table with another man. A boy Jānis's age, maybe a bit older, but with a mature, shiny patch where the hair was thinning on top of his head. Guna came in from the kitchen wearing her best dress. Her father introduced the guest and added: 'If I'd had the opportunity to study medicine...'

Having understood that his presence would interfere with the festivities, Jānis didn't sit at the table, but asked Guna to step outside with him for a few minutes. Guna blushed and looked at her father, at her mother, both of whom urged her: 'Go, go, darling! You have to be polite to guests. Put something over your shoulders and don't be too long.'

Jānis couldn't remember whether it was raining. But it was cold. Guna stood with her arms crossed, fidgeting with the corners of the jacket she'd thrown on, shivering, and told him that's how things had turned out; the wedding was to be in a month.

I tried to ask him about the groom and the reason for the rush, but Jānis clenched his hands until his knuckles turned white and said: 'It doesn't matter. Now she can kiss someone without having to close her eyes.'

Jānis smiled serenely. Mr Konishiki had taught him – you must speak pleasantly of unpleasant things. So as not to spoil the mood of others.

XXIV

Who is this Gibran: the ambassador of mystic misfortune or a dealer sent by Satan to cut the deck?

It doesn't matter! Regardless, he has turned her life so completely upside down, has interfered so overbearingly, that she just wants to see him once and for all! Even if just to confirm that he isn't a ghost that disappears the second the light goes on. She wants to talk to him. Probably talk – what else? It doesn't matter. She doesn't even know what she wants.

'*Mon marquis!* If Monsieur Gibran serves his majesty, is he somewhere nearby?' the baroness gestures nervously around, among the wedding guests.

The marquis doesn't look bothered by Valtraute's nervousness, nor by her curiosity. The whims of ladies no longer surprise the French marquis.

'We would all, of course, be delighted by his presence, but I haven't had the pleasure of seeing him. As I told you, his majesty was not happy to learn the head wasn't ready in time.'

'Please take me to Monsieur Gibran.'

The sly twinkle in the corners of his eyes indicates that the marquis has misunderstood her request. That must explain his eagerness to assist. Sweet, unforgettable Versailles, oh, the lovely Petit Trianon, oh, the Palais-Royal with its secret staircases, hidden bedchamber doors, double-panelled alcove curtains! Oh, court life with its exciting intrigues, elegant games, secrets and mischief. A courtier's heart cannot remain indifferent to those kinds of delights!

Valtraute isn't entirely sure where she's being taken. The hallway loses its splendour. Rows of simple doors leading to barrack-type rooms replace the grand, oaken double doors. The walls are whitewashed in places, blackened with grime or greenish with mould in others. The parquet is left behind for stone tiles on which her heels seem to tap out the beating of her heart.

'The next door on the left,' the marquis says, warily glancing over his shoulder. 'You have to go alone from here. Accompanied only by Amor or Cupid. Don't knock at the first door, but at the second.'

Like a comic opera! All that's missing is a public run-in with Gibran!

Valtraute enters a chamber that looks more like a shed than a room. The outer wall is stacked with birch firewood. To one side is a box containing earthenware. Several empty birdcages are stacked against a wall to the left.

Valtraute is observing her surroundings when suddenly she hears a loud crack. Luckily the rat-trap has only snapped shut on the hem of her dress. Broken furniture clutters the room – wobbly chairs with broken seats, table tops supported by stacks of bricks, a warped and sagging sofa. On her left is a door, apparently the one she is to knock at.

After a moment of suspense spent in the haze of excitement, the door handle swings down, the door opens, and a man in a long linen nightshirt all but jumps out. He's wearing wooden clogs. His face is sweaty. Greasy strands of hair stick to his forehead and cheeks.

'Would you please announce me to Monsieur Gibran?' Valtraute asks in German. The strange man might not speak French.

'Whom have I the honour of announcing?'

'Baroness Valtraute von Brīgen, widow of adjutant Eberhart von Brīgen.'

The man assumes a respectful air – perhaps exaggeratedly so – and bows his already drooping head. The arm covered down to the elbow in the linen shirt sweeps in a jerking motion towards the broken furniture.

'Please, have a seat.'

Valtraute waits. Her agitation boils and bubbles over. She shouldn't have come. She shouldn't have. Why chase after something that happened over half a lifetime ago? There's no reason to carry the ghosts of the past with you.

The door handle swings down again. Out steps a nobleman with his chest puffed out proudly, dressed in rather old-fashioned but fancy velvet trousers and white stockings. Combed, perfumed, with the medal of an order on his breast. But something about him makes her think that this is another encounter with some kind of magic. This same man had stood before her just moments ago as a humble servant in a linen shirt!

'It is an honour – Almustaf Gibran. Currently a baker. To whit, please forgive me for being unable to invite you in further or offer you greater comforts. The bakery ovens are currently running in the quarters. How may I be of service?'

Valtraute has jumped to her feet. Gibran gestures for her to sit, and looks for a chair for himself. He finds one, inspects it. It's quite mangled, so he pushes it aside. Takes another one, which seems to do.

Whatever she will hear or say right away has little meaning. The real conversation happens with their eyes. She studies him, he studies her. The eyes try to assess everything in mere moments. Like the lips in the first second they taste wine.

It's hard to say how long the moment lasts. But something in Gibran's smirking expression calms her. Maybe it's just the noticeable pockmarks at the top of his dusky cheeks. Valtraute looks over the crafty baker once more, from his hair to the buckles of his shoes. Her eyes return to the scars. She doubts a ghost or a demon would have pockmarks. A logger, water-carrier, or baker, dressed in an aristocrat's clothing. *Mein Gott!* He doesn't even look like a barber – they at least have manners.

So she doesn't have to talk about herself, which she doesn't want to do any more, Valtraute twitters about the wedding ceremony, about Edgemont de Firmont's sermon.

'And you, Monsieur Gibran, didn't hear how he dressed with words an experience so analogous to heavenly inspiration…?'

'You are mistaken, madame. The abbé has only one speech. It is, of course, dazzling, but it is worn from use and time like the seat of a clerk's trousers. I haven't forgotten Louis XVI; you don't need to remind me of him.'

'The abbé mostly spoke of the mother, of Marie Antoinette.'

'Ah, so you're here because of Marie Antoinette! That's a different matter altogether. Who sent you?'

Now Valtraute senses genuine interest in his piercing stare. The only other person to have looked at her like that was Count Cagliostro, for whom Valtraute still feels some reverence – may he rest in peace! The Pope had ordered Cophta be thrown in prison, where he – at least so rumour has it – met a mysterious end around four years ago.

'...No, truly! There is a similarity! Come, come closer to the light! Look up! Now look down!'

The baker (Valtraute doesn't want to call him Gibran even in her thoughts) prods her cheeks with water-soaked, wrinkled fingertips, and without the slightest bit of respect or shame. He takes her by the chin, turns her head one way and then the other. At least he doesn't take her by the hair and scalp her. And she simply sits submissively, as if bewitched!

'Similar to what? What do you mean?'

'As if you don't know, since you've been sent.'

Realisation finally dawns on Valtraute and she bursts into laughter.

'With Marie Antoinette? *Mein Herr*, you're too generous with your compliments. Just think how old I am!'

'When she lost her head, Marie Antoinette wasn't a girl any more, either. People tend to forget that. Even today, on Antoinette's daughter's wedding day.'

The baker's black eyes are like spurs; their sharpness doesn't hurt, but it startles her. And then the thought hits her – it's true, even my Johans Amadejs is already of marrying age!

But the baker ushers her from one window to the next and continues:

'Marie Antoinette had one head lobbed off, although she had at least three. In matters of state, she didn't know any more than this butterfly here on the curtain. As a woman, she was gifted with understanding and foresight. That's why the events must be considered both foolish and a tragedy. Don't try to tell me she loved the cowardly Bourbon. Antoinette didn't know love until she met Count Fersen, the Swedish envoy. The young Fersen tried to move the queen abroad, but he was caught. And that was her ruin. Marie Antoinette died because of two men. By not loving one and by loving the other.'

Suddenly, Valtraute's thoughts, which were beginning to calm down, are shaken by a new terror. And what if this ... this ... whatever he may be ... was planning now on putting a very real head ... her head! ...on the silver platter in place of Marie Antoinette's ... *Lieber Gott*! She's at the mercy of a completely mad surgeon. She can scream as much as she wants, but no one will hear her. She must escape...

'Oh ... *mais que voulez vous*?...' In her alarm Valtraute starts speaking in French. 'I'm not well versed in revolutionary operations. The newspapers said the guillotine ... the guillotine was invented as ... as a humane solution...'

Gibran still holds Valtraute's elbow in one hand, and her chin in the other. It's as if his black stare has slithered out from under a rock like a centipede and is crawling over her neck.

'A change in rulers has always accompanied a change of heads. But the French example, which you are speaking of, madame, is educational. This time an unusual change occurred. While the state was without a leader, the crown made a profit. Now the crown sits on a sack of gold. Comfortably, in its own way. You can change currency however you want, it'll always be currency.'

As if what he said has surprised her, Valtraute tears away from his grasp and takes a step back. A maniac, an absolute maniac, all he's thinking of is cutting and changing.

Gibran moves closer again, studies her face and mutters calculations to himself.

'Monsieur Gibran! Monsieur Gibran!'

Her cry is loud and desperate. This time Gibran is the one to take a step backwards.

'Monsieur Gibran! No one sent me! I'm not at all like Marie Antoinette!'

Gibran takes yet another step back.

'I'm here on a personal matter. You served in the Grand Duke Constantine's regiment of cuirassiers, did you not? Does adjutant Baron von Brīgen's name not call to mind a certain incident?'

'Von Brīgen? A certain incident? Not at all.'

'Eberhart von Brīgen, rather tall, with a rapier scar on his cheek.'

'Aaaah, yes, yes! He ran off with Captain Ulste's wife to America! Brīgen and Ulste were injured at the same time. Yes, yes! Brīgen less so, the other more severely. But I was able to mend Ulste. Brīgen ... Well then!'

Valtraute looks at Gibran. Gibran looks at Valtraute. Valtraute is tense, like a duellist raising a pistol. Gibran is contemplative, perhaps slightly annoyed at the sharpness of the otherwise dull memory.

'Have you ever considered that two people could be joined into one?'

'Only theoretically, only theoretically, my lady. I think I even wrote something like that once for a German newspaper in Saint Petersburg.'

'You are mistaken, monsieur. You have done it. You have...'

Gibran turns away swiftly. It could be because of something insignificant – a pesky wasp. But it's as if the movement releases Valtraute from a feeling of submissiveness. She turns and leaves. She's not afraid. There is a constricting heaviness, an emptiness. The emptiness of the world has collapsed on to her. It's a wonder one person can carry so much emptiness.

When Valtraute rejoins the wedding party, Covuer de Montpensier has disappeared. Maksimilians is devoting all his attention to the mayor's wife. That's reason enough for the wine selected from the Russian tsar's cellar to taste to Albertīne of bile; swill served to the crucified from a sponge speared on the end of a lance. Maksimilians hasn't danced a single dance with her. She wants to get up and leave the room. Would Maksimilians even notice if she were gone? Most likely he would, but only after an hour, when the master of ceremonies knocks his staff against the floor to announce 'lights out'.

Albertīne sees Valtraute and knows that fate is here to save the day. Valtraute's appearance makes it clear that she must be taken home immediately. Her face is deathly pale, her eyes watery, her forehead hot.

'Sweet sister, what's the matter? You're ill! Jesus Christ our Lord almighty! Maksimilians, I'm sorry to interrupt...'

Maksimilians exchanges a few more sentences with the beautiful lady, clinks glasses with her, then gets to his feet and comes over.

'*Vous avez toujours des idées surprenantes, ma cherie.*'

Valtraute's appearance, however, is an indisputable argument. Maksimilians gives in.

Valtraute has a fever. Just in case, Maksimilians sends for ice to be brought up from the cellar to cool her forehead. The next three days and nights go by, wavering between nightmare and unconsciousness. Then she slowly resurfaces from the terrors and voids of illness and returns to the accustomed, everyday world.

'Who's this captain you kept calling out for? You've never even been on a ship,' Albertīne chides.

'I don't remember anything. And, thank God, it's all over. No reason to call back ghosts.'

A week later Valtraute heads home to Vidzeme.

Travel has become incomparably more convenient in recent years. She has almost forgotten the days when they were tossed about in stagecoaches stuffed full of strangers. It's a whole new experience travelling in your own carriage with your own driver, only stopping at post offices to rent horses. Even Fräulein Gabriella is nothing like the late Bon Esprit. Valtraute calls Gabriella her fiery archangel. Her feminine frailty is deceptive. In a moment of need, Gabriella could turn a palm frond into a sword. And is that really a surprise? Angels aren't restricted by gender. It only amplifies her virtues.

As for breaking off her visit to her Vidzeme relatives, Valtraute is sure that she wants to get home as soon as possible. She feels weak and exhausted. Home, with the peace and comfort that can't be found anywhere else, calls out to her. She has to gather her wits, compose herself, draw conclusions. Slowly, calmly. Then she'll decide whether or not to accept Klapmeijer's proposal. The baron will wait. It's absurd for a man of almost sixty to play the Romeo.

With Riga in front of her as they drive over the pontoon bridge spanning the Daugava, Valtraute's thoughts wander. She remembers another return from Kurzeme. Filled with just as much uncertainty, and just as smouldering. Many years ago, when she was frantically trying to track down Eberhart, and naively believed that all she would have to do was to find him in order for her life to continue merrily along. What fooled her in the end – Eberhart, Cagliostro or love? Perhaps it was feminine weakness, her inability to separate love from revenge? The flint tinderbox lit the candle for life. Can a candle and a tinderbox even have a common flame?

She wonders how her life would have turned out if she hadn't had that wild notion back then to dash off to Burtnieki.

As if searching for the answer to her own question, her mind recalls the scenes of that trip from her memory. Entering the sleepy dwelling, first the meeting with the armed servant, and then with him. Yes, from the very beginning she had sensed something fateful. Maybe her ancestors had spoken? Before that night, she had on numerous occasions met with men who had caused her to feel frightened. But that night she had been frightened of herself. The dimly lit room had been so hot. She had been sweating, but for some reason it was as if the heat wasn't coming from the masonry but from this Ulste, in whose presence she spent every moment feeling like a woman, wanting to be a woman, unable to be anything else but a woman.

Her entire life, she'd always prayed before going to bed: '...and lead us not into temptation.' Back then, had it occurred to her that what was happening was exactly that from which she had asked the Lord to protect her? She had been infatuated.

After that night nothing else had happened. How could that brief moment of weakness have become the most glaring, unforgettable event? There's no way to escape it. She doesn't love her son, Johans Amadejs – she doesn't. But she doesn't have anyone else. The young Brīgen is an Ulste. Of a *Latvian*. Lord, why have you forsaken me? But if things happened the way You intended them to, why couldn't You have chosen a straighter, clearer path?

These and similar thoughts plague her. She circles them as if she is tethered to a post. As she circles, the tether winds around the post and grows shorter and shorter. And again she's at the whim of God, who is so incomprehensible and unfathomable. Regardless of where she goes or what she tries to undertake, the past will always block her way, and she will never be able to move beyond it. Perhaps it's better to come to terms with the past and accept its burden as a condition of her fate?

There's nothing left to do but admit that she is once again standing face to face with temptation – the temptation to go to Burtnieki. Why and for what purpose, she can't say. She isn't entertaining hopes of capturing the past and tying it to the present. That's out of the question. Simply to take a trip down memory lane. Wander once more willy-nilly, trying to find the place with the strange name, 'Ulstes'. What does it look like now? Back then, she had arrived in the dead of night and by morning she had been too flustered to look around.

So many miles had been travelled in the search for Eberhart. Now, she wants to take a detour to get a closer look at the place that will never be mentioned in the von Brīgen family history, but that will be passed down in the blood of future generations. Why is she bartering with herself?

'Gabriella, have them stop the carriage. There's been a change of plans. We're going to Burtnieki!'

They spend the night at Strīpele manor with Valtraute's immediate, but emotionally lukewarm, relatives. In the morning they drive on. Around noon, they spot the slender steeple of the Swedish Livonian-era church in the distance.

This time they don't get lost. Gabriella asks for directions at the parish house, then climbs on to the box next to the coachman and tells him where to go.

It's a foggy, overcast day, not at all summery. Valtraute childishly presses her face to the window pane and stares, stares. There are the big roofs that, at night, reminded her of the backs of slumbering beasts in a yard. The daylight is harshly revealing; green moss grows over the sparser spots in the thatch, while other spots reveal ragged holes. Grass is slowly swallowing the buildings, and nettles grow freely in the courtyard.

Valtraute wants to get out of the carriage. The footman helps her down the small carriage steps, and stays close to her just in case. She doesn't hear the lowing of livestock, or the barking of dogs. It feels as if the place is deserted. But an old man comes out of the main house, dressed in an ambiguous military uniform. He has a long white beard and long white hair.

Valtraute recognises him immediately. Not by appearance, but by his movements, which are stilted, most likely from some injury.

'A-a-ah, you, madame, came after all,' the old man says. 'My lord always said that you'd be back. You forgot your comb last time. Wait here, I'll fetch it. But I'm not as quick as I used to be.'

When he returns and Valtraute sees the comb – it truly is her comb! *Lieber Gott!* – she can no longer hold back the tears.

'There's no one else here,' the old man sniffles as well. 'The young master Bierns followed his father's steps into the military. The relatives are all dead, the household petered out. Löwenwolde won't let us hire farmhands from the serfs. When I drop, the young master Ulste will likely have the land taken away from him. We're probably a thorn in Löwenwolde's side.'

'Where's the captain?' Valtraute is startled by her own question.

The old man gestures in the direction of the lake.

'The cemetery. Several years already. Directly by the main gate and to the right.'

After a moment he adds.

'After the last tour of Turkey he managed to come home to see his grandson. By the look of it, he was in good shape; but the pastor said that the man he gave communion to was only half there. Imagine that.'

The old man says these last words in Latvian.

XXV

It seemed that Jānis was trying extra hard to make sure he didn't have a minute of free time. He ripped out anything from his life that could remind him of Guna. Once I half-forcefully dragged him along to the cinema to see a legendary Marlene Dietrich and Emil Jannings film. So-called 'trophy films' breathed new life into the ideological Soviet productions. At one point I noticed Jānis was sitting in the dark with his eyes closed, not even looking at the screen. Halfway through the film he got up and left.

The loss was tangible; however, the hours and days rained down and could be divided into work, study and sleep. At work, he was transferred from the drawing room to the planning group. In terms of technology, the Cold War manifested itself as a race for the newest discoveries.

Life at the Manor continued without any big changes. Little things here and there did change, of course. The officers were able to wire the house for electricity. Then half a company of soldiers with shovels worked to dig a long ditch, saying they were going to install utility pipes. That never happened, though. With time the trench was neglected and filled back up.

You could already buy stuff at the shops, if you had the money. Our wallets were usually empty. My income was limited to my scholarship. The only real wage-earner was Jānis. Aunt Alma's gardening let us have as much in the way of potatoes, rutabaga, carrots and cabbage as we wanted.

Then the wardrobe troubles started. Grandfather proudly continued to wear his riding coat and robe. Aunt Alma borrowed a few things from Johanna's collection and turned a blanket into a coat. At the Zvirgzdu Island flea market, a retired alcoholic major gave me a good deal on an American army windcheater and a natural-silk parachute, both good fabrics for shirts. Jānis had the hardest time. The little boy had grown up into a short, yet adult person. He would need to buy everything new. But he was saved by the thrifty idea of making use of the black pelerine capes. Luckily, the tailor – who had in earlier years served Grandfather and claimed to have, in his time, sewn uniforms for General Balodis, the opera singer Chaliapin and the king of Albania, Ahmet Zogu – was fond of rutabaga.

Jānis looked as ceremonious as a Baptist minister in his black suit and jacket. His darker, Vadmala complexion and his glossy black hair, black eyebrows, black lashes and black spectacle frames created an ensemble that was diminished neither by his brown shoes with their rubber soles made from car tyres, nor by the blue shirt he always wore – he'd wash the shirt one night a week so it would be dry by morning.

Jānis and I had our own room, but for some reason we'd always go to Grandfather's desk to study. Even if he wasn't working that night and lay sputtering and muttering on the creaky leather sofa, reading old newspapers by the light of the kerosene lamp fittings, now fed with electricity but still casting their circles of light as if we lived in three separate worlds. We both were and weren't together. We were unified at those times when someone had a question or something to say. Grandfather and Jānis talked most often. Their roles had changed. Now Grandfather asked questions and Jānis gave him answers. For example, Grandfather was shocked by Jānis's statement that electronic calculators had helped the Americans win the war.

'Does that mean semiconductor researchers are to be placed on the same level as the physicists who introduced the world to the atom?'

'No!' Jānis replied as quickly as a fish leaping out of the water. 'Our industry is a step towards artificial intelligence. The important question is what kind of person is more dangerous to others – one with little or one with a powerful intellect?'

'What's dangerous is a person without a conscience.'

'Well, then, there will be order. Artificial intelligence will be given a conscience chip.'

'And they'll take that chip out, or not even install it at all!' Grandfather's voice was furious and confident. He pulled himself up to a sitting position, which was a sure sign that the conversation was far from over.

'It doesn't matter,' Jānis answered flatly, taking his head in his hands like an athlete holding a basketball. 'The history of humanity is one big surrender to progress. My definition is this: the evolution of mankind depends on its ability to adapt to its own inventions.'

'A-ha! Well said!'

'Semiconductors will make it possible to manufacture prosthetic limbs. The internal combustion engine advanced mankind with the automobile and the aeroplane. Man will advance himself, starting with the head.'

'How do you know that?'

'The number of nerve cells in the brain is massive, but limited. We'll be able to increase the power of an artificial brain as needed. Next to a person with an extra head, modern-day *Homo sapiens* will look like a fly next to a genius.'

'Fine, fine, but would God have placed man – created in His image and likeness – on earth with a temporary head? Let him finish his own work! You stay out of it!'

Arguments like this sometimes became quite heated. But somewhere in the wrinkles and creases of Grandfather's pensively drawn forehead there still hid a sly smile, and Jānis would preface even the wildest opinions with the words 'dear Grandfather'.

On Sundays – Jānis one week, me the next – we'd drive to the flea market to sell something: candlesticks, pall-bearers' caps, stable equipment.

The flea market had migrated from the Red Spīķeri neighbourhood to Zvirgzdu Island, which was connected to the city by a single narrow wooden bridge. For years, Zvirgzdu Island was the most curious place in Riga. Poverty combined with the magic of objects, the practical with the theatrical, desire and instinct. The items in circulation here had been sifted out from the receding floodwaters of political change; objects that had wound up in new hands by accident, and had become useless. Or – the opposite – many people were selling family relics just to make a little bit of money. People sold trinkets that were pure junk, and rubbish heaps hid real, God-given gifts for some lucky scavengers. Rain or shine, icy wind or sweltering sun, Zvirgzdu Island bustled and eddied. Beggars sang, thugs played cards, gypsy women told fortunes, thieves picked your pockets clean. Gramophones cranked out schlager music, street-organs trilled, caged birds twittered, dogs barked, chickens clucked in baskets. The smells of mothballs, mould, fried *ponchiki*, vodka, cheap aftershave, sweat and piss.

One Sunday evening Jānis told me about a girl at Zvirgzdu Island who was selling a rock that poisoned cockroaches. She'd lost her entire family to the war; she had survived because when the bomb landed she'd been taking a bath. She'd spent several days buried under the rubble, lying in that enamel coffin. Since her rebirth she saw the world at times in black and white, and at times in full colour.

'Today I was the colour of a champagne bottle. Last time I was black and white, and Liene said I was black with white shadows.'

Survivors of shipwrecks probably don't talk about sunsets over the sea. Jānis had been living as if he had deleted women from his worldview, and now, finally, some piece of skirt had caught his eye.

On my day at the flea market, I laid my wares out on the ground and started to look around for the cockroach killer.

'Poisonous pyroxylin,' she walked past and offered. 'Just draw a line along where the cockroaches walk, and they're goners.'

'Does it really work?'

'Try it yourself.'

There was an aura of dishevelment and carelessness about her that gave her face and body the appearance of being observed through dirty glass. A blue-grey quilted jacket, wide, square cotton trousers. Short hair, like a boy. Her big jockey cap made her look like a drooping mushroom. Later, I learned that the hat was a wallet, with a pocket sewn in for banknotes.

The girl understood that I wasn't going to buy the cockroach rock and moved on. But after a while she came back.

'Are you Jānis's brother?'

'You think so?'

'Last Sunday Jānis was trying to sell that candlestick.'

Her eyes seemed unusual. Wide and very light. As if they didn't have pupils.

'We could use some sun! Everyone's closed in, grumpy, they're not buying anything. I lied to you about the pyroxylin. It's just regular sulphur.'

'You trick people?'

'What I actually sell is the belief that cockroaches can be exterminated. Then people develop the desire to do so.'

'You think?'

'I know. Wishing is the important part. And then it comes true.'

'Okay, let's wish together – shine, sun...'

I waited for her to smile, but she didn't.

'You've got a weak act,' she said.

On Sunday nights I'd ask what Liene was up to and what phase she was in at the time – colourful or black and white. When I went to Zvirgzdu Island myself, I'd always try to run into the cockroach killer and chat with her. It became a little game, in which I included Jānis. But it sucked me in and carried me away like a whirlpool. When we exchanged new information about what we'd learned from Liene, we never came any closer to a tangible answer, just fed each other with new questions that stimulated our curiosity and begged for an explanation. You could even say Liene was not unlike a modern TV show.

For example, she knew some tricks. She'd walk up to someone and make kopeks fall from their nose, the coins jingling as they landed in a glass jar. She could also materialise an ice cream from the pocket of the first person who walked by. When asked where she'd learned that, Liene smiled and answered: 'Pickpockets.'

'Pickpockets?'

'There's little difference between a pickpocket and a magician. And if you've also got some piano skills...'

That was something new. Jānis said Liene struck him as being incredibly non-musical. A week later he'd changed his mind.

'Turns out she knows how to play the piano! And can you guess how? From her father! He worked at the conservatoire!'

We weren't able to learn from what Liene told us how she had ended up alone in the world. We heard about her godmother Hortenzija, and her relative who lived in the Mežaparks neighbourhood in the 'Villa Africa', where escaped birds and animals from the zoo sometimes wandered on to the property. But it seemed as if Liene lived a vagabond's life.

Even that assumption was turned upside down. Liene worked as a stoker in some big building. In the post-war years, people living in statelier buildings kept themselves going with their own heating systems, and stokers were important people. Liene had taken over for Krūmiņš, a poet, guitarist and songwriter; he'd run into trouble with the government institutions and had had to move to a psychiatric hospital.

'What kind of job is that for a girl?' The question wasn't really a question; in my mind, stokers were right in line next to water-heaters, blacksmiths and knife-grinders.

'Liene's fine. She can shovel coal when she wants. Yes, the pay isn't great, but her summer holiday is longer than what teachers get and she gets an employee's apartment in the half-basement. The poet had even installed a shower...'

Jānis explained this in great detail. Such a vivid picture can't be drawn from secondhand information alone. He had definitely been there and seen everything.

For a while Jānis didn't go to the flea market. I was surprised that he didn't ask anything about Liene, either. But in the end it was understandable – it was a short-lived curiosity, like finding a strange bird's egg in the forest or an odd seashell on the beach. I felt partially responsible. The game probably wouldn't have started without my interference – a researcher's game with a girl who sees the world through mystical tones of emotion.

But life likes to deal hands that are unexpected.

Markets are magnets for degenerates and psychopaths. Latvia was hit by a tsunami of immigrants that brought lost souls and bandits from all over. Just as Hawaii was plagued by syphilis, against which the locals didn't have any psychological or biological defences, Riga was overcome with an unfamiliar criminal culture, which the conditions of war had supplemented with a new crop of death squads. Enveloped in vodka fumes, with medals and military decorations on their lice-ridden shirts, invalids stamping the mud with their crutches, Zvirgzdu Island displayed an exhibitionistic shamelessness. An accidental exchange of words would often end with a knife to the stomach. An inattentive, pretty woman wearing earrings easily risked losing her jewellery, not to mention her ears.

Towards evening the crowd thinned out, but the alcohol infused the atmosphere to the point of ignition. A respectable-looking woman approached Jānis and wanted to buy Aunt Alma's silver soup ladle from him. A curious crowd gathered around her. A man grabbed the woman from behind around the waist and lifted her off the ground in jest, while another man tore off her shoes and tossed them away.

Just another typical incident on Zvirgzdu Island. A brief upset, a reason to sigh in relief when the victim, thank God, wasn't you. A show to tickle your nerves. (There weren't any TV shows, after all!) A whistle from an onlooker, a shout or a re-enactment for a neighbour. It was hopeless, dangerous, to step in and get involved. At least as dangerous as trying to get a link of sausages away from a pack of wild dogs.

But Jānis was cut from a different cloth. He described the scene as follows: 'I didn't know that rage could escalate before your brain has time to react properly. I ran after the thief and shouted: "Drop it or I'll shoot! Drop it or I'll shoot!"

'The thief ran, weaving through the crowd of frightened bystanders as if he were skirting trees. As I ran after him, I felt this terrible loneliness. I knew I was completely and utterly alone. I'd never felt that alone before. The thief ran out of breath when we reached the bridge and he stopped. When he saw I didn't have a gun, he was surprised and incredibly angry.

'"What d'you want?" he shouted, shaking with fury.

'"Drop it! Drop it right there!"

'"You bastard, you goddamned Jap! I showered the likes of you in the face with an automatic in the Kurils! You recognise this medal? I shed blood gunning down your brothers! Bastard! The do-gooder wants a beating! You think we won't do it?"

'A few of his buddies had caught up with us. Another group was headed our way. But I was alone. Even when they threw me over the rail and I fell into the Daugava. I hurtled towards the brownish-yellow floodwater and chunks of ice that were more black than white, covered with all the flotsam collected over the course of the winter.

'When I broke through the surface I suddenly realised that I wasn't alone any more. Liene had run out on to the bridge. She was already climbing over the railing and jumped into the water after me.'

That was Jānis's story.

Liene was in hospital for a month, Jānis a bit longer. Soon afterwards they were married.

XXVI

Like an aeroplane, time surfaces above our heads from some unknown distance, flies over us and disappears again on the horizon. When you sit down to eat breakfast, evening seems as if it's oceans and oceans away, on the other side of the world. The years you've already lived are flattened into a plane, spread out like drawings pinned to the wall. In memories, everything is right here, close by.

Today, I can recall every scene from Jānis and Liene's life.

After they'd had their passports stamped at the civil registry office, Grandfather married them at the Manor. As he said himself – for real. He still had a marine licence for the right to cabotage, issued by Latvia's provisional government in 1919 for the trip across the gulf to Ainaži. According to old custom, captains have the right to wed couples, and Grandfather held his rights in high regard.

'...We were expecting our first child, which died not long after being born.'

Before the war, we'd stocked up on office ledgers from Kukurs for the business's bookkeeping; the ledgers had hard, black covers and good paper. Liene had started writing letters in one of the ledgers, without an addressee, and brought them to me once to insert commas in the right places. I still have that thick ledger. The past continues to breathe in her writings.

'...Why was the world created in colour if the majority of living things can't see those colours? It turns out bees, ladybirds and other flying insects can only sense the information contained in colours. My rattled brain has clearly acquired something from bees or ladybirds. I read Jānis the first time we met, without having exchanged a single word with him. It would have happened exactly the same way in total darkness, because the senses in play were beyond the concepts of *like* or *hate*, *smart* or *dumb*, *beautiful* or *ugly*. People think they make decisions unexpectedly, freely, but it's actually more like they've gone to a shop with a shopping list already in mind. Then it's just a matter of whether you do or don't find what you need. My list had Jānis on it, and I found him.

'...Grandma was a strange woman. Her dark eyes seemed to crackle like sparklers. She'd talk to flowers, chickens, birds, and they understood her. One year on my birthday she showed up empty-handed. I felt cheated. There were a lot of guests, and each of them had brought a present. "Grandma, didn't you bring me a present?" I asked. She looked at me with those dark, sparking eyes and said: "Your gift is my face." I thought she was joking, saying the first thing that came to mind so she wouldn't have to admit she'd forgotten to get me a present.

'...Looking in the mirror with each year that passes, I am more and more convinced that my grandmother was telling the truth. I have her face. And when I grow old, I'll probably also have her wrinkles. And even now I'm happy to talk to flowers, chickens and birds.'

The birth of their first child, a daughter they named Irbe, and her death a few months later, was something Liene wrote about in the ledger only years afterwards. It wasn't until she and Jānis had a son, Namejs, and a daughter, Zīle, that she finally had the courage to resume her writing where she'd left off.

'...The air that fills a soap bubble has been here for millions of years and will always be here, even after the bubble bursts. Being born means acquiring new substance. Being born means falling into a lake like a raindrop and turning into a growing ripple. The world is like the surface of a lake during the rain, full of larger and smaller ripples. One ripple fades out sooner, another later. But the rain keeps falling, keeps raining, and new ripples take the place of the old ones, growing, touching, flowing.

'...The doctor held up Irbīte, still unbathed, slick, shiny, and said: "What a beautiful little lady." I saw the round little face, scrunched up in a cry, and thought – it's the face of the moon. Irbīte broke from my surging girth like a bloodied moon from a mass of clouds on a stormy night. I was like a cloud, torn open by the moon. The glowing white walls rocked and waved. The round, multiple light fixture hung over me, luminous pressure, pain ripped me to pieces and, when I felt as if I had no more strength left and I wanted to die, she slid out calmly, easily, unstoppably. My scream caught in my throat, as if I were choking. I don't remember the rest, just that sliding, surprising movement which, in relation to the time that had passed, felt as if it lasted forever.

'...At the cemetery where we buried Irbīte, she slid once more. But in reverse. Grandfather and Jānis slowly, slowly unwound the towels to lower the little casket. The grave was like the wide-open belly of death, taking back what had come into the world through me one night two months before.

'...Dying. Is it easy or difficult? If it is difficult, that hasn't stopped anyone from doing it. Dying can't be easier than being born. Why should going out through those gates be any harder than coming in through them? A person is made to live, but with the knowledge that death is inevitable. A plane, for instance, has wings, but it also has wheels. A person isn't built for tasks unsuitable to them. It's our job to die. Just like it's our job to live.

'...Jānis isn't home tonight, and I can't sleep. Moonlight filters into the corner of the room like a silver, glowing rat. Irbīte is standing by the door frame and watching me, as if she's waiting for me to draw a line to show how tall she's grown. I know these are waking dreams, but what does that change? Shakespeare's tombstone supposedly reads: "We are such stuff as dreams are made on."'

Liene raised their children in her own fashion. They'd all pile into the car and just take off – towards Piebalga or Valmiera, or Liepāja. They'd stop to eat in some roadside restaurant, cool the engine with water at a petrol station and drive on. Back then, they could afford a few extravagances. Jānis was co-creator of an invention that, as Liene saw it, overlapped with reality in only one aspect; that is, in salary.

'...We parked the car at the edge of the forest and walked further on foot. We found a boat by the lake, and oars hidden in the bushes. The dark water smelled of autumn. A lake is actually just a kind of garden – with its periods of emptiness, blossoming, ripening and coming in. It would be odd if a lake in autumn smelled just like a lake in spring. After living in Riga, my sense of smell grew dull and one-sided. Exhaust fumes smell the same in March as in May, as in August. Your nose only truly enjoys itself in the countryside.'

It's hard to say whether Liene continued to see colours differently from the rest of us. One entry touched on the topic in passing.

'...Autumn is light. The once thick, dark canopies of leaves now glow thinly like a transparent lampshade. The edge of the forest by the horizon is the lightest – birches, maples and lindens decorate it like golden rivets. The wind floats the leaves in October waters and plasters the black roads with them like ridged autumn postage stamps. At night, when we returned to the city, the full moon was shining brightly.

'... "Is the moon gone when we can't see it?" Namejs asked.

'... "No, why would it be? It's there."

'...What a childish question and what a childish answer! What does *there* mean, what does *gone* mean?...'

Jānis's career wasn't meant to develop gradually. In order to have the right to work on the kind of research where each blueprint was stamped in a corner with the words 'Top Secret' in Russian, one had to acquire the highest level of clearance and complete a form of almost one hundred questions. Having noticed that the form didn't permit the use of dashes or other symbols, but required everything be written out in full, Jānis got to the 'Father, grandfather, great-grandfather and other paternal relatives' section and wrote that his father had died abroad, he didn't know his paternal grandfather, and had absolutely no idea who his great-grandfather was. And that was enough for the up-and-coming industrial enthusiast to be wrapped up in their tentacles. Jānis was summoned to the factory's head office, where he met with a high-ranking official from a higher-ranking institution who had made the trip from Moscow specifically to speak with him.

'Fine, let's assume that your maternal grandfather raised you from the age of twelve onwards. But that doesn't mean anything,' the official said. 'Every person is made up of two parts – his mother's and his father's. Both of these parts exist objectively, whether we know it or not, whether we want to admit it or not. But because they exist, we have to take them into account. Fine, your father is dead, but somewhere out in Kyushu or Kawasaki he may have brothers or sisters. They are your blood relatives. We don't have the right to give the all-clear to a person who knows absolutely nothing about one side of his family. Let me be frank – it's a dangerous uncertainty! It could still prove questionable if it were a matter of quarters or eighths. But we're talking a whole half! A person is a scale with two trays. A person has two eyes, two hands, two feet, two lungs, two kidneys, two sides of the brain ... Do you think this is all a joke?'

The conversation was drawn out. In the end, the high-ranking official from the high-ranking institution said the following: 'Here, in Riga, you have no hope of continuing in the position you currently hold. There are many circumstances against it. However, approached differently, they're circumstances that could end up favourably.'

'What do you mean?'

'Have you ever looked in a mirror? You could work as your own boss in Tokyo, Yokohama, Kyoto. You probably know that until 1854 foreigners who wandered into Japan were given the death sentence.'

Jānis replied that, while one half of him truly was Japanese, the other half was still Latvian. The trouble, apparently, was that the Latvian half was at the bottom. His mind might consider moving to Japan, but his feet wouldn't follow.

He didn't wind up unemployed, however. The university offered him a position as a lecturer.

...On Sundays after Aunt Alma and Liene had cleared the table after lunch, the children would run outside to enjoy the space they missed while in the city; Grandfather would stretch out on the creaky old leather sofa, and Jānis would take his usual place on the top step of the library ladder. I took my usual spot, too – the chair we at the Manor called the Ulste Chair. It's the only piece of furniture Grandfather brought with him when he came to Riga.

'I think there's a mistake in the Bible,' Grandfather says. 'God's wisdom is revealed through the miracle of creation. Of course, when He created man, horses, dogs, cats and so on, God displayed great creativity and artistic inspiration. But all that is trivial compared to his ability to order his creations into specific relationships so they serve each other and are useful.'

'Why did you list only animals?' Jānis isn't pleased. He takes off his glasses and covers his eyes with his hand. 'In the chain of connectedness, there's room for both the puffball in the forest and the star in the sky.

Even stars have a lifetime, with signs of youth, their prime, and ageing. Lifelessness can be born, and lifelessness can die.'

'Lately, I haven't spent a lot of time looking at the sky with my binoculars,' Grandfather laughs. 'There are these black holes that have opened up and they're pulling everything into themselves, even their own appearance.'

'We determine what's living and what's not like clodhoppers,' Jānis says, not letting up. 'Poke it with a stick – if it runs, it's alive! If it does nothing – it's not alive! Biomedicine and virtual humanoids have no use for old concepts. Where does it say that the meaning of life is to eat and excrete? Life is possible even on a computer screen. It's entirely possible that atoms are cosmic bodies in a system with totally different parameters.'

Who knows if Jānis is expecting answers to his questions, but he pauses for a bit, which is enough for me to give him a sign.

'Pssst!'

Jānis opens his eyes, puts on his glasses, looks at me.

'Pssst!' I wave my hand at him. 'Talk quieter, Grandfather's sleeping.'

And that's how I remember Grandfather. Sleeping on the sofa, his features relaxed, his hands clasped on his chest. Jānis and I keep talking. But I watch Grandfather and I am so tempted to throw something on the ground or to move my chair to wake him up. To make sure he's only asleep.

'Is that all?' Grandfather suddenly sits upright.

I breathe.

'You weren't even listening,' Jānis says.

'Why d'you think that?'

'You were snoring.'

'Not true. I sleep as silently as a fish in water. I heard everything. Ever since I found out that God made man in His own likeness, I feel like his relative. And now you're telling me I'm a speck of dust in the corner of some numbered galaxy.'

'It takes courage to know the truth.'

'No! Don't say things like that to me! I'd rather be snoring.'

In academic circles, Jānis is dubbed the 'alternative professor'. Move however you like, but it's impossible to get anywhere without running into him. Some think he's a lunatic visionary, others think he belongs to the virtual reality avant-garde, others still think he's involved with an emissary preparing a revolution against Kant's philosophy. More precisely, against Kant's thesis that the material and spiritual worlds exist apart from one another. I've heard a few of Jānis's lectures on the layers of reality – the seventh layer is an absolute void that contains nothing but creates everything. The world has been turned on its head on more than one occasion, so why couldn't it happen again now that the world is on the cusp of its third millennium? It's been a hundred years since Einstein; something new had to happen.

Grandfather died before his seventy-eighth birthday. He never complained about his health, at most growled about how his heart 'was plodding along heavily'. He kept a bottle of 'Zelenin' drops on a shelf in the kitchen. The familiar smell signalled the times when Grandfather didn't feel well. But that happened rarely and Grandfather had a ready excuse: 'It's worth living if you get to taste life, not because you're afraid of death.'

The night before he had been reading journals from before the war. The next morning we found him with his glasses still on his nose. His arm had slumped over the edge of the sofa, but the copy of *Repose* lay across his face.

The catafalque, which in its time had carried at least three famous poets, an archbishop, a millionaire, two opera soloists and four ministers, was in the carriage house as if waiting for something, covered by a thick layer of dust. We were able to borrow horses from a *kolkhoz* on the outskirts of town. Liene washed and mended the black mourning coverlet. Several of Jānis's students wanted to be pall-bearers, but the pelerine cloaks had been reused and we could only find two black, eighteenth-century, crescent-shaped hats.

Funeral processions hadn't become entirely foreign to the public at large, and the older Rigans took their hats off to honour the deceased. A sizeable group of mourners followed behind Jēkabs Ulste. Jānis and I sat on the box. In tailcoats, and with top hats on our heads. I couldn't shake off the feeling that Grandfather was watching us to make sure we were doing everything properly. I felt his presence all the time, just as I feel his presence as I'm writing these words. My view extended over everything Grandfather had seen, his words flowed under mine, his thoughts stood alongside mine.

...Liene passed away around five years ago. Grandfather is in the spirit world. The longer a person spends on earth, the closer they become to the group of friends they can now only meet in memories. Children live among the living. Middle-aged people live between the living and the dead.

Recently, some centenarian said: 'Now every day is like the Song Festival; I sit down and watch for hours as the parade goes by ... a parade of shadows.'

In just a few months it'll be the start of the twenty-first century. Latvia has regained its independence, but we're having a hard time adjusting to this unfamiliar state. The spirit of submission has been beaten into our backs and hearts. We've spent so long being bent right and left that standing on our own and standing up for our rights feels almost like a transgression. Our drive to serve has become second nature. We are one of Europe's oldest cultures and this continent's aborigines. The Baltic States – the last colony in Europe. The truth is shocking, and the 'real' Europeans mitigate their sense of guilt by making us out to be malicious barbarians. We're still pawns, easy to push around from one side to the other in a game of political interest.

It would seem logical for experience to steer mankind in the direction of reason, but the spirit of absurdity conjured by Edgar Allan Poe doesn't lie dormant. The wave of progress that washed forcefully on to the beach of civilisation receded quietly after a moment, its waters just as swift, stealthy and powerful as when it had arrived. Degeneracy, if well salaried, turns from a hateful evil into a daily source of income. Sodomites and necrophiliacs with flags of freedom in their hands search for the road back to Nero's Rome. People who have been pieced back together show up at every step: ex-communists who go mad at the slightest attempt to limit the greed of capital; the judicial Minotaurs with the faces of judges and the stomachs of criminals; half-women, half-panthers with fanged maws at both ends.

The nation lacks a stable upper body. Different countries are tested in different ways. Some with earthquakes, others with tsunamis and floods. Latvians are tested with a ribbon of freedom tied to the end of a string, that we have to catch again and again, and that we have yet to learn how to hold on to properly.

XXVII

In an abandoned villa on the outskirts of Montevideo, a man's bloodied corpse is found in a large trunk. The note pinned to his jacket explains in English that the man is a war criminal from Latvia, who was responsible for the death of thirty thousand Jews. Signed, 'Those who do not forget.'

The world's media broadcasts the murder widely, and Germany's Bundestag even decides to extend the statute of limitation on the prosecution of Nazi war criminals by five years. There are several ideas about the incident, but the investigation leads nowhere. When the press and broadcasters calm down, everything gradually fades into oblivion.

A while later, one of the avengers goes public under his assumed name, Anton Künzle, and publishes a book providing a deeper account of forgotten events: 'I had to get close to Satan,' the Avenger writes, 'to deceive an intelligent, guarded and deceitful enemy.'

The man called Satan is well armed, his home in São Paulo is surrounded by a high fence and guard dogs roam the yard. He deals in boat rentals on the picturesque lake and flies tourists over the city in a small seaplane.

One fine day, a respectable-looking businessman shows up at the lake. A bushy moustache under his nose, old-fashioned spectacles, a pocket-watch chain hanging below his round belly, his hair greased and combed over the bald spot on the top of his head like a lid on a box.

The visitor introduces himself as an Austrian businessman who wants to invest some capital in the South American tourist industry.

The businessman makes appearances in public places, chats with people idling about, hands out business cards, buys rounds of beer. He writes cheques for larger expenses: a respectable person, he has a bank account.

One day he walks to the boat rental dock and starts a conversation with the woman working at the register. The Pilot's daughter-in-law is a German from Dresden. She finds her father-in-law's wariness silly. But it's nice to meet someone abroad who is basically a fellow countryman and to get the chance to speak her native language.

'*Gnädige Herr*,' the woman opens up to him happily, 'where business is concerned, you should talk to that older gentleman over there.'

'Already from afar I could tell it was the Butcher of Riga,' the Avenger writes. 'He wasn't particularly friendly. I asked him to fly me over the city and he softened a bit. He was a fantastic pilot. When the flight was over, I turned the conversation back to tourism and investments. Then he unexpectedly invited me to join him for a drink on his boat. Our talk wandered to the war. He asked if I'd served. "Yes, on the Russian front," I responded. I folded back the edge of my shirt and showed him a deep scar I'd been left with after an operation at Beilinson hospital. He saw it and assumed I'd been a German soldier. Then he invited me to visit him at his home. I knew he'd taken the bait.'

The Pilot's house and its unkempt yard aren't much to look at. The exception is the host's rich collection of weapons and international medals and badges of honour from the days when he crossed entire continents, oceans and deserts, winning acclaim for his accomplishments in long-distance aviation. But the Pilot's next move is a surprise – he invites the businessman along to his banana plantation in the jungle. The Avenger accepts because he hopes the Pilot hasn't grown suspicious of being lured into a trap. The businessman expresses delight at the invitation, but first double-checks his pocket calendar. In truth, the Avenger is not in the least worried about the date. He's wondering what to do if, with the two men spending a longer time together, the Pilot should notice the German soldier's circumcised penis.

There do end up being a few tense moments in the wilderness, where they stay near a river in which crocodiles float like logs from a broken raft.

The Pilot suddenly whips out a revolver. 'That's it! It's over!' The Avenger's nerves fire rapidly, leaving his consciousness empty, as if overexposed. Frozen in fear, the Avenger saves himself merely by not doing anything that would give him away. The Pilot, as it turns out, wants to shoot at the crocodiles, to see if he's a good enough shot. He takes a few shots first, then tosses the gun to the Avenger.

Maybe this was the time to act? 'A bullet to the head, a bullet to the heart and be back in Europe before they even find his body. I also had the chance to kill Satan at the plantation. We were together for an entire day and spent the night in a shack. But it was important to stick to the plan, which included a real trial, the delivery of a verdict, and then the administration of said verdict.'

The trip to the jungle is the point at which the Pilot's attitude to the businessman changes. Now they meet at restaurants, drive around, research locations for a tourist centre. They agree to establish the business not in Brazil but in Uruguay, where the atmosphere is supposed to be more prosperous.

The businessman heads for Montevideo first. The Pilot arrives later. It's the first time he has left Brazil, the country whose government has promised to protect him. The Pilot knows he's exposing himself to danger, but he is driven by his adventurous spirit. This turn of events in his tediously dull life is a breath of fresh air and makes him feel young again. Of course, he brings his gun with him. The uncomfortable pressure of the holster against his ribs during the flight is like a safety belt, a support for his nerves, which are rattling even him, an experienced risk-taker. The Pilot and the Avenger look for a place to set up, collect information, meet with intermediaries.

A few days later they go their separate ways, intending to meet again a month later. The businessman flies to Paris, where further plans of action are developed. A month later he returns to Montevideo on the scheduled date with a four-man team.

When the Pilot arrives for their company's unveiling, the Avenger meets him at Montevideo airport. The air around the Boeing shimmers. The Pilot is still wearing his coat, despite the swelter. Around the armpit of his coat, bulked up by the revolver, is a growing sweat stain.

'Welcome back!'

'Good to see you!'

Office space has been found in an old villa not far from the city centre.

'The building itself, of course, isn't much, but we'll move when we find a better one,' the Avenger says as they pull up to the villa.

They go up the gravel path to the door. The Avenger turns the key and goes in first, the Pilot follows. He stops for a moment to let his eyes adjust to the semi-darkness. The Avenger pushes the door closed with his foot. The four other men emerge from their hiding places and jump the Pilot. They're dressed only in their underwear. Their clothes are neatly folded and stacked on the table.

Despite being outnumbered, the Pilot manages to break free and grab the doorknob. His attackers hold the door shut with their combined weight.

The doorknob comes off in the Pilot's hand.

'It wasn't easy to subdue him. He thrashed about like an injured animal, tried to pull out his gun. "*Laßt mich sprechen!*" he shouted. "*Laßt mich sprechen!*"'

One of the men hits the Pilot across the head with a bricklayer's hammer. There's blood. Someone steps on the Pilot's glasses, which have fallen to the floor. The Pilot is holding his gun. The man standing closest to the barrel can't take it any more. He pulls out his gun, too, puts it to the Pilot's head, and shoots.

The room is filled with the sound of five men breathing hard, as if after a mad dash. The youngest one is trembling so hard his teeth chatter.

After they hide the Pilot's body in the trunk, all five carefully wipe the room clean of their fingerprints, put their suits back on and leave the villa. A few hours later they're on a plane for Europe.

There was no trial. There was no verdict delivered, no administration of said verdict. Revenge has been satisfied and a man murdered.

In his memoir, the Avenger writes that the image of the execution haunted him for a long time after the fact. With time it got better, but he still believes he wasn't the right person for the job. 'I learned that your personality changes when you assume a new identity. I became someone else when under stress, I forgot about my fears and about all danger. For many years afterwards this thought worried me, and I went to university to study psychology in order to understand, even a little, what was happening in my soul. I can't say I succeeded.'

...In the morning I take Toms to school. A man passes us and mutters, maybe to us, maybe to himself, 'The day before yesterday they murdered seven people in my building, yesterday it was eleven.'

'The poor guy must be confused,' I try to explain to the boy.

'Why confused? He's been watching TV.'

Another time the boy asked: 'How many people did the fascists kill in the prisons and camps?'

'Who knows? Maybe six million, maybe seven.'

'And how many did the communists kill?'

'They say around twenty million. Why do you want to know?'

'Vaļera and Maksims call us fascists. They want to be communists – communists are the heroes in films.'

Since it's become clear to me that the Nuremberg trials didn't rid the world entirely of violence, I've become more interested in the change of consciousness that transforms *Homo sapiens* into a werewolf.

During the French Revolution, hadn't those people who wiped out the aristocracy as a class – drowned them, guillotined them, lynched them – once sat side by side with their victims in church, praying to God and repeating 'Thou shalt not kill'? In 1917 in Russia, hadn't the soldiers who hammered down their officers' shoulder straps with nails been side by side with them in the trenches, slurping cabbage and sharing lice? And those who released the poisonous gases in the concentration camps and those who had exited the crematoriums as black smoke, hadn't they gone to the same schools, sat side by side in the theatres and watched Schiller's plays, sung the words to Beethoven's 'Ode to Joy'?

The Avenger writes about the Pilot: 'An educated, intelligent person lived in peace and harmony with his Jewish neighbours and suddenly turned into the worst kind of monster, a mass murderer.'

Satan's name doesn't bring us any closer to the truth. As a myth, Satan symbolises the force of evil. The Pilot was a person with a biography and a personality. What turned him into Satan? And what manner of devil, Beelzebub, Belial, Lucifer or Diabolus? At what point does a person become responsible for a crime in which, one way or another, the majority of society was involved?

Is one person, in this case the Pilot, responsible for the murder of thirty thousand people? What do the words 'on whose conscience' mean? That he gave the order to kill these people? Or that he killed them with his own hands?

We know from the published articles that there were no documents found proving the Pilot's guilt. When the commander of the executioners, Arājs, was being tried in Nuremberg, he testified that the Pilot worked primarily in the ghetto transportation division. Primarily. That means, not exclusively. What did he do in addition to that?

Records indicate that, in the 1960s, the Pilot agreed to meet with his accusers face to face on Brazilian television; they never showed up, so the Pilot spoke alone.

He was an outstanding pilot, a journalist, a talented plane builder, air force officer. And adventurist. But his was an orbit that it was difficult to imagine as being connected to the corkscrew trajectory that characterises a professional killer.

A trajectory doesn't change on its own. Where did that forceful push come from? The Pilot had risked his own life to rescue and save one Jewish girl. Back then, few people did such things. The girl he saved stayed with the Pilot's family until they moved to Brazil, at which point she married a local Jew.

The perspective on years past is subject to change as much as a wind-sculpted desert. There are no signposts marking the truth. Whole stories are created from little pieces of information. Are they fact? Fiction?

...The Second World War started. The core of Latvia's air force consisted of Gloster Gladiator biplanes bought from Britain. They were soon to be replaced with the modern Hurricane and Spitfire fighters. The British ceased deliveries. The Latvians were left to do what they were already doing on a smaller scale – build the planes themselves. With support from the state, the experienced Pilot started constructing the C-6bis dive-bomber. The prototype was revealed to the committee towards the end of 1939. The pictures still exist; they show a distant relative of the German Stuka.

That was a normal orbit. The system of values broke down, perhaps, when Latvia was occupied by Russia. The commissars who arrived from Moscow took a liking to the plane. They asked the Pilot to continue working for the Soviet army. Everything in relation to the plane had to become invisible. Every action had to be coordinated with people who made sure no channel could develop between the visible and the invisible, between the existing and the non-existent. After the German invasion, the work-obsessed, fame-hungry Pilot dangled like a lobster over a pot of boiling water. He had been living without worry, taking his achievements and failures in his stride. Until the moment he was told: 'You're through, you were on their side!' And the side on which he had found himself, without even wanting to be there, could have proved the reason for a horrible death. But now another side had shown up, just as foreign as the first one, and this new side promised he'd be safe. He didn't have time to mull it over – things could go wrong at any moment; the water was boiling.

The risk-taker and adventurer had more than once felt the fingers of death pluck at his nerve strings, but he still had his masculine composure, of which he was secretly proud. This time he was pricked with the unfamiliar, unpleasant realisation that fear had gained the upper hand.

The separation of a unified whole into halves had also, apparently, happened to him. It was as if he were made of two people, or – more precisely – of an accused and a vindicated party. The accused party reminded him: you gave into fear, you're a coward, you're scum. The vindicated party argued: it's payback, an eye for an eye, tooth for a tooth.

The stagecoach of history clunks forwards along a beaten path, but it's always the same view whipping by. And Lenin Ulyanov, Hitler Schicklgruber, Stalin Dzhugashvili, Trotsky Bronstein and Rozenbergs Sgrebnezors all occupy the same seat ... Each of them has his arms wrapped tightly around himself to keep his separate pieces together. They all wanted retribution, they all wanted vengeance. They all tried to silence the voice of mankind.

What is mankind? *Homo sapiens* includes Saint Francis, Schweitzer of Lambaréné and Mother Teresa as well as Genghis Khan, the Marquis de Sade and Ilse Koch. You, me, we're beings that have no shortage of hidden strengths which, in certain situations, can bring our evil doppelgängers forth from the depths of our instincts.

In the twentieth century, civilisation saw the planet on a global scale. For the first time, the atrocities of mankind were made known to the entire world. If we tally up the number of human lives maliciously extinguished around the world over the course of the twentieth century, we would be appalled by the Himalaya-like mountains of victims. Once you comprehend how great a percentage of humanity is made of murderers, you'll shudder in terror. Behind every victim stands a person who turned his fellow man into a victim.

The clock inside the Eiffel Tower counts down the hours, minutes and seconds left until the third millennium since Jesus Christ, Pontius Pilate and Judas Iscariot. Maybe someone should build a clock that shows the number of victims mankind uses to mark each hour, minute and second on its way to the future.

In the Pilot's case, there was an opportunity for reason legally and fairly to judge the irrational. But that didn't happen. There was no court, no proof beyond reasonable doubt. What happened was the revenge-fuelled shedding of blood. A crime to punish a crime.

The battle between momentary truth and eternal truth continues. Power can't turn a fiction into fact. Victory and justice are not one and the same.

XXVIII

I frequently return to my memories of the Manor. At the final stop I jump down from the tram and walk along the quietly humming wall of the textile factory. The street isn't cobbled. Now and then they bring slag from the factory's furnaces and use it to fill the deeper potholes. In the winter the tightly packed snow would creak underfoot. An alley of linden trees starts a good distance before the Manor gates. The fat, centuries-old trunks are covered in grooved, cracked bark – the perfect material for fishing floats. From here you can't see how the open spaces go on for hundreds of kilometres, as far as the sea, but you can sense them on a lingering breeze.

The Manor reveals itself gradually as a tangible reality, with character and its own life story. For a very long time it was the only place where I spent my days, the backdrop for my first interactions with people, objects and emotions.

Each of us enters this world as if waking up in darkness. Once we make our way to a small light, we see faces and our immediate surroundings. As the light grows, other things come into our line of sight, things we can't yet reach, but are already observing.

I haven't been able to find out in which year the Manor was built. The eighteenth-century buildings were obviously a continuation of a much older ensemble that had burned down shortly before the end of the Great

Northern War. The Baroness always believed that its beginnings could be found in the time when Riga fought alongside the Order and Archbishop Stefans Grübe took the Daugavgrīva Fort and established a new order for city land.

Manors back then – forts were being replaced by manors – were economic enterprises. The answer to the riddle might be found in the saying from the old chronicle: 'The success of Riga's residents was ensured by the cavalry.' The infinite fields that spread out around the Manor were the ideal setting for raising horses. I believe Grandfather's idea to establish a 'business' in this exact location had been a bud, a root that had grown over the years. This direction of thought was also influenced by the Manor's unusually large stalls, which were only partly used to house the horses; Grandfather used the remainder of the space as the carriage house.

Oh, that mighty, all-encompassing kingdom of horses has disappeared into the past! Teams of horses, carriages and gigs ruled the roads instead of cars – even trams were pulled by horses! From the plough to the cannon, from the outhouse to the firemen's water pumps, there was a single driving force – horses. Everything was founded on the horse. And the horse carried everything on its back.

It's true, the magic words had already been spoken in my childhood and youth, and the changes started. But I don't think anyone could have imagined that the age-old division of roles would change so quickly and fundamentally. Not just Riga, but all of Europe, all of America, still depended on horses at the beginning of the twentieth century. You don't even have to look at the paintings of Pissarro or Manet to know this. You can stop at any of the grandest buildings on the largest boulevards in Paris and Rome, London and Vienna – every one has a gateway for carriages, standing like a noble monument to the era of the horse.

When the German army blitzed Poland and France at the beginning of the Second World War, the newspapers reported: 'This is what technology can do!' In the first days of July 1941, Jānis and I watched the deployment of German troops in Riga. Heavy Ardennes horses with feathered fetlocks and broad haunches pulled large wagons that had a handbrake next to the coachman's seat. An orchestra rode by on horseback. The drummer sat on a tall bay horse with timpani drums like large pots saddled on both sides; the man drummed, lifting his sticks high above his head.

About five thousand years ago people made an important discovery – the wheel. Over the years the skills of wheel manufacturers became remarkably refined. The hubs have to hold the spokes, and they mustn't break. The frames have to be perfectly round, shock-resistant and impervious to moisture. The spokes can't be thick, the rim can't fall apart. Thousands upon thousands of wheels are made every year. Big, small, cheap, expensive, ornate and simple. Wheels for carts for manure and carriages for monarchs.

That's all gone now. But I can still smell the acrid odour of steamed ash wood, when the rims of the wheels were soaked in a special bath before being moulded. I remember how sharply the sawdust flew when Mārtiņš hammered sockets for the spokes into the hollowed-out rims, and how he could tell kinds of timber apart by their scent: oak from ash, apple from pear, linden from black alder.

There was another wonder-tool in the odour- and steam-filled room that Mārtiņš looked after – a wringer for laundry. Of course you could find wringers almost anywhere, but ours, an old model from Germany, already seemed like a strange, old-fashioned object back then. Sheets, tablecloths and other larger items were wrapped around wooden rollers and rolled back and forth with a hand crank, under a box filled with stones. I had to carry the rollers and turn the crank. The smell of scalded timber mixes in my memory with the scent of clean laundry.

I'll never forget the day Grandfather first took me up to the attic of the Manor. We stepped into what looked like a giant, upside-down boat, pierced by the brickwork of the large bell-shaped chimney and intersected by complicated wooden constructions. In the windowless dusk, I could see that the tiled roof was cracked and porous.

'That's baroque,' Grandfather said, 'the high song of the carpenter's art, the battle with the weight of the material. Do you understand how heavy a clay tile floor like this is and how precisely sawed and hammered the wooden construction holding it all together has to be?'

I didn't understand. I listened to what Grandfather told me about the lead roofs of Venice, the natural slate of the Louvre, the copper-tin of the Jelgava Palace, which in more difficult times were replaced with good old straw; but I couldn't understand why the Manor's roof would have to be torn down and replaced with galvanised tin. No one nowadays has the means to do that and everything will end with the collapse of the rotten wood.

Grandfather's prediction came true. The roof determined the Manor's fate. Those were different times, times that allowed for such a complicated structure to support a roof.

When the starry nights twinkle brightly above me I remember the 'upside-down boat' of the Manor's roof and I am also overcome by a reverence towards the Great Architect and his skill in creating the world. I'm a newcomer who, tilting his head back, gazes upwards, sensing that the fate of this roof is also my fate. A roof that grows infinitely and expands, opening itself up to us through Ptolemy's celestial spheres, through the mathematical orbits of Copernicus, through Hawking's singularity – the last more relevant to our modern-day comprehension – and up to the hypotheses, still temporarily shrouded in mystery, about the super-torsion computer of the universe and the universal library of the cosmos.

October 1998 comes after a capricious summer that caused rural residents no shortage of headaches, and is reminiscent of a chaotic intermission on the stage when they're setting up for a new scene but curtain-up is delayed by some unforeseen situation. The American nation, which worshipped TV shows, was surprised to see its president acting as a hero not just on film, but also in real life. Studies carried out in space show El Niño's trajectory is still circling the earth and that new, unusual natural disasters are yet to come. The worldwide financial crisis was predicted. None of it seemed possible...

Of all the months, October is my least favourite. October rain isn't refreshing rain. It's rain that falls on the still-warm corpse of summer. In November and December the bare tree branches will sway in the wind like sterile, polished skeletons that are no longer frightening. In January and February the branches will once again flow with sap, starting up for the new buds and leaves; externally, they don't change, but your senses know it's happening.

I receive a phone call from a man who introduces himself as a visitor from Germany; he speaks Latvian well. I don't catch his surname. He says he's a doctor of history looking into his German roots in Latvia. Politely insistent, he asks to meet me. Of course, only if I don't have any objections.

I don't like these kinds of things; I'm used to spending my time moving forwards. I'm about to decline when the caller mentions the Manor. Yes, he's working on a catalogue of Riga's Balto-German architecture. Because it's no longer possible to photograph the Manor, would I happen to have a picture of it?

His comment changes the conversation. I'm intrigued. Look, he knows my background!

The hotel in downtown Riga has a Germanic feel to it and is bustling primarily with Germans. It smells of cigars and coffee. Like a homely monument to antiquity in a modern interior, a Biedermeier clock in the lobby strikes seven times. I'm on time, despite the rush-hour traffic.

I approach the reception desk and raise my hand in greeting, winded from the quick trip. I ask the name of the man staying in room 315. The receptionist looks at me with a professionally vapid smile, but then suddenly something in his face changes. He must recognise me. In a way it's understandable, if you've been milling restlessly around society for seventy years. But he greets me in German, and the end of his sentence has that same surname I'd heard over the phone. I don't catch it this time, either, unfortunately.

'*Guten Abend, Herr Brrrnnnenn ...*'

Turning nimbly, the man takes a key card from a shelf and hands it to me.

'*Guten Abend!*' I reply, and try to smile just as kindly, but don't take the key.

The receptionist's eyes size me up again.

'I'm supposed to meet with *Herr Brrrnnennn* ... If he hasn't arrived yet, I hope he will be here soon. Perhaps he's left a note for me?'

'Oh, my apologies,' the receptionist is surprised, very surprised. You could even say embarrassed.

There isn't time for an explanation; a gentleman my age flies in through the automatic door. His eyes dart from the Biedermeier clock to his wristwatch. Just like me, his grey hair is parted above the left ear, and he's wearing a black coat. Our noses even look the same – they stick out, sharp and straight like a whetstone.

'I must be late! Forgive me! I was in Pārdaugava and got stuck at the end of the bridge.'

As he extends his hand to shake mine, his left hand takes my elbow; he cocks his head to one side and studies my face. Like someone in an art gallery looking at a painting, or in a shop looking at a desired object.

'You know, you look just like you do in the pictures! Incredibly so!'

The receptionist once again reaches for the key card and hands it to the other gentleman.

'Thank you! Let's not go to the restaurant just yet. The writer and I will start from the bottom, with the foundations.'

The bar is in typical hotel style – comfortable, and with a contained cosiness. We sit in a niche with a plastic tree and armchairs that look as if they're made for the organist Fritz in the *Max and Moritz* illustrations. Except we're not wearing caps and we're not smoking a pipe that looks like a porcelain saxophone.

They bring us coffee. What the good doctor wants is unclear to me. I'll keep to the ancient warriors' principle – as long as I don't take advantage of his hospitality, I'm not a guest, and we have no obligation towards one another.

I place the photographs of the Manor from the Baroness's albums on the table. The doctor falls on them enthusiastically, but he tempers his excitement. This man of society who has the upper hand reveals himself to be a man with polite manners and a childishly deceptive naivety in his way of speaking and looking.

'It feels strange saying it, but Latvia is a lovely country. I'm truly happy that Riga grows more beautiful every year!'

'Why strange? I think the same.'

'No.' The doctor looks me in the eye, and his thin cheeks let his chin drop thoughtfully. 'It can't be compared. When a German says Latvia is a nice country, there's a subtext. History has created a complicated relationship. Last night I saw a play called *Riga*. A very complicated relationship!'

'Relationships are always complicated. The play you mention is a dramatisation. The novel was written almost immediately after the 1905 revolution. Revolutions have a characteristic in common with orgasms – your brain stops working during one.'

'A nice aphorism,' the doctor's eyes flash jovially, 'unfortunately also partially true. The essence of an orgasm is the tendency to overflow, whereas revolutions grow from the tendency to repress.'

'Regardless, in both cases reason follows after the fact. You, from what I understand, left Latvia after the Molotov–Ribbentrop Pact?'

'Sadly, yes...'

The doctor stirs his coffee with a spoon, as if trying to thicken the black liquid into a syrup. But the coffee does nothing, and the gentleman nods his head sadly. 'Yes, yes, yes, a big mistake. We shouldn't have done it.'

'You think so?'

'Without a doubt.'

'In which case you – most likely – wouldn't be sitting here. The majority of bones uncovered in Siberia next to those of Latvians were of Germans.'

'There were countless victims anyway. Bombings. The front. Prison. But you have to broaden the scope. Germany lost one of its most valuable diasporas. An important national accumulator. I've read that Latvianness is under threat in Latvia. Let's assume that the rumours are based on fact, I'm not going to argue. But, as strange as it sounds, Germanness is under threat, too. Germanness as it used to be in the Baltics, and how it could be in Latvia – you can't find that anywhere else in the world. At most in Germany. Yes, yes, yes...'

The doctor's eyes grow dreamy and hazy.

'We lived in the Āgenskalns neighbourhood and frequently crossed the Daugava by boat. At midsummer, or the *Līgo* holiday as you call it here, many passengers were wearing carnivalesque paper hats. Turkish turbans were particularly popular. Made of red crêpe paper decorated with black bows. It all seemed so playful ... That sudden, heightened oriental mentality all around ... I think back on it a lot these days, in Germany. Good Lord! In Latvia, in Riga, the ruckus was just plain fun...'

'But it's hard to compare Germany and Latvia,' I say. 'United Germany has once again become Europe's most influential power.'

Of course that's just a saying, but I purposely try to undo the stitching in this man's way of thinking.

'That depends!' The doctor leans in over the table. 'That depends. Sometimes, a thick blanket of snow melts faster than a light dusting in a ditch. "Giant gherkins, hollow centres." I learned that from the Baložu Street boys. They called me Gherkin, not Kurts. It didn't bother me.'

The doctor is thrown into contemplation. His expression reveals the habits of a professor.

'The true qualities of nations lie within their diasporas. Do you think the nation of Israel was built by the Jews of Palestine? The nation wound up with some powerful reserves. For example, their first prime minister, Golda

Meir, grew up in Daugavpils. Their first president, Weizmann, grew up in Russia. It's an objective regularity. Even modern-day Russia retains little of its Russianness. In Riga, Paris, New York, yes, you can still find some pristine material. It's left over from a nostalgic memory separated from reality.'

'Are you saying that England is no longer the real England and France not the real France?'

'England is coming around the slowest. They're still driving on the left side of the road. The French apparently didn't take note of that when they agreed to build the Channel Tunnel.'

'When I was a boy there was a joke: the last five men on earth to wear a crown on their heads will be the kings of hearts, diamonds, spades and clubs, and the king of England.'

'Jokes age, too, unfortunately. You already know – there are no English left in England. No, no, no. England is inhabited by the British of the United Kingdom.'

The good doctor is unable to hold back his curiosity any longer. Once again he turns to the photographs, studies them and asks questions. I can tell he knows a thing or two about architecture. Suddenly, with a theatrical gesture, he slaps his hand to his forehead.

'Listen, does the interior of a dining room remind you of anything?'

The hint in his words is appropriate to the moment. Our conversation has touched on things but hasn't finished anything. I don't object.

The windows of the top-storey restaurant open on to a view of the heart of the city centre, from Bastejkalns Park to the Opera. There aren't many guests – an older tourist couple with an arsenal of cameras and a video camera on the chairs next to them, and a visibly intoxicated group of business jackals. A broad, bearded pianist mans the piano, improvising popular melodies.

The doctor takes the ordering of dinner and drinks very seriously. Discussions about the types of wine, sauces and vegetable side dishes are drawn out. The city centre shines with bluish-white and yellowish lights behind the rain-spattered windows. The headlights of cars, buses and trams flow like lava from an invisible volcano. The trees along the canal bank appear like X-ray images against the fluorescent boulevard.

And right here, nearby, a building is burning. Quietly, calmly, to the piano's accompaniment. If the fire engine's ladder were turned towards the hotel, the Martian-like men could see right into our mouths; but the ladder is angled towards the burning attic, and the flames quenched by the water try to hide in the billowing black smoke. The fire engines come and then go. A traffic jam blocks the road below. Police in reflective jackets glow like little Santas taken out of their boxes, ready to be hung on the Christmas tree.

We drink wine. The doctor continues to study the photos of the Manor.

'You know, it may sound absurd, but' – his manicured finger taps a photo of the Manor taken from in front – 'I have a certain intimate connection to the Manor. Yes, yes, yes. We'd take the tram to the last stop to go skiing. There were wonderful, gently sloping hills nearby. We'd pass the Manor on the way, and the best way to get to the Ozolkalns Hills was to cut through the Manor park by a strange, warped tree with a heavenly scent. A very, very particular, beautiful fragrance. A few years ago I'd still wake up some nights thinking that that tree had to be somewhere nearby; I could smell that strange scent...'

The doctor looks embarrassed, even a little guilty. As if he's not sure whether what he's just said is relevant to the conversation.

'And now the smell is gone?'

The gentleman rearranges and again spreads out the photographs, but he stares fixedly out of the window.

'Everything has changed. Tall buildings everywhere, buses on every street...'

Isn't it strange, I thought, I've crossed back and forth through the Manor park thousands of times, but I have no memory of this fragrant tree. I can't forget the incense of Mārtiņš's workshop. I can't forget the scent of melting snow under the wind-ravaged black alder trees in the spring. How the large puddles drew me like magnets, until my feet were muddy and the legs of my trousers soaked. Frogs' eggs like transparent peas float in the flooded ditches, turning later into black tadpoles with little tails ... The French are right – two people sleeping in the same bed won't have the same dreams. Memories grow on their own.

The doctor and I have lived back and forth alongside one another. Do we come from the same world? Can we even talk about a concept like 'the world'? Even the very moment we're in means something different to each of us. To the doctor, to me, to the bearded pianist, to the tourist couple, to the close-cropped businessmen. To those whose building is on fire, and to those who have a candle burning on the table in front of them. To those whose glasses are half-empty, and to those whose glasses are half-full.

The fire has been extinguished. The Martian-like men are rolling their hoses back into coils. The piano is closed and the pianist has left. New guests have entered the restaurant.

The doctor thanks me profusely for the pictures and explains how he'll get them back to me after he has made copies of them. He hands me his business card with his German address, almost like some kind of collateral. We head downstairs. The receptionist takes the key card from the shelf and hands it to me.

'*Bitte schön, Herr Brrnnnennn...*'

I smile. The doctor laughs out loud and takes the card. The receptionist fidgets, incredibly embarrassed.

We say our goodbyes. The doctor shakes my hand with both of his, looks me in the eyes and says how the hours just flew by. Can he call me up again the next time he's in Riga? I say yes, why not, surprising myself a little.

'Well, then, until next time,' he says with a smile. One of his front teeth is slightly crooked.

I experience a sensation as if I were standing in front of the bathroom mirror. I know this crooked tooth very well. Jānis used to say, God didn't put your tooth in straight.

Once outside the hotel door I'm tempted to look and finally to see what his name is, this gentleman I've spent the evening with, who looks so much like me. I take the rigid card out of my pocket. The man's name is Kurts Baldūrs von Brīgen ... Von Brīgen ... Kurts Baldūrs.

On the way home I come up with a plot outline; all I have to do is sit down and write it.

XXIX

Papers and dust both have the tendency to accumulate. My wife says she can name three unions: the Soviet Union, the European Union, and the paper-dust union. It would be blasphemous to say anything negative about our flat on Suņu Boulevard. We get offers in the mail daily to sell the apartment, for all sorts of benefits in exchange, from a new flat in the peaceful suburbs to help with moving. We don't bring these flyers inside, but forward them directly to the rubbish chute. All the flats on our floor are privatised. But the stairwell itself isn't, nor the rubbish chute nor the roof. In other words, our private property glides freely among the chaos of privatisation. And fills steadily with papers, leaving less and less room to live.

The entire family has grown fond of the presence of paper in our home. 'We found the contract for some property called "Ulstes" signed by the baron of Burtnieki. You collect that kind of stuff.' – 'I don't have anywhere to put Aunt Alma's songbooks, I'll bring them for you.' – 'Would you be interested in some handwritten Moravian Church sermons? You can't just throw cultural property in the bin.'

Namejs brings piles of letters, newspaper clippings, minutes of meetings, drafts of articles. He gathers them, collects them, stacks them and brings them over 'until things clear up'. Things are always clearing up for Namejs. He goes through women like a president goes through Mercedes. Married, single, engaged. Then he breaks it off and is a bachelor once more. And starts looking for another bachelor pad, some hovel in which he can just barely turn around. And then, just as quickly, he'll find a new better half with luggage and clothes.

Looking through the papers Namejs has brought me, I find a rather recently written letter.

'Dear Doctor, Professor, let me begin by saying that the history of the world as it has been written up till now, the Holy Scripture and mythical literature inclusive, is fiction and delusion. Not a single author has weighed events by taking into consideration the impotence of men. Based on current research – as you probably well know – this affliction affects one quarter of the world's men and is progressing rapidly. The fact that the recently released sexual stimulator Viagra topped the list of most-requested prescription drugs indicates we're dealing with an underestimated phenomenon that, in retrospect, requires another look at history.

'Ancient Babylonian texts tell us it was only through cunning and great effort that Gilgamesh escaped the wrath of the goddess Ishtar for refusing to engage in carnal relations with her. Isn't it strange how, four thousand years later, men view the decision of poor Gilgamesh as a heroic act? But for some reason, a logical, entirely possible explanation such as impotence is either consciously or unconsciously ignored.

'In the same way, the Bible story of Potiphar's wife and Joseph is questionable in every respect. Let's consider the conditions. Dim candlelight, just the two of them. Potiphar's wife – a fortress with closed gates. Joseph, too, has already undressed. What happens next? Joseph suddenly pulls away from the gentle caresses and runs naked from the room. Please, just try and find a believable explanation! Impotence, pure and simple – impotence!

'The story behind the relationship between John the Baptist and Salome evades the truth even more. According to the official version, King Herod's stepdaughter's bloodlust isn't the least bit comprehensible. Everything falls into place if this event is explained realistically. Salome, upon hearing John the Baptist's heroic sermons, imagined him to be an all-powerful man and fell madly in love with him. But she was deceived. What could she want from this weakling, who had been pulled from the prison pit and before that had survived in the desert on dried crickets? John the Baptist, who was capable of entering so many people through the Holy Sprit, but incapable of entering Salome as a man. After this disappointment, Salome's bloodlust becomes understandable. A sexually aroused woman and impotence are two incompatible concepts. In nature, the males of several species of spider are only virile temporarily. And how does that end for them? The female eats them.

'I'm talking about a deceitful malady. I had spent ten years as a happily married man; we had a son and a daughter. One day I was sent on a business trip. A colleague and I decided to use the free time we had during the conference to go to an art museum housed in a medieval castle. We were the only ones there. After the Babylonian and Egyptian rooms came a section on Ancient Greece, with casts of classical sculptures. Having glanced quickly over the bright white horde of nudes, I was already heading towards the door to the Roman exhibits, when laughter suddenly filled the room. "What's so funny?" "Oh nothing," my colleague dismissed my question, but the seal had already been broken and he couldn't stop laughing even harder. "Just imagine what's going on here! Aphrodite Melainis is standing naked in front of Apollo, Poseidon, Hermes and all the rest, and they don't care either way! They're all still soft as pudding!"

'I came back home. In a moment to which memory and contemplation were ill suited, a moment that required action by affirming my love for my wife – whom I hadn't seen or felt in a week – those flaccid white sculptures swam before my eyes. And poof! Done! My stiff wand of manhood, my rope of flint, was shrivelled and dormant, hanging limp like a sleeping bat.

'The following night I was determined to erase the failure from my and my wife's memory. Hell, I'm a regular guy, not some castrated opera singer. It was as if I were watching myself from afar, and I had only one thought on my mind: am I at all like Apollo, or not? Am I like Hermes, or not? And the answer beat down the man in me – just like them! Just like them! Just like them!

'Half a year has gone by since then. My marriage is ruined. I only take comfort in the thought that impotence has been the worst plague of mankind since the beginning of time, and that there are millions of others in the world just like me. Maybe science will let us return to our lives and free us from the punishment we don't deserve. Wishing you success in your holy work and with the request for a house-call regarding the new medication...'

The text stops there. The sender's name and the end of the letter have been torn off. Of course, I could have said: not my sow, not my cornfield, not my problem. But the phrase 'one quarter of the world's men' sticks in my mind like a sliver. Could mankind really be threatened by a tidal wave of terror? Long, long ago apocalyptic disasters were described as the Great Flood, as pitch, hell-fire and brimstone. The arsenal of Providence is undoubtedly much larger. Does anyone know what truly hides behind the concept of 'the plague'? It cropped up and covered Europe with piles of corpses. A disgusting, fetid outcome. Impotence – that's a different matter! Agony on a bed of clean sheets.

When reading a newspaper, it doesn't take the eyes long to find a headline that normally wouldn't have caught their attention. Strange things happen here and there – men in their prime, regular men, on the whole respectable, polite members of society, will suddenly, as if bewitched (and here the clichéd phrase seems irreplaceable), crawl out of their skins and become someone completely different: bankers no longer know their multiplication tables, diplomats wind up in jail, sea captains start basket-weaving clubs, etc., etc., etc.

Take this one, for example.

'On the evening between Saturday and Sunday, Police Colonel of the Sovereign Republic of Latvia Staņislavs N. arrived at the residence of one academic X, produced his Soviet State Safety Committee captain's badge and, despite the protests of X, proceeded to search the apartment, during which time he appropriated a silver case with a golden monogram. Following the incident, a large and valuable collection of silver cigarette cases was found at the home of Colonel Staņislavs N. which – it was learned – he had acquired in searches during the period between 1978 and 1988. The colonel was unable to explain his actions at the home of the academic. The unfortunate incident had taken place after the colonel had been to see the considerably younger Solveiga M. It is suspected that Solveiga M. secretly slipped Staņislavs N. Viagra.'

Namejs has a fairly hectic job, one without specific working hours. The best place to find him is at the hospital, past the old *Jugendstil* doors, that some former patient, an artist in glasswork, decorated with a philosophical quote embedded in the stained glass: 'The preservation of movement means the preservation of life.' In conversation, Namejs explains the mentality of old philosophers like Hippocrates, Avicenna and Paracelsus in contemporary terms: mankind functions under the cinematic principle of flow.

The head nurse lets me into Namejs's office – the professor is in the operating room at the moment. The word 'office' is almost too big an adjective for this space. It's more like a shoebox. Nothing has changed since the first time I was here. A jumble of the practical and the aesthetic. Framed medical certificates on the walls. Flowers in vases year-round. Diplomas, awards, congratulations sent in the form of poems and pictures. Photographs and paintings received as gifts. Stacks of paper, X-ray printouts, medical texts in colourful covers. The only thing that told you anything about Namejs himself was a small statuette: a bronze spire resembling the steeple of Saint Peter's Church in Riga, the tip of which, instead of the famous weathercock, displayed a kidney stone with a kind of raised crest. It looked as if the statuette had been knocked over at some point. Only half of the crest was left. Now the kidney stone's similarity to the Saint Peter's weathercock was questionable. I suppose Namejs didn't think so; his imagination knows no bounds. As a young boy, for example, he liked to hang upside-down from the exercise bar and swing back and forth, so it was as if the sky and clouds and birds spread out below him, while the sand, the grass and his sister's legs flew above.

Namejs comes into the office. He's the complete opposite of his father – a real bear of a man, with a shaved head and a wide girth. His green surgeon's smock, linen trousers and wooden clogs on his bare feet make him look more like someone fresh out of the sauna, allowing his overheated body to cool off slowly on a bench. He even seems to smell of soap and sauna brooms soaked in hot water. This impression is enhanced by the relaxed manner in which he falls into his chair – his arms hang over the sides and his legs stretch out. But his dark eyes have already cut into me like the teeth of a saw pressing into timber.

'...Once, a long time ago, before your father came to Latvia, our grandfather taught me lessons through riddles. I remember one such lesson word for word: "So children come from seeds?" – "How else? Of course from seeds." – "And where is the seed sown?" – "In the furrow of life, dummy ..." Turns out that, after seventy years on this earth I still don't have a proper understanding of these things. Just think what hides behind that little word, *seed* – generations of our ancestors, a line of spiritual and physical characteristics, the modulation of appearances, biological restructurings. Can two olive-sized glands on the male body really collect and develop such magnificent information, such detailed strategies? If they can, then it's easy – the improvement of mankind has to start with a testicular transplant. The only thing that's unclear is why no one's thought of it until now. But if we're talking about this in earnest – it's all rubbish. Man is a more complicated mechanism. Hasn't your field proven that the miracle of birth itself isn't something tangible?'

Namejs listens, twisting his mouth this way and that as he usually does, as if he were in the middle of shaving his face.

'The idea of transplants is worth taking into consideration. For now all we do with those little onions is take them out, peel them and put them back in. Or remove one and leave the other. And it's fine. They can still have kids, and they still have their drive. Politicians might be interested in transplants. They always want more than they can handle.'

'Don't dodge the question! I'm asking which organ makes a person. Or more precisely – what determines what kind of person will be born? The part of the body that, according to general assumption, has the honour of creating man only participates in the process through secondary functions.'

'You're asking me, so I'll ask you. Which organ created your books? Man hasn't figured things out that far. And thank God, maybe! As soon as we understand something we want to break it down and put it back together any way we see fit. I'm completely content with mankind being an enigma.'

He laughs, and tosses the lighter he's been playing with on to the desk. He adds: 'An enigma with impeccable flow.'

We go on talking like this for a long while. After the events of the last days, I'm actually testing out the conversation between a doctor and a writer for my novel.

When Namejs has to go back to the operating theatre, we say our goodbyes. I'm convinced that my nephew will disappear from view for a longer period of time, like Halley's Comet. And he'll probably swing into view again once he's amassed yet another pile of papers he can't bring himself to throw away.

But that wasn't the case. We ran into each other at an event to honour employees of culture and the sciences. The handing out of diplomas and awards was topped off with champagne.

Events like these don't have chairs; everyone is standing, walking around, socialising, wandering.

Namejs and I, having spotted each other during the ceremony, come together in a familial molecule. We discover a common trait – both of us have a strong aversion to eating from a buffet. Even a fancy one. We exchanged a few words about this and that, until Namejs was approached by a slender man, who wasn't exactly old, but not exactly young, and who blushed bright red upon saying hello. Blushing is a rare phenomenon in Latvia in the last quarter of the twentieth century. Especially among men. He was a real asthenic. His wiry neck was marked by a pronounced Adam's apple which bobbed up and down as he spoke. I understood that the newcomer was a patient of Namejs's, and stepped away for a moment.

I directed my attention elsewhere for a few minutes, but, as their discussion dragged on, I started to observe them. Like watching a play on the theatre's lobby monitor, with the sound turned off. What a sight! A few words here and there drifted over to me like autumn leaves plucked off and carried by the wind, turning the missing dialogue into a curious crossword with a few clues filled in.

And suddenly – literally suddenly, because I don't have the slightest idea how it happened – I realised that Namejs was speaking to someone whose sob-story I already knew. It was him! The author of the letter, the epistolary theoretician who wanted to rewrite history and suffered from the influence of Ancient Greek sculptures. One hundred per cent!

When the event was over and Namejs and I were heading down the stairs, I asked him, as if in passing: 'That was the person who wrote that letter, right?'

'Yes … It seems your professional organ is in perfect working condition.'

'Don't worry. I'm not interested in him personally. I'm interested in what happened. You can't tell me everything is all right with him.'

'No, I can't.'

'Is he still haunted by those Apollos?'

'No. Now, on a daily basis, he feels as if he's turning into a tiger. Or a lion. In any case, into an animal that is freed from a cage and down a corridor leading to an arena.'

'Well, then, that's amazing!'

'Yes, yes. But the corridor doesn't lead to the right arena. You have to know his background for it to make sense. In short, in those moments he feels as if he's with his first wife, not the current one.'

'Maybe the drug affects one specific thing, while the root of the issue is connected to the roots of other issues?'

'Are you talking about pharmacology, or curing society at large?'

'I don't see a big difference.'

'And what do you think the answer is?'

'To grasp a broader range of things.'

'Well, sure! At one time society was all about building canals, but not repairing the sewers.'

'Haven't you ever been overcome by a strange sense of the unknown during surgery? Like – what is matter? Reality or just an idea? And if it's real, then where did everything come from when there wasn't anything? And what if this is all the show of some master magician – and luck, misfortune, health and disease are just illusions?'

'I suppose kidney stones could be seen as a kind of phenomenon – but they have to be taken out! For real, without philosophising.'

'Stones can interest you as a surgeon, but responsibility for the future should interest you as a person.'

'I don't get a lot of time not to be a surgeon. And then I'm mostly sleeping.'

We went on like this, sitting in the ground-floor lobby of the Latvian Society. The large building had slowly settled into silence, like a bell after its final ring. The staff on duty kept glancing over to us from their desk. They probably wanted to lock up. Namejs said he'd give me a lift home.

'Thank you! As long as that matchbox of yours doesn't lose all its screws halfway.'

'It'll survive.'

Namejs's car was parked on a street between the university and the Latvian Society. It was a hellish contraption, a Pontiac that was at least fifteen years old, one of those so-called roadsters. Though in its own way it was a special car, because it boasted the kind of extremely expensive number plate that rich company owners would buy for their newest model of luxury car. The plates display letters in place of numbers. The one on Namejs's car spelled out the name 'ANSIS'.

'You're a fool, Namejs, a fool!' I'd say each time, reclining in the kid leather seat of the Pontiac. And each time Namejs would answer: 'So? A certain someone from our family once had a favourite horse named Ansis.'

XXX

There will be a fireworks show at the Daugava riverbank in honour of Latvia's Indepence Day. Pyrotechnics are one of Jānis's obsessions, one that has burned in him since his childhood days in Spain and Italy, where he was first showered with sparks in the circus. The circus often uses fire to supplement its acts: tigers jump through burning hoops, jugglers juggle torches, acrobats fly through the air with their tails on fire. Jānis's face would light up like a lantern whenever he heard words like rockets, Bengal fire, pinwheels, *pot au feu*. We've never officially planned it, but I know that Jānis will come over every Independence Day, without fail, with astronomic precision. An impressive panorama of Riga's old town skyline and the Vanšu Bridge opens up from the roof of our seven-storey house, which sits at the edge of the former airfield.

The doorbell rings ten minutes before the fireworks show. Jānis, frozen, his head burrowed into the upturned collar of his jacket. He doesn't usually wear a hat, but wraps himself up in a scarf as long as a motorway. But this time he has a hat; in one hand he is carrying something like a leather pail with a lid. I know this strange container well – the original has Grandfather's favourite silk top hat in it. By the hat-maker Tonak Valmin, 1799. Why didn't I think of that?

'Wait! Mine's packed away somewhere.'

And soon I have mine in my hand. A party top hat, a Borsalino Tenuto, as thin as a record, but knock it against your elbow when you need it and it pops open to full size.

We each down a glass of cognac for warmth, right in the front hall. Then we roll our shoulders back, stand straight, put on our top hats and head up to the roof.

The dark and endless night sky is unusually clear, but completely starless. The red glow that normally hangs above the city is gone, too. It's like standing on the deck of a ship, but without the whispering field of blackish waves all around. A garden of lights has sprouted in the weedy darkness below – long strings of lights, lighted billboards. Illuminated façades of buildings in a serene rapture, like the faces of the choir on the Song Festival platform. We could almost reach out and touch the cluster of spotlit old town church towers: the lofty Peter, the stout Māra, the slim Jēkabs and the coral-red Anglican. Or reach out and grab Riga Castle's Tower of the Holy Spirit like a chess piece and move it to another square a bit further along that side of the river.

'Have you seen a more beautiful steeple than Saint Peter's?' I point to the highest tower, which the spotlights separate from the night.

'I haven't, no,' Jānis replies. Breathless from the climb, his hand searches for support on the roof railing. His glasses are fogged up. Anticipating the fireworks, which should start any second, Jānis nervously tries to wipe the lenses clean with his bare fingers.

The opposite side of the Daugava lights up with a bluish-white flash; the night is torn from its foundations and thrown upwards, for a moment baring a blinding brightness. The rumbling sound of the explosion follows a moment later. Another fireball shoots up into the sky, followed by a thunderous boom and the shattering of tiny stars that scatter the night with a slowly snowing blanket of colourful sparks. Fans of light streak open before our eyes. Long needles of light stretch out. Glittering bundles flash, break, blossom and layer over each other. Light streams in arching fountains. White, yellow and red billows of smoke filter and collect amidst it all. The Bacchanalia multiplies itself in the lenses of Jānis's glasses like a wall of televisions in a shop. He comments immediately on what he sees.

'See, the yellow is sodium oxalate ... the green is barium nitrate ... The glittering is caused by mercurous chloride, minium or ammonium chloride

... The sparks are caused by iron or brass, maybe copper and zinc fillings. A lift fuse, several casings tied together with a Bickford fuse ... Shellac mixed with lactose ... black powder, stearin, sawdust...'

The fireworks move across the sky in leaps and bounds. And with increasing volume, increasing vibrancy, increasing power. There are no moments of darkness between them. The multicoloured lustre booms, gallops, hisses, shatters, thunders. More! More! More!

And then it's over. The lightless sky is adrift with smoke which quickly dissipates like the rings of foam chasing after a speeding ship. We stand in a darkness that is eddying, black, desolate.

'Wonderful how mankind can change the heavens for a little while.'

Jānis starts to say something, but a strong gust of wind whips the top hat from his head and tumbles it away into the night.

'Look,' says Jānis, 'Grandfather chose mine on this important day. How could we forget about him?'

'You forgot about him? Don't be silly. You've never once forgotten him.'

It seems Jānis doesn't hear me. And how could he hear me if he's not even here? But then his mind wanders back.

'No, it wasn't a different sky. It was the same old one. That's the trick, that we have access to both possible and impossibly possible variations. You don't like steam? Skate on mirror-clear ice. You don't like ice? Enjoy the way the Daugava flows! As dependent concepts, they give us an idea of conditions. But the essence doesn't change – it's all H_2O.'

XXXI

No, Grandfather, I'm not bored. With the onslaught of this whirlwind of information, the mental rotor has to keep turning whether it wants to or not.

Regardless of whether the skies break open to unleash unparalleled floods, whether wells and river beds suddenly dry up, the amount of water on the planet doesn't change –surprisingly. And isn't it the same with a lot of other things? Evil can't be eradicated, good can't be the only building material, change happens in a play of combinations.

The wise Solomon already knew there was nothing new on earth. As did that snake in the Garden of Eden which gave Adam and Eve the chance to choose. The poison and the antidote are within the same arm's reach.

Each life is the sum of its preceding generations, and the layout for the generations to come. Construction-wise, the Eiffel Tower is nothing compared to me. Remember how, in Cape Town in December 1967, surgeons removed the ailing heart of fifty-six-year old Louis Washkansky and replaced it with that of a woman who had died in a car accident. That was the first time such a transplant had taken place, and the young woman's heart was a little too small for a man. Washkansky died eighteen days after the surgery – not because the heart was too small, but because of a biological incompatibility. Scientists were far less interested in the basic concept of a barrier of incompatibility created by nature than they were obsessed with the idea of turning man from a final product into a combination of parts. Countless institutes around the world searched for ways to circumvent the natural defences of the human body. And to everyone's surprise, embodied in millions of dried-up and decomposing corpses, AIDS cropped up. How can we tell, Grandfather, if it's coincidence or punishment?

Grandfather wears a white linen shirt and grey cloth trousers. His feet are bare, the bottoms of his trousers are rolled up. His black Tonak Valmin top hat sits back on his head. As he listens to me, he rhythmically taps the handle of his black-lacquered whip against his shin. The lacquer shines in the sun.

'I'm thinking, I'm thinking. Can you imagine a ship that's leaning to one side? From what I understand it's important to remember Buddha's last words: "All compound things are bound to fall apart."'

We're at the Manor. At first I'm afraid to look, I don't want to see the ruins. But the buildings are all in order and the sun shines so brightly that their contours shimmer, as if drawn by a shaky hand.

The sun is blinding. The blossoming row of cherry trees along the Manor's stone wall creates a white wave across which, it seems, you could almost ski.

The Baroness sits in her usual place in the office. In front of her is a medium-sized television, Japanese or Korean. Judging by her disinterested expression, she's not paying much attention to what's on the screen. She dips her quill into the inkpot and writes in the thick order ledger, glancing up only now and then at the television. I'm surprised to see she hasn't aged at all. You could even say she looks shockingly young; I've never seen her like that. Only once in a photograph in a knotted wooden frame on her bedside table. It was a small picture with several people in it; a fancily dressed, bearded man stood next to the Baroness, most likely just back from the Boer War.

The Baroness stops writing when she notices me. It seems the quill is clogged.

'Sometimes the faraway things the television shows us are very close,' she says, partly to me, and partly to herself. Then she adds with great gravity, 'When mice go to paradise, they need to pay attention so they don't accidentally wind up in cat paradise.'

'Johanna, you're mistaken!' I have no idea at what point Grandfather entered the room. His black top hat and shoulders are wet. It must have started to rain.

'You're thinking logically, and that's a tragic mistake. Sooner or later, logical thinkers are going to run into deception. The order of the world isn't simple or logical. Defining moments rarely happen the way you'd expect.'

Now I see Jānis is in the room as well. His thick, bushy hair – which was once black – shines white. He's taken off his glasses, which is maybe why his face looks strange. Even more likely is that the strangeness arises from the way Japanese features make it difficult to discern a person's age. Jānis still looks like a teenager, but a grey-haired teenager. Liene is there with him, along with Zīle, all grown up, and the lumbering Namejs. Behind Liene is a young, slender woman – she has an uneven hairline, thin lips and low, almost straight eyebrows.

'Who's that woman behind Liene?' I whisper as I lean close to Aunt Alma.

'That?' Aunt Alma is confused for a moment. She blinks her red eyelids and studies the stranger. 'Why, that's Guna from Čiekurkalns! My word!'

'After so many years?'

'You can't cut anything out of your life. Don't you know that yet? Look, little Irbe is there, too. Small and brittle as a bird.'

'But isn't time a forward movement over a horizon, behind which everything disappears?'

'But not while you're living it. A lifetime, like a river, flows forwards along with everything that's filtered into it.'

Grandfather has definitely heard our conversation. He doesn't look our way, but what he says is doubtless aimed at us.

'The horizon was probably created as a by-product of everything else God created. Because the world is round. You wouldn't have the same questions about the horizon if we were talking about a cube. But a cube-shaped world would require more material, a sphere is more economical...'

And without segue: 'Now that I don't go out as often, you could say I'm beyond the horizon. But I don't feel that way. I still have horses and people. Alive, dead, near, far. As if something dead is no longer an active player, as if something living couldn't go stiff and reek. Each continent has its plane. And there's no leering into another country's space – there are boundaries.

Fair and convenient.'

'Grandfather, I've got more news,' Namejs announces. 'I'm getting married again.'

'And so you should. A two-horse carriage is the best kind. A four-horse or six-horse is more for show. The two-horse is for serious business. This is one thing God did right. Man is a two-horse carriage. My fondest memories are all associated with a two-horse carriage.'

The Baroness lowers her eyes and glances at the television.

'Something's going to happen,' she says. 'They're reporting from downtown. There's a crowd at the central station.'

Irbīte is quiet, but Liene still energetically bounces the child on her hip. Jānis's face has made room for the expression of curiosity; though his eyes are half-closed, they still show the excitement of anticipation and the joy of hope. Grandfather removes his top hat and runs his hand over his thinning hair.

'What's going on there? Police ... People with flowers ... Excited faces ... Fidgeting bodies...'

At least two or three police officers are swimming in the city canal among the swans and coltsfoot leaves. Three men are running in circles round a newspaper kiosk. It's not clear who's chasing whom and who's running away from whom. The branches of a linden tree across from the station are laden with people like heavy, overripe fruit.

Suddenly, a cry of 'They're coming, they're coming!' is heard from the murmuring crowd. The bodies sway like a stack of dishes on a jostled tray. Everyone runs in the direction of the central market. The police try to keep people on the pavements, but they get shoved aside, sucked in and eventually carried away like gates from their posts in a flood. Like fence posts in a tornado. The crowd disperses in all directions, but it doesn't thin out. There is the pounding of running feet, the flashing of hands, the whites of eyes. Trams brake carefully and become stationary islands among the thickening mob. Buses become stuck and their engines idle.

'They're coming! They're coming!'

A police horse without a rider, its nose bloodied, rears up on its hind legs, whinnying and sputtering, trying to find a way out. The loudspeakers aren't matched up, they echo back at each other, telling everyone to remain calm and orderly. But it's ambient noise. Like a bright light over the city, like lush, green lawns along the canal. In the foreground are mouths shouting 'They're here, they're here!' and ears that hear those words alone.

A giant luxury Land Rover rolls out from the viaduct, heavy as a tank and white with road dust. It's boxy, with nickel-plated bull bars on the front, as thick as drainpipes. It runs on what look like four rubber-clad wheels from a watermill. Black tinted glass. Antennae on the front and back. A large spotlight on the roof. A turbo motor, no less than 250 horsepower. At least ten gears and twenty litres to one hundred kilometres.

The transport the escorts have is just as awe-inspiring. One carriage is even decorated with a flag, hanging limp in the windless air. The colours change like the multicoloured watermark on a banknote – there's a flash of a sea-blue, then a fiery red and perhaps even a sterile white.

The first person to run to the Land Rover is a young woman with a bunch of roses, followed immediately by a young man with a torn-off sleeve. They fall to their knees next to the large tyre, stroke and kiss it. 'We've been waiting for you! We've been waiting for you!' The crowd around the vehicle sinks in like the jaws of a bulldog on a bone. It takes the passengers some time to push open the doors.

A thin-faced journalist with glasses slides out with a microphone in his hand. 'The National Channel is starting its live feed…' Heavenly music fills the air. A choir is singing. The camera cuts to a pile of flowers.

Grandfather's face is white, his breath catches in the hot room. He's using the top hat to fan himself.

'Listen,' he says, 'I don't understand. Can someone explain to me who showed up in the end?'

And it's only now that I notice a tall man standing behind the black cupboard decorated with a wood carving of two curved waves about to crash into each other. He's wearing a linen shirt, grey cloth trousers and heavy cuirassier boots folded over beneath the knees. His fair hair is straight, shoulder-length, parted in the middle. The narrow ends of his moustache are curled up impishly, but his nose sticks out, sharp and straight like a whetstone.

'Who showed up?' The question has surprised the Freiherr. 'Why, it's Cagliostro! The Great Cophta!…'

The final moment is brief, the beginning is already here again. And the final word is only that there is no final word.

Afterword

In literary translation, a common question is whether to include footnotes appearing in the original text in the translated version. Opinions on this great 'footnote debate' vary widely, from translator, to publisher, to the authors themselves. Each work ends up being an individual case, and final decisions are made accordingly.

The footnotes in the Latvian version of *Flesh-Coloured Dominoes* range from brief notations on historical figures (such as Greek physician Hippocrates and French painter Édouard Manet) to foreign language words and phrases (such as the German *guten Abend* and the French *s'il vous plâit*) – footnotes that, when Skujiņš completed *Flesh-Coloured Dominoes* in 1999, may have been necessary in its Latvian original, especially in light of recent socio-political changes and the respective circulation of informational texts. But a mere fifteen years later, at a time when readers are more familiar with international literature and have instant access to information, the use of footnotes in this particular novel in its English translation did not seem 'in place'. English readers today, who have access to myriad world cultures (through film, literature, media, sports), are less likely to find the presence of an untranslated phrase, or a cultural reference, jarring – even if we do not absolutely understand the phrase or know of the historical figure.

The decision to forego footnotes was one discussed at length and agreed upon with both the author and the publisher; as often as possible, I incorporated the formerly footnoted information into the narrative itself, with a concentrated effort to clarify what must be clarified without compromising the content or the rhythm of the story, and to leave foreign words (i.e. 'untranslated'), which either did not need translating (the above French and German phrases, for example), or which felt more situationally or tonally appropriate to leave in the respective foreign language, thus retaining the multi-cultural essence and history of the story itself.

The late-eighteenth century and Second World War storylines portrayed in *Flesh-Coloured Dominoes* are two well-known periods of history into which Skujiņš does a beautiful job of transporting the reader. He contextualises each period, with great attention to historical detail and by applying his personal experiences, thus creating a rich and immersive text for the reader to experience. It was ultimately due to this richness that we believed the English translation of *Flesh-Coloured Dominoes* would be best served by allowing the reader to experience it without the addition of footnotes that are no longer culturally necessary.

The goal of this translation is to provide English readers with access to one of the most interesting and enjoyable works of contemporary Latvian literature, and the choices I made with regard to the original text were done with this in mind. *Flesh-Coloured Dominoes* does what great literature always does; it provides the reader with a fascinating entryway to a specific personal and historical situation. Hopefully this translated version is as charming and engaging as the original.

Kaija Straumanis (Translator)